NO NAMES

ALSO BY GREG HEWETT

Red Suburb
The Eros Conspiracy
darkacre
Blindsight

NO NAMES

GREG HEWETT

COFFEE HOUSE PRESS

Minneapolis

2025

Coffee House Press books are available to the trade through our primary distributor, Consortium Book Sales & Distribution, cbsd.com or (800) 283-3572. For personal orders, catalogs, or other information, write to info@coffeehousepress.org.

Coffee House Press is a nonprofit literary publishing house. Support from private foundations, corporate giving programs, government programs, and generous individuals helps make the publication of our books possible. We gratefully acknowledge their support in detail in the back of this book.

LIBRARY OF CONGRESS CATALOGING-IN-PUBLICATION DATA

Names: Hewett, Greg, author.
Title: No names / Greg Hewett.
Description: Minneapolis : Coffee House Press, 2025.
Identifiers: LCCN 2024044748 (print) | LCCN 2024044749 (ebook) |
    ISBN 9781566897259 (paperback) | ISBN 9781566897266 (ebook)
Subjects: LCGFT: Novels.
Classification: LCC PS3558.E826 N66 2025 (print) | LCC PS3558.E826
    (ebook) | DDC 813/.54—dc23/eng/20240924
LC record available at https://lccn.loc.gov/2024044748
LC ebook record available at https://lccn.loc.gov/2024044749

PRINTED IN THE UNITED STATES OF AMERICA
32 31 30 29 28 27 26 25   1 2 3 4 5 6 7 8

for Tony Hainault, my lodestar

I've been scanning the ocean all morning long through a blind of rain. Still no sign of the weekly postal ferry. More than three hours late. Mountain after mountain of water speeds past the kitchen window. This could go on for days. The wind presses through the glass, even through the stone walls. The sound relentless, desperate, though the desperation is obviously just mine. Days like this I wonder how big a wave it would take to wipe this island that's not even on most maps off the map. Or at least this part, the few low acres not taken up by the mountain. Living on a volcanic afterthought keeps me aware of how precarious the border between land and sea really is. The mountain's rooted way farther down in the ocean than it reaches up into the sky. For sure, *island* should be a verb, meaning something like, *to be of the underworld and overworld all at once.*

In front of the peat stove the dogs twitch in their sleep.

Right before the storm rose yesterday, the ocean turned jade then lead, meaning winter has arrived. It's taken basically all my fifteen years here, but I'm finally learning to read these signs. Maybe I should cut myself some slack. There's no ocean back home.

If the ferry does come through, it will likely be the last till spring. That always puts me on edge.

Right when I'm about to call it quits and go fry up some of the sausage Abraham made, I make out a faint blip on the blurred horizon, like on a radar screen. I lay the spatula down. The ferry gradually comes into focus. In fits and starts it climbs up one steep slope only to get tossed down into the following valley. I pull on one of Daniel's fisherman's sweaters from the shelf by the door and some rainboots from under the bench, then push my way out into the gale. Rain's going sideways. Alpha and Omega follow at my heels. I can barely keep upright and stagger my way down to the landing. Waves explode against the cliff, making it too difficult for the ferry to dock. A blast nearly blows me into the cauldron. The shipmate loses his balance, falling onto the deck, yet somehow manages to toss the canvas pouch. I leap up, snatching it from a gust just as the ferry pivots back out to sea. Sheer luck. The captain gives his usual salute, though fainter this time, like he feels sorry for me out here alone for the long, dark winter. I savor one last whiff of diesel as the boat spins away. Rain and salt-spray slap me hard. The dogs look up with their china-blue eyes, almost forlorn. I bend down to pat my fellow inmates, to let them know it's alright, it's alright, as the last people we'll see for possibly up to six months disappear in the channel. It's only about two miles across to the main island, Stream Island, but, as Daniel warns me every time he leaves at the end of summer, it's as treacherous a stretch of sea as any on Earth. Even on a calm day it's tough to row. Tomorrow morning the last passenger ship of the season departs from there for the Continent. Doesn't make any difference to me, though. With the postal ferry gone, it might as well be on the other side of the world. I muscle my way against the wind back up to the squat stone house. The sod roof shivers in the hard wind. It should comfort me that these walls have withstood a millennium of storms, but sometimes it just doesn't.

In the pouch there's the sheet music I ordered from Boosey & Hawkes. That's a relief. The Boccherini, Giuliani, Villa-Lobos, all there. Best of all, the Bach *Lute Suites for Guitar*. Enough to last the whole winter. Easily. Plenty of back issues of *Soundboard* and *Classical Guitar,* too. Plus, a thick manila envelope from Daniel.

As it turns out, Daniel's letter is only two sheets of his gray stationery. Inside the manila envelope is a white business-sized one, addressed to me at Daniel's studio in Copenhagen. The return address I don't recognize, but it's from back home. Doesn't make sense. Who even knows that I know Daniel? Who even knows *me* anymore? To say the least, this freaks me out.

2 November 1993

Dear Michael,

Yesterday I returned from the two concerts in Paris that were still up in the air due to a musicians' strike. Well, the strike ended in the nick of time. Paris is always great money and an intelligent audience, but frankly, I would not have minded the cancellations as I am simply drained. Since leaving you 30 August, I have had only fifteen days without performing, including the four days sailing back. The appearances don't let up until Christmastime, then pick up again after the New Year through the entire spring. Next year is already scheduled, but I have got to scale back for '95. I am going to insist the agency give me one full month on the Island when they start talking schedule again.

I have arranged for Abraham to row over and resod the barn roof before the rains come and the sea turns too rough. I only hope that it's not too late. If you would like to help him, you are of course welcome to. He said your work on the farmhouse roof last year was excellent!

I am relieved to hear that all the winter supplies arrived. Judging from what I saw before I left, the potato harvest should be somewhat better this year, so hopefully you'll not have to resort to the instant, though I did send a few boxes just in case. So glad to hear you are enjoying the salt licorice. I almost forgot to pack it!

Now to more important matters: your new songs. They have stayed with me, haunted me, really. I have tried them out on the piano as I pondered your question about how exactly, in a technical sense, they work. Pardon me if I sound like the Village Explainer, but here goes. All the songs have at least one unconventional chord progression. Often there is more than one, and sometimes they come close to destroying the song's musical comprehensibility. However, that is what makes them so exciting. You have maintained a harmonic structure beneath these unruly chords that prevents their collapse. In addition, each song has a tight relationship between the cluster of chords and the semantics of the lyrics, a quality any songwriter would envy. As the meaning of the words changes with each verse, the chords offer a flexible way of shifting the emotional meanings. These songs are impressive, to say the least. They seem to tune in to an otherwise inaccessible and universal undersong in which the ordinary becomes strange or almost taboo. What Haydn said of his own work seems to be true of yours as well: "There was no one near to confuse me so I was forced to become original."

That said, I do hope you will consider coming here for Easter. I will be home, giving only one recital at the cathedral. I know it is a lot to ask of you to leave the Island, but I think it would be good to finally have a change. Maundy Thursday falls on 8 April this coming year.

I, perhaps more than most, understand the importance of solitude. It is, I believe, nearly as much a religion for me as it is for you. The hundreds of hours I spend alone at the piano every year are not only rewarding but constitute my very being. The same is certainly true for you and the guitar. And yet, I cannot help wondering if being too devoted—being too rigid in one's orthodoxy—has the potential of making a fetish out of solitude. I feel as though I did exactly that my final year at conservatory, as well as the year after my parents died. I suspect that coming out of your hermitage will make it all the sweeter when you return. Please don't take offense at my suggestion. If you choose not to come, I will of course respect your decision. You have said that I am all the society you need, which flatters me, truly, but that may not be the wisest thing! Your companionship is not only a great privilege for me but a necessity as well.

I am enclosing a letter from the States that, oddly enough, came to the studio here, addressed to you. The return address is from your hometown.

With Love,
Daniel

The rain has finally stopped, though the wind continues even stronger. Overhead, the pair of usually confident sea eagles are getting tossed and battered around like plastic trash bags as they try to reach their aerie on the mountaintop. The sun flashes on and off as slate clouds pass over, startling huge stretches of ocean and mountainside to bright shades of green and then, just as suddenly, returning them to black. Wind shoots over the sod roofs in short bursts at warp speed, rippling the green grass. Same over the woolen backs of the herd. The dogs chase cloud-shadows as if they're gigantic stray black sheep. With every gust, the waterfall pouring down the mountainside writhes like an enormous serpent.

The past has arrived in an envelope I never expected, never wanted. Hard but also not so hard to believe it's the only letter to arrive for me in all these years, not counting the regular ones from Daniel. From someone I don't even know. A writer, he says. His questions confront me with things I've tried to forget. Remembering is like untangling the waves in the ocean. As much as I wish it were possible, a letter can't be unread.

I head inside, sit down at the table to reread the pages I mostly skimmed but instead tear them up and toss them in the peat stove and head back to the kitchen to finally cook the sausage. I wish I could change some memories, or better yet, I wish the past wasn't so persistently the present no matter how long and how hard I've tried to keep it the past. I examine my cuticles for traces of the black stain from picking walnuts. A weird, involuntary response because these islands have no trees, walnut or otherwise, and the last time I picked walnuts was over twenty years ago with Dad and John when I was a kid and happy for at least that one day a year. I laugh out loud. The dogs look over from the peat fire, cocking their heads.

With the last boat gone till spring, maybe I'm just feeling wistful. It will pass. For all these years on this roadless island, cruising down endless roads of music with my guitar and contemplating the moment-by-moment changes of ocean, sky, and mountain have been enough. World enough, this hunk of basalt stuck down in ocean as deep as imagination.

The night's moonless, starless.
Can't sleep thinking about the letter.
Like it slipped in from another dimension.

No, you can't unread a letter.

I get up and pace from room to room without turning on a light. The dogs let out short whimpers before leaving their rag rug at the end of the bed to join me.

I'm angry that this letter's having such an effect on me.

I stop my blind pacing. The dogs rub against my legs. I squat down to scratch them behind the ears, and they lick my face all over.

SEPTEMBER 1993, ISAAC

As soon as Vashti took off for work, I missed the bus downtown accidentally on purpose so I could search the attic. Need to find my birth certificate so I can get a passport. The only place I haven't looked. For some unknown reason the attic's always been verboten. She swore to God she'd searched absolutely everywhere. She had no idea in the world where it could have possibly gone. Right. Miss Organization doesn't misplace shit, let alone her precious son's birth certificate. She just doesn't want me to leave. Simple as that. She said she'd kill me if I did. We have this sicko bond. One minute we're screaming that we hate each other's guts, the next she's sobbing about how much she loves me and can't live without me.

A few weeks ago, she put it all together: *Motorcycle Adventure: Latin America* and *The Motorcycle Diaries* on my nightstand + new bike + passport application = bad news. But seriously, who gets their spoiled-rotten kid the classic '69 Kawasaki H1 Mach III that he's whined and begged about forever for his eighteenth birthday and doesn't expect trouble? Big fight about no college. She's still in denial. Since graduation last year, it's been Patagonia here I come! Gonna do my Che thing, except in reverse. Hop on my very own La Poderosa and ride, ride, ride, following the compass south.

Like the rest of the parents up here in the Heights, Vashti always assumed her absolutely gifted son would go to college. I'd literally cringe when she'd tell me, "Your friends all say you're a brainiac." Not true and not her lingo. She's even started applying *for* me again this year. Ivies and the like. As if. She's got Ivy on the brain. She marks the beginning of my downfall from the moment I bought the guitar, after which I quit Scouts (three merit badges shy of Eagle) and hockey (right when I made starting lineup). Sometimes she adds drugs and sex into the equation, but mostly she doesn't want to think about those things.

I haul the aluminum ladder from the garage all the way upstairs. It's bent from when she pulled her car in one time and rammed into it leaning there against the back wall. Classic. It starts wobbling as I'm climbing to the attic. Next thing I know, the damn thing's falling out from under me as I push open the trapdoor. I barely keep from plummeting and somehow manage to pull myself up into the huge space. Huge but filled with stuff. And I mean *stuff.* Like another family's hiding out up here. I haven't been in the attic since I was a little kid. Most of the things date back to when I was a baby and we lived at Aunt Cindy's before she got married and moved to Hawaii. There's the puffy green-velvet sofa with matching recliners, some dressers, beds with perfectly good mattresses. To be honest, it feels a whole lot cozier than the *Architectural Digest* space we occupy below. I plop myself down on one of the recliners. On the dining table are stacked dishes from her grandma, with apples painted on them. The handles of the creamer and sugar bowl are in the shape of twigs. Cheesy, yeah, but also cheery, homey. Cheerier and homier than us, that's for sure. And the clothes. A couple decades of female fads. Mini-, maxi-, midi-skirts, etc. Shoes galore: platform, spiked, loafers, sandals, you name it. In the center of the space sit two huge, empty aquariums, stained brown by dried algae, with my baby toys tossed inside. How symbolic. I remember crawling up to the aquariums when they were downstairs, filled with water and fish and miniature forests. She was into aquaculture back then. I'd press my face against the glass, escaping into an underwater world that seemed way more interesting than the one of air fate had trapped me in.

After nearly two hours searching through boxes of papers, still no birth certificate. I sit and stare out the window. The skyscrapers way downtown sparkle in the morning light. Even though we live in the Heights-iest part of the Heights, we don't have a view of the skyline except from up here because another so-called executive home, pretty much identical to ours, went up right across the street. At this point, there's no use catching a bus to the internship. Missed half the day already.

Bored, I flip through a couple of milk crates of vinyl: Crystal Gayle, Peaches and Herb, Three Dog Night, Chuck Mangione, Captain and Tennille. Barry-fucking-Manilow. No Beatles but what looks to be every McCartney and Wings release. I guess I'm supposed to go, like, *Look at all this crazy '70s shit,* and think it's kitschy-hip, but I don't. It's just plain sad. Billy Joel's about as edgy as she got. I ought to haul the whole lot down to Rongo at the Vinyl Heart and get a few bucks or some weed for them.

There's one record that's totally unfamiliar. The jacket's a plain brown wrapper. Like porn. It's called *Invisible City.* The title's spelt out in weirdly faint lettering, as if you're looking through venetian blinds. The band's called the No Names. No picture of them or names. Guess that's the point. It's from '78. The label's Dangerhouse. Never heard of it, either, and I feel like I know tons of obscure bands and labels from back then. Some of the titles sound pretty cool: "Altared Boy," "Pissed Off!," "Bench Press," "All Your Finery at the Refinery," "Strong, Silent, and Loud."

I'll give it a listen. With no ladder, I have to drop like a commando down through the trapdoor, mystery record in hand. My turntable's busted, so I head down to the console in the living room. It was my grandparents' and is the only old thing not relegated to the attic, though Vashti never uses it anymore except to play creepy Bing Crosby at Christmas. She's all into CDs now since her '93 Audi came with a sound system.

I lift the lid, throw the disk on, drop the needle. Within five, six measures, a phantom sensation comes over me, like my synapses stop firing and I stop breathing. The music puts me in a state of suspended animation, and I'm not even stoned or anything. It's punk, for sure, but also not punk. It's more than either punk or not-punk, if that makes any sense at all. I crank the volume. It's so fucking sublime. Like nothing I've ever heard, yet it feels like I've been hearing it—or maybe always been wanting to hear it?—my whole life. It's like entering that schizoid void when I'm daydreaming about math problems and the whole universe explodes into equations. I go down on my knees, like the stereo's a fucking altar. September out the picture window shimmers all golden, like going to heaven or tripping. I stay in this position for the next song and the next song and the next. Chaos as order, order as chaos in every single measure. I roll onto my back, close my eyes. The two guitars fly as fast and sure and wild and high as anything by Johnny Ramone or Tom Verlaine. Who are these bastards? Why haven't I ever heard of them? Usually when I hear something I dig, I run for the trusty Gibson Dark Fire and try imitating a few licks. Not with this, though. It's too awesome. *Awesome* the way God meant it. I flip the record, put the arm on repeat, and lie there horny in what's maybe my soul and for once not my dick. It's a fix of something way beyond anything I've known. It's escape from myself and the dull story of my life trailing after me.

Somewhere under the layers of music I hear the garage door grinding open, followed by keys jangling all angry as they hit the soapstone kitchen island she's usually so worried about scratching. Sounds so far away. And then she's shouting, "What the hell, Isaac?" I keep my eyes closed as she repeats, "What the hell?" She's come home like a million times before when I'm blasting music and hasn't freaked like this. I get up. She tries grabbing me by the hair, but I dodge her. I swear to God she'd be a homicidal maniac if she didn't meditate and do yoga obsessively. Voice slicing right through the music, she demands, "Where'd you get that goddamn record?"

"Vinyl Heart." I lie.

She mumbles a *bullshit* or two, glaring up toward the ladder fallen over at the top of the staircase, beneath the trapdoor. "I hate that goddam music," she says, obviously for her own benefit. In the past, for my edification, she has given dissertations on the antisocial, nihilistic nature of punk. "And stop digging through my shit," she adds, moving toward the console. I instantly know what's about to happen but am, tragically, too far away to stop her, especially in her full Fury Mode. The needle goes flying, and a wicked screech rises out of the vinyl. Never have I been so pissed off but am 100 percent determined not to show it. At this point, she starts looking around for something. She eyes a legal folder on her treasured aerodynamic Noguchi coffee table, swoops in, snatches it up. As she heads back toward the garage, she turns her head to glare at me, red hair flaming in the sun pouring into the kitchen. "You didn't go to your internship today, did you Isaac?"

"What does it look like, Vashti?"

"Dammit to hell. I pulled strings to get you in there. It's my reputation. And by the way, it's *Mom* to you."

She changed her name a couple years ago, after spending a month at some bogus ashram in Iowa, and I get a kick out of saying it any chance I get. As for the internship, it's not like there's much incentive. It's unpaid, and all I do is xerox legal briefs and make coffee.

"It's called being responsible." She looks at her fake Cartier. "I'll deal with you later. I have yoga tonight, so you're on your own for dinner." Then she's off, officious in her Brooks Brothers suit. Yoga and Brooks Brothers. Right.

As soon as I hear the garage door closing, I slip the injured album into its sleeve and put it in my knapsack. And because the Kawasaki's waiting for a part, I have to hop on my old Miyata. I pedal down the hill, all the way around downtown and along Sauletaux Avenue, with its pawnshops and boarded-up businesses, to the Vinyl Heart. It's already crazy hot, the wind off the Plains blasting me in the face the whole way. I arrive drenched, lean my bike against the front of the store, and head on in.

Rongo greets me with his usual, "I-sack, man, how's it goin'?" He's my source for all things music. And weed. We high five. I've been coming here since I was like twelve, for records and guitar lessons, and he's never treated me like a kid, which is exactly why I like hanging out here. Vashti thinks he's a bad role model. No surprise there.

I wipe the sweat off my face and pull the album out of my knapsack. As I'm laying it on the cracked glass countertop, he murmurs something into his grizzled beard and looks like he's having one of his acid flashbacks. Before I even ask if he can repair the record, he's asking me, "How much you want for it, I-sack?"

This tells me it's something good. I'm feeling smug. "Sorry man, not selling. Besides, it's my mom's. Found it in the attic." Rongo's visibly bummed. "Just wanted to see if you can repair it." I take it out of the jacket, pointing to the deep gouge.

"That's fucked up, dude."

I don't explain how the wound was inflicted.

He unfolds a soft cloth, spreads it over the glass, then lays the disk down. Applying distilled water, rubbing alcohol, and photographic developing solution, he very gently, very carefully, goes over the indentation again and again with a chamois. Every now and again he lifts the vinyl up to the light, eyeing it. At last, he nods, lays it on his B&O turntable, and wow! It plays like new. We high five again and start grooving to "Altared Boy."

Rongo lifts the record off the turntable, puts it back in the sleeve, and hands it to me. "Take care of it, nimrod, you've got yourself gold there."

I look at him kind of confused.

"Well, not gold as in gold record, but as in it's a rare one. You know the No Names are from here, right?"

Embarrassed, I shake my head.

He shakes his gray dreads back at me. "I'm not big into punk, but you, my friend, have stumbled upon what is for lots of folks the Holy-fucking-Grail." Nostalgia filters through his smoke-torn voice. "At least around these parts. Some bastard ripped off my only copy years ago." He starts moving his arms in a wide arc above his head, like some prophet from an old-timey biblical epic on late-night TV, as he proclaims, "The No Names blazed across the music scene for maybe nine months, back in '78. That was it. One album, and this is it. Rumor has it they cut another in Europe, never released. First decent punk band from here and, in my considered judgment, the best. The guitarists, they were among the bitchin'-est ever, right up there with Greg Ginn. The drummer, unreal. They burned this town down and, after that, blazed through just about every underground club in the country."

So, the coolest band I'd never heard of was local. My delusions of grandeur about becoming a rockstar suddenly don't seem all that insane. "Why've you never mentioned them before?"

"Don't know, man. Didn't have anything to play for you? Besides, it was, you know, brief and some time ago." With a certain amount of pride, he adds, "Before the band formed, when the guys were still in school, they'd stop in here from time to time."

My eyelids nearly unhinge. "You're shitting me."

"I shit you not."

I get all jittery. "What were they like?"

"What were they like?" he echoes, rubbing his chin philosopher-style. "Mysterious cats. Serious. No banter onstage. But that sound! It was the two guitarists that came in here most. Badasses, I suppose. Cool. Not posers. The front man, especially. Quiet as death. Even if you asked if you could help him find something, he wouldn't say a word, would just give you this fuck-off look. The other one, the second guitar, seemed more outgoing. Though a little volatile. He'd flip through a bin and announce right out loud, so the whole store could hear, how this one blows his mind or that one sucks. One morning I come to open the store and there he is, taking a leak right in the doorway. Doesn't give a fuck. I say something, and he says, 'When ya gotta go, ya gotta go.' I unlock and he pushes right in, tracking piss across the floor but then buys three records."

Time sucks. Time walls me off from the scene the No Names ruled when I was like three.

"Can I have a listen to another song?" Rongo asks.

"Of course, man!"

He takes the album back, slips the record out of the jacket again, puts it back on the turntable, and places the needle down:

You thought you could alter me with your religion.
Goddamn your God, I'm making no concession,
Goddamn your God, I'm my own religion.
I sacrifice at the altar of my own confession,
I get sacrificed at the altar of violation.
Violence is my religion.
I was an altar boy, now I'm altered, I'm an altared boy . . .

"My God. Or my gods."

"Lapsed Catholic that I am, that's my favorite," Rongo tells me as he gets back to the archtop jazz guitar, a Gibson ES-175 he was restringing when I came in. For how callused his fingers are, they're amazingly nimble. Without looking up, he says, "The No Names simply disappeared. The European tour was the end of the band. Heard they became junkies. Rough times. That was many moons ago."

This news destroys me. Suddenly, I have got to know where they are. I plead with him, "I need to find out if they're still around. You gotta have some sort of lead!"

Rongo looks at me all skeptical. "Lead?" he says right back at me. He's seen his share of crazed fans, those who, as I've heard him say, put the *fanatic* back in *fan*. With not an ounce of enthusiasm, he offers, "The guys grew up over in the Flats. Got no idea if any of their relations are still there."

I ask the names of these No Names, and Rongo pretends his memory's burned out more than it actually is. After some not-so-pretty begging on my part, he offers them up. Mike Abramczyk, Bobby Godek, Pete Lac, and Matt Lachapelle. "Mike was the singer and lead guitar. Wrote most of the songs, too, with the help of Pete. Pete also played guitar. I'd say he was co-lead. Both were great. Bobby was the drummer. The brains. From what I heard, he's responsible for turning them from just another garage band into serious musicians. You could see it when you went to their practice sessions down at Dreamland, him stopping the action to make comments. Matt was, plain and simple, a damn fine bass player."

From under the counter Rongo pulls out a beat-up phone book and hands it to me. Abramczyk. There's one. A Stanislaw. The father, I guess. There's no Godek. A Richard Lac. A whole clan of Lachapelles. I figure it's best to go in person, as it's a whole lot easier to hang up on someone than it is to slam the door in their face. The Flats is the opposite side of town. Rongo lets me borrow his Datsun pickup, a total rust-boat.

Though it's part of the city, I've never actually been to the Flats before. It always looked pretty grim from the interstate but in fact looks way grimmer up close. The refinery rules everything, like some evil castle. About fifty stratospherically high smokestacks rise up, a couple with flames shooting out like colossal roadside flares. A chaos of pipes and tanks and scaffolding surrounds the stacks. The air smells bitter, chemical. The river flows by, looking muddier here than it does other places, though that's likely my imagination. Enormous cottonwoods, many broken or shattered, line the banks.

Abramczyk's is on a street called Magnolia, off Petroleum Avenue. Now that's poetry for you. There's petroleum here, for sure, but not a magnolia in sight. Do magnolias even grow around here? Theirs is the last house on the street, caged in by the razor wire fence of the refinery on one side, the chain-link fence along the highway on another, and the river on a third. Plastic bags caught in the fence by the highway flap wildly in the rush of traffic, like terrorized birds. High-tension power lines crisscross overhead. The house looks smaller than our garage. Paint peeling. Front lawn all weeds. Plastic covering the windows, though winter's long past. The aluminum front door is dented in, like someone's kicked it but good. There's a hole where a doorbell was, so I knock, wait, knock again. I'm about to give up when a woman comes to the door. She blinks and squints like she's been asleep a hundred years. Her face is hollow. She's white as a rose, thin as a snake. Probably thirties, with long hair the color of tar. A sister of Mike Abramczyk?

"Hello," I say.

"You must be the judge."

I shake my head. "No, ma'am. Just looking for Mike Abramczyk."

It's as if she doesn't hear me. "The lawyer said the judge would be coming by with the money." Her voice gets intense, loses pitch. "Have the check, Mister?"

I'm eighteen, in torn jeans, ratty T-shirt. Even still, I have to tell her again, "Sorry, I'm not the judge. Just looking for Mike Abramczyk."

For a moment she seems to tune in to what I'm saying. "Haven't seen him in . . . in years . . . My mother and father might know."

"May I please speak with them?" I do polite well.

"They're not here."

"When might they be back?"

She glances skyward, scowling.

"Hello?" I say, but she's gone up into the clouds.

At this point, another woman, who might be her healthy twin—with a little flesh on her bones and color in her cheeks—comes up behind her in the tiny foyer. "You looking for Mike?"

"Yes!" I sound way too eager. Got to level the voice off. "Yes, I am."

She shakes her head. "Haven't heard from him since . . . well, since maybe forever."

The thin sister slips out of the crowded entryway, back into the dim interior. The other one tells me, "A letter came once. To our mom. Not much of one. From someplace foreign."

"Do you remember where from?"

She pauses. The hum of the highway fills the space between us. "Come on in," she tells me. "I'll give a look."

I take three careful steps into the cramped foyer as she heads to the back of the house.

Now the thin sister returns, handing me a ragged plastic tumbler of ice water, which is nice of her, it really is, though it tastes kind of like refrigerator.

The other sister comes back. She hands me a gray envelope. The stamps say *Danmark*.

"You can have the letter," she says nonchalantly, without, bizarrely enough, even asking who I am or what I want her brother for. I could be mistaken for an undercover cop way easier than a judge.

In her other hand she holds a wine bottle, which she also gives me. The label's a piece of masking tape with *Nocino 1970* written in green Magic Marker. I have no idea what nocino is. "If you see him, it's his favorite. We can't stand the stuff. Our dad used to make it. Just been collecting dust in the basement."

That's nice of them. They're nice. Sad seeming, but nice.

Once back in the Datsun, I pull the letter from the envelope. It's a single handwritten sheet of gray stationery. The fact that it's in Mike Abramczyk's hand works on me like a fetish. I've never seen what the guy looks like, but, crazy as it seems, hearing his voice and his playing has given him power over me in the few short hours since I found the record. The words he wrote are few and simple:

July 17, 1978

Dear Mom,

Been all over Europe by now. Know you've always wanted to come here, Paris especially. Someday I want to bring you. You'd love it. The ladies are so fashionable. I'm tired but happy.

Your Son,
Mike

Though the Lacs' house on Geranium is pretty much the same as the Abramczyks' and all the others around the refinery, it's also the opposite. Like it was built yesterday, not right after the War. White paint so fresh it looks wet. Windows like water. Lawn green and dewy, even though it's a hot summer afternoon. Flower beds chock-full. The yard's all garden, like in a magazine. I open the gate—a wooden one instead of the Cyclones everywhere else—go to the door, ring the glowing bell. No answer. I count to thirty before pressing it again, then wait a minute more before leaving for the phone booth at the gas station on the highway. I call a bunch of

Lachapelles. No answer at five of them, three hang up on me, two never heard of Matt, and then, finally, a woman with a deep crack through her voice tells me, "He's deceased," hanging up before I can get a question in. I stand there, zoning out on dial tone. Something inside me collapses. When I get myself together, I return to the Lacs'. Still no one there.

Back home, I head upstairs to my desk to write a letter to Mike Abramczyk at the return address on the envelope from Denmark, despite the fact he probably hasn't been there in all these years. That is, if he's even still alive. I feel like I can't not mention how I got the address (on the chance my visit might prompt his sisters to write to him). I ask if he would please be so kind as to get back to me, a young writer researching a book about the early punk scene here, because, hey, you guys started it all. I do upbeat well. The book ruse is the best I can come up with. I mention Rongo, the Vinyl Heart, the River Club and anyplace else here in our shared home-town of Hallein we might have in common. Between every stilted line I write flow unwritten lines telling him how I want more than anything to jam with him, learn to be an artist from him. Even to myself, this fantasizing gets a little creepy when it reaches the point of wanting to hang with him. That said, my lust is pure. As in, not sexual. Not like I have any choice in the matter—I don't have the slightest idea what the guy looks like—but still, I deserve at least some credit. I ask if he could possibly tell me where Bobby Godek and Pete Lac might be, and if he would please tell me about how they all met, how the band formed, etc. The letter's getting long so I wrap it up, closing most cordially. That's me, cordial.

There's a fake-ass polite knock on my bedroom door, and before I can even say "come in," Vashti's just-poking-her-head-slash-barging-in as usual. Boundary issue #39. Another minute and she would've witnessed me in manual overdrive. That would've been pretty, very pretty.

"Peace offering?" She holds up a bag from the Golden Dragon. She's in her yoga getup, hair in a do-rag.

It's after nine and I'm only now realizing that I am hungry so decide to play along with whatever scenario's filling her head. "Sure, I'll be down in a sec."

As I mosey into the kitchen, rubbing my sleep-deprived face, Mom's pulling cartons with the familiar writhing red-and-gold dragon out of the bag. She sets them in a row on the island. "Sorry," she offers, "if I overreacted this morning."

"Sorry about going through your stuff." Truce comes easier when I'm tired and hungry.

She opens the cartons, sliding one, along with a pair of chopsticks, toward me. "Your potted eel with bitter melon."

This is major. Along with various dishes featuring jellyfish and chicken feet, the eel is one of the ones I order to get back at her for ordering lame things like chop suey, chow mein, and egg foo yong. Unlike most people, we never share Chinese. No common ground. Under normal circumstances, she wouldn't on her own order anything remotely like this for me. To be honest, I don't even like the eel all that much. Smells pretty atrocious, actually, and there's something grim about it, glowing brown and black and green under the low-hanging light. Fortunately, she also got eggrolls that she won't touch because they're deep-fried.

She sets a plate down in front of me before I can start eating straight from the carton, then nods at the two cartons of rice. I grab one.

I put some rice and eely goop on my plate, keeping them separate. I'm still preoccupied/obsessed with the record. I say, "Those guys—I mean the No Names—are from here, went to school here."

"I guess they did." She chopsticks some chop suey onto her plate.

"That's so cool." I grab both eggrolls along with two packets of Chinese mustard. "Did you know them?" I squeeze the mustard on the crisp golden shell and shove half an eggroll into my cakehole.

She hoists a mess of chop suey to her mouth, chewing a little before answering, "No, I didn't. Same as now, it was a big school. Nearly six hundred in my class. We ran in different crowds." She swallows. "I don't think they were even my year." Then, her expression changes, like she's trying to figure out some big-deal mystery. She lays her chopsticks down with maximum deliberation, close to full-on dramatic. "How do you or anyone know anything or even care about this random, obscure band?"

Mouth stuffed with the other half of the eggroll, I answer, "Rongo." I swallow big. "Went down to the Vinyl Heart. He told me about them."

She drops her voice an octave. "You're telling me you never made it to Buboltz and Stadler at all today?"

"I'm not telling you, but you can infer that if you'd like." So much for the truce.

"Look, I know you don't give a shit about whether you do anything with your gap year or not, but that's not cool." She pushes her plate away.

She likes calling my not going to college a gap year. Softens the blow. I raise another good hunk of goopy, squishy eel, and arc it artistically into my wide-open mouth, chewing with faked relish. Tastes better than it smells. What she doesn't seem to understand is that I *do* give a shit. I want to get out of here, get away from her and ride as far south as humanly possible. "Don't you worry about a thing, Vashti."

She can't sit still. She gets up and starts clearing her place and closing the lids on the two cartons that are hers, though she's eaten next to nothing. She puts the food in the fridge before turning to look at me. "You've already blown off college and now the internship. In which case, you can get yourself a job, because if you think I'm underwriting any goddam motorcycle trip you've got another thing coming."

I'm surprised she didn't end the sentence with *young man*. The sad fact is, thanks to her indulging my every desire, I've never even had an after-school or summer job. I'm the only kid I know who's given carte blanche with the parental credit card. If she cuts it off now that would most definitely put a serious dent in my plans. "Right," I say with a laugh, thinking she'll think I'm calling her bluff.

"Look," she says, moving back over to the island. "I know you think I'm a major downer, but I'm worried. Worried you're going to get killed, either in an accident or by bandits. I've read stories." She puts her arm around me.

I stay seated on the stool while at the same time shrinking away from her.

She tousles my hair. "And where you going to go without a degree?" She pecks my cheek. "Remember, you're gifted."

What she really means is that I'm an investment and she doesn't want to take a loss. "Don't patronize me," I grumble.

"It's called parenting."

I get up, leaving her arm dangling over the back of the stool. I take my nearly full cartons of Chinese and dump them in the trash.

1973, MIKE

Never had a best friend before—was always a loner—but from Day One Pete and I have been solid. I still don't get it. I mean, he's the outgoing type and, when he moved here, looked like one of the rich kids from the Heights, though in fact he came from the Flats, just like me. Just like me, only different. His family moved from California for a job his dad took at the refinery as a safety engineer, which puts him pretty far above my dad who works as a scrubber. His dad went to college on the G.I. Bill; mine didn't even finish high school. There's a hierarchy at the refinery. There's one everywhere. When they moved here, Pete was still wearing 501s with creases ironed in them, loafers without socks, and Alligator shirts, not the Wranglers, sneaks, and Fruit of the Loom T-shirts most of us guys from the Flats wear. Sure, he looked pretty much like he came from the Heights but somehow cooler, nothing stuck-up in the way he carries himself. Within a few weeks of moving to Hallein, he made starting JV quarterback and had a bunch of rich girls following him around.

We met first day of school. Music class. Everyone's worst. For most of the period I didn't notice him across the room on the other side of the double horseshoe of desks because I was seated right behind Doi Sargent with her big, beautiful halo of an Afro. She and I had been paired to perform "Sloop John B" together. Everyone was forced to do it, paired randomly, boy-girl, boy-girl, with the boy strumming ukulele and the girl shaking maracas. The duos before us pretty much mumbled their way through the song, missing every beat. I was not looking forward to our turn, but glad I was with Doi. I like her. She and I are among the kids who stop under the railway trestle for one last cigarette on the way to school. None of us smokers really speak at that hour of the morning, and I didn't really know her, but the spring before she had made a comment about *Hamlet* in English class that I thought was brilliant, so I got up the courage to tell her that the next morning. I spoke right as the salt cars rumbled overhead so had to repeat myself like three times. Her comment in class had been about "to thine own self be true." Polonius's advice sounded good on the surface, but she wondered how anyone—especially young people like Polonius's son or Hamlet or Ophelia—could even know oneself, let alone be true to it, and what if it was a no-good, evil self? As she smudged her butt out on one of the steel pillars, she nodded and thanked me for the compliment, adding that she didn't know anyone, except the teacher, was paying attention.

Doi and I took the makeshift stage in front of the piano. Only because of her was I even going to try at all. From the very first note, her voice lit the entire room. It had power, it had beauty. After the first couple of measures, my awe turned to inspiration. My murmur became audible words, and my Tiny Tim strumming the ukulele got a dose of Hendrix whaling on electric guitar. Doi was putting her heart and hips into it, so I did too. In any case, I thought we were doing great. And the audience of classmates that had been sitting there like zombies started clapping and cheering. But Doi and I didn't even make it much past the second verse when Mr. Garvey leapt to his feet to cut us off, practically apoplectic, because no, no, no, this wasn't R & B, this wasn't rock and roll, this was *calypso,* and you, young sir, are no Little Richard, and you, young lady, are no Miss Aretha Franklin. Doi scowled at him as he shooed us back to our seats. Good for her. We sure as hell weren't his Beach Boys, and maybe that was our point. It was only then I saw Pete. He was grinning and called out to Doi and me, "Far out!"

The calypso death march through the roster was interrupted. We were going to have a very, very special treat. A senior by the name of Cindy McNabb was dropping by to inspire us lowly sophomores as to the possibilities of music. The kind of girl still wearing light-blue cat-eye glasses and curling her hair, she had the tremendous honor of being Mr. Garvey's pet. So, this Cindy McNabb came twirling into the classroom, dressed in a blue-check dress with a matching ribbon in her hair, carrying a hurricane lamp, and singing "O-o-o-klahoma!" at the top of her lungs, like a cartoon opera singer, while Garvey pounded away at the upright, an arrogant grin smeared across his face. Doi whipped around in her seat, shaking her head, mouthing to me, *Fuck this shit!* while at the same time laughing, raucous but silent. It was as she was turning back around that Pete was fully revealed to me. We looked at each other, both shaking our heads, both grinning wide. We'd never seen each other before so of course had no idea how intense each other's interest in music was. Good music, that is. Anyway, we were bonded forever by Cindy McNabb *proceeding*—as Garvey put it—through an incredibly long medley from *Oklahoma!:* "I'm as corny as Kansas in August . . ." Exactly. Lucky for Pete, time ran out and he never had to do his "Sloop" duet.

After that first day, Pete and I did the cool-guy nod passing in the halls. Then, second week, he got transferred into Mrs. Homer's English class, the only college-prep class I've been in and by far my favorite. She's the only teacher I've ever really liked. Definitely not one of those mellow hippie teachers telling us how it is, just a lady in horn-rimmed glasses and tweed suit with a big love for literature that she loves sharing with kids. She's not the kind who feels she has to relate to you or that the books have to relate to our lives, at least not directly. They only have to be great and written by geniuses. She also loves words and makes us learn long vocab lists and etymologies, which I actually like a lot. I'm now kind of obsessed with new words, what my mom complains are *five-dollar* ones. I also like Mrs. Homer because she doesn't either like me or dislike me. All other teachers are one way or the other. They either like me because I'm a good-looking kid (according to the grown-ups) who seems troubled, so they want to help me, or else they dislike me because I seem like trouble. It's kind of hilarious, given my rep as a disaffected youth (Mrs. Homer's term for Holden Caulfield), that the Lady in Tweed should be my lodestar.

I remember so clear the day Pete joined the class. We were doing Emily Dickinson. Mrs. Homer was finishing reading aloud "I Felt a Funeral in My Brain," and I was sitting there totally mesmerized:

As all the Heavens were a Bell,
And Being, but an Ear,
And I, and Silence, some strange Race
Wrecked, solitary, here–

And then a Plank in Reason, broke,
And I dropped down, and down–
And hit a World, at every plunge,
And Finished knowing–then–

Mrs. Homer was so into the poem she hadn't so much as looked up when the door opened, even though everyone else turned to see who it was. The new kid. He stopped and stood there under the threshold, like his breath too had been taken away by the poem. Some months later he told me that's exactly what had happened. Maybe Pete and I and Mrs. Homer were the only ones in the room who felt moved, but that's all that mattered. *And I, and Silence, some strange Race / Wrecked, solitary, here—* Those words played over and over in my head, saying to me all that needed to be said about what Mrs. Homer calls "the human condition." In that moment, I felt I finally had someone to share the company of Silence with.

Third week, though, I nearly murdered Pete. It was the school's annual slave auction. It's so wrong on so many levels that we even have a slave auction and definitely a huge mark against me that I know this and yet still got involved. The auction is to raise money for activities, so the guys in AV Club pressured me into getting auctioned off because we needed money to buy a better turntable for DJing school dances. They were sure girls would bid on me like crazy.

My head hung in shame as I walked from my place in the audience up onto the auditorium stage. In the back row sat the handful of Black kids at school, all girls except Ozby Hancock. The guys had either dropped out, been sent up to Camp Comstock, or spent their days down at Golden Gloves. Like all assemblies, the slave auction was mandatory. The Black kids slouched down in their seats in the back row, arms folded tight across their chests, defiant looks on their faces, none more so than Doi Sargent. For sure, any chance I ever had of asking her out, or of even being her friend, went right down the toilet when she saw me up there. I didn't blame her if she never talked to me again. Not at all. I had only myself to blame for taking part in such an incredibly twisted event.

The guys in AV were right, though, the girls got a bidding war going on me. The giggles and shrieks flew around the room. Only trouble was, halfway through, Pete, who I'd never exchanged even one word with, joined in the bidding, eventually outbidding them all. He bought me. Pete actually bought me. Always—and I mean always—a guy buys a girl to do something like bake him brownies or eat lunch with him, or a girl buys a guy to carry her books, walk her home from school, etc. Guys don't buy guys. It's just not done. I was standing on the stage thinking, *What the hell?* There were catcalls accompanying "Going, going, gone!" that continued as I walked down off the stage and up the center aisle to my master, as required. I could barely lift my feet. Doi Sargent, sitting there in the back, was shaking her head. I avoided her eyes but thought I heard her amid the laughter of the crowd, throwing *Hamlet* back in my face. "So, *this* is your true self?"

I'm definitely not the type of guy who takes kindly to being put in embarrassing situations. I wanted to punch this California kid out, except he was giving me two thumbs-up as I approached, like I was in on the prank. He was laughing full-on, which made everyone understand he knew it was so gay for a guy to buy a guy but that he was guy enough to pull it off.

As Pete and I were walking out of the auditorium, he turned to me, and the first thing he said was, "I'd like to see your record collection." A joke pickup line? I was about to tell him where to get off, when he added, "I hear you're the music guy." That flattered me enough to almost forgive him for the whole fiasco. I'm that pathetic. For my slave duty I had to have him over to my house after school to see my record collection and then go over to his house the next day to see his. In the end, mine was the cooler of the two, if I do say so myself. My Deep Purple *Who Do We Think We Are* and New York Dolls beat anything he had.

Not long after our friendship began, in the school cafeteria, where other kids could hear, Pete asked me, "What do you think our place in history is going to be?" Right there, eating sloppy joes and wilted green beans, sucking chocolate milk from wax cartons with red-striped straws, and with eight other kids at the table, he asked me this like he was some professor in a movie. No one had ever asked me a philosophical question before, not to mention the fact I'd never heard anyone ask anyone else one either, at least not in real life. I'd soon find out he had this nerdy interest in philosophy and ancient history. When he was like ten, he saw *A History of Western Philosophy* and the first three volumes of *The Story of Civilization* at a rummage sale and for some reason had to have them. He begged his mom to get them for him, and she did. I couldn't picture that going down with me and my mom. Not ever. Anyway, in the cafeteria he told me, "Just like ol' Julius Caesar, you've got to make your name in the provinces, then you cross your Rubicon and take over the whole damn show, which in his case meant the whole empire."

"Wasn't it true, though," I asked after pausing, "that Caesar's buddies killed him because he turned into a tyrant?" I remembered that from Shakespeare.

"Minor detail." He was smirking. "But seriously, man, you've got to have a vision and a mission, so you don't lose your way and wind up being one of the plebes." Gesturing at the tables around us, he proclaimed, "'It is a rough road that leads to the heights of greatness.'" I flashed a confused look, so he added with a laugh, "That's what Seneca tells us."

Seneca? The name didn't help. I thought it was a kind of grape juice or an Indian tribe. I didn't ask him to clarify, though afterward I made the rare trip to the school library to look it up. Stoic philosopher.

Another day, we were walking along the riverbank when he asked me the meaning of life. He actually asked me that. It was October, the air cold, and I was wearing only a jean jacket over a T-shirt, so I told him the only thing that meant anything to me right then and there was staying warm.

"That's the problem with you," he said, "you're no better than an animal." He blew his nose onto the back of his hand, flicking the snot into the dead weeds.

I wasn't sure how to take what he said. I touched the bark of a cottonwood as we passed by. It felt like Styrofoam.

"Look," he said, stopping dead in his tracks, "you and I and everyone are accidents of chemistry, and this river an accident of geology, gravity, and whatnot, but that doesn't mean we can't imagine something else, that we can't be fucking profound. 'The unexamined life is not worth living.' That's Socrates."

I put my cheek on the trunk of another cottonwood and shrugged as I told him, "Okay then, if Socrates says so." My sarcasm was clear, but what I didn't tell him was that I actually did like it when he brought me out of my blindness and blankness. *Accidents. A happy accident meeting you, Pete Lac.*

Though I've never worn Alligator shirts like Pete does—and in fact never knew they were really called Lacoste after a guy nicknamed the Crocodile—some people think we're brothers. A few even wonder if we're twins. Which is a riot because he's half Japanese. I guess if you want two people to look alike, they will. That said, we do resemble each other somewhat. Both about five-ten. Both wiry, though he has more decent muscle than I do. Both have kind of long, what you'd call black hair, pale skin. But if you really look, our coloring's different. My skin and hair have more of a bluish hue to them, his more coppery—his hair the color of root beer. We have the same black eyes, which are really just super-dark brown. Weird thing is, he claims mine are more slanted than his. One difference between us looks-wise is that he has this sharp left canine tooth that slightly overlaps the incisor. It makes him look fierce. What really separates us, though, isn't any physical trait. When you meet Pete, it's obvious, he's at ease in the world, that he doesn't look back on any mistake. With me, it's the opposite.

Our voices have a similar dark tone, except we definitely do not speak the same. Despite being a philosophy buff, Pete swears a lot, uses slang, and finds it hilarious that I hardly ever do. I don't know why I don't. All my buddies do, my family does. I guess I've always just tried to speak plain. Not as proper as I'd like—grammar's not my strong suit—just kind of neutral. I suppose that I'm fooling myself into believing that by doing so I can somehow escape the time and place I'm living in. Along with the swearing, Pete also makes things sound really formal in a wacked-out kind of way. I know that sounds like a contradiction. Maybe it's more him making fun of formal language? For instance, instead of saying, "Let's go!" or "Hurry up!" he'll say something like, "The advision of hustle is upon you." Or instead of, "The food tastes great," he'll comes up with, "The excellence of the grub is made manifest."

I practically live with Pete's family now. My house is impossible. Impossible, though probably not any more impossible than most others in the Flats. Company houses. Built by the refinery and sold to workers supposedly for cheap. Postwar, two- or three-bedroom ramblers. A two-bedroom with five kids is not that unusual. The Doctovics have ten kids in a three-bedroom. I've got three older sisters and had a brother. We all lived together in our two-bedroom until John died in Vietnam when I was twelve. Jeannie, the oldest, got married the following spring and left. My two other sisters, Anne-Marie and Terri, are still at home. Plus, we now have Anne-Marie's kid, Blake. She got pregnant by her boyfriend P.J., but then he got sent up for stealing cars. I slept in a dresser drawer in my parents' room till I was nearly three, though Mom usually brought me into bed with her when Dad left for his shift. She'd say the rosary a lot or talk on and on, either to me or to herself. As a baby, I couldn't tell which. Sometimes I'd crawl out of the dresser and to John on the couch, where he slept. He'd pick me up and cuddle me against his stomach until I fell asleep. At four, I had a rollaway in the girls' room till John died, after which I moved to the couch. When Blake came along, and was caterwauling all the time, I retreated to a corner of the basement. Pretty dank, and there are spider nests up among the pipes that come back no matter how often I vacuum them out, but at least it's private, except when someone comes down to do a load of wash. I try to give a little life to my space. I set up a black light to shine on posters I've taped on the walls. My favorite one's of this beautiful girl with long, flowing hair, riding on the back of a giant psychedelic butterfly through outer space. One other good thing is the only books in the house are down there. I found them, all dusty and mildewed, thrown in an open box with a broken pair of binoculars, some extension cords, mousetraps, and lids to canning jars. The titles are random. Two volumes of the *Grolier Encyclopedia* (G, H, I and Q, R, S); *Reader's Digest Condensed Books, 1958, volume #4* (*Preacher's Kids, The Steel Cocoon, Women, Thomas Harrow, Green Mansions, Tether's End*); *The Holy Bible;* and *The Blue Poetry Book*. So, I have encyclopedic knowledge of all things *g, h, i, q, r, s*, and the Bible (which has way cooler stories than those condensed novels). I have no idea how a poetry book from the 1800s ever got into this house. Nothing poetic here or in any of us. But that book saved my life. When I needed to escape, "To a Skylark" and "Kubla Khan" took me far away. I memorized them. And "Annabel Lee" the week after John's funeral.

Not sure I understood much of any of them, but they hit me hard, and "Lycidas" is maybe the best and saddest thing I've ever read: "For Lycidas is dead, dead ere his prime . . ."

Dad's always trying to keep the house picked up. It gets kind of crazy, what with Blake's baby stuff strewn everywhere. Dad works night shift, scrubbing pipes and tanks. He comes home grimy from petrochemicals, then, after showering, cleans the house. When he's home, he's as silent as his saxophone that sits on a shelf in the basement collecting dust. He was in a dance band before marriage and kids derailed his music dream. There are pictures. He looked slick in a red tux jacket, letting loose on his horn. When I was little, I begged him to play. Once in a great while—maybe half a dozen times?—he'd bring the sax out and played jazz that came out of him like an incredible dream, filling me.

Pete's house has a totally opposite feel. First off, he's the only only-child in the Flats, so there's room to breathe. And his mom keeps the place immaculate. No clutter. Not a speck of dust on the coffee table—and it's the glass kind—or streak on any window. She's a certified Master Gardener, too, so theirs is the only house in the Flats with flower beds all the way around. Plus, they're weeded. The place looks right out of a fairy tale. The bushes are pruned into cool shapes, what jerks around here say is *Jap style*. I was actually surprised the first time I came over to find out that Mrs. Lac is Japanese. Pete hadn't mentioned it. As he joked, I look more Japanese than he does. First time I heard him speaking Japanese with her, it was like he was someone I didn't know, a complete stranger.

Mrs. Lac's the only Oriental in the neighborhood, which has got to be hard, though she's never said a word about it, let alone complained. No one talks to her. It's like they're afraid of her. They say she's a war bride, and all these years later people still have something against the Japanese. But she's not a war bride. Pete's dad was stationed in Japan a decade after Hiroshima. Besides, she's way too young. For sure, hasn't hit forty. She's probably the most beautiful woman I've ever seen in real life. Slim, though not bony. Everything about her seems soft and good. She's got that same overlapping canine tooth Pete has, only hers is a little more prominent. He tells me that in Japan it's considered a beauty sign for women. I'll say. Also, she's nice to me the way most other adults are not. Talks to me like I'm a grown-up. I'm welcome in their home anytime. And she uses the word *home*. The rest of us around here say *house*.

It was maybe only my fifth time over to Lacs', a Sunday. I went because I was feeling down, didn't want to be alone, wanted to hang out with Pete. I opened the gate and was heading up the walk when a bird flew low overhead and smacked right into the front window. It dropped onto the yew hedge. I hustled over to see if it was still alive, which was totally unlike me. I'm usually the guy trying to pick birds off a telephone line with rocks, and there I was lifting a regular old grackle from the top of the dark hedge, cupping the oily body in my hands. It was knocked out cold but still warm, still breathing.

Mrs. Lac had apparently heard the bird hit the glass because she was already at the door, holding it open for me. "Oh, Mike, come in, please. Bring the sweet thing."

She led me back into her sun-yellow kitchen. From beside the fridge, she took a stepladder and climbed up to get a breadbasket down from way on top of a cabinet.

"Peter is out with his father," she explained as she came down.

A gun was lying on the table—a not-small pistol—taken apart for what I guess was, given the rags, cleaning. Aside from in a policeman's holster, I'd never seen an actual gun. Why was there a gun?

She took a red-checked dish towel from a drawer and folded it so it fit perfectly into the basket. "Poor creature," she whispered to the bird or to me, taking it from my hands and placing it in the impromptu nest. To keep the bird warm, she placed the basket under the jug-lamp on the table. Then, with her delicate pinkie, she stroked its side. "Beautiful, no?"

And it was. I'd always thought grackles were as ugly as their name but guess I'd never seen one up close. It had iridescent blue feathers around its throat and forehead that highlighted the brown-black body. Its eyes were brilliant, light-yellow. Really striking.

"I think it will survive," she said, "I do."

I shifted from one foot to the other, mumbling, "Guess I'll be going now."

She looked at me kind of surprised. "Oh, they won't be much longer. You may wait here, if you'd like. Have a seat, please."

I felt like I was interrupting her day, though I have to say just being in her presence, even with the gun there, made me calmer. She has that effect on me, she definitely does. I shrugged.

"They're picking up a cord of wood." She gestured for me to take one of the yellow chairs. "At a farm, out near Bethel Grove."

That's the village my dad's people are from. Not sure why, but I didn't mention it.

"Would you like a cup of tea?"

Such a simple thing, but just her asking this nearly overwhelmed me. Like a moron, I again only shrugged. The kettle was already steaming. With a spoon, she pried open a metal can with a pattern of flowers and ladies in kimonos on it. Her slim fingers pinched out some dark leaves. I'd only ever seen tea in tea bags. She put the leaves in a tiny basket and rested it on the edge of a blue-and-white china teacup that didn't have a handle. After pouring hot water over the tea, she placed the cup in front of me and told me to let it steep.

Meanwhile, she picked up a rag torn from a man's undershirt and resumed cleaning the gun. I guess I must have been staring because she glanced over at me, laughing, "Don't be so surprised!" She then admitted that guns are an unlikely hobby for a Japanese person, especially a woman. "They are . . ." she said, then paused, grabbing a well-worn Japanese-English dictionary from the windowsill. She flipped through the pages ". . . They are . . . they are . . . *anathema*! Yes, they are anathema to the Japanese people." When she first came to the States, she explained, Mr. Lac had taken her along to the shooting range where he practiced and, as a kind of joke, let her try. To everyone at the range's surprise, including her own, she turned out to be a natural. And then, to their continuing amazement, in the following year she moved quickly from qualifying as "marksman" to "sharpshooter" to "expert."

"I have to practice later today at the Rod and Gun Club," she said, removing the little basket from my cup and resting it on a tiny and very beautiful plate patterned with blue and yellow flowers. "The state action-pistol competition begins in only two weeks."

I sipped the tea, letting it burn my upper lip to distract me, to keep me from staring at her.

"Have you ever gone shooting, Mike?" Out of my silences she was trying to weave conversation. If she only knew how much there was that I wanted to say.

"No," I mumbled, shaking my head slow and stupid.

"You might like it. Would you want to try sometime? Peter doesn't care about it."

"That might be fun," I said with a dullness in my voice I couldn't seem to shake. When I was a kid, I'd wanted a BB gun, but Santa couldn't afford one. Then I almost bought a .22 when I was fourteen and started earning money but decided to save up for a motorcycle instead.

"We'll arrange it."

"Okay."

"You seem down," she said, examining the gun. She held it up to the window for better light.

This time, I didn't so much as shrug.

"School okay?"

"Sure."

"Work?"

"Busy."

"Oh, Mike, I'm sorry. I'll stop pestering now." She wiped the barrel. "They shouldn't be much longer."

"No!" I practically shouted, panicked that I'd wrecked one of the most perfect moments of my life. "No, I'm sorry. It's just that . . . I don't know . . . that's the problem."

She placed the gun down on the table, now focusing entirely on me. Normally, I'd hate the attention but not from her, no, not at all. "Would you like to talk?"

I met her eyes, gathered my thoughts, nodded. She responded

with a smile I'd never seen on anyone else, a smile that told me the world wasn't such a scary place but was in fact a place that might welcome even the likes of me. I practically whispered, "It's really not such a big deal."

"That's okay." She folded her hands on the tabletop. "Sometimes the small deals are the ones that matter."

I took another sip of tea. It tasted smoky, it tasted good. "Well, they're teaching me how to paint cars at the shop—even custom work—and that's great and all, but I just don't know . . ."

She waited before asking, "What don't you know?"

"The thing is, I really do love cars and motorcycles. How they run, how they look. And, at least to me, the paint's a miracle." I had told her this, like the second time we met, when she asked where I worked. Pete was shaking his head and laughing as I explained to her that it's not as if the invention of car paints is up there with the invention of the wheel or penicillin, but when else in the history of civilization has there been so much color, and so many amazing colors? Like jewels, I had only half joked, monster-sized jewels. Except, unlike jewels, they're everywhere, for everyone! Maybe I was trying to impress her with my goofing, but underneath that's how I truly felt and pretty much still feel, and yet, I just don't know if I want painting cars to be my entire future. I breathed in slow, then sort of held my breath before answering on the exhale. "The purpose maybe?" I wanted to give her more than this. I forced myself to add, "I never thought there'd be a real purpose to life— you know, *purpose* purpose—not till recently." I didn't tell her that it was Pete who had changed this for me, that it was Pete who had made me discontent with life in the Flats and to think beyond it. Now I want to try other things, see other places. Before Pete, I'd never been either content or discontent. He was the unpredicted, random factor in my life that came along and made it what you maybe could call a life.

She seemed to consider what I'd said carefully, before responding, "In some ways, the problem you mention—one's purpose—is never, or so it seems, answered, at least not completely."

That got me all panicky. I wanted her to be as certain as that gun. "But you've found purpose, right?"

She frowned slightly, profoundly. "In large part, yes." Then she kind of blinked or winced. Pete had told me that as a child she'd survived the US firebombing of her hometown by crouching the whole night with her mother in a pond behind their house. The details he described changed me in ways I still can't account for. The lotuses floating on the water withered. The school of calico— calico?!—carp under the surface either suffocated or cooked. And yet, she and her mother survived. Survived, only to discover when the air raid was over that her father and brother never made it out of the burning house.

"I have a husband and a son to care for," she continued, "a house to keep up. These are essential. They bring me joy. Most of the time." She laughed softly. "And, for myself, I have my garden and my guns." With a smirk, she lifted the weapon. "And now that I've finished the certification for Master Gardener with the university extension, I can help people with their gardens. I'm going to enjoy that. Did I have bigger dreams? Certainly. I dreamed of becoming a Japan Airlines stewardess so I could see the world! Only I didn't realize that girls from poorer families such as mine weren't considered. The daughters of big-company executives got those jobs. I was even so naïve as to dream that once I was a stewardess, I could work my way up to pilot! Given circumstances . . ." Her voice trailed off. "This is why you boys have to dream big, as they say here. This dreaming big is what I love about this country." She clasped her hands together. "So, dream big! There's nothing at all to be ashamed of about working on cars, but if there is something else you want, make that your purpose."

The bird was now trying to move its wings, almost as if it was wanting me to recognize it as a symbol. An obvious enough one, for sure.

"What if that's not clear?" I coughed into my closed fist. "I mean, the purpose." What I didn't ask was, *What if everything about this world except for you and Pete makes me sick and angry?*

34

She reached over and placed her hand on my forearm. "Maybe it will never be perfectly clear," she answered, "but something will come to you. Of that, I am sure."

One of the first things Pete and I ever did together involved major arson. He of course saw it different, saw it as rebellion. As was usual, after school we were roaming along the river by our houses, getting high before dinner. He'd just picked up a bull snake with his bare hands—a good four-footer—from a flat rock where it was trying to get what little warmth was left in the day and the year. They're sluggish and easy to catch when the weather gets colder. He wrapped the red-and-yellow reptile around his neck, like a scarf, as he took a toke. Freaked me out a little, the snake that is. Hadn't yet gotten used to this thing he has for them. Unlike just about every other primate on the face of the earth, he's not wired to be afraid of snakes. In any case, the river and bluffs have always been a place away from the crazy of my house and the ugly of the Flats. Pete and I call it our own private Walden. As the two of us were walking up the bluffs, we noticed how fast the condominium development was going up a ways downriver. At the exact same time we both declared that was bullshit. The more we talked, the more pissed off we got, even though we didn't really know what a condominium was. Nobody around here did, not till they started building these. We only knew we hated what they were doing to our sanctuary. Rich people were taking over everywhere.

The construction crew had gone for the day. As usual, they'd left a huge pile of scrap lumber and other construction debris burning. Before I realized what was up, Pete had grabbed a burning two-by-four from the edge of the blaze and, with that snake still around his neck, went charging into one of the already framed condos, shouting, "The revenge of Prometheus!" He began torching the place. I couldn't believe it—he was torching the place. I was scared, I was excited. "Come on!" he yelled. I hesitated before pulling a torch of my own out of the flames. I ran into the next building, touching off fires along its entire length. Would-be rooms burned all around us. Pete's face turned insane with something resembling laughter, but different. It was the first time I'd seen that maniacal look that, for some strange reason, I've learned to love. By then, he was surrounded by huge, twisting flames, swinging his torch in great arcs. When all six buildings were finally on fire, we retreated upriver to watch our handiwork. We didn't think we'd done anything criminal, at least not at the time, not until his dad mentioned it in his concerned citizen voice while reading about it in the paper. He had no idea it was us.

We'd acted in defense of nature, of that Pete was positive. "Fuck their progress," he said, finally taking the snake off and laying it on the ground. "Gotta burn Carthage before Carthage gets built." Whatever that means.

NOVEMBER 1973, MARIKO

It was like nothing I had ever seen. Not in Japan, not in California. Swans—tundra swans they're called—filled the sky above a great bulge in the Steel River where it forms a bay of sorts. Hundreds of different flocks of them, or perhaps smaller divisions of one enormous flock, flew in from all directions, at all different heights, wings lit gold by the lowering sun. The countless calls—some whistling, some bugling *oo-oo, oo-oo,* while still others were *click-clicking*—blended and yet remained distinct, creating an ultimate music that blotted out any thought of a self I had separate from the birds, the river, the sky, the sunlight. My soul opened wide.

Mike took Peter and me to see them, the two of us being new here. We had never heard about this spectacle of nature. He came bursting into the kitchen, shouting, "Mrs. Lac, the swans! The swans are back!" I had never seen him so excited. We hopped in the car and drove downriver half an hour. He explained how the swans stop at that particular place on their yearly migration, to feed on the tubers of wild celery and arrowhead. Last year, more than fifty thousand birds came! I am grateful to him. I am grateful *for* him in our lives. He makes Peter happy. He makes me happy. He is so full of life. Not usually in an obvious way, as he was with the arrival of the tundra swans. More often quiet and thoughtful as he takes in the world around him. Funny to think that when I first met him, I misinterpreted his quiet as sullen or surly. I thought he was a bad boy.

Viewing the swans made me miss Cousin Keiko. She loves birds. She would be taken by this sight. She would burst into laughter over how amazing the world is! She loves everything and everyone. When I first moved to California, she took me to watch the swallows of San Juan Capistrano. We drove all the way from the Bay Area with our babies, and without our husbands, and camped. The thousands of swallows arrived on the same day, all the way from Argentina, pouring from the sky and entering their nesting places in the cliffs and in the eaves of the Spanish mission.

Long distance is expensive, but I will call her later tonight to tell her that next year she must come for the tundra swans. Seeing the friendship between Peter and Mike makes me long for her. With her I always feel more myself. I don't have a friend like her here. At times I do feel lonely.

MARCH 1994, ISAAC

Got home from the latest idiotic internship Vashti wrangled for me, wolfed down some sketchy leftover sushi, and headed up to my room to study Spanish for my Latin American odyssey. Unfortunately, I wasted my time with French in school. Vashti had told me it was a classier language. On the desk sat an envelope propped against the lamp. The rare letter for me, Vashti must've set it there so I'd notice it amid the chaos of the college applications I'm never going to fill out, model motorcycle parts, NHL cards, and sheet music. It was from the same address I'd written to Mike at way back in fall!

Wow. I'd given up on a reply, especially after having found out on *The Gazette* microfiche at the library that Bobby Godek died in '80. With two down, the fate of the two remaining band members didn't look great, especially given what Rongo had said about them being junkies and all. I sliced the envelope open with my Swiss Army, careful not to tear the cool stamps from Denmark showing castles and ruins. There was no letter inside. Only a brochure for a classical pianist. Total bummer. A preprinted note read: *Dear Music Lover, Daniel Beck thanks you for your interest. Please find below the schedule for his North American tour.* Probably no one even read what they thought was, oh, just another rambling fan letter in schizoid handwriting. On the outside of the brochure there's the kind of glossy picture you'd expect: this Daniel Beck, in tails, attacking the keyboard of a deep-space-black grand piano on the stage of a hall lit by a crystal chandelier big·as a merry-go-round. He has *classic looks,* as Vashti would no doubt say. Not a positive thing as far as I'm concerned. The schedule listed more than a dozen appearances—from Carnegie Hall to San Francisco—including one at our very own Hallein Orchestra Hall, in two months. Maybe he'd know something about the No Names? A scrap of hope.

I went down to the Vinyl Heart to find out more. "Ever heard of Daniel Beck?"

Rongo's face got all twisted. "You nuts, amigo? Only one of the greatest pianists on the planet."

Like I know classical? Famous for Beethoven, Chopin, and so on, Rongo informed this ignorant slut. He then led me to the classical section. Five Daniel Beck albums in stock, all on the biggest classical label. I studied the covers. Yeah, those classic looks to go with the classical music, but also something intensely serious about him I found myself kind of digging. His thick mane—wavy, gold—and star-blue eyes are, I'll bet, a big selling point for the females and gay guys. In any case, I bought all five.

"What's up with that?" Rongo wondered.

"Heard he's coming to town." Not exactly an explanation. Rongo looked skeptical. I smirked.

Can't say I'm a convert to classical, but after listening to the albums a few times I'm getting into Daniel Beck's Chopin Preludes and his Beethoven's *Emperor* Concerto. You'd have to be an idiot not to hear the genius of his playing.

By the day of the recital, I still hadn't figured out how I was going to get to Daniel Beck. Send a message backstage? He'd obviously assume it was from some deranged fan, which isn't far off the mark, though he'd have no way of knowing it was a deranged fan of a long-forgotten punk band, not him. Tell him I'm a reporter? That's a possibility, even though I have no credentials to flash and am only eighteen and probably look it. Stake out his hotel? I bet he's at the Grand, right across from Orchestra Hall, where important people stay. This was all getting to sound stalkerish. No, it *is* stalkerish.

The crowd at the recital went crazy the way polite people go crazy. *Clap-clap-clap, bravo-bravo-bravo.* Like a hundred encores. I paid enough attention to be able to flatter Daniel Beck if I managed to get to him. The Albéniz *Iberia,* for instance, was kind of amazing. The Mozart sonata was also cool: math made into art. I wasn't as bored as I thought I'd be, though I dig his music more listening to the recordings in my own space with a little bump from some good weed.

After Daniel Beck takes his *final* final bow and exits the stage, I'm feeling confident. As the audience files out, I stay behind, study-ing the possibilities. Stagehands come out and put the thick quilted covering on the piano and roll it away. If I look like I know where I'm going, I'm sure I'll succeed. It's all about attitude. I take the stairs up to the stage, three at a time, then head stage right, the direction in which Daniel Beck disappeared. Some bulky old guy in a boxy suit comes bustling toward me. He asks if he may help me. As inno-cent as can be, I reply, "I'm a young artist and would like to ask Mr. Beck's advice." I love that phrase, *young artist.*

This official informs me he's afraid that won't be possible, and promptly—and, I have to say, kind of abruptly—escorts me out to the lobby from where the last of the crowd is dispersing into the night. It's all about attitude. Not. If my charm didn't work on a nobody, then how's it going to work on a somebody? To be honest, I'm a little surprised by my failure. I mean, I'm wearing a brand-new CK suit bought on Vashti's dime. Right. I drop down onto one of the upholstered benches, resting my face in my hands, contemplating a next move. If Daniel Beck had only answered my letter from months ago about Mike Abramczyk and the No Names none of this tomfoolery (as Vashti would deem it) would be playing out.

When I've just about given up and am going to leave, I glance to my side, and who should be striding along but the star himself, with handlers of course. Bingo! He glances at me as he passes, probably with no particular interest other than noticing there is, aside from him and his people, someone else in the otherwise deserted lobby. There might be an electron of a smile in his eyes, or not, but I'll go with the charge.

I jump to my feet, asking with enthusiasm so over-the-top it stuns even me, "Excuse me, Mr. Beck! Would you be willing to answer a few questions? I'm with the . . ."

Before I can even finish my lie, the suit who appears to be in charge interrupts: "Mr. Beck gave all his interviews this morning. He looks forward to reading your review."

I'm about to say it's a quick question, when one the other goons steps between me and Daniel Beck. He totally cuts me off. "Thank you, but Mr. Beck has a schedule to keep." What a loser. I swear, Daniel Beck was about to say something to me when the head cheese starts ushering him and the group through the revolving door. I count to ten before following them out and across the plaza toward the Grand. I don't know if Daniel Beck senses me or not, but he glances back. Only then does it dawn on me just how crazy this stalking an international star is. Sure, it's only the classical music world, but still, what am I thinking? That he's going to say to some random, disturbed teenager, "Let's grab a drink?" Hell, why not? Got to stay positive.

The doorman nods as Daniel Beck and his crew pass into the hotel. He of course doesn't in any way acknowledge someone so obviously lowly as me. I keep my distance, staying in the bright lobby as the group enters the low-lit bar. I take a Louis-the-something chair in a corner, pretending to be reading my program. I'll wait them out.

Maybe an hour later the party emerges, less uptight, falling all over Daniel Beck with sloppy idol worship. The four shake hands with their star in that gropey kind of way business-types do, especially after a few, and then they leave. When Daniel Beck moves toward the elevators, I dart over, barely managing to slip in before the doors close. Three other hotel guests had already boarded. Buttons for floors light up—5, 9, 12, 17. If we were alone, I'd start up a conversation. Either he doesn't recognize me or he's following elevator etiquette and stares straight ahead at the door, silent. One person gets off at five, another at nine. Hopefully Daniel Beck is on seventeen, but no, he steps out on twelve, and so I, of course, do too. Trailing after him down the otherwise empty hallway feels even sketchier than following him on the street or hopping on the elevator with him. He stops in front of room 1211. I slow, almost to a standstill.

As he's unlocking the door—before I can even turn the charm on—he pivots to face me, asking, "You would like to come in?" Which is obviously different than *Would you like to come in?* in its assumption as opposed to invitation. Maybe it's simply stilted English? At least he hasn't threatened to call security. His question, though, has not only thrown me off my game, it has thrown me out of the freaking arena. Only now do I register what I've gotten myself into, though I can hardly play innocent. After all, I bought the CK suit for the occasion and, insane as it is, followed him into his hotel, to his room even.

After an absurdly slo-mo second, he answers for me: "Sure." He tilts his head and raises his right arm to usher me in. "Come in, but your questions will have to wait while I make some notes on tonight's performance."

So, he does recognize me as "the journalist," though I doubt he could believe I'm a real one. Basically, he sees me as harmless. At this point I'm not sure who's pursuing whom. He motions me to a wing chair as he crosses the crazy-big suite and sits down at an ornate writing desk, his back to me, a stack of sheet music in front of him, and starts writing. Never one at a loss for words, whether a remark (smart or otherwise) or a full-blown speech, I'm dumb-struck in his presence. It only occurs to me now, this late in the game, that he probably thinks I'm just another groupie looking for a star-fuck. Like rockers, I suppose classical artists have their share of fans offering themselves up like room service. I keep glancing at my Johnny Guitar Swatch, which suddenly looks ridiculous.

Almost exactly half an hour later he stands up and turns back around to face me. "So," he says, clapping his hands together, "now that you have my full attention, let's begin." He pauses, looks at my empty hands, then says, "Oh! Do you need some paper? Something to write with?" After an embarrassingly long moment of me uhm-ing and him smirking, he asks, "Or is there something else you would like to do?"

If nothing else, the guy gets to the point. There really should be something more mocking in his tone (that I've definitely earned). After all, he's calling me out on my lie and exposing me as the hustler I am only just now realizing I am. I didn't know my own intentions, not really. I thought I came here to get intel about Mike Abramczyk.

Fortunately, or unfortunately, the phone rings loud and fast the way only hotel phones do. He answers, face brightening, tone light-ening. He speaks into the receiver all lovey-dovey in obscure syl-lables. He doesn't turn away from me but doesn't look at me either. He's focusing beyond me, out the window, maybe down into the park below twinkling with little white lights, or further, to the dark river, or across the continent and across the whole damn ocean. He talks for over fifteen minutes, then offers kisses into the mouthpiece before placing the receiver back in its cradle.

"And so?" he asks, obviously not having forgotten his question from before the phone call.

I wonder who he was talking with. I almost want to ask in a cheeky kind of way that might help me regain a scrap of my for-mer joker of a self. Instead, I decide that, at this point, silence is probably my best option. He walks over to the sink at the wet bar.

Something about his hand turning the faucet really floors me. A whole ballet in that one gesture, and I'm not even high. He fills a glass, takes a long gulp, then hands it to me with a nod. I shake my head, so he downs the rest, throat pumping as elegantly as a throat can pump. He gathers up the sheets of music from the desk, placing them in a leather folder.

His response to my continued silence is to simply carry on, "But let's not have sex."

This time his directness throws me for a loop. I can't manage even so much as a fake laugh.

"Certainly not under these circumstances," he continues. His attempt to clarify only manages to obscure things. Maybe that's the intention? He comes over and takes the program from my lap, holding it up as if it's evidence. Of what? The circumstances? Of a star-fuck in the making? Sitting down on the arm of the wing chair, he adds, "You wouldn't want that, either."

I should be offended. I'm not even attracted to him, or at least not that much. Anyone else would take his words as those of an arrogant bastard, but I'm hearing a weird kind of sincerity, sincerity paired with pragmatism. Like there's a problem to solve. Makes me jumpy, confused. I tilt my head back and decide to come clean, or sort of clean, or at least a little less dirty. "Actually," I say, swallowing hard as I force the words, "I'm here for another reason."

His face turns serious as God's. He flexes one eyebrow.

"Don't know if you read it," I say, pausing, "but I'm the one who sent the letter to Mike Abramczyk. I'm the one writing the book about the No Names."

MARCH 1994, DANIEL

It was already the middle of the night when I had this fellow Isaac bring me here to one of the caves at the salt mines I know from Michael as a place so central to his past. Now dawn advances into

43

the abstract space with precision, with momentousness. It's as if it were a neolithic site for some astronomically based ritual, the significance of which is now lost, and not simply an abandoned mine. The darkness turns star-white. Walls, ceiling, floor all shimmer like an epiphany I cannot discern the meaning of.

This curious, young, would-be author lies curled by my side, asleep in ultramarine shadow. I am not sure that I have slept at all. I dreamed but I did not sleep. It's as if I were meant to keep vigil over a dreamworld not my own. Whose, though? Isaac's? Michael's? Peter's?

I should have dismissed Isaac straightaway at the hotel, but his appearance was so curious and out of the ordinary that I played along with him. First off, his eyes are different colors, the left one brown, the right one gray, giving the impression that he's looking in from another world. And he moves through the world as gracefully as a deer. But my attraction is more than physical. When he talks about things that are important to him—especially mathematics—he becomes excited and mischievous at the same time. It's as if he feels he is making mischief with the order of the universe.

Once Isaac revealed his book project, I saw him as a key to better understanding Michael's past, or at least someone who might show me the places Michael once frequented. I did, however, make it clear that Michael has no desire for any contact with him or anyone from his past, let alone interest in such a book. My first mistake was even letting him know that Michael is alive. He asked, I answered, and then he echoed me, though with question and joy flooding his voice, "He's alive? He's alive! He's alive?!" So why, then, have I entangled myself? Even our brief attachment will certainly give him false hope of reaching Michael. I will not give him any more information about the band.

My flight to Los Angeles leaves in a few hours. How am I to reconcile this simple fact of scheduled time with how, here in this glimmering cave, time has been suspended and distorted by dream and memory that are not my own, not my own and yet holding me captive?

The lake pulses below.

Isaac—red hair flecked with salt crystals, navy-blue suit white with salt dust—shimmers as rays reflecting off the walls now strike him. His bare feet start twitching with dream. Something about him disturbs me. I cannot pinpoint what it is. A few short hours ago, we lay down here together, to sleep. He wrapped himself around my back, reached down, placed his hand between my legs. Even as I was starting to get hard, I played dead until I could tell by his breathing that he had fallen asleep.

OCTOBER 1974, MIKE

Down by the river there's a keg, some weed, a bonfire. The usual Friday night. Maybe fifty of us, the ones who didn't go to the football game. Me and Pete because we got kicked off the team for pretty much doing what we're doing right now. A cute girl I don't really know named Debbie is looking up into my face, like one of those smiley-face buttons. She sticks her hands into the front pockets of my jeans because she's cold, she says with a laugh. But I'm wishing I was with this girl Lisa I see through the gyrating flames. I've never talked with her but saw her plenty at Mass when we were kids and I was an altar boy and watched everyone come and go from the pews, and we've exchanged glances in the halls at school ever since she came to public after Immaculate Conception closed. A guy I don't know has his arm around her. In the bright dome of firelight everyone seems happier than me. Louder too— shouting, laughing—too loud for my mood. I move downwind into the smoke and sparks because I don't want to join in the yakety-yak and the goofing, and also so Debbie won't want to come be with me. She does anyway, coughing from the smoke, asking why I'm always so quiet, even though we've only just met so it could hardly be *always*. She giggles as she asks this, but the giggle's fake, nervous. I make her nervous. She seems like a nice enough girl,

45

though. I can tell she's thinking I'm either a bad boy who's a nice guy or else a nice guy who's a bad boy.

Pete and I have the bad half of this rep because we smoke cigarettes and pot, and skip school, but mostly because one time we beat the shit out of (as Pete proudly puts it) a couple of rich jocks, soccer players. We call anyone who has more money than us rich, and what kind of losers except rich kids play soccer? People think we jumped them for kicks, but that's not true. It started last summer. It was hot as hades, and houses in the Flats don't have AC, so we were going for a swim in Deep Lake to cool off. We went to a weedy scrap of shore between the Yacht & Country Club and the rich people's so-called cottages, which are bigger than our houses. We'd always thought of that beach as a kind of no-man's-land. That day, the cops showed up and kicked us out for trespassing. This had never happened before. It was for sure those two soccer guys who called the cops on us. We could see them sitting over by their club's swimming pool, swilling bottled beer—most likely on their parents' tab—watching as the cops showed up to kick us out. We didn't actually see one of them go to the phone, but they were laughing like crazy, like it was the most hilarious thing ever. Some prank. Next time we saw them was maybe a month later, after school started, in the parking lot by the football field, and they were about to get into this sweet Triumph Spitfire done in that classic British Racing Green. They grinned when they saw us, showing off their straightened teeth. That's all it took. I led the attack and, I swear, it was directly to their faces. Pete reminded them in not-too-polite terms of the shitty thing they'd done. He took the one guy, I took the other. They acted all girly, screaming, trying to run away. Gave up fast. We pummeled them on the blacktop for only a few seconds. Bloody noses, nothing more. No big deal. Didn't matter, though. News spread like wildfire and got more and more tabloid with every telling.

So, this Debbie asks where I live, and when I say the Flats, she says, "Wow!" like I'd said Outer Mongolia or something. "Wow!" she repeats, then tells me, "From the highway at night it looks like a fairyland, or an outer-space castle—or something!—what with like millions of lights twinkling on all those towers."

"It's a refinery," I tell her. She looks hurt. Girls like her, rich ones from the Heights, would hold their noses at the chemical smell of the Flats, that is if they ever walked through. But I suppose I wouldn't know what the Heights smells like, either. Hallein is that way, divided. Us from the Flats almost never see any of the landmarks and areas the rich people and the tourists see. Likewise, the Flats is invisible to the rest of the city. That's why Pete and I call it Invisible City, after the cool title of a book that recently came out, *Invisible Cities*. Neither of us has read it, but Mrs. Homer talked about it in English class one day, and we dig what she digs. Besides, the name fits. Hallein, the biggest city between here and there, between somewhere and nowhere, might as well be invisible.

The moon comes on big and bold and bright. I've lost track of Pete. Some of the kids have paired off and are disappearing into the shadows. I toss my cigarette down in the sand and tell Debbie I've got to take a leak. I don't really have to, not after only two beers, but I want some space. And I don't want to go make out. I wander off into the sumac thicket, letting her hands get cold, I suppose.

After going only about a hundred yards into the thicket, I turn a sharp bend in the thread of a trail and suddenly there's a couple right there on the ground in front of me, naked. I think it's Pete—his backside—but it's hard to tell under the crisscrossing of shadows made by the bare sumac branches. It is Pete. He's on top of the girl. I can't see who she is. They're really going at it. I stop dead in my tracks in the deep sand. I've never even seen a picture or a movie or anything of anyone having sex, let alone right in front of me, in real life, let alone someone I know. It's real life, sure, but it feels like I'm making it up. Pete's ass flashes like a deer's and the girl's splayed under him, gasping every time he pumps. Her hair's spread over her face and across the sand, like waterweeds; her eyes are blotted out by the silver light. I still can't make out who it is. One of those rich girls, I think. Maybe called Jill or Kim? Her blouse is pulled up, jeans pulled down. What seems totally bizarre, though, is that it's cold out and Pete's buck naked. Not just his jeans pulled down, like her, but clothes flung every which way, some in the sand, some in the sumac branches. Maybe the scene's hotter than I'm making it sound, but also maybe not. She shifts her eyes to me, or past me.

I'm getting hard and feeling sick all at the same time. I stand there, stock-still, yet somehow Pete senses me and turns his head around. He flashes those black-diamond eyes of his at me while continuing to drill away. He then gives me a weird kind of grin. I can tell I'm supposed to give a thumbs-up, so I do. Like an idiot, I do. He turns back to this girl and at the same time reaches behind for my hand. He takes hold of it. I pull away, but he pulls harder and places my hand on her breast. Now I don't pull away. I should but I don't. Her eyes, suddenly legible, meet mine with what I read as scorn. Now I do pull my limp hand away, but he takes hold of it again, guiding it downward. Gutless creep that I am, I let him. "Grab hold, grab hold," he whispers. As if I know what I'm doing, I fix my palm and fingers around the base of his cock. It's slick and sticky at the same time as it moves in and out of her. Christ, what am doing? For maybe three breaths I hold my hand there before freaking out and jerking it away. He looks at me again, seductive this time, and I get the idea I'm supposed to join in, like take a turn or something. I shake my head slightly, murmur a feeble no, and step back. Something like a laugh, a very short laugh or maybe a yelp, comes from the girl. I turn away, wishing I hadn't let him do any of what he did to me, wishing I hadn't done any of that to her.

I'm pretty dazed as I head farther on through the sumac maze. I still don't really have to take a leak but should try anyway so I can at least tell myself I haven't lied to Debbie. When I whip it out, though, I'm too hard to get a stream going. So I wander around like my dad does when he tells my mom he's going out to get some air. I think about things, and I suppose Dad does too. I wish I knew what he was thinking at those times, and I also wish he knew what I was thinking right now. I'm thinking about how confused I am about girls and everything. I'm thinking about how what just happened probably bonded me to Pete forever and maybe also fractured that bond forever.

Here I am, wandering among the sumac—branches velvety as new buckhorns—when out of nowhere Debbie appears. Like she's hunted me down. Stands right in front of me, blocking the only way forward. She moves in closer, so we're practically chest to chest, then, quick as a gunslinger, gets her hand down the front of my jeans. She starts kissing me like crazy with her beer-mouth, sucking the breath right out of me. She pulls me down onto the damp sand, and even though I'm not wanting to, I'm kissing her back. We're Frenching and she lets her breasts out of her blouse and wriggles herself free from her jeans. Next thing I know, she's forcing my hand between her legs. I'm still hard and have a condom in my wallet but do not want to screw her. Definitely not.

I can't help but think about Pete and that other girl so close by.

Debbie flips me onto my back, and I kind of go with it. That is, until she's straddling me, at which point I freeze up. She pulls on my dick and starts working it into her. I whisper-yell, "No way," and try squirming out from under her. She succeeds at pinning me down only because there's no way I'm going to treat a girl rough. So I don't do anything at all. That is, until she starts riding my dick. I get mad—no, not mad, more like upset, confused by her determination—and then—I can't help it—I push her off me—like *wham*—and she goes flying across the small clearing, landing on her back in the sand about a body's length away. I can't believe I just did that to a girl. I jump to my feet, tugging my jeans up. I don't know why, but I say, "Sorry, I'm so sorry," and stalk back to the bonfire.

I want to be out of here now, I want to be alone, I want to not have to wait for Pete, but he drove.

When Debbie returns to the circle a minute or so after me, she's all bouncy and chipper. Saving face with a party face, I suppose. She picks her plastic cup up from a log, goes to the keg. All loud and sassy, she asks one of the guys to pour her one. Like she needs another. She's chatting him up, even as she starts moving in my direction. I'm embarrassed. Also scared, scared that even though I was barely inside of her and didn't come inside her—or come at all—maybe somehow some leaked out.

About five minutes later a couple I don't know wanders out of the thicket. A little while after that, more people—some together, some alone—appear, as if there'd been a secret signal. They head toward the fire, Pete among them, alone. He's forgotten to fasten a couple of buttons on his 501s. I either don't see or don't recognize the girl he was with among those returning.

By now, Debbie's back next to me and I'm ignoring her, which doesn't stop her from nuzzling into my denim shoulder. She murmurs something I can't quite make out. I think she wants me to say that I'll take her home. Not going to happen. She's a girl from the Heights, I'm a guy from the Flats. By some bump of fate, our totally opposite cliques have overlapped here tonight. Not sure why these rich girls weren't at the game.

Soon after Debbie and some other girls leave, everyone else starts drifting away. Except for me and Pete, the other guys trail after the girls.

"Following tail," Pete remarks, his voice lazy.

Right now, though, I'm feeling too weirded out about what happened in the sumacs with me and Pete, with Pete and that girl, with me and Debbie, to care about who's following who or what. It's going on midnight. Pete and I throw a couple hunks of driftwood onto the dying fire and sit down on one of the big logs. We take in both the warmth from the blaze and the cold of the sky above. This makes me feel a little better. I'm hoping there's enough history between me and Pete that we'll make it through this.

Nightjars—shadowy, spooky—soar all around, nabbing insects in midair. Pete and I track the sparks from the fire as they push through the smoke and eventually mingle with the stars.

"Whoa, my Mike!" Pete shouts after one humongous spark rises spectacularly. "That one's never gonna die!" He starts throwing rock after rock into the flames. Suddenly, out of nowhere, he asks, "Are you happy?" like it's a normal question.

I pull one of the last Marlboros from the pack in my shirt pocket before answering, "Yeah, sure." I light up. "I'm happy."

But he doesn't let things go at that, doesn't ever let me get away with anything. "But what does that mean, camerado divine?" He reaches over and punches me lightly on the chest. "What does it mean to be happy? What, my comrade in arms, is happiness?"

Somehow, his words are making what happened with the girls start to drift away up into the sky. I take a few quick puffs and shrug. It's involuntary, I swear. He of course won't accept that as an answer, either. He snatches the cigarette right out of my mouth, takes a good long drag, then starts lecturing: "Socrates was the first guy to say happiness is obtainable through human effort and not a gift from the gods. So, anustrious anus-brain, you should make the effort to at least think about what happiness might be." He hands the cigarette back.

Though this is the Pete I like, inside I'm squirming.

"So?" he asks.

Didn't realize he meant for me to think about it right now. I take a few more nervous drags before responding, "I suppose being out here thinking about the stars and outer space and life is happiness. And answering dumb questions." I smile but don't tell him what I'm really thinking: *Being here with you is happiness, because otherwise I'd be hurtling through the universe totally alone.*

"But wouldn't you rather be out here solo contemplating all of this?" It's like he's read my mind.

Then I do tell him, I tell him what I've been thinking. I don't look at him as the words stutter out but can feel him smiling.

After one of those long, easy silences we have lots of, I look over. With a slow wink he asks, "So, did you and that babe get it on?"

I hope the wink's ironic but am not so sure it isn't just plain sleazy. Until then, I'd been happily on my way to forgetting all that happened in the sumacs. One of the rocks he's been chucking into the flames explodes. I shield my eyes, then shake my head and tell a lie. "Didn't have a rubber on me." I'm too ashamed to tell what really happened.

"Didn't have one either, but there was no stopping us. When it was time, I pulled out, shot my load in the sand."

There's something in his bragging that's forced. By the way he glances away I can tell he knows I know this. He also knows I was there witnessing what was going on, so he adds, "Chicks are just plain weird. It's a whole lot easier hanging out with you."

For some reason those words kind of help. They shouldn't, but they do. Truth is, we both want some imaginary girlfriend that doesn't exist, someone like his mom, though obviously we don't say that.

At the edge of the river, a pair of small amber lights appears.

"Hey, a fox!" Pete shouts quietly, as only he can. The fox is standing flank-deep in the current, staring at us. The fire illuminates Pete's face gold. His eyes glitter fierce. The fox turns and trots down along the bank, away from us. Then, almost as if his voice is coming out of the silent dark all around, Pete asks, "Do you believe in reincarnation?"

I pause before answering, wondering what kind of trap he's setting for me. "Um, never given it much thought." That seems like a safe thing to say, and true. It's strange because I'm wishing I had a better answer, wishing maybe I had at least wondered even a little about reincarnation before.

He looks all dreamlike before speaking again. "That fox makes me think of this kid I swam with back in Cali. Keith Hernandez." He sneezes into his fist. "Swam a wicked butterfly. Also had this perfect memory, so he functioned as our nonstop jukebox between reps. One day after practice Keith hopped out of the pool singing Stevie Wonder—"My Cherie Amour"—and went running across the lawn toward where he'd laid his towel down." Pete took a long pause and stared at me. "Next thing you know, Keith's rolling around in the dry grass like a mad dog, howling. We all looked over. I was in the shallow end, leaning against the side of the pool, still catching my breath after the series of sprints he'd just smoked me on. There was a fucking snake stuck to his foot. A rattler had bit him on the bottom of the foot and was hanging there by its fangs. Keith and the snake were whipping around like they were caught up in a tornado. I jumped out of the pool, sprinted over, yanked the snake out of his foot, and tossed the motherfucker over the fence. By that time, Coach was there. He swept Keith, who was a big boy, up into his arms, like he was made of foam rubber, ran him to his truck, and rushed him to the hospital." Now Pete turns his stare downward into the sand between his feet. "A couple hours later, Keith was dead." He stares into the night, eyes on fire like a demon's.

"Jesus," is all I can say. What is it with Pete and snakes? Some rocks go *pop-pop-pop,* sending burning shrapnel everywhere. We duck for cover.

"Crazy as it sounds," he continues, "I swear Keith's spirit lives on in that fox." His voice is calm, certain. "Not because he was clever like a fox, or foxy like a girl, or looked like a fox, or anything like that. And not because I think about him all that much anymore. Keith was just there, in that fox. I mean, it would be cool if we all migrated into some other being." He gestures to what I guess is supposed to be our voices and thoughts—or possibly our very beings?—floating in the dark space around us. In any case, things that are hard to gesture toward.

"Yeah," I say kind of lamely, "it'd be nice."

"Well, the Greeks—or at least some of them—believed in reincarnation, only they called it 'the transmigration of souls.'" He snatches the cigarette from my mouth again, takes a sloppy suck, nodding as he exhales. "The religion around Orpheus, the poet guy, and Pythagoras, the geometry guy. Anyway, supposedly Orpheus's soul entered the soul of a swan after he died."

At this moment, Pete looks fierce and noble, like a warrior from the ancient times he loves so much. He hands the moist cigarette back to me.

I can't help asking, "Do you really believe in all that?"

He answers immediately, "I do." His eyelids flutter real slow, and then, without raising his head, he looks straight up into the sky, like one of the saints in the paintings at St. Ignatius I stared at as a kid. "I feel it, I really do." He lets out a sigh that's more like a hum. "Don't you ever?"

I shrug and stick the cigarette butt in the sand.

"For instance," he says, turning to look at me, "your brother. Don't you ever feel him in all the things around you?"

Except for John resurrected, more than anything else in the world I'd love to feel his presence. In a fox, a grackle, a bull snake, a cottonwood—anything. But I haven't. Not once in the four long years since he died. Something in me wants to tell Pete that I do, but I can't. Like Emily Dickinson when she was a girl and getting pressured by her school to say she'd been "saved," I can't perjure my soul, not even for Pete. I shake my head.

I'm not looking his direction but sense his face moving in closer to mine. "You've never told me about him," he whispers, "about what happened."

Truth is, I've never talked to anyone about John. Never wanted to. Now, for the first time, I do, or at least I think I do. Except words feel impossible in my head, let alone my mouth. We stay in our same positions in front of the fire, not saying anything. I light the last two cigarettes at the same time, hand one to him, and stare hard into the flames. I can't look at him.

"Hey man, you don't have to talk about it if you don't want to." He places a hand between my shoulder blades.

I cough. I do that when I'm nervous. A fake cough, my mom says. After a while, I force some words to come: "He was the best brother." I cough again, then go silent for a while before starting again, slow, with simple things, like how I looked up to him, idolized him really. Easy stuff: how John was a laid-back kind of guy, confident without being a jerk. How everyone said he was loyal, how everyone loved him, especially my dad. Plus, how great a mechanic he was. Had this amazing Kawasaki he treated like a baby. I don't tell him how the happiest I ever felt was with John on that bike. Before I was old enough to hold on behind him, he'd put me between his legs and we'd cruise slowly around the Flats. He'd ask, "Having fun, champ?" He called me that, champ. Later, when I could hold on, we'd ride up Deep Lake and onto the salt flats. He'd open the throttle wide, and we'd hit top speed without any thought of danger.

So free. We were so free. He'd tell me that when I got my own bike, the two of us would ride the nearly two thousand miles to California—and right across the Golden Gate Bridge—and camp among the giant redwoods.

I think, but don't say, that if John could tell his own story it would be way better than any I could tell about him, not to mention better and more important than any story I might tell about myself. The guys who came just a few years after the draft, like me and Pete, are kind of left without stories, or maybe it's just that our stories get eclipsed by guys John's age. Which only makes sense, what with the war and stuff. I don't tell how John's death turned me into what people say is sullen, sullen or moody. One thing I know for sure, though: since his death words have always come hard for me.

"He was drafted and shipped out before I really understood what it all meant. I was young, in my own world." I swallow hard. Feels like there's a baseball in my throat. "Next thing I know, we get a soldier at the door telling the family he's dead. My parents completely lost it. Didn't speak for what seemed like weeks." I don't explain that in some ways my dad hasn't really spoken since.

This time it's Pete who says, "Jesus," only he adds, "holy shit." He lifts himself up and turns so he's kneeling in front of me, his back close to the fire. He looks me right in the eyes, murmuring, "I'm so sorry, man." I have to close my eyes, afraid of crying or going crazy. He places a hand on my forehead, like my dad would when I was a kid, to check and see if I had a temperature. My breath stops. Everything in me seals up. Because I never cried as a kid, my mom would tell me that not crying's worse than crying. I don't know if I believe that.

When I finally get myself back together enough, I start breathing. I start breathing and I tell Pete about John's funeral. "It was November. Leaves all gone from the trees. John's best friend Kevin Tanner was the only one who seemed to notice me, silent there in a pew all by myself, away from the family. He came and sat beside me. We were bathed in the colored light that pours down through the long windows of St. Ignatius. The totally useless words of Father Brozek droned through the nave. Everyone else was crying their eyes out but I couldn't pump out a single tear. Kev and I just sat there." What I want to describe for Pete, but can't, is what I thought about while sitting there looking up at the sun-filled yellow-and-gold-and-white window depicting the Good Shepherd. In this version, Jesus looks like a teenager—no beard, wearing one of those Greek tunics, not the usual robes. He carries a lamb over his shoulders. I thought how He hadn't protected John, so damn Him, and damn the sun for illuminating Him like he was something so great.

"Maybe," I go on, "Kev saw my silence as something like his own."

A dense swarm of sparks rushes up from the flames and spirals away.

After the funeral, everyone drove out to the cemetery in Bethel Grove, where Dad's family is buried. Graveside, I was about to freak out. Kevin could tell. He put his arm around my shoulder and led me downwind from the grave site. There, behind the trunk of one of the giant walnut trees they have out there, while Brozek was going on with his stuff about meeting John again in heaven, Kevin lit a joint. It was my first time getting stoned. I don't tell Pete these things, or that Kevin told me that he'd loved John. The fact that Kevin had loved John has always been kind of a relief for me. It's allowed me to consider, despite massive evidence to the contrary, that love might actually exist, and that maybe, somehow, Kev's love remained with whatever part of John's body or soul that may or may not have carried on out into the universe. Not exactly reincarnation but maybe my brand of hope does a similar job? At the very least, John had not been alone while he was here.

But I do tell Pete, "Kevin hung out with me till his number came up. It was only after he shipped out that I finally cracked up. I'd head down to the river late afternoons and think about not coming back." Suddenly, I feel kind of strange, like sick. I can't recall ever having said so many words in a row in my entire life. Not to anyone.

Pete flops an arm around my shoulder. "You know, my dad was an Army guy, but I hate the fucking military. What a waste. I'm no hippie, man, but they got that right, peace."

I nod. "At least the draft's over."

"For sure," he says, looking straight up into the sky. My eyes follow his. A long silence blankets us while we do nothing but stare and stare at stars and stars and more stars. His voice returns: "Hoping for falling stars." He then puts his arm around me and kind of shakes me. "The Romans took them as signs."

"Of?"

"Events. Great events." He leans in so his face is right in front of mine. "Like the upcoming events of the two of us making history!" He turns to me and smiles. "To make John proud."

I'm about to tell him it's too late in the season for meteor showers when, unbelievably, at that very moment a star shoots across the sky. *Flash.* And then another. *Flash.* As if he's willed them. He laughs like a little kid.

After a longer, less easy silence, he says, "I have something really tough to ask you."

I'm not sure if I say "Yeah" or not, but he goes on, warning me, "It might ruin what we have." The breeze shifts. He blinks from the smoke. "But I've really got to know something, Mike."

The two of us have hung out together virtually every day for the past year, and I've slept at his house more than half those nights, yet I've never before heard this uneasy tone in his voice. You think you know someone, but maybe you don't, maybe you're just making them a consistent character in your head—like in novels—because inconsistencies get too hard to deal with. Plus, me being me, I don't have a clue as to what he could possibly want to ask that might ruin the surest thing I know in this world, by which I mean our friendship. All of a sudden, I feel like gravity's gone and I'm floating up into the starry sky above.

A few more times he starts to say something but winds up only mumbling then stopping.

"Come on," I finally say, "it can't be that bad." Out of the corner of my eye I can see he's turned his face towards me again. I don't turn towards him.

In the next second he blurts out, "Jesus, I just have to know, do you think this is the best thing ever or am I just dreaming it all up?"

I'm not exactly sure what he means. Somehow, at this moment, nebulous me wants exactness.

He reads the confusion on my face and attempts to make it clearer, "You and me." He starts tossing rocks into the burning coals again. "Will we be together like this always?"

That's exact enough. I look at him and can't help grinning like an idiot, a scared idiot. I don't know how or why, but I match crazy for crazy, and proclaim, "For sure, for the rest of our lives." Another rock pops out of the flames, blasting straight up into the sky. I've never told another human being I even like them. I have no idea what's gotten into me, but I do know that what I said is right and true. Maybe strange for a guy to say to another guy, but I'm not thinking that. I'm only thinking it sounds kind of wonderful. I think how I am just me and he is just him and we are just us and how I'm down with that.

Next thing it's like a bomb's about to go off, Pete jumps up, pulling me along with him toward the riverbank. "Come on!" He starts tearing off his clothes—for the second time in one night!—as we go, though there's an even more definite nip to the air than before. He stops at the water's edge and orders me to do the same, to strip.

I don't know why I obey him but, as usual, I do, except unlike him, with each piece of clothing I hesitate before dropping it onto the sand. Of course, we've seen each other naked in the locker room and sharing a bedroom, but that's somehow different, it is. We stand there, away from the firelight, in starlight, with probably nightjars and foxes and raccoons and surfacing carp and maybe even creatures from other planets and solar systems watching us, knowing us.

"We're going to make a Roman promise," he announces, "what's called a 'testimony.'"

I have no idea what he's talking about. Besides, I'm shivering. He puts one hand on my shoulder and instructs me, like it's something totally normal: "You hold onto my balls, I hold onto yours." And then, seriously, before I know it, he grabs me by the balls. This flips me out. I jump back, nearly castrating myself. He's laughing like a madman, telling me, "Be cool, be cool." I'm sputtering and swinging at him, glaring like I could kill him because I could, while he's all the while hushing me like you do an upset kid or a spooked animal. He goes right on explaining, "I swear to God, Mike, a Roman promise is when you take hold of the other guy's testicles, and he takes yours."

I stop moving, clenching my whole body so tight it's like not having a body at all. The animals and the aliens must think we're crazy.

His voice becomes less manic as he informs me, "You then look the other guy right in the eye to see if there's truth there, or not. It was a real thing, I swear."

At this point, I'm hardly listening. I reach for my underwear. I should be laughing in his face or punching it in.

"Just listen," he whispers, like we're in some kind of conspiracy together, "*testimony* comes from *testicles*." Even in my state of fury I'm not sure I buy this etymology. "Just relax," he says in a low voice. He now pulls my right hand gently—and I'm such a freak that once again on this night I let him put my hand on his junk—so it's under his balls, palm up.

The only thing I can manage to think to keep myself from going crazy is how it's like cupping a warm rabbit kit. Which is totally weird, insofar as it was John's and my job to do the culling when there got to be too many in the hutch for the family to eat. John would pick me up and place me in the hutch, which stood about four feet off the ground, on stilts, so foxes and weasels couldn't get at the rabbits. I would lift the kits in my palm, one at a time, and hand them to him. He would then hold each one underwater in a galvanized steel tub till the count of twenty. Afterward, we'd bury them all together under the burn pile out back. God knows why, but thinking about this helps right now.

In any case, this Roman promise is a lot weirder—not to mention scarier—than the conversation we'd been having, and yet because it's Pete, I'm once again letting him do it. *I am doing it.* It's weird, not in a sex kind of way like it was in the sumacs with that girl, just weird as in unthinkable. Unthinkable, except for the fact it's Pete Lac and he's always saying and doing what's unthinkable.

Without a trace of a smirk on his face, he tells me, "It's a trust thing, like, I'll crush your nuts if I detect you're lying, and vice versa." So, there on the river, under the light of a moon just past full (that's got to be, I'm hoping, the cause of this lunacy), away from a dying fire, holding each other by the balls, he speaks like he's reading from some document, "We promise to keep what we have forever." He stares me right in the eyes. "Promise?"

I squint tight, wondering who the hell this person is and who the hell I am. At last, I answer, "Promise," my tone a little defeated but also a little defiant. I swallow hard. With that, he undoes his grip and I drop my hand.

Just when I thought all was said and done, he grabs me by the hand again. I'm pulling away but he pulls harder, and we're running into the river, both of us whooping from the cold, though in reality the water's warmer than the air and feels kind of good. He loves to swim. I don't. In fact, I'm a little afraid of water. He was the captain of the swim team—our star swimmer from California—before he got kicked off that team, too. I doggy paddle. He jumps on me, pulling me under. I'm thrashing like mad to escape and manage to struggle to the surface, starved for air. He stays under for a long time yet, bringing me almost to the point of flipping out, which, I wonder, might be his goal.

JULY 1976, MIKE

We're in Lacs' rose-filled backyard; it's Bicentennial Fourth of July. Pete and I are letting our guitars rip, really rip. We got an extension cord for the amp though we keep it turned down pretty low because Mrs. Lac's out grilling chicken teriyaki on this tiny kind of grill, a hibachi she calls it. Not that she's ever said she minds our music— even loud—but something about her makes you want to be courteous. She's so fine, squatting there in her sundress, managing those bamboo skewers. She's made other kinds of Japanese food for the day, too, like sushi. I don't think that it's not right to not be having burgers, baked beans, potato salad, Jell-O and all that stuff for the Fourth, like I know my mom will say when she asks and I tell her what we had. No one around here has even heard of any kind of Japanese food. Mom will screw up her face when she asks me again what sashimi is and I tell her it's raw fish. Pete's dad is sucking down cold ones, one after another, not feeling he has to take charge of the grill like dads around here do. Maybe that's Japanese-style cookout, and though he's not Japanese he's going with it. I try not to stare at Mrs. Lac for too long. Even though it's hot as hell out, she's smiling and Mr. Lac's smiling and Pete's smiling and I'm smiling. Pete and I work our guitar strings. I still can't help glancing over at his mom from time to time, mostly because I've never seen anyone so happy or felt so happy myself.

Pete's dad captures our Bicentennial in color on Super 8. Red, white, and blue bunting all around the fence. The hibachi smoldering orange. Amber bottles of beer glowing in the sunshine. A rainbow of roses on the trellises. And two recent grads, stripped to the waist, doing their Hendrix thing. But we'll have to remember the soundtrack because Super 8s don't have sound. It's us imitating Hendrix doing "The Star-Spangled Banner." Lame, I know.

This past Thanksgiving, Pete and I got guitars, Univox Hi-Flyer electrics—Japanese knockoffs of American guitars at about a fifth the price. But good knockoffs. Mine's black, his white. I had money from pumping gas at the Sinclair and working at the body shop, money I'd been saving for a motorcycle. Pete somehow managed to scrape some together. Not sure how. His parents didn't give it to him, I know, and he's mowed lawns and shoveled snow only once in a while. At first his parents were none too

thrilled about him purchasing a guitar. He was supposed to be saving for college, even though his grades had nose-dived and he
hadn't applied anywhere. They keep thinking he'll apply, maybe
to the new community college because everyone's heard they'll
take anyone. Getting kicked off football and swimming caused
Pete to not do well in school. He's the kind of guy who needs
to be busy. The less free time, the better he did. Not that I was
the model student, but most of my classes were vo-tech. His were
college-prep. College isn't anything most families from the Flats
think about. His is different, though. My mom works across town
at the university, in the laundry, washing sheets and towels for
students, yet it never occurred to her that one day her kid might
be one of them.

Without football, and before we got guitars, Pete and I definitely had time to kill, or, to give it a better spin, we had time to
pursue other interests. It took a year, but making music became
our interest. Pete knows music in a traditional way, which helps a
lot. He played cello from when he was like four until right before
moving here from California. When he started, his mom told me,
he was so small he had to play what they call a one-eighth, a
cello about the size of a violin. Must have been one of those pre-
cocious, adorable kids, like I never was. He has a huge advantage over me in knowing how to read music. He's tried teaching
me, without much success. But some of the discipline from both
sports and cello has stayed with him and rubbed off on me. He
claims I'm a natural because I can hear something on the radio
or a record and imitate it right off the bat. I wasn't aware that's
anything special.

Some days we sit for hours, either in his bedroom or on the
bluff above the river or at the old salt mines up the lake, trying to
write songs. Like it's something that's going to be important to the
history of the world, Pete records all our sessions with a portable
cassette player he got from his folks for his birthday. Sometimes it
seems like we have the same tune in our heads and it comes out
at the same time. With only a few notes from one of us, the other

one picks up on the pattern and offers a couple chords and it goes from there.

Writing music makes me feel not so much a stranger in the universe. It carves out a world of sound and echo that has more meaning to me than anything else. Music reveals everything about everything, or almost. I write most of the words. I say things in song that I would never say in real life. Sometimes I feel that singing these things keeps my life from exploding. Pete and I started writing songs by putting some poetry we liked from English class to music. Emily Dickinson's poems were, as Mrs. Homer told us, based on hymns, which in turn were based on ballads, so using those was a no-brainer. A fun one was:

I'm Nobody! Who are you?
Are you—Nobody—too?
Then there's a pair of us!

We thought that was absolutely hilarious *and* true. In the scheme of Hallein, not to mention the world, we're definitely nobodies. Our rendition of the poem didn't sound too bad. Dickinson goes electric. And then there's our other favorite, Thoreau. Prose wasn't off-limits. From just a single quote of his—the famous one—"Most men lead lives of quiet desperation, and go to the grave with the song still in them," we hammered out a decent song. That sentence became kind of a credo for us. We saw so many lives of quiet desperation in the Flats—my dad's, for one—and felt almost like a responsibility to let their song out for them. These adaptations were mostly us fooling around, but they gave us footing song-wise.

We did the Romantics, too. Pete especially liked Byron because, according to him, he was a badass, full of both bravado *and* bravura. Couplets of *Don Juan* were easy and fun to play with musically. Wordsworth made sense to me, which is probably why I liked Keats better. We managed to turn "Bright star! would I were steadfast as thou art" into an anthem. Pretty great, if I do say so myself.

Our favorite poem on earth, though, is Shelley's "Mont Blanc," even if it was impossible to make into a song and Shelley probably was, as Pete puts it, a douchebag. The guy was talking to a freaking mountain and comes up with lines like these:

> And what were thou, and earth, and stars, and sea,
> If to the human mind's imaginings
> Silence and solitude were vacancy?

Can't beat that. Can't beat it, yet it's kind of weird when you think about it, a poet going for silence.

One time when we were both feeling pretty quiet and pretty desperate ourselves, our songwriting really took off. Pete and I had hardly said a word to each other all day. I was sitting on the floor between the twin beds in his room, strumming, while he was on the one bed, propped up by a few pillows, also strumming. He asked, "What's up?"

"Nothing."

"What are you? Practicing to be the strong, silent type?"

He meant it as a joke, but I automatically came out with this song, melody and all: "Maybe I come off as strong and silent, but I'm not that type . . ."

He picked up on it: "Maybe I come off as strong and silent, but inside me there's a lot to fight . . ."

Within half an hour, tops, we had a new song down and were singing it like it was an old familiar tune:

> One day I'm gonna break out and be strong, silent, and loud.
> One day I'm gonna be strong and break out,
> Gonna break out of this world that makes me silent and keeps
>   me down,
> Then I'll be loud, I'll be loud, I'll be loud, loud, loud . . .

It's not easy to explain how hard I fell for the guitar. Nothing really made much sense before it, or before Pete. Before both. And, as I suppose he is for most guys, Hendrix is God for Pete and me. But we're also into metal: Zeppelin, Deep Purple, Black Sabbath. Straight up rock, not so much. Folk rock, no way.

I got home to the Lacs's from work late, pretty beat after priming a sweet '63 Corvette. I'm lying propped up by pillows on the twin that's become mine, relaxing, jotting down lines for possible songs, messing with chords to go with them. It's about an hour later when Pete comes in from visiting this girl he likes, this Cheryl. He's all hyper, bouncing off the walls. He'd been hanging out at the counter at Friendly's drinking a bottomless cup of coffee while she worked her shift. Last time he did this, she sent a wrong order—a Fishamajig—his way. Same thing with a scoop of peppermint stick ice cream. Fish with cheese kind of grossed him out, and he wasn't a fan of peppermint, but he ate both anyway. With a laugh, he told me that's true love. He's stoked about a record he just bought. The hippie at the Vinyl Heart told him he had to listen to it, and now I also have to, like this very second. "Totally blew me away!" he proclaims three times.

The cover shows four guys leaning against a brick wall. They're dressed in super-tight jeans, T-shirts, leather jackets, sneaks. They have dark hair, rocker style. Two are wearing shades. One has a bare midriff, which kind of weirds me out. *The Ramones* is the name of both the album and the group. Eponymous. Pete's grinning ear to ear as he puts it on the turntable and cranks the volume. With the very first notes I have to stand up or I swear I'll be dead. Can't believe the force of it. Pete flops down on his bed, whaling on air guitar. The songs are fast and clear and loud and jump off lots of cliffs. *That's us!* is what comes to me in a rush. I feel like this is true but also feel like everything in and about me is under assault. I stand there completely still for the whole first side. When Pete turns the record over and drops the needle, I grab my guitar but don't plug in. I play along, silent as a ghost, and Pete gets up, grabs his instrument and does the same, song after song:

Hey, daddy-o
I don't wanna go down to the basement
There's somethin' down there
I don't wanna go . . .

This time when the record ends, Pete's so crazy he's shouting, "See! I told you!"

I think I'm smiling, or at least I'm smiling inside, because I *do* see.

"We gotta make a pact, my Mike, a pact." Pete's big on emphasis, big on pacts. I'm only worried he's going to grab me by the balls again, or possibly something worse.

I give him my well-aren't-you-going-to-tell-me-more look, and he does: "I want us to swear to, from now on, practice hard—not just dick around. Practice every day and come up with some stuff and see if it all adds up to 'band.' Let the fortune of musicdom be ours!"

"Okay, man, okay." I'm busting out laughing.

"Nothing short of excellence nonpareil!"

And I repeat his ridiculousness in an even more ridiculous tone: "Nothing short of excellence nonpareil." He punches me in the chest.

Before we get serious about our band and future stardom, though, we've got to go pick up Cheryl. She'll be getting off work. She's going to see if her friend Lisa can come along. The same Lisa I've always liked from a distance at church and school, so that's cool. The four of us will drive up the lake in Mr. Lac's turquoise Dodge Dude pickup, a lame vehicle if ever there was.

"We can all squeeze into the cab, nice and cozy," Pete says, leering. "We'll stop at the salt mines, get high, have a six-pack, and, if we're lucky, get us some pussy."

I shake my head, and he laughs nasty-like, knowing I don't like that kind of talk.

The girls seem happy to see us. They're pretty chatty on the drive up the east shore of Deep Lake. We park along the perimeter of the salt flats, in the dry weeds, and trudge across the illusion of snow. The turquoise truck glows, a little iceberg. A couple of guys buzz their Honda CB750s across the glittering white plain. Pete and I gaze after them longingly. Dream machines. Memories of me and John here on his Kawasaki nearly choke me up.

Cheryl and Lisa take their Dr. Scholl's sandals off and shriek, "Motherfucker!" in unison because the salt's burning the bottoms of their feet. Pete gives a *rat-a-tat-tat* laugh. I shake my head. I do that a lot.

We climb a bank of salty sand then scoot around to the cliffside, inching our way along a shale ledge maybe thirty feet above the surface of the lake. Today, the water's aquamarine as a postcard. We enter one of the white caves. The mines are about the only place on this whole huge body of water where people like us can go, except for Dreamland, but that gets crowded and the beach there turns kind of muddy. Like just about everywhere else around the shore, it's also private property here, but the salt company that abandoned the mine doesn't lock the gate or patrol. Technically, we're trespassing, but us kids from the Flats have been coming to the mines on both sides of Deep Lake since forever and think of these places as ours. The trains pulling the salt cars run through town slow enough that all us guys, before we got our licenses, would catch hold of a ladder on the side of a car, hop on, and ride up one shore or the other for a day of swimming and hanging out.

The four of us get high and polish off a six-pack pretty quick. These girls are so fine, especially in halter tops and hot pants—legs, bellies, shoulders, all nice and tan. We shoot the breeze for a while. Cheryl says she's kind of glad we're getting a second shopping mall because it will be on our side of town and is going to have some pretty cool stores.

With that cute giggle of hers, Lisa adds, "Just another place to waste my dough."

They're both psyched at having finally graduated. Cheryl announces, like it's some incredibly bold opinion, "I hate school, just hate it."

Lisa adds, "I'm glad it's over, too, but wouldn't mind taking courses somewhere. Useful ones, that is." She's sensible. I like that.

I'm not much for school either but my future is so vague that being back there might be okay.

As usual, I take cues from Pete. When he starts making out with Cheryl, I start with Lisa. She smells good. Mouth tastes citrus. Watching Pete and Cheryl going at it ten feet away dials me up. As Lisa wriggles out of her halter top, unzips my jeans and tugs them off, I start getting a little scared. I mean, perfect timing, right? Graduate, get pregnant, get married, live happily ever after. In the Flats. As always, there's a rubber in my wallet, but I swear I'm not going all the way. This fear is probably why, contrary to popular belief, I'm still a virgin. Hate to admit it, but sometimes I admire Pete's confidence with girls. Nothing clumsy as he gets it on with Cheryl. It's kind of beautiful, especially in the light reflecting off the lake into the cave. The crystal walls glow. At certain moments, though, it does feel like he's performing. He keeps looking over my way. For what? Approval? Sure. Probably also to egg me on. He nods encouragement when Lisa goes down on me. It's not like an orgy, though. More a parallel kind of thing, where he and I are having our experience with each other while we're each having an experience with someone else. What will it be like when we actually do find girls to marry? Do we ask our fiancées if they're down with us being so close, so to speak? If they'll put up with our nonsense?

Pete shakes like a dog coming out of water as he climaxes and then, pronto, pulls his jeans back up. He doesn't button them, though. He lights a cigarette, kind of leans against Cheryl and watches Lisa work on me. Not helpful. I start losing my hard-on. I turn away from him and Cheryl, and let Lisa go at my dick for a minute or so longer. But I can tell nothing's going to happen. I murmur low, so only she can hear, "It's okay," and zip up. Hopefully, Pete thinks I came quietly. I'm a quiet kind of guy.

Lisa says, soft as velvet, "No problem," and I can tell she means it. I'm liking her a lot.

For some reason, Pete's in a hurry to leave and drop the girls back at Cheryl's. It's not that late. I can tell the two of them feel let down about not going out somewhere, like to a bar or something. It is kind of rude of us. After all, it's Saturday night and we've just played them.

As we pull up to Cheryl's house, she asks, all pouty, "What's the matter?"

Pete doesn't respond.

Lisa tries to brighten the mood. "Why don't we drive downtown?" She says this like it's an exotic destination, which for kids from the Flats it sort of is.

Keeping his eyes straight ahead, Pete murmurs, "Sorry. Got a lot of stuff to do.

Cheryl's silent as they get out of the car, but once they're on the sidewalk I hear her mutter to Lisa, "That burns my ass."

Lisa doesn't seem angry at all. As she shuts the door, she says, "See you guys!" like a regular buddy, which is nice of her, it really is.

As we drive off, Pete peps up, looks me right in the eye, and tells me, "We have promises to keep and miles to go before we sleep." I like it that he likes that Frost poem—or that he even remembers it—because I like it too. He wants us to have our first real serious jam session tonight. He actually says that: *real serious*.

I wonder where we're going to hold this jam session, though. Turns out, he doesn't know either. Definitely not my house. His folks are usually cool with our playing but it's getting kind of late for them. Somewhere outside would be fine, except we need electricity.

Out of frustration he announces, "We've got to get a studio this week." Like we can afford one. Suddenly, his eyes grow super wide, and he shouts, "I've got an idea! A most brilliantized notion! The fucking basin of all desire!"

Then in normal English he explains that he still has keys to the high school pool from when he was on the team. The coach wanted his star to have all the practice time he wanted. It seems kind of weird, the coach giving him the keys in the first place, and him still having them, and us going to a swimming pool to practice music.

We stop by Pete's place, load our portable amp and guitars into the back of the Dude, and head out. It's one of those amazing nights when the sky stays kind of blue and the stars shine more yellow than white and appear to bulge right out of the sky.

I suppose we're trespassers at the pool, too, but Pete talks like we're entitled to the space. It's a public school, we're taxpayers. Anything for music. Inside the hall it's dark and warm and smells of chlorine. I remember hating this place that long winter freshman year when everyone had to take swimming. They made us wear school-issued bathing suits, the faggy Speedo kind. I mean, I suppose a Speedo's okay if you're on the swim team but otherwise definitely not cool, especially the school's, which are either too baggy or too tight, the nylon worn thin in all the wrong places.

Pete knows the hall, even in the dark. He flips a switch that turns only the underwater lamps on. Beams of light play through the rippling water, reflecting in wild patterns off the walls and ceiling. It's like another world. He starts setting up on the starting blocks, never considering we could easily be electrocuted. I can just see him getting overenthusiastic in his playing, like he always does, and falling in with his guitar. *Zap!* He's also brought the cassette recorder along, rests it on a third starting block, and presses *record*. We strum a few chords. They echo crazy, mimicking the light. Maybe not the best acoustics in the world but definitely radical. We work our way into a decent jam. No songs, just chords and riffs that jump and curve through the cavernous space. We're nodding and grinning at each other. Then it's like we've been touched by the ghost of Hendrix himself. We break into "May This Be Love" at the exact same time, or possibly Pete recognizes the very first bar I play and follows, or the opposite. I don't know what gets into me, but I start singing full voice out over the glittering, glowing surface of the pool.

Waterfall, nothing can harm me at all,
my worries seem so very small with my sweet waterfall . . .

For the first time in my life, I feel like I'm singing for real. I fly down into a groove so deep I disappear:

So let them laugh, laugh at me,
so just so long as I have you
to see me through
I have nothing to lose long as I have you . . .

Pete has now pivoted on his starting block to face me directly.
He's no longer grinning or even smiling. His expression opens wide,
like he's letting the whole universe in, and he starts playing deeper
and deeper, and I sing into his depth:

Waterfall, don't ever choose your ways.
Come with me for a million days,
oh, my waterfall . . .

It's a fairly slow, mellow song, but going into the second verse we
glance at each other and, without exchanging any signal at all, pick
up the tempo. At this point something happens inside me, in a place
I don't know, and then, without any will on my part, I start hearing my own voice like it's someone else's, and that someone else
is breaking into a rage that's as familiar as it is unfamiliar, a rage
unexpressed till now, and this not a rage kind of song at all.

I'm as lost in myself as I'm found.

After the final verse, as the last chord goes shimmering away,
we stand like mannequins, not saying anything at all for a long
while. Pete then lays his guitar down, leaps on over to my starting block, and gives me the most mauling bear hug ever. "That was
amazification to the maximum! Your deified voice! That's what's
going to take us to the pinnacle!" For once in my life a compliment
doesn't embarrass me. He shouts, "Orpheus lives!" Whatever that
means.

Next thing I know, he's whipping all his clothes off and arcing
high into the air, like a dolphin. His body hardly makes a splash as
it breaks the surface. He torpedoes along the bottom of the pool,
surfacing only at the other end with a holler: "Get the hell in! Your
rocked-out Triton awaits you!"

Just how deep Deep Lake is becomes as clear as it is unclear on this clear day. I mean, you can see down into the water forever and still not see bottom. I sit on the ledge and lean back against the shale bank as Pete dives in. It's quite a drop, higher than the high dive at school. He doesn't come up for a long time. This makes me more nervous than it should. After all, he's Aquaman. But the fact that no one—not even scientists—knows how deep the lake is, and that it connects with all sorts of dark, starless underground rivers, unnerves me. A drowned body can show up weeks or months later in another lake miles away.

He finally surfaces and takes off across the lake. Here at the salt mines, it's about a mile across. He can swim back and forth in under forty-five minutes, easy. Right before diving in, he was rambling on. Something about imitating Lord Byron imitating some myth about these ancient Greeks, Hero and Leander, but I wasn't really paying attention. I'm writing down words and notes I hope will become songs. The sight of him in the water distracts me. The sun shines off his body like he's made of metal.

When he returns, for God knows what reason he's laughing like Flipper as he pulls himself out of the lake and climbs back up to the ledge. He shakes off on me. I know he wants me to say "asshole" or tell him to cut it out, but I don't. My body feels so lazy around his vigor. He lies his naked self down on his side, turned toward me. He once told me he's so comfortable being naked because that's the way the Japanese are, with their neighborhood bathhouses called *sentos* and hot springs called *onsens*. People are naked together and it's no big deal. All this nakedness, he jokes, is getting me out of my Catholic upbringing. It's true, I've almost become okay with being naked, at least around him.

He dries his fingers on his crumpled green T-shirt, digs a box of Marlboros out of his jeans, lights up. "So, what is your educationalized opinion of Lady Lisa, milord?"

I pause to translate, not his words but his thought. "She's okay," I answer slowly. And she is. And a whole lot more.

"Well, I'm not so crazy about Cheryl," he confesses. I nod in agreement. She's kind of a not very nice person, though that might just be me not really knowing her. I do get the feeling she already wants to get married to Pete and we've been double dating for only a few weeks. Next, right out of the blue, he asks, "You mind if I go out with Lisa instead?"

Any other guy would probably at least say, "What the hell?" or blurt out, "Fuck you!" Instead, I answer in a calm voice, "Sure, just so long as it's not a swap." I have no idea why I agree to this. And so readily. Maybe because it came totally unexpected, and my default is pure wimp? But it's not like I own Lisa or am even officially going with her. She can make up her own mind who she wants to go with. Only after some long seconds does it occur to me that I should feel possessive or jealous.

"Thanks pal," he says, resting his right elbow on my stomach, cigarette twirling in his fingers above me. "This won't change what we have at all. Lisa will still hang out with the two of us." I shrug. Deal done, he puts his cigarette between my lips and drapes his arm across my chest. "If you and I are going to make it, we can't go on playing as a guitar duo. We need a bass-player and a drummer. An assemblage supreme of rock 'n' rollers!"

"You mean a band?" I ask, joking, as if I need an interpreter. He nods. It's funny he has it in his head that we're not just daydreaming anymore about this music thing.

We retreat into the cave to write some lyrics together. It's become our routine. What makes these caves so amazing is the light. Even during the night, they're never truly dark. The slightest moonlight, or even starlight alone, can fall in through the opening and play off the salt walls, illuminating the space. During the day, either direct sunlight, or sunlight reflected off the lake, flows in, making you feel like you're breathing light. You feel, well, *enlightened*. It's the perfect place, this cave of light, where ideas and dreams take off.

The next day Lisa broke it to me that she was going with Pete. She was super nice about it, so I muttered that I'm cool with it. We agreed that we hadn't been really going together anyway, at least not officially, and it was for the best. On the other hand, Cheryl was none too pleased when Pete informed her about him and Lisa. I don't blame her. Being dumped and having your friend take up with the guy who dumped you has got to be rough. Unfortunately, I was in attendance for the drama. It went down at Friendly's, while she was working. Not cool. I could've told Pete that wasn't the right time or place, but no one asked me. He didn't even warn me he was going to do it. He made his little pronouncement right while she was pouring us refills. He's lucky she didn't smash the globe of scalding-hot coffee on his skull. Instead, she stuck her middle finger right in his face and shouted so the whole restaurant could hear, "Sit on it and rotate, motherfucker!" As I said, can't blame her. He tried laughing it off. I stood up fast and dropped a huge tip on the counter as Pete and I headed for the door, him moseying, me slinking. Out in the parking lot, I told him that was an asshole thing to do. To my surprise, he totally agreed. He said he was just trying to be honest and direct but had misjudged the situation. I'll say.

Pete, Lisa, and I do in fact start hanging out together, and, weirdly, I actually like Lisa more as Pete's girl. She's funnier and smarter around him. Maybe it's my downer ways that made her seem a bit of a drag when she was sort of my girl. Oh, she's not anyone's girl! She's Lisa. She decides what she wants. We drive around aimlessly in the Dude, Lisa seated between us. Sometimes we go to the salt mines or to Dreamland. We also go to lots of movies. Each of us gets a turn choosing. Pete goes for blockbusters, like *Rocky* and *King Kong*, but he also makes us watch *I, Claudius* on PBS, a Roman emperor thing that goes on and on. Lisa's the serious one. She picks *Network* and *All the President's Men*, both of which put Pete and me to sleep. I choose *Carrie* because Sissy Spacek's my kind of girl, and *The Man Who Fell to Earth* because of Bowie. Sometimes we go for Chinese after getting high. A few times we've even split a room at the Lakeview, the cheapest motel in the area, which, we laugh every time, doesn't have a view of the lake at all. That way, we can hang out together all night. No sex, just the three of us on a king-size bed watching TV, getting stoned, talking about everything under the sun. Lisa's smarter and has more sense than the two of us put together.

The best thing, though, is Lisa doesn't hide things. That first date at the salt mines—when she didn't even know me—when we were curled up together in the glittering white dust, she told me in a soft voice how sorry she was about my brother. She knew what happened from church. She told me how her brothers looked up to him. I didn't know that or that she even had brothers. Made me feel good. Another time, when she and I were lying in the grass at Dreamland, waiting for Pete to show up, she told me how her older sister had disappeared the same year John died. She didn't leave a note or take anything with her, not even her wallet. The last time she was seen was leaving her shift at the register over at the A&P. The police never got a single tip to go on.

DECEMBER 1977–JANUARY 1978, MIKE

It's Christmas. Pete and I are lying head-to-toe, soldier-style, on my rollaway bed in the basement listening to Blondie's *Plastic Letters* while getting stoned: ". . . I nearly fell, I feel like a lowlife in hell . . ."

We spent the morning at the Lacs's opening presents, drinking eggnog, and eating stollen Mrs. Lac made from Mr. Lac's mom's family recipe. Right now, she's preparing a Japanese feast for later, so we're putting in time at my place. No one seems to much care that we're here, though—not so much as a "Merry Christmas"—so we've retreated down to my lair, as Pete calls it. You wouldn't even know it's the holidays here except for the scrawny spruce Dad cut down above the river and dragged home. It's got a few balls and some tinsel on it, no lights. Everyone's doing their own thing, which means the girls and little Blake are watching some Christmas special featuring one of those has-been crooners, Dad's trying to repair the refrigerator before all the food goes bad, and Mom's doing bills.

Later, Mom comes down with a basket of laundry. With a cigarette hanging from her lip, I doubt she can smell the pot. She loads the machine. On her way back upstairs she mutters, "Merry Christmas to you, too." Before I can respond, she says what she's been saying to me for a couple of years now: "When are you going to start acting like a human being?" There's really nothing to say to that. I don't get mad. I get sad and wish I could get inside her head and know her a little, so I'd maybe understand what makes her say things like that to me. Am I that rotten of a kid? Or is it random anger, like I sometimes feel?

A while later Dad comes down, heading for the pantry under the stairs. He's either oblivious to the weed or ignoring it. Likely he's after a bottle of the dandelion wine he made last year. Every spring he picks the dandelions from the huge lawns around the refinery. God knows how much weed killer is in that cocktail. Either that, or he's after a bottle of his homemade nocino. Pete's seen my dad only a few times before, but I'm not sure they've ever actually met. This fact suddenly makes me incredibly sad. On his way back, nocino bottle in hand, I say—not like an animal but like a real human being—"Hey Dad, this is Pete." Dad turns to us. "Pete, this is my dad."

Pete says, "Hello," not "Hey" or "Hi," because he isn't an animal, and because he can even be quite the gentleman when the situation calls for it.

Dad nods. He looks so exhausted. He looks so exhausted and it's Christmas. I'm not sure he even knows I haven't really lived here for nearly two years. Him not knowing might not be as weird as it sounds, though, as he works third shift. After a pause, Dad says, "Merry Christmas, fellas," almost cheerful, like a TV dad. He trudges back upstairs. A minute later he returns with juice glasses and the bottle uncorked. We stand up. He pours the dark, syrupy nocino, hands us each a glass and offers a toast, "Cheers, boys. Here's looking to a new year."

In unison, the three of us practically sing out, "Merry Christmas!" Bottoms up. Dad leaves. We lie down again.

Truth is, things are none too merry for me and Pete lying there on the rollaway. We've got nothing. After all this time, the band still hasn't gotten off the ground, even though we have Bobby and Matt. They're amazing. Trouble is, Bobby's still in school, caught up in all kinds of music stuff there—marching band, orchestra, jazz ensemble, you name it. But we're betting he's worth the wait. It was like magic when we first heard him, and in a marching band of all things. Pete and I had gone to watch my cousin Steve quarterbacking, and there was this elfin guy with long red hair and a snub nose going wild on the snare during halftime. He totally transcended the lame "Up, Up, and Away" the marching band was struggling through. He's got enough freak in him to counter the elf thing, plus he knows more bands than Pete and I put together. We found Matt totally by chance too, playing with a cover band of old guys at the Palms, right outside the refinery gate. We already sort of knew Matt; he graduated a couple of years ahead of us. He's a crane of a guy. Bent over his instrument he looked totally bored, but still, it was obvious listening to just a few licks and watching his hands move across those strings that he has talent to spare. It became totally clear when Black Sabbath's "Children of the Grave" found its way into a set with a Billy Joel song and "I Can See Clearly Now" and his playing kicked into gear. Problem is, he's now doing ninety for a third DWI. If all that's not enough, Pete and I don't really have girlfriends. Lisa's got herself a good job in the steno pool at the refinery and at night goes to the community college for computers. She's insanely busy, but even when she's with us lately she seems kind of distant. We think she's starting to see us as losers, which isn't so far off the mark.

Just when I'm thinking all this negative stuff, Pete delivers truly terrible news from out of left field. As matter-of-fact as can be, he announces, "Hey Mike, you know, I'm thinking . . . I'm thinking of joining the military."

I fight the reflex to bolt upright. "The military?" I echo after a pause, trying hard to sound calm.

At first, he doesn't respond. His breaths are long and steady from all those years of swimming. At long last he says, "We can't go on just pumping gas, getting stoned, and playing guitar." I had gotten him a job a few months ago with me at the Sinclair so he'd have some money.

I don't get it. He's the one who's been so gung ho about the band. "This is crazy," I tell him. "You've always said you'd never join up."

Funny thing is, he agrees with me, then comes out with a great big BUT. "But my parents want more for me. If I'm not going to college now, Dad likes the idea of the military, then college. That way it gets paid for. It worked for him."

I feel threatened. At this moment, it has become absurdly clear that Pete's the only thing I've got going for me. I remind him of our ball-squeezing vow down by the river centuries ago. He smiles, all sad. Somehow, smiling is the default expression for him, or maybe it is for everyone except me. A smile can mean a million different things, I suppose.

"The promise is still good, comrade," he claims a little too eagerly. "It's only a three-year hitch. You could enlist too. We could become our very own Theban Band."

Ignoring the reference I don't know anyway, I tell him, "You're not serious." For the first time in my life, I'm jealous, jealous not of someone but of the world, of circumstances that could take Pete away from me.

"Don't worry," he responds like a parent to a little kid, which only makes me worry more.

When we're finishing Christmas dinner at Pete's house it starts snowing steadily. We're stuffed with sweetened black beans, herring roe, grilled prawns, sushi, and more than a dozen other dishes Mrs. Lac has made. The four of us are hanging out in the living room, opening presents. Pete gives me a cool hardback 1931 edition of *Moby-Dick* he must have had to go downtown to find. It's got dramatic illustrations, in color. I give him a bottle of British

Sterling aftershave, mostly because he jokes about my Hai Karate and this is, I guess, classier. He opens the bottle and sprays me all over, making me sputter and cough. Then he paraphrases and mimics the snobby British voice-over in the commercial (the one that has a castle in the background and shows a lady from the Middle Ages on a horse and, weirdly, a man in a modern tuxedo helping her down): "Make me a legend in my own time so we may both go down in history."

I reply with a grin, "That's the plan, man."

When we're all done unwrapping, Pete goes and stands in front of the picture window, looking out on the world for the longest time. He's gone so far away. The tip of his tongue pushes out between his lips, like he's trying to catch a snowflake through the glass.

It's the first workday morning after New Year's. I'm alone at the Lacs'. Mr. Lac's of course at the refinery, Pete's working his shift at the Sinclair, and Mrs. Lac is off doing the weekly shopping at A&P. I hear the clink of the mail slot. I slurp down what's left of my soggy Frosted Flakes. On the way from the kitchen, I pick up envelopes and flyers scattered at the front door and put them on the sideboard. My eye catches an envelope addressed to Peter Ichiro Lac. It's from the United States Army. My body tenses. I pull the letter out of the pile, hold it up to the light coming through the window next to the door. Can't read it. I neaten the pile into a stack, leaving Pete's letter on top, and head upstairs to get ready for work at the body shop. As I wash the sleepers out of my eyes and try taming my shock of hair with a comb and some spit in my palm, I can't stop wondering about that envelope. I get more and more curious, or suspicious really, as I pull on my paint-stained work jeans and a clean black T-shirt.

I give myself a longer than usual look in the mirror, trying to find something resembling a conscience. Evil things, I suppose, sometimes happen spontaneously, aren't premeditated, or at least not exactly so. I feel myself becoming as conniving as Lucy on TV, only this isn't a comedy. I jump down the stairs four at a time, grab the letter, and head into the kitchen. I put the kettle on, bringing the water to barely a simmer so only the faintest plume of steam rises from the spout. The plume glows opalescent in the sunbeam falling in through the window. I hold the back of the envelope pretty far above the spout and start pulling the gluey flap apart millimeter by millimeter. It's hard to keep the paper from wrinkling. Takes patience. Seems to be working. The envelope opens pretty decent. I remove the official stationery, unfold it, read. The letter congratulates Peter Ichiro Lac on finishing the preliminary enlistment procedure. It goes on to instruct him that, on the following Tuesday, a recruiter from the Military Entrance Processing Station will arrive at nine hundred hours to escort him there. The MEPS, as they from then on refer to it, is a three-hour drive. The testing will take all that afternoon and the following morning. He should pack an overnight bag.

That bastard did it. In fact, he'd already been to the Army recruiter over at Arrowhead Plaza and enlisted before Christmas, when, on Christmas Day, he told me he was only thinking about it. I don't feel betrayed exactly—or not only that—more like abandoned, superfluous to his existence. To be honest, I'm flat-out desperate. I take the letter with me and head up to the bluffs to get high before work. I sit there, staring down into the river's complicated current. After rereading the letter, without pausing for even a second, I light both it and the envelope on fire with my Cricket. I hold the flaming papers up, watching the big ashes unlatch and fly away like mini bats high into the sky before gliding back down and landing in the muddy water.

I'm scheduled to work at the Sinclair Tuesday morning and Pete's off. I'll ask him to switch shifts. Once in a while we do that. He won't be suspicious.

While Pete's in the shower, I slip his driver's license and Social Security card out of his wallet on the dresser and put them in my wallet and then put mine in his. He won't notice. He doesn't usually carry a wallet anyway, unless we're going to a bar.

After he's gone off to work, I get dressed in clothes of his he has pretty much not worn since he started hanging out with me: khakis, blue-striped Oxford, penny loafers. I feel like a rich kid, or more like a counterfeit rich kid, or really a counterfeit of a counterfeit rich kid. I'm his doppelgänger or something, like in that weird story by Poe. Who am I kidding? I'm just glorifying my insanity with a literary reference. Besides, that story doesn't end so well. The guy winds up stabbing his double, only the double turns out to be himself. No, I'm nothing more than an impostor, the worst kind of cheater. I toss some dirty laundry into the smallest of the set of brown canvas duffels his mom bought him from one of those preppy catalogues, zip it up, and head down the stairs.

From the kitchen sink, Mrs. Lac glances over her shoulder. She offers her usual cheerful, "Good morning!" then does a double take. She's never seen me in anything but jeans and T-shirt so is probably wondering what's up. "Breakfast?" she calls out.

"No thanks, not today Mrs. Lac, gotta run!" I sound fake cheerful—deceitful—like one of those smarmy sitcom-chums on reruns who's always sucking up to the earnest protagonist's mom.

I go out to wait on the front stoop. Through the door I can hear the clock in the entryway cuckoo nine times right as the Army truck pulls up. If nothing else, the Army's punctual. To my surprise, it's a Dodge pickup, painted that tan they call Gatsby Cream, and not an olive-drab Jeep. Even though it's cold out, I'm sweating.

An officer in dark-green uniform decorated with braiding and lots of medals and insignias gets out and heads through the gate toward me. He's got spring in his step. His skin's as gray as the sky. He looks me straight in the eye in a way I'm sure he's practiced in order to get the misguided youth of America to feel something approaching momentousness as they enter the military. "Ready?" he asks before even introducing himself.

I let out a "Yessir!" that comes out way too close to parody.

He extends his hand, introducing himself as Sergeant Battle. A soldier named Battle? Of course. We shake hands and walk out the gate to the vehicle. Mrs. Lac's looking out the window, puzzled. The sergeant tosses the duffel into the bed of the truck. When he grips the passenger-side door handle, I want to bolt. Instead, I take a deep breath and get in. He shuts the door and I'm going to hell. He goes around, slides into the driver's seat, turns the key, and I'm even more certain I'm going to hell. A flock of sparrows lifts off the dull, salt-stained pavement in front of us. They flit up and swoop across the windshield only inches above the glass before rising into the sky. The truck moves down Geranium.

"Any questions, Mr. Lac?"

There's my opening. What I really want to ask is for him to please stop the truck so I can get out, but I don't. Instead, I answer, "Just one," my voice meeker than I'd like.

"Shoot."

I'm going for it. I dial up the naïve intonation I've been rehearsing in my head last night and this morning. "Does it matter, sir, that I think I might be, well, might be a . . . a homosexual?" Even as I'm saying the words, I can't believe I'm saying them. Not sure I've ever even said that one word out loud before.

As I might have predicted, but didn't, this stops everything. Literally. He pulls over, puts the truck in park. For a good long time the sergeant doesn't seem to know what to say or do. I feebly attempt to fill in the gap: "Does the Army have, you know, help for that?"

His gray eyes blink a few times. I suddenly wonder if I'm going to be arrested—or rather, if Peter Ichiro Lac is going to be arrested. Or get beaten up. Or killed. Homos get killed sometimes for just saying they're homos. I didn't consider the consequences beforehand. That's the way sociopaths are. I feel like a sociopath. Maybe I am a sociopath. I can't believe I've done something so *dastardly*. I've deceived—and maligned—my best friend, my brother, my boon companion (I got that one from *The Confidence-Man*, a book I really love). I'm such an asshole, as Pete would doubtless say. I'm going to lose my friend and wind up in jail for impersonating him to a government official. Or something like that.

It's hard to tell if Sergeant Battle is disgusted, shocked, indifferent, or what. He doesn't reveal a thing. Maybe he's just confused. At least he hasn't assaulted me. When he finally does respond, to my relief he sounds simply matter of fact: "To be honest, brother, this is a first." He turns his head to look right at me. I look away. "In my experience, that is. And I've been recruiting for going on ten years." The word *brother* is unexpected, nice.

I reach down and worry the penny from Pete's left loafer. I turn it over and over between my thumb and forefinger. A 1958, the year he and I were born.

Sergeant Battle clears his throat. "Sorry to say, Mr. Lac, I do not think this is going to work out. The Army probably isn't the place for individuals such as yourself. There would likely be a discharge involved, if you were to enlist and your homosexual inclinations were to later be . . . well . . . detected . . ." He then puts the truck in gear, makes a U-turn, and we head back down the street, this time maybe a little faster. He stops across the street from the Lacs'.

I had originally thought of telling whoever the Army sent that I/Pete smoked pot, which is true, instead of that I/he was gay, which isn't, but that might have led to my/his immediate arrest, or else I/he might have had to go to the MEPS anyway to get a urine test, just in case he wanted me/Pete for his quota of recruits and thought there was a chance of me/Pete testing negative. There's no test for being gay, or at least that was my logic.

Sergeant Battle goes around the front of the vehicle to open my door. Polite. I slide on out. He then shuts the door and lifts the duffel from the truck bed, placing it on the dead winter grass at the curb. He shakes my hand, which surprises me. It's decent of him, really, given the fact that he believes I'm a gay guy. He wishes me luck. Mrs. Lac has come to the window again, probably because the few cars that come down this street almost never stop. Now comes the tricky part. I ask the sergeant, "Will this go on my record?"

He answers promptly, "You have no record. To confirm this, I will send a routine rejection for enlistment."

That's somewhat of a relief, though I still feel sick to my stomach. I'm generally known as the least dramatic person in the world, but right now inside I feel like someone's insanely jealous drama queen girlfriend. I head into the house.

From the kitchen, Mrs. Lac calls, "Everything alright, Mike?"

"Yeah, sure," I answer, unable to rinse the tension out of my voice. She deserves more than that, so I go to the threshold of the kitchen and add, "Just needed to talk to someone about the Army."

She nods, appearing to accept my vagueness, or at least pretending to. She doesn't mention what I'm wearing, though she's got to know they're Pete's clothes. I get the feeling that on some level she knew of Pete's plans and understands I've gotten him out of the Army, and that she approves of what I've done. Though that's probably just my wish to be freed from the monster guilt that's choking me.

I tell myself over and over that I'm saving Pete's life. That there could be another war. That he could wind up dead, like John and thousands of other guys. Or, at the very least, that the Army would destroy the person he is and turn him into someone he is not. Like all deceivers, I think I know better than the person being deceived. It's insane, it's presumptuous. We have our rock 'n' roll dream to make come true, I tell myself. But really, it's selfish, plain selfish. I want Pete with me. It's as simple as that.

"Un-fucking-believable!" Pete stormed into the room with an open letter in hand and threw himself face down on the bed. I immediately knew what was up. It had been four days. The letter dropped from his hand onto the carpet between the beds. He lay there a long time before finally rolling onto his back. He didn't say anything, just stared at the ceiling.

Finally, I asked, "What's up? What happened?"

Still without a word, and without looking at me, he reached down and handed the letter to me.

Dear Mr. Lac:

We appreciate your desire to join the United States Army. However, we regret to inform you that you do not meet our standards for enlistment at this time.

The Army sets and reviews its standards for enlistment based upon particular missions. Our entry rules are purposely tough because in the field the lives of your fellow service members may well depend on your physical and mental capabilities to perform as part of a unit.

There are, however, civilian employment opportunities for which your situation may not be an issue, such as with the US Civil Service. I encourage you to pursue this alternative avenue for serving your country.

Sincerely,
Sergeant Isaiah Battle

When I'd finished, I rested the letter on the floor and waited for him to say something. Eventually he did. He reached across the space between us, touched my arm and apologized for keeping me in the dark. I practically winced. He then said, "I'm such a loser. My 'physical and mental capabilities'! Makes me sound handicapped. Both physically and mentally."

I tried to comfort him, saying it was probably a form letter, and that he had no idea what they were looking for right now. He wasn't buying it. "You still have us, the band," I told him. "We'll make it work."

For practically the entire next week Pete barely said a word. The military thing had been a surprise to his parents. At dinner, they tried to sell him on the community college or insurance business (his father had a friend who had an agency). He didn't do much more than mumble a few maybes. He stayed pretty despondent until I splurged and got us tickets to the auto show out at the fairgrounds.

The band's been going great. Matt's finished doing his ninety, Bobby's graduated. We're practicing under one of the picnic pavilions at Dreamland. A lot of the park remains flooded from the snowmelt, and it's barely warm enough to be outside, yet it feels fine to be here jamming with the boys. Besides, we really don't have a lot of choices. The high school pool didn't last long as a practice space before the night janitor caught us. The only reason he didn't call the cops is because Pete gave him the swim coach's number and told him to call him, and the coach said God knows what but got us off. Why Pete had the coach's home number, I don't know, and why the coach didn't even report us to the principal doesn't make any sense at all. Something about Pete makes crazy things work. After that, we moved between basements. When someone's family wasn't home, we'd go there.

It dawned on Matt at the end of last summer that the picnic pavilions at Dreamland had juice and would be a great place to practice. Although some people get pissed off with us disturbing their picnics with all that goddamn racket, other people, mostly girls, seem to like it, or more like they think we're cool or cute or something. They hang out for a listen.

Bobby's a blast. He loves the attention from the girls and manages to keep them around for a while after our sessions end with his joking. He also brings a six-pack along and hands out beers, which also helps. When he starts talking about music too much, though, the girls start drifting away. The guy's so into what he's saying that he doesn't realize it's a turnoff. He wouldn't care anyway despite the fact he's always talking about wanting to get laid. Which he never does.

Bobby's knowledge of music helps a lot. I go by instinct, and he gives me information to make that instinct better, if it's even still instinct after that. For instance, he showed me that I have the tension of my strings a little too high. Loosening them has made me freer to play dramatic bends. He also got me to change to a lighter string because that makes it easier to play fast. "Don't be afraid of playing each note and singing each word," he coaches. "Don't muddy it. And don't make a mystery out of tone with either the guitar or your voice. Let it come with what's written." He doesn't buy the punk line that punk's antimusic and all about destroying anything that might seem musical. Real punk, he insists, shows what's ugly as beautiful and what's beautiful as ugly.

That said, I still wouldn't tell Bobby about how when I was a kid the most beautiful thing in the world was hearing the Supremes singing "I Hear a Symphony" on my sister Jeannie's transistor radio. That would be taking the beauty thing too far. But Diana Ross's silvery voice singing the words *symphony* and *melody* and *rhapsody*—words that had nothing to do with anything in my life— hit me deep and strong. I didn't even know what rhapsody meant, but somehow, I desired rhapsody—the word and/or the idea—out of thin air.

I swear the Supremes still lurk somewhere way down in my music and in my voice and in myself. When I was like seven, I watched them on our fourteen-inch black-and-white. With her large, dark eyes and glossy lips—plus that asymmetrical haircut and those dangling, glittering diamond earrings—Diana Ross was to me the most beautiful woman in the world. I wanted a woman like that when I grew up, and somehow—though it sounds completely crazy—I think I also wanted to be *be* the guy version of her. Maybe I still want to be the punk guy version of her? Whatever that could possibly mean!

As usual, it's evening and we're under one of the pavilions jamming. We've been playing amazing together the past few months. With only our band to focus on, Bobby's become even more of a wizard on drums. He's punked his red hair out, too. Almost no one else in Hallein has spiked hair. And Matt's so solid. He knows how to make the bass flow between the notes of the two guitars. He usually gets trashed before practice, but that only seems to make his playing even better. Pete's a star. He doesn't want to sing lead but really should. His guitar shines, and his background vocals always sound like they're not just atmosphere but like he really, really means what he's singing.

We're going full tilt when among the shadows the pillars cast on the lawn Mrs. Lac appears. She's never come to one of our practices before. She has a worried look on her face. I glance over at Pete. He's in full ecstasy mode with the chords he's busting and has yet to notice her. She waits until we finish the number before stepping forward into the light, like some phantom lady in one of those forties film noirs on late-night TV. She doesn't go to Pete. No, it's me she wants. I don't get it. She approaches, apologizing, "I'm so sorry, Mike, please come with me right away." Doesn't even look at her own son. This can't be good. Pete starts to say something, but she waves him away as she leads me toward her '67 Skylark. Its paint is called Green Mist. I'm only naming it so I don't flip out. We get in the car, she turns the key in the ignition, slips it into drive. Once we're on our way, as calm as calm can be she tells me, "You need to be with your mother, Mike. It was on the evening news." I look out the window at all the empty picnic tables and trees silhouetted against the darkening sky. "There was a shooting this afternoon at the refinery. Your father was led away."

My mind goes blank. I can't get a word out for what seems forever, only to finally come up with, "Was he handcuffed?" as if that detail were important. She nods.

There's no one else in the world I could hear this news from, except for maybe Pete, but even him I'd probably shove away. Impossible as it seems, at some level I'm not totally surprised, or at least I tell myself that in order to not lose my mind. In the absence that dwelt in Dad's presence I had maybe always suspected tragedy lurking. But that's probably only a kid's anxiety over missing his dad. Maybe I've been detecting something in his silence, something so beaten down, so defeated, so humiliated, something waiting to rage. In all his years at the refinery, he's been confined to crawl spaces for eight-, ten-hour shifts, scrubbing burning-hot valves, pipes, tanks, and I've never once heard him complain. I want to start bawling but can't. Something in me that's been sealed tight ever since John died now seals even tighter. *Hermetic.*

Mrs. Lac pulls over at the park exit. Her hands on the wheel glow pearl under the streetlight. "There may be no explanation," she tells me. She smells like flowers. "Sometimes men are so . . ." Those simple words sound familiar. Maybe from Hawthorne? That's crazy. I'm going crazy. Mrs. Lac isn't quoting Hawthorne. They're just four ordinary words spoken with no reference to literature. In any case, they ring like prophecy, echoing in my mind over and over: *Sometimes men are so . . .*

As we turn the corner onto Magnolia, TV crews and journalists are crawling everywhere, surrounding the house. Freaks me out to *be* the news.

Instead of just dropping me off, Mrs. Lac gets out of the car, goes around to my side, opens the door, and tells me, "Mike, be strong." She takes my arm in hers, and together we run the gantlet. Cameras and microphones hit us as we move up the cracked walk to the house. She pushes through. The door is locked. I don't have a key because no one ever locks their house around here. I bang on the door, shouting, "It's me! It's me, Mike!" Finally, Terri opens it a crack. Her eyes are bloated from crying, crazed with terror.

I look around to Mrs. Lac, desperate for her to turn back time. She faces me, takes hold of my forearms, and shakes me gently as she tells me again, "Be strong." Before battling back through the crowd, she smiles all the love and sadness of the world at me. Last thing she says is to let her know if we need anything, anything at all. And, unlike with most people, I know she's not just saying that.

I slip into the house and bolt the door behind me.

It's a siege. My sisters' words, blurred by their blubbering, don't give me any more information than what I got from Mrs. Lac. Mom's wailing over and over again, "This is worse than death!" She sounds like some character out of Shakespeare, though I can't think which one. I want to comfort her but don't know how, other than to stay with her. I want to tell her I love her, but that's not us, not our family. When it comes down to it, she appears uninterested in having me or anyone around. I get that, I do.

Long before this, Mom had already thought her life was destroyed. At least that's what she'd once in a while suggest. A couple times she almost said so directly. She entered the city beauty pageant in 1951 and won. She only did it, she would insist, "to get the hell out of here." Usually she'd add, without disguising her disappointment, "Then I met your father." If you do the math, she had Jeannie six months after the wedding. But even knowing the situation never really made me feel like I knew her any better. Not that I haven't always craved to know her. Because I have. Still do. I'd picked up other bits and pieces over the years from Aunt Blondie. The two of them had a pretty messed up childhood. Their mom died when Mom was only three. Yes, I wanted to know Mom. But wanting to know someone and knowing them are two different things that maybe never get bridged.

I have to wait till the ten o'clock news to get more details. There's a theory, though little evidence to support it. It goes that my father was only nine months shy of thirty years at the refinery when his supervisor fired him, which would have made him ineligible for full pension. There's no paperwork to confirm this, a spokesman from the refinery says. Mom shouts at the TV one of the curses she picked up in the German neighborhood where she grew up. "Scheisse bastard!" It's not clear who it's meant for. The announcer? The spokesman? Dad? They interview several employees who add a twist. They say Dad and the victim were close friends. I never knew Dad had any friends at all, much less a close one. Apparently, they ate together frequently in the cafeteria or sometimes went out for a beer after a shift. His name is Leonard Dodge, a name Dad never mentioned. A grainy black-and-white photo of Leonard Dodge appears on the screen. I don't recognize him. He's posed by what looks to be the lake, halfway smiling, his thinning light hair blowing in the wind. Then suddenly I do recognize him. Something about the deep corners of the mouth and the way his head is tilted back a little. It was a long time ago. I was maybe in second grade and stayed home from school with a fever. The other kids were at school and Mom left for work knowing Dad would soon be getting home from his shift to look after me. I heard something in the living room and crept out of the bedroom in my pajamas. There on the couch sat Dad and Leonard Dodge, both looking relaxed. They appeared surprised to see me and straightened their backs. Dad stood, sort of chuckled, and introduced me. Leonard Dodge seemed maybe flustered and said he had to get going, and Dad led me back to bed, took my temperature and got me some ginger ale from the fridge. That was the one and only time I saw Leonard Dodge. Were the two of them as tight as me and Pete? In any case, this friendship changes how I've always thought of Dad. It also makes the crime all the more horrible. It's grotesque to even think this way, I know, but the tragedy somehow makes my father more human while at the same time making him inhuman.

The news goes on to report that Dad went home for his meal (something he almost never did) and returned with a pistol. There's a picture of the pistol. I didn't know he had one. He then walked into Leonard Dodge's office and shot him in the head. My guts tighten around what I'm guessing may be my soul. I feel like I'm going to puke. I can't handle the thought that Leonard Dodge is no longer a thinking, breathing, feeling human being. And somehow—I don't know why—I feel implicated.

The chronic sadness I've always felt over the fact that I barely know anything about who my father is now becomes so acute I can't stay here with Mom and the girls. As I rush out of the room, Mom again wails, "Scheisse bastard!"

Huddled on the floor next to the rollaway, I start convulsing. This has never happened to me before. For a long time, I can't stop. There, in the dark basement, I'm barely conscious for a long, long time. Eventually, I'm able to start thinking again. I think about one of the few times Dad and I have been alone since John died. It was maybe three years ago. We were walking along the river on a Sunday afternoon, picking blackberries, when all of a sudden, he stopped. He stood there for the longest time, silent, looking out over the water. When at last he spoke, he said he would like a job as a lookout in a national forest, living up in one of those fire towers. That was all he said. I didn't think much of it, but now it suddenly means so much. It was pretty much the opposite of the work he did, enclosed by pipes and machinery. I try to make some sense—any sense at all—of how the situation he's now in came to be. Unlike how I feel about not knowing Mom, even if I didn't know Dad, I at least thought I knew the ghost of him. I only now realize he's way more complicated and angrier than the ghost I'd created in my head. There's something sentimental to the point of being obscene about how I'd imagined his life as one of Thoreau's lives of quiet desperation, when it has now, for all intents and purposes, ended in a most unquiet way. I used literature to shield myself from real-ity. As I start putting a few of the pieces together, what's so strange is that I'm feeling his story becoming mine. I have become a mur-derer's son.

It's warm for an April night when I finally leave the house. I had to get out. The news about Dad has stopped, and I've given up hoping he'll contact us from jail. His silence has made Mom crazy, which is understandable, but I can't take another day of being confined with her rage and the girls' sorrow. I haven't seen the guys or the Lacs for over a month. Pete stopped by the house a bunch of times. I saw him from the window but didn't go to the door. I did the same with Lisa. On like her third time, she left a card I never opened and a tin of brownies. I feel bad about that, about ignoring her and Pete. None of us answered the door for anyone. Or the phone. Now I head to Dreamland with my guitar, sure that's where the guys are. And I hear them before seeing them, before even pulling into the parking lot. The fact they're here somehow makes it almost okay for me to enter the world again. I walk up to the pavilion, trying to calm the chronic jitters that have plagued me these past weeks. The band's riffing on the Stranglers' "(Get a) Grip (on Yourself)," which is really pretty ironic because I definitely don't have one on myself. I enter from behind, plug in while they're still playing, not sure they've even noticed me yet. Without a signal to them or from them, I join in, tentative at first. Bobby looks surprised when he turns his head and sees me, but he gives an *alright!* grin as he beats out an even wilder rhythm than the one he'd been riding. The other two look over. Matt nods to me in time with the music, Mona Lisa-ing a smile. But Pete studies me, even as he's putting out a series of monster chords, he studies me. A look of sympathy. Or is it empathy? I try to remember the difference. There's maybe also hurt in his eyes, hurt because I never called him, closed myself off from him. Before the last chords fade away, I raise my hand, giving the old *a-one-a-two-a-three*, and play the first measures of our "Strong, Silent, and Loud." The guys come right in. They're looking at me kind of funny. Maybe they're noticing I'm feeling kind of funny. Something has changed. In my playing, in my singing. This something scares me. All three of them are staring at me as we travel into the song, like they're also scared but also like they want to come with me to wherever I'm going or maybe to where I've been. I have no control over what I'm doing, and I have full control. Like a shock, I know it's Dad. All that's been silenced in him for so long is now flowing through me and finding voice. I'm a ventriloquist's dummy, I'm a voodoo doll. I take in all his pain and anger and shame and send it out through the world. This song—that Pete and I wrote—starts sounding unfamiliar. All the songs, one after the other, seem changed. I'm burning up. I tear my T-shirt off. The girls at the edge of the pavilion stare wide-eyed. They take a step back. My father's pain pours down my face and chest. I climb onto one of the concrete picnic tables and, standing there, legs spread wide, feel my eyes roll way back in my head. A trembling begins through my whole body. Now the girls look even more frightened. I feel strong, stronger than I've felt in my entire life. We play and play. We play hard, until nothing's left, until our voices are raw and we're drooping over our instruments. I curl up on the table, guitar shrieking with feedback. Bobby's leprechaun-green eyes glitter with glee. Matt knocks back nearly a half pint of whiskey in a few long swigs. Pete gets down on his knees by my side, whispering, "That's it, man! That's it!" I don't say a word, but I do know that whatever *it* may be, Pete's right, this is it, and yet I'd easily trade all my music for my father's redemption. Everything's changed inside and outside of me, and these changes are definitely what's pushed the music majorly.

Like a lot of guys starting bands, we're influenced by all the new music coming out. Big-name punkers like the Ramones, Blondie, the Clash, and Iggy Pop, but also less famous ones like the Boys, Dead Boys, the Dictators and lots more. But influence isn't everything. As Bobby says, you enter a genre and you develop a style, for sure, but there's life, and what it does and does not do to you makes the music not just music but art. Wise man, that Bobby.

Every day our practicing gets more and more intense. Word gets out and people flock to the park to watch us, only now it's mainly guys. The girls have all but disappeared. Guess I scared them off. One girl saw Bobby at the mall and told him as much, that I seem violent. He loved that. Not so sure I do. The guys who come nod their heads and shake their fists to the beat. Even with a crowd, though, we try to keep it practice and not so much rehearsal. Bobby says rehearsal implies an impending performance, but we've got to get things exactly right musically before we arrange anything like that. He stops to talk about this chord or that note, this measure or that phrasing. He's great.

As usual in the month since I reemerged, we're at the pavilion practicing. Tonight, the sour air from the refinery drifts all the way down here. In my peripheral vision an old guy's standing by one of the pillars. Kind of a beatnik—goatee, dressed in black, wearing wraparound shades even though it's dark out. He stays for the whole session. As we're unplugging and packing up, he approaches Matt, maybe because he's the tallest of us and is a little older. He introduces himself, Jimmy Ryder, owner of the River Club. It's probably the coolest venue in town, though not a place any of us from the Flats go because there's a cover. Jimmy Ryder lights a joint, passes it around. He growls, "Dig your sound, fellas." He's heard rumors we're out here at Dreamland and that we're wild, so he came down to check us out. He takes a long toke. On the exhale, he murmurs, "Had a cancellation. Can you cats play tomorrow night?" He pauses. "If it works out, I'll get you another gig later in the month."

Pete and I look at each other like we've just won the lottery. Bobby looks at us cautiously. It's Matt who, without even glancing at us, nods and tells Ryder, "That'd be cool." He says it in a cool way, too, not acting at all excited. The rest of us follow Matt's lead and nod. "We'll be there, Mr. Ryder," Matt assures him.

It occurs to me for the first time that this delusion of ours might actually turn into something real.

"By the way," Ryder asks, "what do you cats call yourselves?"

Once again, Matt's the one who answers. "We don't call ourselves anything. We don't have a name." He doesn't add *yet*.

The posters plastered outside the River Club read *No Name Band*, which is, Matt suggests, sort of a name. We just might keep it because the more Ryder asks us to come up with one, the worse any other sounds.

The River Club's not a small place—a converted '30s bus terminal—and it's packed with guys. Just a few girls in the back, leaning against the wall or their boyfriends. Some rich girls from high school days I recognize. Though no one I know. I'm hopped up on nothing but adrenaline as we're about to go on. Our first show ever. My compadres have taken speed. I've never given a performance before, and Pete's only done cello recitals in elementary school, so we're lucky to have Matt who's played every dive in town and Bobby who's performed a ton at school. They steady the band.

As Bobby's always reminding us, it's kind of useless to try and describe music in words, let alone a performance, but I *know* that both sets rock the house. For the last song, I find myself moved. I mean moved the way I hear people are moved by religion to do things they might not otherwise do, like shake on the floor or handle poisonous snakes. My body starts vibrating, vibrating but no shaking or twisting hips like Elvis. The crowd goes nuts. They want me, I want them. They start grabbing at me, pawing me, hitting me. It's crazy, it's like those ancient Greek cults Pete talks about, the ones that rip their god apart. Like that, except the god part.

Before we knew it, we were on the road in this '67 Twilight Green Econoline Jimmy Ryder loaned us, on a tour arranged by him. He's become our de facto manager, which is cool because, except for Matt's experience booking local bars, we don't really know the ins and outs of the business. For two months total, we'll be on the road. Forty gigs, twenty-five cities. So far, it's been mostly dives. We've played a Chinese restaurant after hours, a strip club between shifts, a burned-out supermarket, a bunch of apartment building basements. Some legit clubs, too. We drive and drive through inter-state sameness. The landscape looks so far away. We sleep and eat fast food in the van, which very soon begins to stink of four guys who've been partying too much and haven't showered or brushed their teeth. Most nights we earn not much more than beer money. Despite the shitty conditions, I'm loving performing. For most people, I suppose, performance implies acting a part that's not yourself. But not me. I never feel more like myself than when I'm singing and playing guitar, offering myself up to the crowd. Maybe it's entertainment for the audience, and that's cool, but for me it's ritual, it's resurrection.

I'm not exactly sure how people hear about us. There's Ryder's publicity, of course. He has clubs put posters up and place announce-ments in weeklies, but without a record I just don't get it. I'm trying to think if I'd go see us if I hadn't heard a song on the radio. There's what Matt calls the buzz, I guess. He talks about how sad it was playing in bands without the buzz, in bars where the crowd won't shut up and doesn't seem to care about the music.

I'm afraid to think of what life would be like without music, without Pete. I kind of see Pete as the music. He once called me his muse and explained that the word comes from music or vice versa.

I think it's more like he's mine, though. It's not as if Pete and music make me only happy, but they do make things make sense, at least a little. They give meaning, even if that meaning's awful, ambiguous, cryptic, or just plain confusing.

It's kind of hokey, but Pete and I like doing touristy things in the towns we hit. That is, if we manage to drag ourselves out of the van after a hard night's playing and partying. I've never been anywhere so really want to see something of the world. Matt and Bobby aren't really interested.

Today we're at Niagara Falls, me and Pete. We took a tourist jitney because Matt and Bobby were wasted and still snoozing in the van in Buffalo, where we played last night. The couples with us in the jitney all appeared to be honeymooners. They seemed none too happy to find freaks along for the ride, like our presence was somehow a downer to their newlywed bliss. Not that we were in their faces. No, not at all. It's like black jeans and T-shirts do the trick. Well, and that don't-fuck-with-me look Pete says I can get, or how sometimes his lip curls above that prominent canine of his like he's about to snarl. Think mean Elvis.

The two of us are hiking the rim above the Canadian side of the falls. Once we're away from all the tourist traps, it's easy to get high on the bigness and the beauty of it all, like what in Romantic times, Pete says, they called the Sublime. The feeling probably comes from all the charged electrons, ions, or whatever they are that get generated by falling water.

We're sitting right on the edge of the rushing river, about a mile above the falls, when Pete says, "More than anything, you know what I'd like to do?"

I don't so much as nod or shake my head because I know what he's going to say.

"I want to dive in there, swim with the current, then go flying gloryizingly over that motherfucking cascade of the ultimate!"

He leans forward on his haunches, and for a second, I swear he's actually going to do it.

He laughs, "And you, *mio Orfeo,* would have to gather up the pieces smashed on the rocks and sound the elegiac lay on high. Or, if you'd prefer, you can just say, 'Fuck him!'"

Just to be safe, I suggest we hike further upstream. As we're moseying along, I ask, "What is it with you and water?"

He doesn't pause a second before answering. "Sometimes I think I was born into the wrong element. If I'd gotten to choose, I'd have gone with water. Or maybe fire. Possibly air. Definitely not earth."

Late afternoon, we get back down below the falls to take a ride on the *Maid of the Mist.* It's expensive but we want to get right up under the monster falls. The water pounds more and more intense the closer the boat gets in. The force penetrates every cell of my body. My brain tries to measure the power, get the music of it. Impossible. Too big, too complex. When we're almost all the way in, Pete starts shouting like a maniac into what's probably the greatest of all white noises on Earth. He shouts for the sake of shouting, so I start shouting along with him. The other passengers look scared. They move away from us, huddling together on the far end of the deck. When the ship stops momentarily at the farthest point under the falls before spinning back around, we start laughing into each other's mist-blurred face.

Our hike's made us incredibly hungry. For the first time since beginning the tour we decide to eat something besides the usual junk—burgers, wings, chips—and head into a fancy restaurant, not so much because it's fancy but because it's all glass and overlooks the Horseshoe Falls. The maître d' is very sorry, but gentlemen must have dinner jackets. And the customers are dressed up. Suits and ties, nice dresses, even a mink stole or two. But when Pete flashes his gayest smile, the persnickety old guy responds with a wry grin. "One moment, messieurs," he says before disappearing. He returns with two navy blazers. He's beaming as he holds them for us to put on. Perfect fits. The other diners look askance as our newfound champion leads us to what appears to be the best table in the house, the one directly facing the falls. He even pulls the chairs out for us. Our waiter (who happens to look a lot like us, except clean-cut) comes over and opens our menus for us. Never had that happen before. We're grinning at the ridiculousness of us. We order surf 'n' turf because it's something we've never had, something rich kids eat at nice restaurants on prom night.

The lobster's sweet, the steak tender—more delicious than anything I've ever tasted. We down the food with plenty of Black Russians and we toast a lot. "To stardommery!" (that's his); "To camaraderie" (that's mine). We're getting buzzed and totally mesmerized by the grandeur of nature right smack in front of us.

We've missed the jitney back to Buffalo by a long shot, and luckily don't have a show tonight, so after we count up the cash to pay the bill, we decide there's enough to go hog wild and check into a motel. The idea of a real bed after so many nights sleeping piled like puppies in the Econoline sounds amazing. Problem is, neon no vacancy signs are lit up and down the strip. We walk and walk, happy-drunk, until at last we see a place called the Honeymoon City Motel has a vacancy. We smirk and nod to each other, then head into the office. The lady at the desk looks at us like we're aliens who've just landed. I suppose to her we are, and maybe she is to us, what with her bright-yellow poodle-perm and sleeveless blouse with yellow butterflies all over it. We ask for a room, and she's very sorry but all she has left is the honeymoon suite.

Without batting an eye, Pete responds, "I assumed they're all honeymoon suites."

"But there's only the one bed." She blinks fast before adding, "And it's heart shaped."

"Perfect!" Pete smirks.

I feel like I'm in a TV skit rejected from *Love, American Style.*

Poor lady looks like she's about to have a nervous breakdown as she hands him the registration form. "Brothers?"

He answers no without further explanation, all the while grinning at me. I'm too freaked out to offer even a weak smile back at either him or the lady.

When we get to the door of the honeymoon suite, in one fell swoop Pete grabs hold of me and tries picking me up to carry me over the threshold. He thinks it's a riot. I struggle loose and push him away, tell him to knock it off. The room is all satin hearts and gilded mirrors, *tacky,* as my mom would say, but still, nicer than any I've ever been in.

Before I've taken in the whole suite, Pete's already over on the other side whooping, "Far out, man! Just like back in Cali!" He's already turned the big gold knobs on what is, he informs me, a Jacuzzi. "Hust-a-ler-endo!" he shouts. "Get your ass in here." He's already undressing, even though the tub's got barely an inch of water in it. Next thing I know, he's racing across the room, stark naked, shouting, "Minibar! Minibar!" He swings the doors open. The fridge is chock-full of soda pop, juice, beer, even a bottle of champagne. The cupboard has fancy snacks, like smoked almonds, salami and cheese packets, Pringles. There's an enormous fruit basket wrapped in yellow cellophane on the counter. With one hand, Pete grabs the champagne from the fridge, and with the other busts through the cellophane, pulling out an enormous, totally red, perfectly heart-shaped apple. He scampers like a puppy back over to the tub and climbs in. When the water gets high enough, he turns the jets on. I've never seen anything like it. I wait until then to drop my underwear, cross the room, and slowly lower myself into the churning water. Hot as hell but feels so good to my aching bones. Pete pops the cork on the champagne, sending it ricocheting off the popcorn ceiling. Plaster snows down. He puts his mouth over the frothing bottle, sputtering, "Mucho wackoid!" then hands it to me. I'm drunk from the Black Russians but manage to give the green bottle a good swig anyway. New taste. Not bad. With champagne still foaming from his mouth, he takes a horse-chomp out of the too-perfect apple. He then holds the fruit up in front of me, urging me to try it. Snow White, along with Adam and Eve, flicker through my brain. I pause before taking a bite then do it to humor him. I don't swallow. I hold the bit in my mouth, just in case.

We each have a jet massaging our back. We lie there in bliss. His left arm and leg lazily bump into me; my right arm and leg lazily bump into him. Not a word between us. The timer shuts the jets off after half an hour. Three times Pete lifts himself up to reset it as I drift in and out of sleep in our cozy cauldron.

At some point Pete taps my shoulder to wake me. He's all lazy smiley. The water's perfectly still now, lukewarm. He drags himself out of the tub and from a shelf grabs the biggest, whitest, fluffiest towels ever. He pats himself quick all over with one, then holds another out for me to step into. He pats me front and back a few times before giving my head a brisk rubbing. Like a dad with their kid. This should embarrass me but somehow doesn't. He then floats toward the bed, me trailing behind. We're both freezing from the AC so huddle our naked selves together in the middle of the enormous heart, shivering on top of the red satin because he never sleeps with covers. "I'm freezy yumming!" he says like that's the normal way of saying he's cold. Instead of a blanket, he decides to pull me right on top of him, naked front to naked front, holding onto me so tight I can hardly breathe. He's kind of squirming and chuckling and nuzzling into my neck. Eventually, we both stop shaking. I try to roll off of him, but he grips onto me, murmuring, "Not yet, not yet."

God knows how—maybe it was the alcohol—but I somehow managed to sleep till morning, splayed on top of Pete like that. How he could have slept under me I haven't a clue. When I woke up, I lifted my head to see him bright-eyed, looking up into my face. He pats me on the cheek, and I roll off him. I try not to meet his eyes again and also try not to look at his body or, for that matter, my own.

On a tour like this, life becomes what Mrs. Homer calls some novels: *episodic.* Like *Tom Jones,* for instance. It's when one thing happens after another without any of the events seeming to be connected. The important stuff gets mixed in with the trivial on the conveyor belt of time. Even dramatic things, such as fights—I mean fistfights—are simply one more thing. For instance, on a super muggy afternoon in Kansas City before a show I was feeling *anguished* (it was probably the first time I ever really understood what that word could mean) about having left my family in the mess they're in, so I scrounged up all the coins from the glove compartment and floor of the van to call home. Amid burnt-out storefronts I found a battered phone booth. I plugged the machine, studying the world outside through a web of graffiti as the phone rang and rang. On the ninth ring, just when I was about to hang up, came Mom's voice, "Hello?" faint, quavering. None of the usual harshness in her tone. We did the small talk thing, then I asked after Dad. She told me his lawyer had him plead guilty and that he's going to spend the rest of his days in prison. She said it just like that. No sobbing, nothing. The news comes like a fist shoved down my throat. Dad, poor Dad. And his poor friend Leonard Dodge. How did it come to this? The drama of the courtroom, where we might have at least found out something more about what happened, wasn't going to happen. We're all left with nothing, nothing but grief and agony. The coins quit in the middle of the silence between us. I left the booth, crazy with anger. I wound up taking it out on some guy who'd nudged his LeSabre into the crosswalk. It seemed so right to kick the driver's side headlight in. Next, I jumped on the hood, scuffing the Almond Mist Metallic paint job good and scaring the hell out of him. I gave the windshield a couple of good stomps, but it didn't bust.

In St. Louis, me and the guys were on our way into a dive next to the one we were playing later that night, and there were these two jerks standing next to the jukebox staring at us. They kept their eyes on us as we moved to the bar to order. The one with Bee Gees hair and Dingo boots said something. I don't even know for sure what it was and didn't bother finding out either. Without giving it a second thought, or, for that matter a first, I delivered a series of rapid-fire blows to his face that sent him rag doll-ing across the tattered linoleum. His friend jumped in and tried taking me, but I decked him too. By this time, Pete was holding me by the shoulders while Matt and Bobby stood over the two, fists clenched, as they tried to get up.

Pete yelled right up in my face, "Don't give assholes the time a day," as he led me out the door fast because the bartender was shouting that he was calling the cops.

I'm not proud of what I did, going crazy like that. I don't have any real reason. You'd think I'd be more philosophical about this violence thing. I didn't even hate those guys. Sure, they were assholes, but then so was I. And that wasn't even my first fight on tour or the last. Later on, Pete said he didn't get the shit I did. I reminded him of all his stuff he'd done, like back in high school beating up rich kids, burning down condos, etc. He argues that what he does is different. It's planned or political. Not out of control, like me.

Onstage, a different kind of violence comes. It's like I'm busting out of the prison of myself and giving to the world whatever part of me that's worth anything. I get in this weird trance and wind up leaving some shows battered and bruised all over. Most times I don't remember how it all played out. But I do recall how, somewhere in Michigan, some guy in a Lynyrd Skynyrd T-shirt (the one with the skull design) got too enthusiastic leaping up toward me and nearly fractured my jaw with *his* skull. At the same show, another freak thought he was a vampire or something. He made it up onto the stage and was all over me, trying to bite me on the neck, until Matt dropped his bass, grabbed hold of the guy by his jean jacket, and tossed him off the stage.

In Houston, I woke up in the hospital. No idea how I got there. My head hurt like hell. Pete was at my bedside. He started in with this weird police-speak, "You've been a victim of assault." I didn't like that, I told him—the being a victim part—but he insisted. Apparently, some guy drop-kicked my head. "Maybe things have gotten out of control," he added in a calm voice I could tell was forced. "Do you really need to get so out of control?" That was a good question, it really was. He continued—now almost urgent— like he'd prepared a speech and was afraid he wasn't going to get to finish: "Look, guy, I'm right there next to you and even I don't know, but I have got to ask, do you somehow encourage it?" Again, good question.

Should I have told him, "Yeah, sure, I like having the shit kicked out of me"? I'd never thought about it that way. Maybe it's true. I do know one thing's for sure, though: I don't decide to do any of it. It just happens. Maybe there's something in me that brings it out in people? That is, when I'm onstage. On the street, I think I frighten people, or at least that's what I've been told by Bobby and even Lisa. Strangers steer clear of me. I wanted to explain to Pete that it's not an act, but maybe he wouldn't understand, and maybe I don't either. Probably to try and scare me straight, Pete told me exactly what happened. It wasn't pretty. He has an eye for detail, as they say. "The blood was pooling under your skin, then started leaking out, man! There wasn't a cut or anything, it just seeped out of like your pores and eyes." He winced, shaking his head. There was more: "The weird thing is, when you were lying there in this puddle of beer and blood and puke, the guy who'd done the damage threw himself on top of you. He was yelling for everyone to keep back, that you'd been hurt. I had to fucking pull him off you. He kept blubbering how sorry he was, and how he loved you so much."

Crazy as it sounds, I found some beauty in the picture Pete painted.

We're in the middle of walking our way across the Golden Gate Bridge, me and Pete. The phalanx of fog, as he calls it, has retreated out to sea. He stops to look toward Alcatraz. Without turning to me, he says, right out of the blue, "This is getting to me." I look at him, puzzled. "I mean life on the road—not sleeping, eating shit, drinking too much, getting high all the time. Crazy crowds."

I deploy a nod, my usual tactic to absorb bad news I sense coming my way.

He goes on, "It's too much. Hate to break it to you, my Mike, but I've got to leave the band. Need to head home." He's shaking his head real slow.

Before he started telling me this, I was having a rush of completely different thoughts, like how beautiful the world is, and how we're going to be rock stars, and how I can't believe I'm on the

Golden Gate Bridge, exactly where John and I had dreamed of coming, and how I'm seeing the ocean for the first time in my life, with my best buddy in the world, and how the bridge stands for so much in our lives. I was only starting to figure out what the bridge might really mean when he started in with the bad news. I can hear it in his voice, though, that he's dead serious.

I put my arm around him and whisper, "Touring's a grind, for sure." He hangs his head. "Everyone says so. Matt, Bobby, other bands. But it'll be worth it, I promise. We can cut the booze and weed. I'm fine with that. Look, we're almost done. We can go home then, get some rest."

"It's not just that," he says, finally turning to face me, "it's the whole scene. Sure, there's good stuff, like when the music soars and we get ovations, and like when you and I have some time to ourselves. But there's too much of the other stuff. I can't take any more of you getting in fights with random guys and guys from the audience pounding the shit out of you. I need something else. The Army won't have me, so I don't know what, but something else."

He dwells on the Army thing a lot. I feel shitty about what I did, I really do, but swear the deception was for the best. Knowing him, if there was another war, he'd try something heroic and die. I of course don't say anything about that, only remind him I'm trying to be better and haven't gotten in any kind of mess since the hospital in Houston.

He looks me right in the eye, determined. "Sorry to ditch you like this, man. I know I'm the one who talked about fame and fortune, about making history and stuff, but now I think it's just love I want." His eyes start tearing up. He grabs hold of me, nearly crushing me.

I'm desperate for only the second time in my life, and both times it's Pete who's made me this way. Is it that I took the lame adolescent vow we made to each other so long ago down by the river seriously, whereas he took it as just that, lame and adolescent? I guess what he means by love—this love that he says he wants—means having a real girlfriend. Because he's got my love. And he's got his mom's. Maybe he's just homesick? If I had a mom like his, I guess I'd be homesick too.

I have an idea. When we pulled into San Francisco yesterday, Matt wondered what the huge, aerodynamic, white wedge of architecture dominating the hillside in the distance was. Pete told him it was the cathedral, and that it was at the very center of Japantown. I didn't know cathedrals could be modern or that there was another Asian town here besides Chinatown. He told us he has relatives in Japantown. So, in his moment of agony and doubt—and mine of desperation—I suggest we get ourselves over to Japantown and visit his family. This might help, I think, might give him some relief.

His face does in fact brighten. "Sounds good!" He stretches toward the sky. "But first, I want to swim to Alcatraz." He says this like he's just going to take a snapshot of it or something.

"No way. That's crazy." My eyes blink out of control. "It's too far, too cold." But he's smiling at me like I'm the crazy one. "Besides, there are sharks—Great Whites, like in *Jaws*."

"Trust me," he snickers, "people make the swim all the time. But to make you happy, I'll just swim the length of the Bridge instead."

I tell him this is also a monumentally bad idea. I know I sound uncool, but he brings it out in me, he does.

He claims a seven-year-old girl has swum it, that some guy has done it in under seventeen minutes, that he's used to the Pacific's cold from his childhood out here, and besides, the only confirmed killing by a shark in San Francisco this century was in 1959, at Baker Beach, which is *outside* the Bay.

"Do what you want," I say, not able to help coughing my nervous cough into my fist. His leaving the band suddenly seems insignificant.

He tells me he'll go from the Presidio side, where we just came from, and that I should meet him with his clothes on the other side, the Marin Headlands. He points across the water: "That's the cliff I'll be aiming for." Right offshore from his destination a fleet of tiny sailboats drift and dart like butterflies. We retrace our steps.

I don't know why I descend to the base of the bridge's tower with him, but I do. It makes me an accomplice of sorts. There, he strips down to his underwear. I'm a little surprised he doesn't go full-on naked. In any case, he rests a hand on my shoulder and tells me in this unnerving manic voice he sometimes gets, "See you in less than forty-five, my *philos!*"

I look away. This pseudo-heroic prank is absurd.

"Come on," he says with that foolish grin of his, "cheer up! If Leander swam from Europe to Asia every night to meet his Hero, this is the least I can do for you."

I sort of remember him telling me this myth, and how I thought it seemed weird that someone named Hero was a girl. But now that he's making an analogy to us it's beyond weird. Besides, Leander swims *to* Hero. He smirks, and before I know it, he's taking a dive into water that feels cold as iron to even the one hand I stick in. Cheer up? He was the one all gloom and doom just a minute ago.

With Pete's clothes under my arm, I jog across the bridge, keeping an eye on him moving like a torpedo through the water way below. Tourists are pointing down at him, some snapping pictures. I hate to admit it but watching him propel himself through the waves is beautiful. That is, until it starts to look like the current's pulling him off course, at which point everything turns ugly in my head. He goes with the current for a zig, then zags back, making as much progress as not. It soon becomes clear that not only is he being pulled off course, he's being swept away. He'll be taken out of the bay and into the ocean, and that'll be the end. I break into a full run to find help. By the time I reach the Headlands, my lungs are about to burst. I scramble down the embankment, looking for a lifeguard or anyone. I'm in terrible shape from too much smoking and drinking. I'm about to collapse.

When I finally make it down the steep slope to the shore, there's no sign of Pete anywhere on the glaring sweep of water. I run toward four of the sailboats I saw from the bridge. They've just now landed on the beach. They turn out to not be sailboats but surfboards with sails. I'm frantic for air and pointing wildly toward the horizon. I somehow manage to get my message across to these guys. I'm sure I come off as a deranged person, but they don't ask questions, they go to the rescue. I continue along the shore as the little flotilla shrinks in the distance. I don't say prayers or anything. I only think of Mrs. Lac and how hard she's going to take this, and how I can't possibly explain it to her. I squat down, hugging my knees, looking out at the blank ocean.

It seems like forever before the four sails reappear among the waves. I start moving to where it looks like they're going to come ashore. It's not clear whether they have Pete or not. I wave his flannel shirt. I'm not sure they see me. I finally make out a body lying on one of the boards. It's got to be Pete. Drowned. The guys drop their sails and come ashore. Then the body starts shaking and rolls off the board and onto the shore. It's Pete and he's alive! I'm so relieved and thankful I can't get angry at him for his stupidity, at least not yet. You hear about people turning blue with cold. Until now I'd always thought that was a figure of speech, but he's as blue as one of those Hindu gods. He curls up into a ball and seems to be trying to laugh but is unable to make a sound. He grabs hold of my arms, pulling me down close to him, for warmth. I put his shirt around his shoulders, rub hard.

The sunburned rescuers stand around us. The one whose nose is peeled to pink says to Pete, "You're a strong motherfucker. Anyone else would be dead."

They each pat him on the head like he's a dog and tell him to take it easy. Pete's nodding and stuttering his thanks through chattering teeth. I also thank them, though my thanks comes out too quiet, too brief, not revealing a trace of what I'm thinking, which is something about things normally foreign to me, like brotherly love and goodness, and how sad it is to meet such great people when you'll never cross paths with them again. The surfers take off, carrying their boards up the beach.

We stay where we are, not saying a word. Pete smokes one cigarette after another to warm his insides up. He knows this was a close one and in his own Pete way beats me to the punch, asking me to promise to stay with him. "You're my hero," he says softly. I'm not sure if he means *hero* lowercase or *Hero* uppercase. I don't respond. I should be the one making him promise to never pull a stunt like this again. "Promise?" he asks, just like a little kid.

I shrug. He keeps staring at me until I finally speak: "I'll rip your nuts off if you ever pull a stunt like this again."

He laughs. "Not exactly your patois, amigo, but that's one Roman promise I'll keep."

We wander up to the bridge, eventually finding a bus to take us back into the city.

Japantown seems more like a shopping center than a town, only cleaner and sunnier than the shopping centers back home. There are three plazas, one right next to another. There's also a huge modern pagoda made out of concrete. Pete's aunt owns a small jewelry store, in the one plaza called Kintetsu. We head there. She's not really an aunt, though. His mother's American cousin. In any case, she's really happy to see Pete. She bear-hugs him, then shakes my hand like a fireman. She's nothing like his mom, this Aunt Keiko. She's a bulldog of a lady. A friendly bulldog. A cheerful bulldog. A '40s-style bulldog, what with her hair swooped up and lacquered like the Andrews Sisters, only black.

For a minute they talk Japanese, then come back to English. She asks him, "What the hell you doing in Frisco, son?" When she hears Pete's answer, she asks three times, "A rock band?" with varying degrees of amusement. Or is it bemusement? In any case, she's not impressed, and he hasn't even told her we're specifically a punk rock band. She wonders out loud, "Shouldn't you be going to college or getting a job or something?" This is not exactly helping matters, at least not from my perspective. "Got a record? Can I hear you on the radio?"

My whole life's about to collapse. So this is where I intervene. Which is to say, this is where I tell the second whopper of my life. "Hey," I begin in a chipper tone that's totally not me, "this was going to be a surprise for Pete and the guys, but since you asked . . ." I'm formulating a subterfuge as I speak, and then, right there on the sunny plaza of Japan Center, I announce, "We've got a recording contract in LA."

Pete's eyes nearly pop right out of his head. "Really?" he asks with a look so pitiful I barely recognize him. Maybe he's suffering from hypothermia.

I nod and say sure, wondering what kind of miracle I'm going to have to work to make this happen. I improvise out of thin air: "When we arrive there next week, we're going to cut our first record." I cough into my fist three times. "If we can just lay it down for the moguls, like we do in our shows, we've got it made."

Aunt Keiko claps us both on the backs at the same time, braying, "Why, that's a horse of a different color! You're pretty near gosh darn celebrities! Let's celebrate!" She takes us to the sushi shop across the pristine plaza, buying square plate after square plate of whatever we want. Lots of *unagi*—grilled eel—for me, and *uni*—the scary sea urchin—for Pete. Plus, little clay carafes of sake. She announces to the whole place, first in Japanese and then in English, that this is her nephew and his friend, and that we're celebrities. Pete goes around talking to them in Japanese. I nod, feeling myself blush from the publicity of my deceit.

When we're done eating, Aunt Keiko's going to take Pete around to see a bunch of relatives. I'm more than welcome to come along but beg off so I can make a desperate attempt at turning my lie into some semblance of truth. I head over to a newsstand to get change for phone calls. Everything's in Japanese. There are incredibly bright magazine covers and countless comic books—some thick as phone books—with drawings of people with enormous eyes and bangs flopping over their foreheads. I get two pocketsful of coins and walk away from Japantown, just in case Pete and Aunt Keiko happen by.

From a phone booth inside a drugstore, I call Jimmy Ryder. He's surprised, so surprised, and happy, so happy, to hear from me, even though I'm not sure he knows who he's talking to until I mention the band. He sounds pretty stoned. After some small talk, I suggest, "As long as we're in LA, why don't we cut a record?" I say it very matter-of-fact, like it should be a matter of fact.

Ryder doesn't answer my question but says he has of course heard the buzz around our tour. "I'm impressed, very impressed."

I'm afraid the coins are running out, so I push him, "What about a recording studio?"

He must really think we're good enough, or else he's stoned out of his mind, because pretty much automatically he says, "Okay, for you I'll put my neck on the line. For you, I'll call in some markers. This will maybe be your one and only shot, so don't blow it. My guess is that the studio guys will most likely come to your show first, to see if you're something they want."

This is unbelievable. I'm to call him back the next day. The lie is the most initiative I've taken in my entire life. Desperation seems to be a good motivator for me.

The next day I sneak off from the guys while they're napping in the van where we parked on a pretty sketchy side street in the Mission District, and I call Ryder back. He's got us what amounts to an audition with a record company. They'll come to our show. Plus, our reputation's grown enough that our LA venue's been switched to the Starwood Club in West Hollywood. A big deal, according to Ryder. Not that we're famous in the greater scheme of things. When it comes down to it, we're just another underground band. Any night we play in any city there's probably a big act or two or three filling a huge theater, arena, or even stadium, as well as other bands filling, or not filling, clubs of all sizes.

The only instruction Ryder gave was this: "At the Starwood, play them keisters off boys, play them keisters off."

"Yessir, will do," I responded with so much earnestness I was afraid he might think I was mocking him.

When I told the guys, they went crazy. They got all amped up and started imagining some big-deal mogul squiring us around Hollywood. Limos, coke, chicks, the works, as Bobby, who looks about twelve, put it.

The night before the show we headed over to the Starwood to check out the stage and equipment, and to hear a band called Black Flag.

Bobby's heard of them. The lead guitar, this guy named Greg Ginn, played out of this world. The drummer was also excellent. The lead singer is called Henry Rollins. He was quite the performer—bare-chested, explosive. He flew into the crowd, thrashed around, mic in hand. I was a little intimidated. Well, actually, a lot. Until afterwards. Without me saying anything at all, Bobby said, "I'm so fucking glad you're not histrionic like that guy."

I grin. *Histrionic.* Good vocab word. Bobby's an *aficionado,* so I take this as a compliment and feel a little more confident.

Our show at the Starwood went decent enough. Not our greatest but by no means our worst. I became a little too self-conscious about which face in the crowd might be a record executive's. Afterward, though, no one from any record company came up to us. This made me nervous. To be honest, I was crushed. We were about to leave through the stage door when the guy from front of house came out and handed us a note scribbled on a Miller coaster. It said to show up at noon to a place called Dangerhouse Records. There was an address. It was a mystery as to why no one from the company came to tell us in person. Whatever the case, I was relieved. The guys all high-fived.

Next day, we drive around looking for Dangerhouse with a bad tourist map that includes houses of the stars. We get lost but eventually manage to find the place. It's in a neighborhood that's the furthest thing from the stars. Warehouses and cinder block industrial buildings, not a palm tree in sight. We spot a small sign with *Dangerhouse* done in yellow and black, like it's marking a hazard. I wasn't thinking Decca or EMI, but the place looks pretty grim. Matt presses the buzzer. The guy who answers is maybe a few years older than us, nondescript except for a dime-sized mole on the bridge of his nose.

"Glad you're here," he says, almost cheerful. Nothing dangerous about him. "Really dug your show. Sorry I couldn't come backstage. Had to run." He lets us in. "Everything's going to be great," he assures us.

His name's Burt. He's as polite as a businessman, though it's not like he's wearing a suit or anything—worn cords and tattered Oxford, like they're the last clothes his mom ever bought him. The studio's no more than a commercial garage but full of what Bobby declares is outstanding sound equipment. None of us really knows about studios and recording. Bobby, though, picks it up instantly and asks good questions. We don't really get how to use a studio mic, or what we're supposed to get from the headphones. Another guy, Dave, is here to help. He's patient. He shows us how to set up and plug in, and what cues to look for from Burt up in the booth. Dave's a big guy, pale—paler than even us—which makes it hard to believe he lives in Southern California. He has this calm around all the equipment that makes us trust him. Reminds me of some of the guys in AV club back in school.

When we're set up and about to take our positions, I suddenly go dark with doubt. I'm thinking of all the great records for forever, and how we can possibly live up to them. We have only eight songs. Even ten's thin. Iggy Pop did it with eight on *The Idiot*. If Iggy can do it . . . Who am I kidding? Worse, though, I'm not sure I can perform without an audience. I pick up the guitar, knowing to the bone that if this doesn't fly Pete's gone. Bobby gets up from the drum set, all antsy. With him, antsy's good. He's bouncing around, checking the wires and plugs. He has us tune our instruments one more time, making adjustments for each of us. The guy's got an ear—like perfect pitch. He goes over and whispers something to Matt, then to Pete, and finally to me: "It's ours." That's all he says, and then I know it's true.

First number's "Ripped-Off Melody," which starts out by inverting the first three bars of the old standard "Unchained Melody" before flying off on its own, warp speed. In the split second after that initial passage, I'm dead, wondering if I can fly at all. In what's left of that second, I'm back at the swimming pool sessions with only Pete and me. I'm okay, I'm okay. More than okay, I *am* flying. It feels weird with the headphones on, but still, I'm flying. The headphones make another universe. I'm playing and singing deep inside myself, flying up and falling down through caverns of music. A flying fall, a falling flight. I'm seeing and hearing Matt, Bobby, Pete, and know they're in this new universe too. Their expressions go back to something way prehistoric, to like when our apish ancestors were gazing at the lightning or stars above them, or into the fire in front of them, and filling the fear and the void and the loneliness of existence with noise and words and rhythm. A phantom of myself reaches across to Pete—one, two, three times—but he's water through my hands, through my arms. I feel that what we're making is great, and I know that what I feel for these guys goes deeper than love, wherever that takes you.

Between songs, we don't talk. It's as if each of us independently intuits that talking might jinx the vibe. Burt and Dave say a few things from the booth. We nod.

We go over songs and parts of songs for a whole day, though it seems like only an hour has passed. When the session ends, the four of us stand there staring at each other. Bobby kind of shakes his head, meaning *unbelievable.*

Burt speaks over an intercom from behind the glass booth. "I think we've got ourselves a record, boys," and he's grinning as wide as Howdy Doody.

Dave comes over to shake our hands. "Best session I've sat in on in some time."

We're calling the album *Invisible City,* a twisted homage to our hometown. They'll press a thousand copies, which doesn't sound like much when you think about gold or platinum records. If the record takes off, they'll do ten thousand, but we've got to, Burt tells us, tour the album like hell.

JUNE 1978, MARIKO

Cousin Keiko called. Peter visited her in San Francisco! She had not seen him since we left California. She said he has grown to be

114

a fine young man. I am surprised he thought to go and see her. I haven't heard from him in weeks. This upsets me. He knows how I worry. I told him he could call collect anytime.

I keep telling myself not to worry, that he is young, that he is finding himself. And yet, I can't help but feel something is not right. Oh, it's not that he is in a rock and roll band. That bothers Richard, not me. Richard also believes Mike has been a bad influence on Peter, which isn't fair. No, it is something else, a dark star over my son that a *yōkai* of ill will has hung there.

At practice, I aim my Smith & Wesson .357 Magnum at the 50-yard silhouette target and fire, imagining I am blowing that evil spirit away.

MID-JULY–AUGUST 1978, MIKE

We arrived in London two days ago. The record came out fast and did in fact sell. Dangerhouse kept pressing more copies, so Ryder extended our US tour. He then floored us by lining up Europe. Never in my life had I thought about going to Europe or not going to Europe, but now that I'm here it seems way out of my league. As a musician, for sure, but more basically, as a human being. London is punk central and everyone, punk or not, seems so sophisticated. It's in their eyes and how they carry themselves.

We were home for just five days after the US tour. Only Pete had a passport, from the time he went to Japan with his mom, but Ryder had the expedited forms for the rest of us all in order. Matt dropped me at my house before returning the van. I thanked him for the ride. He said, "No, thank you, man, for the ride of a life-time." I grinned. I'm not a grinner. He grinned back. He's not a grinner either.

I walked into the house after months away and Anne-Marie and Terri barely nodded, barely moved their eyes from the TV. *Three's Company* was on, the eponymous three yukking it up, whereas the present company of three didn't so much as crack a smile. Without Dad's attention, the place had really fallen apart. The main floor smelled as musty as the basement. The floors—carpet, linoleum, wood—all had grayed from refinery smoke. Fly carcasses littered windowsills. The dining table was piled high with laundry. Mom's probably at work. No sign of little Blake.

"You guys off today?" I asked. It was the middle of the day, in the middle of the week.

Without moving her eyes from the sitcom, Terri answered, voice flat as a frying pan. "You think we could go back after what happened?"

Right. Made sense. Sad sense. Both had jobs at the refinery. Terri cafeteria, Anne-Marie front gate.

"How's Mom?"

Still not moving her eyes from the hilarity, Terri murmured, "Don't know."

"What do you mean?"

"Haven't heard from her." She almost smiled at something on the screen. "Not since she left for Vegas."

"*What?* Mom never goes anywhere."

Terri shrugged, just like I do. Annoying.

At this point, Anne-Marie did turn to look at me with those silver eyes of hers, though she didn't say a thing.

What with the wreck of Dad's life, I wanted to see Mom so bad before leaving for Europe, to see how she's doing, to let her know what I've never let her know, that I love her. "When's she back?" I asked, unable to get all the panic out of my voice.

Anne-Marie bit her chronically chapped lower lip. "Not clear."

This didn't make sense. She sounded so blasé. "Blake?"

"Gone to live with his dad."

I almost said, "Didn't know he was out of prison," but it's really not my business, and is, I'm guessing, a situation that probably has like a hundred threads to tease out that my sarcasm would snip, snip, snip. I could feel myself becoming outright frantic. No one would consider me a family man, but with ours disintegrating so fast I was feeling I just may be, at least a little. That's human nature, I suppose. Further proof that I am possibly a real human being after all. "How's Dad?" I asked in a voice so strained I almost didn't recognize it in my throat or ears. "When can I visit?"

"Good luck with that," Terri said with a snort. "Even after sentencing, he still won't see anyone. Mom included."

"Oh," was all I could say. I had to retreat or else I'd explode. I went down to my lair to collect my thoughts and to see if there was anything I might want. There wasn't much I cared about or needed, just the cassettes of Pete and me rehearsing. I gathered them up in old paper bags from Vinyl Heart that were lying under the bed. There was, I suddenly realized, one other thing I did want. In the pantry under the stairs, among the remaining jars of homemade sauerkraut, rested a few dusty bottles of Dad's nocino. I wanted one to take to the Lacs. I'm not that crazy about the taste, but still, the nocino means a lot to me. One of the best memories I have of Dad is him and me and John driving out to Bethel Grove each June to visit the cemetery at St. Caspar del Bufalo to pay our respects to his family. While there, we'd also collect green walnuts to make the nocino. Every holiday he'd let us kids have a sip of the sweet dark liquor. It was a recipe from his mom's mom—the Italian side. We did this every year until John died. Even though it was a cemetery, still, it was one of my favorite places—the rolling, manicured lawns, the giant walnut trees full of light and shadow, the peace and quiet. We'd bring the wooden extension ladder from home, and John and I would climb up and on into the branches, fast as squirrels. We'd let the walnuts fall onto a canvas tarp spread below. Dad would pick from the top of the ladder, dropping his into a galvanized pail, the first ones making hollow *pings* until the bottom was covered. The liquid from green walnuts is clear, yet weirdly it blackens your hands, which explains the color of nocino. The stain lasts for weeks. I liked that—the stain—because it would remind me of a day I loved so much. Those were among the few times a year we did something with Dad, and it was always sunny and breezy when we went, or at least that's how I remember it. The whole world appeared animated, vivid. Underneath it all, I'm a sentimental bastard. The opposite of a punker, I suppose.

I took a bottle of nocino from the gritty shelf.

Next morning, I caught the crowded visitors' bus to the prison. When we got there, I waited patiently with all the other families in a long line at the iron gate separating the two worlds. When it was finally my turn, I did, as Terri had predicted, get turned away. I didn't understand. After all, he's my father. The flat-topped corrections officer explained, like he was reading from a script, the visitation program is not mandatory, that any prisoner has the right to refuse visitors. I had pictured one of those moments, like on TV, where Dad and I would be seated facing each other, wire grating or safety glass between us, him telling me everything—not about the murder, no, but about himself—and I would come to some understanding, and it would be cathartic the way Pete's Greeks meant it. I definitely hadn't imagined this, the story just ending. Just ending with nothing.

Mrs. Lac treated us like soldiers returning from war. Over the few days we were home she made all our favorite foods, both Japanese and American—sushi, tempura, green tea ice cream, T-bone steak, meatloaf, walnut brownies. And lots more. There was nothing too good for us, even though she wasn't thrilled when Pete announced we were off again, and to Europe at that. But she's not the type to dwell on disappointment. After taking the news in, she told us, "You boys will have experiences you have never dreamed of, and those experiences will make new dreams for you, bigger ones, bolder ones."

Our first morning back I was up before dawn. Couldn't sleep. The meeting with Dad that didn't happen, and would never happen, had overloaded my dreams. The scenes were so intense they scared me awake more than once. In some, Dad remained silent, staring blank as a mugshot at me. In others, this man who I'd never seen lose his temper, went wild with anger, cursing me for never having been there for him. But in one—just one—he was sitting in the shade of the towering walnut trees at Bethel Grove, mild as Jesus, assuring me that everything would be alright. All the versions, even the ones that seemed a little nicer, hammered me with guilt.

I wanted to write down some of the dreams in order to, hopefully, clear my head a little. Pete was still sound asleep, so I grabbed my notebook and headed downstairs. I was going to write outside at the picnic table. As I was heading through the kitchen to the backdoor, out the window I saw Mrs. Lac at the far end of the backyard, on her hands and knees, weeding. Here it was, still practically night, and she was out there creating beauty. I was about to open the door, when it hit me: Why not make Mrs. Lac a cup of coffee? It's something that shouldn't have had to hit me, it's something most decent people would simply do for someone, a common courtesy. But the truth of the matter was, I'd never made a cup of coffee, peanut butter sandwich, or even poured a bowl of cereal for anyone, let alone a full breakfast of bacon and eggs, or a sushi dinner. How many times had Mrs. Lac made me a cup of coffee or tea? I was ashamed to think how many. With that, I filled the percolator with water, scooped ten scoops from the steel canister into the basket, as I'd seen her do so often, and plugged it in. I felt probably a little too satisfied when the coffee began to percolate into the glass bubble and the aroma filled the air. I brought the red lacquer tray down from on top of the refrigerator and set two cups and saucers and the pot on it. Carrying the tray as carefully as possible (because I wasn't used to it), I kneed the door open and managed to step outside without dropping everything. The moon was growing pale and the sun appeared a gilded strip that had barely edged above the horizon. A bird called, long and liquid, and another answered. A pair of chipmunks tumbled out of the small rock garden and darted across the lawn.

As the door clicked shut, Mrs. Lac looked over her shoulder and waved. I set the tray on the picnic table and called to her, "Ready for a coffee break?"

She smiled, stood up, took off her gardening gloves, and walked the short distance across the grass to the table. She nodded. "Why, thank you, Mike."

I motioned for her to take a seat. We sat facing each other. As if I'd done it a million times before, I set a cup and saucer in front of each of us and poured. We both take it black.

She lifted the cup and took a sip. "Delicious." She set the cup down. "You're up early!"

"Couldn't sleep."

"Oh?"

That one syllable from her launched me into talking about my visit to the prison and all the thoughts and feelings I had about it. Only with her would this possibly happen. As I began, she put both hands around her coffee cup and looked at me intently. I told her everything. Especially about guilt. Guilt for not having shown my father the love that might have made him feel better about himself and about the world. The love any son ought to show his father. I even told her about the dreams in as much detail as I could without faking how much I actually recalled. By the time I was finally done, the sun appeared whole, a bronze disk.

We sat in silence for some time before she told me she had read in the paper about the sentencing and had been thinking about me and my family all the time. She reached over, placing her palms on the back of my hands. "Guilt is only natural, Mike, but don't be so hard on yourself." She told me she still felt guilt over having survived the firebombing of her hometown, when her father and brother, in trying to save the house, had not. She took another sip of coffee, and I took another one too. Then, as if the sharing of coffee had sealed an agreement between us, she continued, "But it really isn't so much a matter of guilt or innocence." I looked at her, confused. She met my eyes. "It's about love. Maybe you didn't always express it or express it exactly how you wanted to—nobody does—but you feel it, that much is clear."

"How does that matter? It's too late."

"It's never too late. Maybe he won't see you, but you can send him letters. Even if he never responds, he will know how you feel." She then took hold of both my hands and squeezed them.

I thanked her. I thanked her, but my thanks sounded way too

simple. How do you thank someone for their giant love when yours is so puny? How do you thank someone for caring enough to give you advice when no one else has ever really bothered?

Several times during our time back home Mr. Lac made it known that he still really wanted Pete to go to college and study engineering. Even so, he was glad we're making a name for ourselves. Never mind that he had to take our word for it. The local papers don't review or even mention us, and it's not like any radio station Mr. Lac might tune in to would play us, or that Johnny Carson was lining us up for a slot on *The Tonight Show*.

Our last night home, Mrs. Lac made Pete's and my agreed upon very favorite dinner, tonkatsu, a deep-fried pork cutlet served with this dark sauce that's kind of like Worcestershire, only thicker, tastier. She also broke out special sake, the kind where the rice is polished some crazy amount, which makes the wine silkier. After a lemon bar for dessert, she opened the bottle of nocino that I'd brought. When she put the tiny glass to her lips, she sighed, "So delicious, Mike." And the four of us, we got a little drunk. Mrs. Lac's face flushed a beautiful shade of pink, almost lavender.

After the festivities, we all headed upstairs to get some sleep. I was sitting on the bed playing on my unplugged guitar one of the new dream songs I'd been working on, while Pete was showering, when Mrs. Lac stepped quietly into the room.

"Thank you, Mike," she said, "for being with Peter." She made it sound like I was doing her a favor. Then it was as if a shadow fell over her. Her voice lowered, "You must promise to look after him. He is sometimes too . . . too—what should I say?—too naive." I looked in her eyes. They glittered, even in the dim light of the bedside lamp, they glittered. "Promise?"

"Promise," I answered after hesitating, though I did have to wonder who needed to look after who. I mean, a jerk getting practically mutilated by the crowd and starting fights with strangers likely needs someone to not just look after him but to control him.

The promoters have booked us at the Roxy, maybe the hippest punk place in the world, according to Ryder. Hippest punk? Those two words just don't seem right together. In any case, we're not really even punks here in London. Everyone else at the club is either straight-up skinhead or punked out in all the best regalia. A whole rainbow of mohawks, some over two feet high. Halloweenish makeup, leather duds, choke chains, dog collars—the works. The crowd is punk, for sure, though the place has a swanky Rat Pack feel: low lights, plush booths, Vegas-y stage.

We're just a bunch of Americans in sneaks and jeans, but that's probably part of our charm. To them, I suppose, we're exotic. The audience went nuts all through our show. Two newspapers used *honest* to describe our music. I liked that, though Bobby wasn't so sure it was meant as a compliment. Another said, "The No Names are tough in that very American way, without the requisite nastiness of our native punk artistes."

The four of us are lying on the floor backstage, exhausted after our second night's performance, when the Roxy people show up. They're enthusiastic. They've seen just about everyone coming through, so their words mean a lot. The three of them are going to take us to a pub to get something to eat and discuss maybe doing a couple of shows at the end of our tour. As we're heading out the stage door, a girl approaches, all perky and efficient, like Mary Poppins if Mary Poppins went hippie, wearing braids, peasant blouse, hip-huggers. She asks if she might have a word. The way she looks at the others, then quickly focuses on me, I think means she wants to speak with me alone. She's not my type. Sure, she's gorgeous, but for one thing she's too tall, and for another she's too perky. I look to my pals to rescue me, but she insists it will only take a moment. The house manager suggests I catch up with them, they're just nipping into the pub 'round the corner.

As soon as the group takes off, the hippie chick introduces herself, Miss Gwen Chambers. Miss Gwen Chambers? Can't recall the last time a female around my age introduced herself as *Miss*. She offers a cigarette, lighting it before handing it to me. Way too inti-mate. "What's your name?" she asks, adding, "It's not on the fliers, or for that matter the record jacket!"

"Doesn't matter."

She smiles weakly in British, meaning, *how quaint* or *how trifling,* maybe both.

We walk a little ways down the street. It's called Rathbone Place. The pavement's greasy with mist. The city's alive the way no American city is. People everywhere.

"You are an e-nor-mous talent," she says, making the word sound like a whole sentence. "Upon the recommendation of a friend at *The Village Voice,* I attended one of your shows in New York while there on business. I was very impressed. My friend had to give me her copy of the record because it was—and how grand for you!—sold out at all the record shops. You have the sound, the look, for today."

I don't respond.

"Why don't you pop by the offices tomorrow and have a chat with one of our producers? Say eleven?" She hands me her card.

The card says she's a talent scout. For a major label. With a list of artists that's a who's who of the music business. This is un-be-lieve-a-ble. I stay cool. Suppose there's no harm in talking with them. I mumble, "We'll be there."

She responds with a sinister little snicker, "Oh, I mean you, dar-ling. We're not really looking for another punk band right now, but you, you'll make a terrific solo act."

I don't hesitate for a second. "No deal."

This Miss Gwen Chambers isn't fazed in the least. She stares at me all starry-eyed. "Think about it, darling. I'll pop backstage after tomorrow's show."

I don't meet her eyes. They're way too sexy. Plus, she's *posh,* as they say over here, way too posh for the likes of me.

With that, she turns to go.

The crowd flowing along the sidewalk swallows Miss Gwen Chambers up and I move on past the pub where the others have gone, wanting to clear my head. Miss Gwen Chambers is not interested in punk bands, but she's interested in me? But I *am* a punk band. I'm nothing without the guys. After wandering aimlessly around this neighborhood they call Fitzrovia, I head to the room I'm sharing with Pete in the vacant flat the Roxy people got for the band. I try to write a few lines of a song about wandering the streets but wind up staring at the wallpaper instead. The pattern's hypnotic. Elaborate black vines with deep-purple flowers that seem to pop right out of the surface. Maybe two hours later Pete finally comes in. I say *finally* because I really want to tell him how crazy this business is, and that I'm so glad I have him and Matt and Bobby to anchor me. And I do tell him, but only the second part—about them being my anchor.

He laughs, all beery, "You're nuts!"

I still don't tell him about the offer. I'm afraid he'd wonder how I could possibly think of *not* taking it. I can just hear him—at his most manic—that deep voice jumping a few octaves up at the end of every sentence. I know Pete wants what's best for me, but I also feel like he'd see me going solo as an out for him. If I were to do it, and it worked out—and that's a humongous *if*—the band would disperse, he'd go home, join the Navy, go to college, find love, whatever.

"What happened with the bird?" He gives me a wink.

After our third London show, Gwen Chambers comes backstage, just as she said she would. This time she's a swirl of gauzy material—a Brit Stevie Nicks—and gives me a dramatic hug and kiss right smack on the mouth, declaring, "You were simply in-cred-i-ble!" It's clear that this *you* is once again not plural, as she doesn't so much as glance at Pete, Bobby, or Matt. One arm still resting on my shoulder, she asks, "Have you given some thought about coming 'round our offices?"

This sets off alarms. All three bandmates turn to me, staring. They're obviously wondering what's up. I can't help but act sheepish, like I'm deceiving them, though I'm 100 percent not. I tell her, "I'm tired," nothing more, and walk away.

Gwen Chambers follows me along the corridor and out onto the sidewalk. She skips in front of me then turns to face me. She's walking backwards. She looks hot and giddy, probably because I'm so sullen and surly. A real turn-on. All manic, she's full-on nagging me in front of passersby. "There's no obligation, simply pop by."

Pop by? To put a halt to this little spectacle, I agree to show up the next day at the record company offices. She's ab-so-lut-e-ly thrilled. I go all delusional and start thinking I might be able to turn the tables and convince someone there to sign the band.

I meander my way back to the flat. It's past two in the morning when I slip in. Pete's still up, still dressed. He's sitting on the floor, trying out some new chords. He gives me the evil eye. For the first time ever, I can tell he's truly pissed off at me. Light from the fixture hanging in the middle of the room reflects off the purple wallpaper, making him look like a vampire. Probably does the same to me.

Turns out, he's learned from the club guys who Gwen Chambers is and what she likely wants from me. Instead of being glad at the possibility of me going solo, as I thought he would, he's crazy jealous. He's not only jealous, but he feels betrayed. He goes dramatic on me, full-on Shakespeare, shouting, "Et tu, Brute," from our favorite play. He's obviously forgotten he's the one who wanted out back in Frisco. He reminds me about the promises we've made to each other. It's a *how-could-you?* kind of situation like in Julius Caesar, for sure, but also like when your girlfriend's found out you're cheating on her only you're not.

I tell him what's up, I tell him the truth: "I was scared, man. Scared you'd encourage me to go out on my own. No way I'd do that. We're a team. When I see those record people in the morning, I'm pitching us, the No Names." I go down on my knees in front of him, like a guy proposing to a girl. I reach up, placing my hands on his shoulders, and vow, "Nothing's going to split us up, not ever."

He looks both relieved and sad and like he might start crying. "I know, I know," he stammers. "I'm such a freak. Sorry I got so out of control."

I put my arms around him. I think we're going to get some sleep, but like it's instinct we both go for our guitars. Through the early morning hours, we work on a not-so-mellow song we started a while ago. It's actually totally aggressive, which is good for right now. We wrap each other up in chords and riffs. I slam him with a variation on the melody and he slams me right back. We rip some chords that lift us far out and away from melancholy.

I hardly slept yet still managed the Tube okay and found my way to the record company. It takes up a whole office building. In the lobby, everything's bright marble and glass. Portraits of famous recording artists line the walls. Stars. Legends. For one solitary second, I think, wow, I could be up there with them. But then I wonder who am I fooling? There's a directory of what looks to be dozens of employees. Gwen Chambers is on the seventh floor.

I slink into an elevator. When I get out, there's a receptionist right there, behind a fortress of a desk, a formidable sentry. She's the kind of perfectly dressed lady difficult to imagine outside of this setting, like in bed or grocery shopping, for instance, or even eating. I say who I am, then ask for Miss Gwen Chambers, and she asks me to please take a seat, she will ring her.

When Gwen Chambers comes out, gone is Hippie Poppins, gone Brit Nicks. Her red hair's up in a bun and she's wearing a man's navy pin-striped suit, only made for a lady. Have to admit, she looks sexy. She acts surprised that I've come, though I'm pretty sure she knew I would. She leads me down a corridor. People pass us in their hurries. I've never seen rich people at work before, except on TV.

As we're walking along, she chirps, "Girls will go positively mad over you!" We enter an office that looks like it could be the president of the world's. Windows that are walls overlook the Thames. London Bridge and Big Ben in view. Gold records mounted everywhere, statuettes on a long glass shelf. I know the little gramophones. The man behind the desk appears tiny, gray stubble on his cheeks and chin, hair like Dylan's, wearing a rumpled wine-colored velvet jacket over a T-shirt. His name is William Richards. Not Bill or even the more British Will. I resist the urge to call him Billy or Willy.

He has listened to *Invisible City* and is sure they can use me. He has loads of ideas, loads. "Gwen has reported on the marvelous shows," he tells me, "and Gwen is never wrong. I'd like to sign you."

Just like that.

He gets up, and without him saying anything, Gwen Chambers signals we should follow him into an adjoining room. Don't know why, but I do. It looks like the bridge of the Starship *Enterprise*. A whole recording studio. The engineers are already in place. Musicians, too. How'd this happen? Was she that sure I was coming?

"I hope you don't mind," he says, "but we've taken the liberty of writing arrangements for a few of your songs. Would you care to try them out?"

This is crazy. How did anyone have time to do arrangements? "Got my own band."

He gives a druggy chuckle. "I know, I know, but please, do give these arrangements a go. I think you'll dig them."

"Didn't bring my guitar."

"No, no, no." That chuckle again. "We only need your vocals."

I'm not sure I *can* sing without holding a guitar. He hands me a mic. My fake cough comes right as the studio musicians start to play "My Cross," one of our edgier tunes. I barely recognize it. They're taking it at less than half-speed, volume way down. They've totally de-punked it, smoothing out the chords so they blend into one another, all friendly like. In other words, they've dulled it. Sounds like a lame Eagles tune. He nods for me to begin. I don't know why I feel cowed, but I do. I start to sing:

We all got a cross to bear,
I'm no different from the rest,
we all got a cross to bear
because we're masochists . . .

At this tempo, it resembles a hymn.

We all got a cross to bear
but I want to call it quits . . .

I sound like Jackson-freakin'-Browne. From their faces, I can tell Gwen and Willy think this is a-maz-ing. But before the next verse is through, I drop the mic on an amp, causing wicked static to crackle big-time through the space. I take off, sneaks squeaking across the polished floor. *Not going to be your David Cassidy.*

After a couple of weeks touring—London, Paris, West Berlin, plus a bunch of smaller cities—we've made it here, to Copenhagen. For laughs, we're calling it Visible City. Visible City because it's the total opposite of where we come from. First off, it's super old, with lots of *sights* to *see*. For hours, the four of us wandered through square after square, each of which seems to have either an imposing statue or a big, old fountain. The city is reflected in all the water surrounding it, so if you don't see it one place you see it another. Even what's underground everyplace else in the world is out in the open here. *Aboveground,* I suppose—*visible.* Drug deals on street corners. Porn in store windows. Hookers cruising the sidewalks in broad daylight. At one porn shop, Matt wanted to go inside into a booth and watch a movie advertised on a big poster outside, of cute girls having a lezbo orgy. We pushed him on because we had to get out here, to the abandoned naval base where we're staying, to meet with the guys who've organized the concerts here.

There's a dilapidated grandeur to the base—it's called Christiania—what with these colossal old brick buildings, some with fallen walls. There are makeshift shops selling pottery, candles, bread, and other homemade stuff among the ruins, right beside stands selling hash. The dealers ask us in English if we want to buy. The druggies get mixed right in with the hippies. Matt read somewhere that they've been squatting in the half-wrecked buildings for some years now. Raggedy vegetable patches grow all over the place.

We find the palatial ruin where we'll be crashing with a bunch of punk squatters. Inside, a couple of people are making what looks to be soup or stew over an open fire. A chubby hippie-punk hybrid seems to be in charge. She comes up to us, greets us half-heartedly, like we're the millionth band to have stayed here. She shows us to an arched alcove where we'll be sleeping. Tie-dye hangings decorate the broken brick walls.

The four of us are lounging around in our den when the impresarios show up. They introduce themselves, Jean-Luc and Jean-Marc. They moved here from Paris a few years ago, own a couple of clubs in town. They aren't much older than us. They're cool in that skinny, shaggy kind of way that makes our cool, skinny, shaggy kind of way look square, husky, and clean-cut. They take us to the building where we'll be playing. It's cavernous. Lots of deep, irregular shadows and crumbling arches, like in old prints of ancient ruins in one of Pete's rummage sale books back home. Matt guesses they built ships in here.

This might be the biggest space we've ever played in, and soon it starts to fill. The crowd seems to have more women than most of our shows. "Biker chicks," Bobby decides. There are, in fact, a bunch of bikers. They look like the Hell's Angels back home. When I go out behind the stage for a last smoke, there's a whole lot of what my brother always called piece-of-shit Harleys. Didn't expect Harleys over here. They seem so American. Anyone who knows anything about performance, John taught me, would prefer a Japanese bike to a Hog. Also like the Angels back home, these guys would probably kick your ass just for riding a Japanese.

Three songs in, the show seems to be going okay, not great. The bikers are acting kind of crazy, shouting random stuff. A couple of them are fighting. It pisses me off, them not paying attention. Some bearded maniac is screaming at me something I can't understand and starts pulling himself up onto the stage. I stride forward and give him a good swift kick to the chest, sending him back into the crowd. Pete glares at me.

By the fifth song, with lots of people yelling who knows what, a disturbance of calm appears out of nowhere. If that makes any sense. Amid bikers going berserk, skinheads shaking their fists, and random hippies trying to get a groove on, a solitary figure leans, formal as a statue, against a steel pillar. I can't make out details— not even whether it's a guy or a girl—only this eerie tranquility. From this point on, the show seems to get better, or at least it does for me.

We start winding the last set down. I feel like going out with our only slow number, or at least as slow as we get. I'm not talking "Stairway to Heaven" tempo or anything like that, but not our usual frenetic beat. I signal to the guys. They nod. So, "Guitar Scream" it is. We play deep and strong. The song ends with feedback and the lyrics:

My heart's a guitar,
each chord a scream,
and all you there watching,
wrapped in your own sick dream,
wrapped in your silence so safe,
wrapped in your silence so great,
you want to smash my heart,
you'd love to hear me scream,
because that's your thing, that's your sick dream . . .

I throw my head back, staring up into the rafters, letting the last chords reverberate. And then, amazingly, there's total silence. When the silence has extended about as far as people can stand it, they all start going insane. They're shouting and whistling, which is like booing over here.

Pete leans toward me, shouting over the din, "They want an encore!" I shake my head. He starts "Altared Boy" anyway. I refuse to play or sing. "Come on!" he yells, "You're gonna get us fucking killed!" I shake my head, this time more gently. A few guys, muscular and fat like pro-wrestlers, charge the stage. Security blocks them. Two others right below the stage try grabbing my legs. I kick them both in the face. Another pair of fools leaps onto the stage, fists clenched like comic-book villains. Pete drops his guitar and flies over to grab me. Guards pull the attackers away. Pete looks shaken. He picks up his guitar and gets back into position, expecting that I now understand the consequences and will play. He stares at me, and in that stare there's also a lot of hurt. But I can't help him. I'm certain this is how the concert has got to end.

Bobby speaks directly into my ear, his voice confident, "You're the artist, man." That's my drummer boy.

The crowd starts chanting. They start throwing beer bottles. We dodge them but don't hide. Matt makes a one-handed catch and chucks the bottle back, hard. I look out on the hundreds of people and, despite everything, feel something resembling love for them. Maybe not love. Something else, something I can't name or even know. It's all fuzzy inside my head, yet I'm so filled with it, this feeling, I'm afraid I might explode.

Pete steps in front of me, putting his face right up to mine. "Never again," he hisses. I look at him like I don't know what he's talking about, even though I sort of do. "Never again," he repeats. He's shaking his head. "If you ever get into it with the crowd again, it's over. You're going to wind up in the hospital again. Or dead. I can't deal. Try being a little more of a Stoic: 'Most powerful is he who has himself in his own power.'"

In the midst of this mayhem, he's quoting philosophers. That's why I love him. Truly. But I'm also freaked out because I'm not sure that I *can* control myself in these situations. It's like there are two mes and the one refuses to obey the other.

The techies finally get the idea that there's not going to be any more, and the lights go up. Now I can make out the disturbingly calm figure that's been standing all night by the pillar. It's a guy, and he appears totally oblivious to the chaos around him. He's smiling—no, it's like a smile but also not, more like a trace of knowing something unknown to others drifting over his features—holding a black briefcase—no, a *satchel*. He holds it in front of himself with two hands. It's weird to be holding a satchel here, at a venue like this—or holding a satchel anywhere. And he's wearing a dress shirt, navy cords, and black loafers, pointy, not like loafers back home. No one like him has ever before been at one of our shows. His hair's blond. Not long or short, which, along with everything else, separates him from the long-haired hippies and skinheads that make up the audience. Nothing menacing or intrusive about his presence, yet still, his attention bothers me.

The stage lights shut off all at once, and security (basically a crew of old hippies) starts herding the rowdy crowd out the wide archways. My senses are in overdrive. There's the banging as the stagehands start taking scaffolding and equipment down, and in the distance the dull roar of people heading out. Bobby is here. Matt is here. Pete is here. And then this figure with the satchel comes up, all chummy, and announces, "That was quite a show! You fellows were marvelous!"

Fellows? Marvelous? He's a handsome guy, and I don't mean that as a compliment or in a homo way. I mean handsome as kind of old-fashioned, his look being one my grandparents might appreciate. *Handsome* is the word they'd use. Not the way guys considered attractive look today. They're something besides handsome today. Today they've got this fallen angel look—wide eyes, full lips—like say, Jim Morrison, Peter Frampton or the guy in *Love Story*. This *fellow* doesn't have that. His eyes are deep set, mouth small. He resembles an engraving of a philosopher from one of Pete's old books. He's tall and thin, with the attitude of someone who's never had a worry in their life.

Pete's the one who responds. "Hey man, thanks," and claps him on the back. It's like this guy's serenity comes as a relief to him after all my antics.

He tells us his name, Daniel Beck. He looks from Pete to me and back to Pete, then asks, "Are you two brothers?"

Matt somehow feels the need to be the one who answers: "No, they just act that way."

Everyone laughs, except me. I don't get what's so funny.

We introduce ourselves as Pete, Matt, Bobby, and Mike, but right off the bat he's calling us Peter, Matthew, Robert, and Michael. He tells us this is a country without nicknames, like it doesn't matter what we'd prefer to be called.

Pete has taken to this guy immediately, probably seeing his former preppy self in him. They're best friends in like five seconds. Pete's already telling him the saga of the No Names, like he's giving an interview. All this crazy affability is more than likely antidote to me.

I'm heading out. Bobby and Matt say they're coming with, and hey, let's go for some brews. Pete asks this Daniel if he wants to come along, which annoys me. Hate to admit it, but it does. He thanks Pete very much, but he really must catch the last train home. Then, in his overly correct, softly accented English, he asks, "Would you fellows like to come sailing tomorrow?"

He's got to be kidding. Pete's and my history with yacht clubs isn't the greatest, and besides, who do any of us know that goes sailing, period, let alone inviting strangers to come along? Before I can stop this from happening, Pete, Bobby, and Matt are all on board, so to speak. "Cool, man!" they chime, practically in unison.

Daniel writes down directions to his place on a piece of music composition paper. A musician? Composer? He then disappears into the night that's really night out here on the abandoned base because there are no streetlights. The others don't seem to wonder what this guy might want from us. When I say I'm not sure it's such a good idea, they dismiss me as paranoid.

"He's a fan," Bobby says. "It's way cool having fans."

Jean-Luc and Jean-Marc approach. One of them—I think it's Jean-Luc—says, in his heavy French accent, "That show was intense." They have a case of beer stashed where we're staying, if we'd like to head there.

Back in our alcove, one of the two—Jean-Marc?—passes bottles around. They've also brought their skinny girlfriends with them. The other Jean asks if we want to get high. We all nod, that's cool.

He then whips out a glassine envelope containing white powder. He doesn't mean pot or hash.

"Freaking smack," Matt mumbles.

And I am freaking out. Don't know how or why we haven't run into heroin by now, given the music scene and all.

I kind of stare at Pete, trying to get him to leave with me. When he at last does notice my mute panic, he says, "What?" with a self-conscious laugh. I don't know how or why I'm expecting him to read my mind—we've never talked about the junk—so he'd have no way of knowing how I feel about it. I don't say a word, don't know if I have one to say. I just keep looking at him, but now he won't look back. He's watching Jean-Blank mixing the powder with lemon juice, heating it in a silver spoon, filling the syringe. Matt and Bobby are both grinning like this is the coolest thing ever. When one of the Jeans asks who wants a hit, I say, "I'm good," though I'm not, not at all. Pete nods. At first, I think the nod means he's with me, but no, he's signaling he's in. I intensify my stare. He responds with an expression that's maybe one of defiance. Whatever it is, it does the job of distancing me. Matt and Bobby say, "Yeah, sure." Jean-Luc—yes, definitely Luc—does Pete first, tightening a scrap of lace around his lower bicep. His veins stand out naturally, so the tourniquet makes them look like the Incredible Hulk's. He doesn't even blink when the needle goes in. A red cloud rises in the syringe, like a sudden thunderstorm during a brilliant sunset. The liquid turns pink as it's plunged into his arm. Pete's eyelids flutter, his eyeballs roll back in his head, and he shudders, like when he's totally into some guitar riff or like the time I saw him having an orgasm with Cheryl in the salt cave. He nods kind of slow at Jean-Luc who's steadying the syringe, then at Jean-Marc, then at Bobby and Matt, but not at me. As Jean-Luc withdraws the needle, a ruby forms, glinting on Pete's pearly skin. His eyelids flutter again, right before a slow, lazy smile spreads across his face. Then, all of a sudden, he turns away. One of their chicks has anticipated what's happening. She quickly and calmly hands Pete an empty vase with

Egyptians painted on the outside, into which he throws up. He wipes his mouth and shakes his head, like he's apologizing. Jean-Luc then shoots Bobby up. His vein is hard to find. It takes a few pokes. Once the drug's in, he too vomits. When it's Matt's turn, he's calm as calm can be. No vomit. Finally, the French guys shoot themselves up. Their girls don't. The five get mellower than dream, and I'm wide awake. Pete murmurs how, inside of him, it feels like the ocean hissing on a stony beach. His head nods, like a baby drunk on mother's milk.

I pretend I'm just hanging out drinking beer and not sticking around to keep my friends safe. An unasked-for guardian, to be sure. There's something that resembles conversation going on around me, but I'm only hearing warnings from faraway.

Pete, Matt, and Bobby are still sobering up on the early morning train Daniel Beck instructed us to take. Except for hopping freight cars up to the salt mines back home, and the London Tube, I've never been on a train before. This one seems fancy. The compartments for six have red-leather seats and lace-covered headrests. We're heading up the coast. It looks abstract, like a modern painting. Turquoise water bordered by a gold band of sand and a thicker band of bright-green trees. The houses we pass resemble small palaces—white, yellow, and pink stucco—perched above the water with a view to Sweden. Daniel Beck calls it a sound, the Øresund, in his note. The area looks way richer than the Heights or any place I've ever seen.

This fantasy view helps take my mind off the guys shooting up last night and my fear that we'd crossed some border we shouldn't have. It's got to be a one-time thing.

We get off at the stop Daniel wrote down and walk through a village of half-timber houses with thatched roofs. A fairy tale, except the people look yacht club. They all seem to be tall and tanned—Bermuda shorts, sailor stripes, boat shoes. The four of us, ragged and hungover, definitely look out of place, though the nobility's too discreet to so much as glance our way.

Past the village, we go on to what in his note Daniel calls a *lane,* an unpaved road, narrow as an alley, brick walls on either side. Never been in a lane before, except in nursery rhymes. The lane runs behind the pastel mansions, inland a hundred yards or so. We find the address—the brass numbers arranged vertically on a post—but there's no house in sight. From the lane a narrow trail winds down through woods. We melt into white-green shade cast by incredibly tall trees with great spreading branches and thick, smooth, silver trunks. A half-sweet scent comes up from the floor of dead leaves. A building gradually begins to appear. Not stucco, but glass. Not a palace at all, more like a suburban bank branch, except no suburb. It's as if the windows are walls and doors or vice versa. Not the kind of place it seems anyone would actually live. A house that's not a house. An invisible house that makes every-thing inside of it visible from the outside. The glittering waves of the sound can be seen right through the structure. In the center of the space a shiny grand piano appears to float. Daniel Beck is seated there, hands running up and down the keyboard. But it's silent, the music sealed in behind the glass.

This place is everything I am not.

Bobby, all eager, knocks on the expanse of glass that looks most like a door. When it opens, classical music comes pouring out. The music distracts me so much that, for a few moments, I barely notice the woman standing there, saying hello, shaking our hands. She's the first person I've ever actually met that I would call *aristocratic.* Daniel's mother, obviously. Like him, tall, thin. Her graying blonde hair is coiled like a snake on top of her head. She's wearing what my mom would call a mod dress, like a tent, with a huge abstract pat-tern of vines and flowers in bright colors—magenta, orange, lime green—on a white background. On her wrists clang lots of bangles, some silver, some made of glass or maybe stone. A chunk of amber set in silver dangles on a chain around her neck. Her tan face makes her light eyes all the more startling. They're the color of liquid mer-cury. Her lipstick and eyeshadow look like frost. She's how a queen of another planet might look.

She says in English only slightly stiffer than her son's, "I am Daniel's mother." Graceful as a ballerina, she motions us in. "Please, wait here in the kitchen. Daniel will be finished with practice shortly." Her greeting's not warm, not cold, just perfectly polite. The house smells exactly like nothing.

Pete's the only one who responds, "Pleased to meet you, Mrs. Beck." He sounds like a real gentleman.

I'm still too bothered by the music to say anything at all. Something about it that I can't explain is getting to me. Daniel's most definitely not just some kid practicing piano. As he plays, he looks serene and intense at the same time. Maybe that's what's agitating me, his—what is it, confidence? Poise? No, those aren't right. Something more. *Transcendence*? I've never seen anyone playing classical music before, except on cartoons, or when changing channels and there's some guy at a keyboard in tails pounding *like* a cartoon character. Daniel's different, though. He's steady, with precise movements, and yet, I hate to admit it, he plays with obvious passion. Maybe that annoys me too. His playing starts playing tricks on me. The notes swirling around the glass box create an intricate pattern that feels like it's about to pull me into a killer vortex. I shake my head hard so as not to fall in.

It's a blessing when Daniel's mother starts serving tea. The tea distracts me enough. Did he ask her to do this or does this kind of thing come naturally to people like them? She pours from a sleek silver pot into sleek white china cups. The guys are acting abnormally polite, saying *please* and *thank you* like the Royal Family. It would be kind of hilarious if I wasn't so suspicious.

When the music finally stops, I can't believe how relieved I feel. It's like I've avoided some great crisis that never fully revealed itself. Daniel comes bounding over to us, his small, white teeth glinting. He's wearing pastel-blue Bermuda shorts with a light-yellow Lacoste shirt and on his feet are what I think are called espadrilles. Maybe he's spiritually related to Pete after all, and the alligator is their shared totem? We're our usual black-and-blue denim selves, unshaven mugs, uncombed hair, and, at least me, sullen.

"Good morning, fellows. Ready to set sail?" Daniel's all alacrity, unselfconscious of the fact that, even dress-wise, he's the odd man out.

"Dig your Chopin," Bobby says. He really does know music. Impressive.

Matt adds, "It was smokin'."

Something about *dig* and *smokin'* sound so not right about classical music that they're exactly right.

"Thank you," Daniel nods, "I appreciate that."

Pete has slipped out of happy puppy mode and grown quiet. I can't tell if he's intimidated, awestruck, or what. My silence is a different matter.

"You preparing for a recital or something?" Bobby asks.

"Yes," Daniel answers, pouring himself tea, "a tour, in fact. Berlin and Vienna in September are the big ones." He takes a careful sip, adding with sickening cheer, "I have a lot to work on before then!"

I blow into my tea, wary as to why this apparently big deal classical guy would be hanging out with lowlife punkers such as ourselves.

When Daniel stands up, it's apparently time for us to set off on our adventure. His mother has prepared an old-fashioned picnic basket that he calls a *hamper*. It's full of wax paper packets and bottles of colorful soft drinks with unfamiliar labels. Unfortunately, no beer. Without being asked, Pete and Matt each take a handle of the basket, and the five of us walk out onto a lawn mown short as a putting green. Several huge abstract sculptures in bronze and marble dominate the yard. Like a museum. One of the bronzes looks like a female giant lying on her side. We go down a long flight of stairs made of white stone that leads to a dock where a sailboat of thirty or forty feet is tied up. It has two masts. *First Movement* is the name of the boat, written in gold script along its bow. All across the Øresund dozens of white sails move among the whitecaps.

"Probably none of us has ever sailed before," Matt offers, "so just tell us what to do."

"Thanks," Daniel says, raising the sails, "I can manage. You fellows please just enjoy yourselves."

We climb aboard. As a kind of joke, Matt pulls Bobby from the dock, catching him right before he tumbles into the water.

"Dick!"

Daniel has us sit two to a side for balance. He undoes the lines, trims the sails. We take off with more of a start than you'd think a sailboat would have. Pete murmurs, "This is the life." Daniel, apparently hearing him, nods.

I'm thinking exactly the opposite. I'm thinking how much this is not the life, that this is someone else's life, or at least it doesn't resemble any life I've ever known or ever really wanted. I'm not really disappointed in Pete, more surprised. This is, after all, the guy who burned down rich people's condos. Would he want to live in a museum made of glass above the sea? It is, I have to admit, nice zipping along with salt spray on my face, but I don't know. Maybe I'm envious that Pete finds it so easy to enter this world. It must look hilarious from the outside, though, a prepped-out guy sailing over the waves with us punks. Like we've crashed his Ralph Lauren ad.

"Wow!" Matt calls out, "Never seen so many sailboats!"

Pete murmurs again, all sappy, like he's lovestruck, "I could sail on like this forever."

Daniel laughs, at which point Pete becomes more his usual self again. "I bet I could swim the sound!" Usual and predictable.

"A lot of people do," Daniel tells him. "It's not terribly difficult. The narrowest swim is about twenty kilometers north of here, right at the opening of the sound. It's about eight kilometers across there." He asks Pete, "Are you interested?"

"Hell, yeah!"

"The crossing point can be reached," Daniel explains, "by going farther along on the same train line you took this morning, to the final stop, Helsingør. You can rent a rowboat there, so someone can follow."

"Oh, I don't need anyone following."

"You really should. There is a lot of ship traffic, and the current can sometimes be tricky."

"I'll follow," I volunteer, recalling all too clearly the San Francisco Bay fiasco.

"All right, then!" That's Pete's first real acknowledgment of me since last night's show. We decide we'll do it the day after tomorrow, early in the morning following our third and final concert here.

All of us take our shirts off. The sunshine lights up our various shades of milk. I mean the four of us, not Daniel. He's got a country club tan. Have to admit, the sun does feel great.

Now that he's taken his shirt off, one thing doesn't fit the picture of Daniel I have. It's this electric-blue dragonfly hanging from a thin leather cord around his neck. It rests on his clavicle, like a pagan cross. If nothing else, it's hippie-ish.

"This is the life." This time, Matt's the one who says it.

Daniel continues tacking our way across the Øresund. Bobby pumps him for information. I'm surprised to hear he's Pete's and my age. He seems older, or at least he acts that way. He finished conservatory two years ago. Conservatory? Now that's one more thing way outside my world. Maybe I'm jealous? Or is it envious? Like us, his first record came out recently, though on a famous label. A Schumann piano concerto, he tells us. I'm not even sure what a concerto is.

"Had circumstances been different, I'm sure I would have been in a band," Daniel says.

I'll bet. If that's not condescending, I don't know what is. With his sky-blue eyes he keeps looking at Pete. I bet he's a queer.

Bobby suggests, "Maybe sometime we can all jam together?" That's just plain embarrassing. Too naïve to be for real.

Daniel smiles—again, a little patronizing—making me wish I'd had the sense to not board this ship of fools. He maneuvers the *First Movement* toward what appears to be the only island in the sound. It's small and low, with dunes of yellow sand. He steers us into a secluded dock. Not a house in sight.

We tumble out of the boat. As Daniel's securing what he calls the starboard side to the dock, he points up a low hill, announcing, "We'll luncheon up there." Didn't know *luncheon* was a verb. This time Matt and I lift the picnic basket—I mean *hamper*—following Daniel and Pete up the slope and across a field. Bobby takes up the rear, whistling the Chopin. A herd of cows like I've never seen grazes at the far end. They're golden. Golden cows. It's not hot out—not like it gets back home—but I feel hot, almost like a fever. Too much sun or the rocking boat, I suppose. We come to a group of scattered boulders. A few trees have grown up among them. Daniel stops. "Here," he says. We set the basket down. Daniel opens the lid and lifts out a blue-and-white-checked cloth, the kind nice people have, and spreads it on the grass, the way nice people do, like we're nice people.

Pete runs his hands over the stones. He leans in, as if smelling them. He turns to Daniel and asks in a weird, distant voice, "What was this place?"

I have no idea what he means.

"The center of the universe," comes the answer wrapped in that polite laughter rich people have.

I have no idea what he means, either, but I'm tired, not tracking. Bobby and I sit down on opposite edges of the cloth. Daniel hands Matt a bottle opener.

"They're ruins, right?" Pete asks.

To me, it looks like a jumble of rocks in a cow field.

"Exactly!" Daniel answers, like a teacher pleased with his student. "Believe it or not, on this spot was the most advanced observatory in the world back in the Renaissance. But for me, it's simply the place I used to come with my girlfriend."

"For sure," Bobby adds, all goofy enthusiasm, "great place to bring chicks!"

Matt deadpans, "Ain't that the truth."

Pete's crazy eyed as a martyr saint. He looks toward Daniel and utters this gem: "'As far as death is concerned, we men live in a city without walls.'"

"Where does he come up with shit like that?" Matt wonders aloud, popping a cap off a bottle of purple soda and handing it to Daniel. Matt and Bobby aren't usually subjected to Pete's philosophizing the way I am.

"Epicurus," Pete manages to answer out of what's fast becoming one of his full-blown reveries.

Waves hitting the shore aren't quite loud enough to block their voices out entirely, like I wish they would.

Daniel adds fuel to the philosophizing fire, "And don't we spend much of our lives trying to deny that fact by building those walls anyway?"

Pete's brow furrows.

Bobby starts up with the Chopin again, this time blowing the tune on a long, thick blade of grass he's pulled out from between the rocks. The rest of us go silent. Matt opens more bottles and passes them around.

A city without walls. I turn that phrase around and around in my head, probably either not getting the original meaning or distorting it. Despite my cynicism, I find myself falling into thoughts that are probably bogus, but at least they're bringing some other self out of my petty, jealous one. I can now see that these seemingly random rocks were in fact once walls. A place to study the sky. Nice. The sky has no walls. The sky is, I suppose, a city beyond all of us. The stars are pretty much the same now as they were back in the Renaissance, and though it's daylight, I imagine I can almost see them, can almost make out the endlessly complex architecture they create. Out among that invisible castle of stars, the five of us are all visible, and we are repeating our every breath, our every word, our every gesture, thought, and emotion, in every light-year for light-years and light-years to come, out toward wherever infinity is. And right here I can, in this very moment, almost delude myself into thinking that, at least here among these ruins, I'm seeing the truth of everything. In the leaves flickering in sunlight, in the flock of birds, wings iridescent as they fly across the sun. It's one of those moments where you want to see or notice everything at once in order to get at the truth. And you maybe do get at it—the truth, or at least *a* truth—for a millisecond, if you're lucky, but in your desperation to sustain it you wind up with only a few pitiful impressions, nothing but rubble. Then again, maybe this is true of every single moment of our lives, but we just don't register truth or the loss of truth all the time. We can't, or else we'd go insane.

"Could eat a horse," Matt announces. His totally normal voice derails my inward spiral, for which I'm grateful.

The guys all lean in toward the hamper as Daniel hands out wax paper oblongs. Inside these packets are all kinds of cheese and sausage and fish, on different types of bread, all open-faced, with different toppings, such as beets and pickles, as well as a creamy spread with peas and carrots. Some of the bread looks dense as meat and nearly black, some white and airy. I nibble at a slice of smelly cheese on white bread but am feeling more tired than hungry. The air's so clear that I'm seeing too much. I suppose that's what's drained me. I take a swig of orange soda, lean against a fragment of the observatory, and close my eyes.

When I wake up, the sun has shifted noticeably. Matt and Bobby aren't too far away. They're lying curled in the blue shade of one of the larger rocks, sound asleep. Bumblebees bob and hum above the abandoned picnic. Cicadas have begun their unnerving rattle. No sign of Pete or Daniel. I get up, scan the field, but still can't find them. I light a cigarette and walk back from where we came. They're not at the boat, either. A kamikaze horsefly divebombs me over and over again. I sit on the dock trying to finish my smoke in peace, but my antagonist wins, and I toss the cigarette, half-finished, into the surf and head back to the ruins.

I'm kind of out of it and kind of irritated. After what must be an hour, Pete and Daniel eventually reappear at the far end of the field, walking side by side toward us, faces turned toward each other. Their hair's wet. They look like they're deep in conversation. I can't help thinking they look like a couple, a romantic couple. Just an observation. Matt and Bobby stir awake when Pete and Daniel greet me.

"Would you care to go over to the beach for a swim?" Daniel asks. He gestures in the direction they came from.

"Water's great!" Pete chimes in a little too enthusiastically.

I shake my head, annoyed and ashamed by my annoyance.

"No thanks," Matt answers.

Bobby says the same.

Pete gives it another go, "You guys should! Seriously!"

"Let's head back," I say, my voice monotone.

After docking back at the glass palace, Daniel asks, "So, would you fellows like to go to the studio in the city and have a session?" He's finally responding to Bobby from before we got to the island. I seriously don't get what's in it for him, except for maybe hanging out with Pete. He holds the boat for us to climb out.

Bobby's eyes bulge. "Boy, would we! That'd be a blast!" He thinks he's answering for all of us.

Matt, understated as ever, adds, "Cool."

Pete looks at Daniel, like a servant grateful for some scraps off his master's plate. "Are you sure, man?"

I don't say a thing.

Daniel secures the boat. He's practically staring at me as he coils rope, like he's expecting an answer, or maybe he's trying to hypnotize me.

Not wanting to be a total prick (as Pete would likely say), I grumble, "Sure."

"Great," says Daniel, "then I'll ring up the studio."

The studio's located on one of those narrow, cobblestone streets they have here, in one of those old houses with crooked window frames and doorframes. Inside, though, the place is all modern.

"State of the art," Bobby declares, looking around at all the equipment, wide-eyed.

I suppose it's because Pete has told him I write most of the songs, or else because he's trying to butter the sullen one up, that

Daniel turns to me as soon as we're in the door, and asks, "Do you have any new material?"

I bristle. All eyes are on me. I cough into my fist. "There is some new stuff."

"Yes?"

"About ten songs, mostly not done. Works in progress."

"Sounds perfect."

I was trying to communicate the opposite. "We've gone through them only maybe twice." I'm hoping this puts the kibosh on the whole thing.

Instead, Daniel responds with nauseating alacrity. "That's fantastic! This way, there will be fewer preconceptions about what the music should sound like. Let's go with them."

Again, all eyes on me. I would put the brakes on the whole thing but don't want to be the prima donna (the worst thing in the world, according to my mother).

We set up. Daniel listens to us go through the first song, "Star Boy," and when we start a second go through he joins in on the piano. I sing, "Star Boy, far boy, come close and be our sun, Star Boy, bar boy, come out and have some fun . . ." Of course, he picks up the music instantly. Not like it's Chopin or anything. We're talking three chords, fast and loud. I hate to admit it, but right off the bat he gets the ratio of ugly to beautiful we strive for. And the piano somehow works. Daniel makes it work, keeps it punk. I was sure the piano would make the music too smooth or else sound like jazz or, worse, honky-tonk. His playing joins the parts without making them too unified. This classical guy keeps the anarchy. And he doesn't go solo on us, which is, Bobby's always said, antipunk. I look over at Daniel, he looks back. I nod.

We're in this perfect chamber for hours. We go through all the songs a couple of times. The piano—I mean, his piano playing—does stay punk but also seems to be making it a new genre. I'm liking this and start thinking maybe Daniel's a decent guy after all.

When we've been rehearsing for what seems a light-year, Daniel asks, "Ready to record?"

I blink hard a few times. "Hold on a minute. Record? I thought we're just jamming."

"Who's got the rights?" Bobby wonders. I'm glad it's him asking and not me. He's bordering on aggressive. I like that.

Daniel laughs it off. Dismissive yet polite, polite yet dismissive. Either way, I'm not impressed. He clarifies, "I was only thinking as a memento of our time together. I was going to have the studio press copies so we each could have a few."

Bobby looks to me, then Pete, then Matt. We each nod. He last turns to Daniel and tells him, "That'd be cool."

Daniel readies the equipment to record. He suggests we run straight through, not stopping between songs, like a symphony. Crazy as this sounds, that's what we do. It's the opposite of how punk's supposed to be, what with short songs and all. But at some point, I find I'm going with it completely, and the others seem to be going with it too. At least for a while I feel like I've gotten past all the crap that is me. I want music now more than I've ever wanted it. I guess this is how art's supposed to be. Unexpected. Possibly, or hopefully, transcendent. All thoughts of us as part of society evaporate. It's ecstasy, what's happening here, and I swear it's important.

When we're finally done—when the last notes have completely faded away—we stand there drooped, like a platoon after a fierce battle won. Daniel walks up to each of us and shakes hands, like a commander or something. That's probably what he does when he plays with an orchestra. We unplug and flop down on a couple sofas to listen to the reel-to-reel. Bobby, all jittery, keeps saying, "Wow!" and when it's over, Pete shouts, "A new manifesto!"

Daniel laughs his well-patrolled laugh and thanks us all. "Let's call it *Undersong*?" he suggests. The guys—especially Bobby, who has to explain to us what that means—dig this. Then, once again, like a good boy or a businessman on a tight schedule, Daniel has to leave to catch the last train home. On our way out, I grab some stationery and envelopes lying on a desk. The gray paper feels expensive. I don't know why I do it. A souvenir? A way of making the place and what happened in it more real? A bout of kleptomania?

Bobby and Matt go off to see some girls they've met. Pete and I do shots at the first bar we see, before heading back to the squat to get some sleep.

When we hit the beat-up mattresses on the floor, he turns toward me and says, "This is totally dreamatory, my Mike, not to mention scary as shit."

"Good scary?"

He reaches over and gives my cheek a sarcastic pinch. "Good scary."

AUGUST 1978, DANIEL

I once again manage to slip into the last car of the last train right as the doors are closing. I've got luck down to an art! On the outskirts of morning the city becomes a passing thought, buildings and streets splinter as we gain speed. Faces in the windows of the train moving on the next track become clear and almost familiar for the moment or two our velocities synchronize, then, in the next moment, blur.

It has been one of the best days of my life. The American fellows are wonderful. It would be so great to jam with them again. I don't consider myself a sentimental person, and yet already I am missing them. I have never considered myself a lonely person either, but now I begin to wonder.

It's a foreign feeling for me to want camaraderie in anything more than small doses, but confronted with the four of them leaving I find myself wanting more. My impossible dream would be to sail the five of us all the way to the Færoes when their tour is done, stay a few weeks, play music and hike the mountains, then continue the voyage on to America. I have to remind myself that my chosen profession has made me so solitary a soul. Practicing long hours, studying scores, taking private lessons instead of subjects with classmates, and so forth, have all of course been necessary for success. As the maestro reminds me every now and again, music demands complete devotion. It is also, I must admit, in my nature to want to be alone, and that could be, at least in part, why I chose to become not simply a musician but a soloist.

It is strange, because at conservatory anyone would have said that I had friends—they might have even gone so far as to say I was popular. Of course I did refer to certain people as friends, and they considered me theirs, but, antisocial as it sounds (and as difficult as it is to admit), I would never have called anyone *friend* to my inner-most self, not really. The exception was the mason's apprentice, and he, like these four Americans, had nothing to do with my world. I never even learned his name! How preposterous is that? To call a nameless near-stranger *friend*? Maybe the absurdity of the situation had to do with us having been seventeen? Or is the absurdity what made the friendship work for a loner like me? Hard to believe we met nearly every weekend night for a year on this very train, in this very car, and yet it was more than a month into our friendship before we realized we hadn't exchanged names. Somehow, he convinced me it was meant to be, declaring that not calling each other by name made our friendship more profound. It hurts to recall that he used that word, *profound.*

If it hadn't been for the mason's apprentice, I would certainly never have met the No Names. If nothing else, I owe him that. He introduced me to punk. Before meeting him, I hadn't even heard of punk. Inexplicably, I took to the sound immediately. Was it as simple as punk serving as a counterbalance to classical? Or was it the connection with my stranger-friend? He and his music most definitely brought me out of myself, my routines, and for that I am grateful. The couple of times I got off with him at his stop, and we listened to his records all night long, definitely took some of the good-boy veneer off of me as far as my parents were concerned.

Only once did I have him over to listen to classical. I usually try to avoid thinking about him but tonight I cannot. I chose popular selections—a Brandenburg concerto, "Eine kleine Nachtmusik," the opening movement of Beethoven's Fifth—but the piece that moved him the most was the overture to *Tristan und Isolde*. The impossibly deep, sustained tones of those sublime chords seemed to paralyze him. It was as if I could see his innermost self float out of his body. When the music stopped, he shuddered and looked at me with damp eyes, embarrassed, as though he had forgotten I was there witnessing such an intensely private moment.

I still don't understand what happened. After that day, my nameless friend simply disappeared. It's hard to believe I have not seen him, even by chance, or heard from him since then. His unexplained absence continues to hurt deeply. I can't help thinking of him now and even found myself scanning the crowd at the No Names show for him. It's ridiculous, but I still wear the dragonfly amulet he made for me. I shouldn't, as it is a sad reminder of him, but it is quite possibly the most beautiful thing anyone has ever done for me. It still seems unreal, and yet no matter how hard I try to stop it, the night of the dragonfly plays over in my head every time I step into this last car on this the last train of the night. It is still so vivid, that sapphire-blue dragonfly following us into the train and staying, hovering above our heads, even after we were seated and the train started moving. Then, suddenly, the mason's apprentice leapt up and, lizard-like, caught the insect in his mouth! It was unbelievable. I don't know what I thought when, after a few moments, he pulled the stunned creature out and, without a word of explanation, slipped it into the pocket of his jacket. He simply continued our conversation as though nothing had happened. Sometimes I think I imagined the whole thing. The next weekend when we met on the train, he presented the dragonfly to me. He had embalmed it by dipping it in polyurethane, after which he affixed it with a metal clasp to a leather cord. He fastened the amulet around my neck, telling me it was a symbol of change.

Only lately do I understand why, after the mason's apprentice abandoned me, I avoided friendly overtures from most anyone. I had grown cynical. This only intensified when, after winning two international piano competitions and releasing a recording that has received strong critical praise, I suddenly discovered I had many new "friends." With fame, friends began to multiply like loaves and fish. Due to this miracle, I became even more of a loner. This is, I think, why it has come as quite a shock that the No Names have brought about a sense of change in me, a flowering of fellow feeling. Especially after so short a time. They have changed my sense of self in ways I cannot yet account for. They have brought me out of myself—my orderly, rational, solitary self. When we played music together, I was brought to a state where, at least momentarily, I apprehended new, as yet unnamed, truths about myself. These fellows have made me happy, which may well be the dangerous part, as very soon they will, like the mason's apprentice, disappear from my life.

AUGUST 1978, MIKE

The old naval building is even more packed tonight than it was for the first concert. There's a restlessness, like it's the same crowd come back for the big-bang finale they never got.

Daniel's in the audience again, which surprises me a little. Seeing him gets me to give my all. It seems like the guys are following suit. Playing with him yesterday has changed me—changed us, I think. At least it's helped me think beyond what we've been doing. The show moves like a dream. My whole body goes perfectly still, except for my hands flashing over the guitar. Then I sense myself starting to vibrate. Always a good sign. We play to the limit. We do three encores. The audience wants a fourth. Three measures into "Pissed Off!" I step off into the crowd. This time no one hits me, no one mauls me. I catch Daniel's eye through the wall of frenzied bodies. He's leaning against the same pillar again tonight. He nods and smiles, like he approves. Given how much respect I have for him musically, that means a lot. I still don't get him but have grown to want to connect with him.

As we're leaving the stage, Daniel comes over. He congratulates us and asks if we'd like to go to a bar to celebrate. Bobby and Matt have other plans. They're going to meet their girls. I'm pretty sure they've been shooting up with them. I tell them to take it easy. I wish I could make that phrase mean more, a lot more.

My body feels like it's collapsing after the show, but I tell Daniel, "Sure."

Pete says, "Maybe we can check out Jean-Luc and Jean-Marc's place."

That makes me nervous, though there's definitely something about Daniel that makes the idea of shooting up in front of him not even an option.

The three of us head out to the old harbor, which for some reason is called Nyhavn, or New Harbor. There are lots of bars along the water, mostly sailors' dives. As it turns out, Jean-Luc and Jean-Marc's place isn't a sailors' dive or any kind of dive at all. It's not even punk. It's the kind of club where Pete and I don't belong, and Daniel does. *Sophisticated*, I guess you'd say. Its name is a reference, Daniel explains, to a poet who was a revolutionary or a revolutionary who was a poet, more than a century ago. A historical reference, yet it's got big abstract paintings on the walls and modern chairs and sofas made of hard plastic.

Pete's impressed with all the lovely women. I think they look bored and say so. With a sly grin, Daniel remarks, "That's the way girls here show their interest." He insists they are definitely attracted to me and Pete. We sit around one of the low tables. The hard egg-chairs force us to slouch.

The beer in this country is incredible, so that's what Pete and I order. Strong and full of flavor, like nothing back home. Daniel orders some other drink. We don't understand what he says to the waitress. The clear liquid that arrives could be water, vodka, or anything really.

"You fellows were especially on tonight," he says in his oddly formal way. Odd, though not awkward. "Your guitars interlocked perfectly." I like that, when he gets specific.

"Thanks," Pete says, "we dig playing together."

I go one further and tell him I couldn't play without Pete.

At Pete's request, Daniel analyzes more of our playing and music. I'm interested but have to force myself not to listen to the background music—an uninterrupted flow of pop. That's the trouble with me and bars—or me and anyplace—I get distracted by the music, whether it's great stuff or crap. Daniel's got something of the teacher in him, always asking questions and then giving the answers, usually long ones. That could, I suppose, come off as condescending, but with him it doesn't. He's just inquisitive and likes to bring that out in other people. I'm glad for whatever knowledge I pick up from him. What makes Baroque Baroque? What makes jazz jazz? What makes punk punk? I know genres when I hear them but not what in a technical sense makes them what they are, so this is useful.

After a second round, someone sends over a third. Like an idiot, Pete thinks it's one of the fine ladies, but of course it turns out to be Jean-Luc. He follows the waitress to our table.

In English he welcomes us, then takes a seat. Before we finish our beers, he signals to the waitress, and she brings a bottle of clear liquid and four shot glasses. "His national drink," Jean-Luc says, nodding at Daniel, "akvavit." It's unclear whether they know each other or not.

We start doing shots. There's one of those lulls in our conversation, as well as in all the conversations around us, that sometimes happens in noisy places, which makes it even easier to get lost in the music. After two shots on top of the beers, I'm feeling a little blitzed. The alcohol has also taken its toll on Pete (always a lightweight). Daniel and Jean-Luc still seem to be sober, though. By now it's almost one in the morning and the place is packed with beautiful people. Pete's zoning out. I'm zoning out. Like the times before, Daniel announces he's leaving to catch the last train. I find myself trying to reach for his arm, to ask him to wait, to stay, but my limbs don't move, my voice doesn't work. I feel like I'm falling away from him faster than he's leaving, and that soon, for some reason I can't explain, Pete and I will be lost.

At this point, Jean-Marc shows up with their two girlfriends. After greeting Jean-Luc and Daniel with cheek kisses, the girlfriends leave to talk with some other girls at the bar. The French guys are talking to us, but in the state I'm in it sounds mostly like a lot of heavy accent and laughing. As far as I can tell, Pete's not even registering that much. Then, all of a sudden, I'm wide-awake when Jean-Luc asks, "How would you like to make a film?"

"A movie?"

"Yes," he grins.

Jean-Marc, nodding with too much energy, adds, "An adult film."

Takes me a second to register this. "You mean a porno?" The two nod. I actually laugh. For a second I'd thought he meant a concert movie of the band. The music playing beneath the buzz of the crowd presses through to my brain, and suddenly it seems vital that I recognize the song or, really, recognize anything outside of what's going down. It's in English—"Livin' Thing" by ELO. I nudge Pete: "We've got to go, man." I've never even watched a porno. *Deep Throat,* which the whole world seems to have seen, never made it to Hallein because of protests by the born-agains. I'm also laughing because these guys have no idea that I'm the last guy virgin in the world.

Suddenly Pete appears alert. To my amazement, it becomes apparent he's been following what's been going on. I thought he was blotto. He says, "Sure," as if they're merely asking if we want another round. He then asks, "But how much are we talking?" followed by, "Do we get to pick the girls?" He gestures at the crowd.

I'm not sure why but the absolute insanity of the idea starts evaporating as Pete blathers on, pretending he knows the business.

Jean-Marc suggests, "Let's go upstairs to discuss details."

"Someone left the cake out in the rain . . ." Donna Summer sings beneath the buzz and hum of the crowd. I could never figure out whether the song is a parody or not. If not, it should be. ". . . and I'll never have that recipe again . . ." I murmur to Pete, "Let's get out of here, now," but either he doesn't hear me or is ignoring me because he keeps nodding to the French guys.

Jean-Marc and Jean-Luc stand. Then Pete stands with less difficulty than I might have expected. I'm the last. I whisper in Pete's ear, "Come on, this is crazy, we need to go." He responds right out loud, "Yeah, crazy fun!" I plead with him some more, quietly. It's no use. He's not leaving, and I can't leave him here. I attempt to brainwash myself into thinking this counts as an adventure and sure beats wasting life away in the Flats, but sophistry's not really working right now.

Upstairs, there's a bed in the middle of a roomless space. Lights and cameras are set up around the periphery, waiting for action. The wooden floor's dusty, badly scratched.

There's talk of money. I'm in fight or flight mode; Pete's all about negotiation. He takes control: "What you're offering's not enough, not by a long shot." It translates to about five hundred dollars each, which doesn't sound bad at all if one were actually going to do something as stupid as this. Five hundred amounts to more than the whole band has made at any one gig.

I'm staring at the stained bedsheets when I hear Pete asking, "Like what you see?" I turn around to find he's whipped his dick out. Unreal. His attempt at sounding like a pro? The French guys nod approvingly. Next thing I know, he's got them up to what's a thousand dollars apiece.

"Where are the girls?" Pete wonders, tucking his junk back in. "We want to make sure they're hot." That sounds less like an old pro and more like a kid in a candy shop.

Jean-Marc answers with a wicked smirk, "There won't be any." Pete wrinkles his brow.

"It's a gay shoot." Jean-Luc says this like "We don't serve Coke, only Pepsi."

"Pete," I say right out loud, "let's get out of here."

Without missing a beat, and either not hearing me or else ignoring me, he tells them, "Then we want double," as if that's also a regular thing. "And, I'll only do it with him." He points at me, giving the very same grin he first flashed at the totally unreal slave auction where we first met way back when.

No one bothers asking me what I think. Any other guy would be out of here. But once I stop thinking about the mechanics of it and start thinking about two thousand apiece, I'm thinking I could do it, I'm thinking I could be bought.

Pete leans toward me, speaking low, "Me and you could live off that for an entire year over here! Get one of those boats and live on a canal." The old, chummy Pete is back in full force. Bizarre as it seems, this turn of events is also serving as our reconciliation. He then asks the French guys, "What about the script? We need to approve the script."

Once again, Jean-Luc's smirking. "No script. Only a—how shall we say?—a situation."

Pete laughs out loud, like we're all in on the same joke.

Jean-Marc offers, "The situation is that you are two American guys traveling around Europe."

"We are two American guys traveling around Europe," Pete replies, now in full wise-guy mode.

Big laughs all around, except for me.

"Then it should be easy," Jean-Luc concludes, folding his hands in front of him.

They bring out two backpacks on aluminum frames. The nylon's threadbare and smeared with what looks to be axle grease. Are they real props or things left behind by other losers like us, those naïve enough to get themselves into a *situation* like this and who then just disappeared? In any case, we're supposed to be backpackers who meet in a youth hostel and get it on in the showers. They point to a doorway.

Not especially wanting to disappear, as I fear the actual backpackers might have, I freeze in place, looking toward the opposite doorway, the exit.

Pete whispers, "Let's do it, guy."

My legs are about to give out.

"*Come on,*" he pleads, pulling me gently by the arm. Gently, yes, but still he's pulling.

Jean-Luc seems impatient and suggests we get started, only it sounds more like an order. He and Jean-Marc adjust the studio lights before lifting bulky cameras to their shoulders.

"The one rule is," Jean-Marc warns, "never look into the camera. Oh, and another, let us know when you're about to come." He instructs us to go to the far side of the room and put the backpacks on. I activate autopilot and follow Pete. The packs are super light, like they're filled with nothing but tissue paper to make them look full. The cameras start rolling and we're told to take the packs off, as if we've just arrived from the train station. I think of all those college kids from the States we've seen in Europe and imitate their no-worries attitude, or at least I try to. We're then given the signal to strip and head into the showers. It's our last chance to back out. I hesitate but Pete, true to form, gets naked in a flash. The being naked with Pete's not weird, the being watched is. My whole body's shaking. I can't help it. I turn my back to Pete and the cameras and undress slow, as slow as possible. I fold each item of clothing neatly and place it on a chair.

"Great, simply great," Jean-Marc crows, "the reluctance adds to the sexual tension."

Feeling nakeder than naked, I walk into the showers after Pete. It's like we're going to our execution.

"At first, pretend you're not noticing each other as you wash," Jean-Luc tells us.

We each turn a pair of faucets in the gang shower on. At the squat where we're staying there's no running water, so having warm water pouring over my greasy hair and down my waxy skin happens to feel great. It feels real. Yes, this is real, I think, but the next second I think the opposite.

Jean-Marc tells Pete, "Start noticing him, start getting yourself hard."

I'm not supposed to notice what Pete's up to till they say so. When they finally do, there's Pete, impressively erect, cock flat against his belly. I say impressively because I'm not sure I can get it up at all.

Jean-Marc directs us to look at each other *meaningfully* before Pete approaches me. Not sure what *meaning* the look's supposed to be *full* of.

Like a barker at the county fair, or a Roman emperor at the Colosseum, Jean-Luc announces, "Let the games begin!"

Even through the terror, I want to laugh when Pete, as ordered, starts kissing me. It's for sure funny, us making out, but the surprising thing is that Pete's really going at it. It feels weird, though not necessarily bad weird. After all, it's only Pete. It's not like I'm suddenly realizing, *Wow! Pete's a gay guy, after all,* or *Wow! I didn't know that I'm gay until right this second.* I love him, and we've been intimate in every way but this. The real intimacy, I guess, is that we're doing porn together.

They now want me to go down on Pete. Once again, mid-panic, I have to stop myself from laughing because in my mind I'm hearing a declaration he's made more than once in the past: "I'm not a blow job kind of guy." I squat on the tiles. It's maybe a little like drowning, blowing him with water pouring over my head and down my face. Like drowning, but not as difficult as I would've thought.

They keep telling us to think about our girlfriends. As if.

The blow job goes on until Pete is ordered to lead me to the bed. We don't dry off. Who knew youth hostels had king-size beds? One camera comes in close to get our faces. It's like Pete wants to make sure to give them a good shot, so he starts acting all frantic with desire, deep kissing me as we move towards the mattress and he tumbles us down onto it. At this point I don't know what to pretend.

Both directors coax him on, "Great stuff, great stuff."

Jean-Marc wants to know, "Who's going to top and who's going to bottom?"

I'm confused.

Jean-Luc sees this, so translates from the English, "Who's going to be insertive and who's going to be receptive?"

I get it and I don't.

Pete volunteers, "I'll top," like it's tennis and he'll serve.

He takes charge. He lays me down on my stomach and starts pressing his dick against my ass, and all I can think is, *That thing's going in there?* I try squirming away, but he pushes me into the mattress.

"Butt-fucking," Pete says right in my ear. "They want us to butt-fuck."

Call me the densest guy in the world, but I swear I did not really know anyone did this until right now. Seriously. Of course I know the slang "butt-fucker," but till this moment it was only something guys called each other back in junior high and didn't refer to anything actual. I'll be the first to admit, I'm truly out of it about lots of stuff when it comes to sex. And this time I don't just think, but whisper, "That thing is going in there?"

I'm freaking out. I twist my head around to see Pete smiling—not wry or sly or goofy but sweet, like the sweetest smile I've ever seen from him, like he thinks this is funny and sweet and that I'm funny and sweet, which is crazy because no one's ever thought I'm funny or sweet, let alone both. Then it hits me: he's for real in love with me. Through the fakeness of the porn, it hits me: Pete's in love with me.

He whispers back, "Just relax. And breathe." I hear him rubbing Vaseline—or whatever the goop in the tub on the nightstand is—on his dick. *Squish, squish, squish.*

At this point even the scared has been scared right out of me.

He starts slow, very slow, pushing his dick into my butthole. The head's not even all the way in and it's excruciating beyond belief, disbelief, and unbelief. I wince massively, barely keeping from gnashing my teeth in front of the cameras. He pushes the head all the way in and that's it. I yelp—for maybe the first time in my life, I actually yelp—and force myself out from under him. I jump up from the bed, shouting, "Holy shit!" over and over.

Pete laughs all wholesome like a Disney character. "Then you top me, if that'd work better."

I'm thinking I've wrecked everything, but Jean-Luc and Jean-Marc say this is all great, simply great, it makes the straight amateur first-time thing more real. I want to tell them that, for Christ's sake, the straight amateur first-time thing *is* real.

Pete gets up from the bed and starts kissing me again. I'm guessing he does this to get me over what he's guessing's a crisis. Which it is. I wouldn't have thought him kissing me would help matters but somehow it does. It makes me reconsider everything I've ever thought. His mouth is powerful, unlike any girl's I've ever kissed. It feels like I'm going to be swallowed. He continues urging me on, "Just let go. It's nothing either of us hasn't ever thought about before." I look at him like he's crazy. With a glittering look, he adds, "At least subconsciously."

Truth is, I'm *consciously* thinking I don't know anything about my *subconscious*.

He then starts going down on me because any pathetic erection that I might have had has since withered. I try to get back into character, so to speak.

I'm still standing by the edge of the bed when Pete flops down onto the definitely-not-youth-hostel satin sheets and spreads his legs like a girl. He dips his fingers in the tub for a gob of goo, rubs some on my dick, and then, with three whole fingers, puts the rest of it inside his butt. Can't imagine doing that. It's almost like he's done it before. I notice for the first time how the hair on his belly forms a perfect whorl. A good distraction. So are his hands. I've never really seen how graceful they are, especially in motion, like herons on the river back home—what a brilliant epiphany at a moment like this! Real poetry. It's scary how he seems to know how to do what we're doing and scarier still that he's so matter of fact about it. It's probably because he's so at ease with his body (and, apparently, with mine). I don't know why but I think it's funny in a cartoon kind of way when he pulls me by my dick. He raises his ass at the same time, and I find myself inside of him easier than I would've thought, if I'd ever thought about it. His hole grips my dick, takes it in. I try to tune out all the psychological crap in my head by focusing on details like the runs in the sheets—as if a cat has clawed them—and the pumpkin pie aroma of his armpits and his crotch.

I start thinking too seriously about how this is my first time having sex with anyone and I don't even know if it's real because I'm with someone I love, or fake because it's porn and with a guy. It's weird, but maybe it hurts that this person—my best friend in the world—might be thinking only of the money and the mechanics. I start going all negative. I'm losing it, by which I mean my mind, my heart, my confidence, and, once again, my hard-on. I've got to make this have meaning. All my feelings for over four years have been directed toward this guy lying under me. I hesitate almost too long before making myself press my hips against him. I just have to believe Pete's really into this sex act outside of the porn act or else it won't work. He's kind of moaning and keeps murmuring, "Man, oh man." I've got to not think it's fake and not think about Mrs. Lac or any of the girls I've ever made out with or want to make out with. I watch his body turning underneath me—really watch it—and suddenly being with him becomes like playing music together. Sex and music, music and sex. That's of course a thing, like universally, and now I'm understanding that thing for the first time. Our bodies start responding, one to the other, like when we're jamming and intuit what the other's about to play. I find myself in a maze of rhythm, and soon I'm really wanting to get off with another person for the first time ever. Even with one camera in my face and the other focused on my dick going in and out of him, I'm feeling real feelings, like when we fall into a song. I look down into his face, sequined with sweat and twisted into what looks like real pleasure, and I love him. I think *pleasure,* and in that instant he announces for the directors that he's coming, he's coming, and starts gushing a mass of pearls, and in the next instant I start vibrating, like during a show when it's going great, and I keep on vibrating until I heave and heave and collapse on top of him, panting.

Jean-Marc snaps me out of my reverie: "You came inside of him?" He drops the camera to his side.

I nod as I roll off Pete who starts licking his own spooge off my sticky-wet ribcage, like a puppy, which should probably be grossing me out but for some reason isn't.

"We told you not to," Jean-Luc complains. "Now we've got only the one money shot."

Jean-Marc shakes his shaggy head. "It will have to do."

Pete reaches down between his legs. His fingers come out gooey. "Pretty!" he laughs.

The heron now in the muck of a marsh.

"Right from the start you've had me soul-wise, Michael A., and now you've got me body-wise." I can actually feel Pete grinning as he sings these words and nuzzles into my armpit.

Jean-Luc and Jean-Marc are already putting the cameras away and taking the lights down. When they're done, they place the money on the bed and leave. Perfunctory.

Pete sits up, cross-legged, and starts counting the bills. "That was better than junk," he opines, scratching his nearly hairless chest vigorously, "which is saying a lot!"

I ignore that one.

He then gets all serious, pupils huge, and announces, "I'm so apexically psyched about the honorification of the mere fact of being with you." He flops over on top of me.

I suppose what he says in his weird lexicon is clear, but it's also not. This state of being together—that long-ago night by the river when we promised we'd be together—remains a mystery to me. *Being* is so deep yet so vague. I take a nosedive into my own thoughts. Next thing I know, Pete's snoozing right on top of me, our bellies glued together.

Dawn's already filtering soft and silver through the windows. It's unlike any light we have back home. I scooch out from under Pete without waking him. I lie there watching him sleep. Hundreds of nights I've seen him sleeping but have never before *watched*. Maybe it's a faggy thing to do. I don't care. His face flickers. I try rappelling down into his subconscious, to know him completely. As if that's possible. As if that's possible with anyone, even with oneself—myself in particular. I have no weird or guilty thoughts or feelings about the two of us having had sex, or even having had sex with a guy, which is surprising given my leftover Catholic stuff. He's not only the only guy I would ever have done porn with but also the only person. How's that for intimacy? One thing scares me, though, as I'm falling asleep: maybe he's the only person I would ever have sex with. *Ever,* meaning *at any time,* and *ever,* meaning *in any way.*

Something wakes me with a start. Not sure what. At first, everything seems as it should be. Pete's asleep next to me, outside the covers as usual, on his back, naked, his cock and balls resting on his hip, like a rabbit kit. It takes a longer moment than it should for me to register that he's not sleeping, that someone's on the other side of him, kneeling on the floor. I lift my head, glance over, blink hard. It's Jean-Luc. Jean-Luc, with that same dirty lace tourniquet from the other day, now knotted around Pete's arm. He's poised, needle in hand. Jean-Luc nods to me with a faint grin. His whole hipper-than-though existence makes me sick. I don't so much as shout, "What the hell!" or anything at all, before I'm leaping over Pete and am all over Jean-Luc's scrawny French self, whaling on him. I shove him so hard he lands on his back halfway across the room. In three strides I'm there, straddling his chest. I'm punching his face in and he's screaming, which makes me punch even harder. Pete comes flying after me. At this point, I'm choking Jean-Luc so tight his face goes plum. I lift myself up then thrust my knees down onto his chest, hoping to crack him wide open. He's about to pass out, all expression leaching from his crow-like features. Pete grabs me from behind, shouting, "You're gonna fucking kill him!" He tears me off the still body.

Jean-Luc's barely moaning. I smash my bare heels on his concave chest as Pete's dragging me away, and I'm yelling, "I want to kill him! I want to kill him!"

Pete throws me on the bed. Jean-Luc's quiet now, looking pretty much dead.

"Get dressed," Pete says, almost gentle, but nervous too. "Let's get out of here."

"What the hell was going on?" I ask as I pull my clothes on.

Pete's not answering, and not just because he knows that I know the answer. He gathers the colorful money up from the bed and shoves it in his pockets.

Jean-Luc twitches, mumbling something neither of us can understand. I give him a swift kick to the gut with my now sneakered foot, then reach into his jeans and take his wallet, fat with cash. He reaches feebly toward me, like the money means more to him than his life. I wish I had killed him.

As we head down the stairs and through the dark, deserted club, I ask again, "What was going on?"

Pete unlatches the door, then, without turning around, answers, "Some people just like to get high."

That remark ignites every nerve in my body. I grab hold of the door and slam it closed before he can pass through it and out into the world. I turn him around, hard, and, half shaking him, half hugging him, shove him against the wall. He's looking scared, not because he thinks I'm going to hurt him, I'm pretty sure, but because I'm sobbing. That's something he's never seen. I'm pressed against him, gripping him, undamming years of sorrow. We slump onto the floor together. He holds my convulsing body, trying to soothe me. "Hey, hey, my guy, I'm sorry, so sorry I got you into this mess, sorry."

My head falls onto his lap. Through the blaze burning up my mind, I eventually am able to stammer, "It's John, it's John . . ."

"What? What do you mean?" He strokes my cheek, his palm surprisingly cool. "Your brother?"

I nod.

"What about him?"

Bile rushes up into my mouth. I spit it out on the floor and pause for a long time to try and get both my breath and wits under control. "Like I told you. In Vietnam. He died." There's this terrifying image of John shuddering in the hot-dark jungle. I pause again. "But I didn't tell you how."

I can feel questions pulsing in Pete's fingertips as they move across my forehead and into my hairline. I take in as much air as my lungs can hold before blurting, "This same shit, the junk." I lift my head. "Over there." I bury my face back down in his lap. "He became a junkie over there. OD'd in the jungle." Like a million times before, I try and fail to imagine how it was for John as his last thoughts flickered out. It's more terrible than anything. I picture him all alone. "Goddammit, goddammit."

"Whoa." Pete exhales big, shaking his head. "I am so sorry, pal, so, so sorry." He bends down, kisses my cheek lightly, then starts licking up the tears sliding down my cheeks. When he's taken up all the salty mess, he says, "No wonder you flipped out." He rakes his fingers through my hair. "That's the saddest thing I ever heard." He places his palm across my face, like a mask. A weird gesture, yet somehow right. "It won't happen again." I've never heard him so solemn.

We're quiet for a stretch before Pete says, "We better keep moving. Before he gets up." He cocks his head toward the ceiling.

We pull ourselves to our feet and together we step out into the colorless light of morning here in Copenhagen. We wander the streets, ignoring or absorbing what's happened. After walking blocks in silence, Pete says, almost boisterous, "Lend me your aural appendage, my Michael Angel."

I nod, relieved our love didn't break last night, relieved there seems to be a new bond between us. Really, he had as much reason to be coming down on me as I had for coming down on him. I nearly killed a man. We're both reckless, just in different ways.

"With all this dough," he says, "we really could get one of those little barges and live here, me and you. It would be sweet." His eyes go wide and wild with desire. "Or Matt told me about these guys he met who drove a van to Katmandu, then on to Thailand, sold it there and flew back with more money than when they left. That'd be the road trip par excellence! You and me, we'd out-Kerouac Kerouac!"

Because I don't respond to his fairy tales, he turns even goofier. He jumps on me, piggyback. "Let's take one of those city boat tours! Heard they include a smorgasbord—including coffee, beer—the works. Perfect remedy for a hangover."

We're popular enough in Copenhagen that for our last night they've moved the venue outdoors, to a park in Christiania. Though they call it a park—*People's Park,* in Danish—it's really more of a hole in the earth amid the dilapidated naval buildings. It's where, we're told, a munitions dump used to be. The place is weedy and kind of wild, with random slabs of concrete and piles of bricks.

When we met up with Matt and Bobby back at the squat to huddle over the playlist, the two of them seemed too mellow. Definitely the horse talking. Bobby showed us a telegram from Ryder that somehow found its way to us here: *Japan next. Records selling there like bikinis to coeds on spring break. Details to follow.*

To sober the guys up, I led them to a Greek café I'd found when we first arrived, for this thick coffee, strong as paint thinner, served in tiny gold-rimmed cups.

As he sat there stirring tons of sugar into his, Matt confessed he's exhausted from back-to-back tours and wouldn't mind staying here for a while when we're done. "Fuck Japan," he said, spinning a gold filigreed spoon around in the sludge.

Bobby agreed, adding, "We should use the time off to finish the new material for a second album. I say we go to Japan after that."

When this tour's over, I'm pretty sure that Matt and Bobby want to come back here to Copenhagen because of their girls and also probably because it's easy to get ahold of heroin. The girls live on a barge moored in one of the quieter canals. That's where Pete got the idea. We're both a little jealous of Matt and Bobby—of the girls and the barge but not, at least as far as I'm concerned, the junk. The barges do look romantic. A lot of them have flower boxes along the decks. In my imagination, their girls are hippies growing vegetables on their deck and cooking up vegetarian stews. Maybe they're like this dream girl with long hair the color of sunshine I've seen playing mandolin beside a fountain in one of the squares. Like a lot of the girls here, they probably don't wear makeup. Something I really like.

I've got to get real. For all I know, their girls could be skanky, strung out punk chicks, with vampire makeup, serving up frozen pizza.

Bobby and Matt left me and Pete at the Greek place to, in fact, go meet their girls. Over this weird wine that tasted like Pine-Sol, Pete wanted to finalize plans for his swim across the Øresund to Sweden. He asked if I know how to row.

I laughed. "What, you worried I'm going to capsize?"

"Just wondering."

"I haven't rowed since I was like fourteen, the last summer I went fishing with my dad, but it's not like it's something you forget." We agreed we'd leave from the main train station super early, at six, so we can be back to leave for our next city, Hamburg, by noon, because it's a six-hour drive and our gig's at eight.

It's a perfect night. Not hot and muggy like Hallein in summer, though not too cool either. Venus floats above the ruins and I'm feeling powerful as we hit the opening chords of our not quite parody cover of "You're So Vain." As I scan the audience, I nearly stop playing. A few rows back from the makeshift stage, standing by one of the scraggly thorn trees growing up in the Meadow, is Daniel, and leaning against him, none other than Gwen Chambers. They know each other? I get totally paranoid. How much clearer could I have been when I walked out on her and her boss in London? Pete sees her, too. He gives me that what-the-fuck look of his. I told him what happened, but by the way he glances at her again then back at me it's clear he doesn't believe me. This woman has become my nemesis, relentless as the ones the Greeks had. I feel like I'm being dragged along by a chain of events I have no say in. At this moment, it's also as if I'm in that poem about Icarus falling into the sea and no one noticing.

After a single encore (which tonight is, appropriately enough, "Pissed Off!"), but before the applause has even hit its peak, Pete's unplugging and taking off. I go after him, leaving Matt and Bobby to acknowledge the audience. Like good soldiers, they do, raising their arms, waving, bowing.

I catch up to Pete, grabbing him by the shoulder right as he's slipping into the shadows beyond the lighted area. He whips around, knocking my hand away.

"Leave me the hell alone!" He lifts his hands like he's going to shove me.

"Look," I try to explain, "I didn't know she was going to be here, or even that she knows Daniel!"

He's not listening. He sprints off through the dark outskirts of the park. I'm shaking. I run after him, calling his name, but he has slipped away among the ruins. I stop and look around. He is nowhere. I fall on my knees and start sobbing. I can't help thinking that our making porn together has something to do with the new rift between us. Maybe not the idea that it was porn, but the vague everything else around it, like what we mean to each other. When I can breathe again, I get up and head back.

Behind the stage I find Matt and Bobby with their girls, who, it turns out, are not at all how I pictured them but nonetheless cute in a freaky kind of way. The one's got bleached hair and is wearing a plaid Catholic school skirt, a man's undershirt, and combat boots. The other, with black hair, has got on super short cutoffs and a leather jacket. Bobby's arm hangs around the blonde; Matt's deep-kissing the other one.

Matt sees me and pulls his face away from his girl's. "What's up with Pete?"

I give that classic and annoying shrug of mine. And then, my nemesises (or whatever the plural is) appear, all smiles, unaware—or maybe too aware?—of the discord they've sown among brothers, just like in the proverb. Daniel appears his usual princely self, in pressed shirt and trousers, shined shoes. Gwen Chambers is not Hippie Poppins or Brit Nicks or Business Lady tonight. She's wearing a short leather skirt and lacy tank top. As much as I hate her, she's hot. In unison, they say, "Terrific show!"

I turn away from them, to Matt and Bobby and their girls. I need company. I ask them what they're up to.

"We've got to split," Bobby says. "Meeting up with friends."

Heroin aside, those two seem to have a pretty normal life here. They don't invite me along, but I don't take it as a slight. They usually go off and do their own thing, Pete and I ours. I try my best to tune Gwen Chambers and Daniel out as I change my T-shirt and pack up my gear. The audience has become a dull roar beyond the park. The stars pulsate. Now I'm paranoid that the whole porno thing was arranged by Daniel to blackmail me into whatever it is Gwen Chambers wants me for. Even the sailing expedition seems like a ploy to impress me, so I'll sign a contract, and the guys were only invited along for cover. How did I ever let Daniel record with us? That's going to come back and haunt the band and me. The two of them keep going on about how great the show was. I don't so much as look at them. I lay my guitar in its case.

When I'm ready to leave, I look at them. "I didn't know you two knew each other." I sound like I'm on a freaking soap opera.

Gwen Chambers responds, "Of course we do. Through the record company, my dear. Daniel is on our classical label. I of course told him he absolutely must attend your concert when I knew you were coming to Copenhagen."

I'm too paranoid to think straight.

"Come dine with us at my hotel!" Gwen mentions the name of the hotel. Sounds French and this isn't France.

Daniel chimes in, "Gwen has got fantastic news for you, Michael." He sounds like a dad, and he's my age for Christ's sake. "Come with us, please," he says, placing a hand on my back like we're old chums.

What more have I got to lose?

I lag behind them on the walk to the hotel, which, through the windows, looks like a French palace, all glittering chandeliers and mirrors and white woodwork trimmed with gold. The doormen are right out of Cinderella—white wigs, breeches, the works—and greet us—or at least the two of them—like royalty, bowing deep. I'm waiting for my rags to turn into a ball gown. It's by far the classiest place I've ever stepped foot in. And the scariest.

It's way past any dinnertime I've ever known, but the dining room's packed with people way more dressed up than not just me but even the rich people back home. The men's suits are darker and more severe looking. The women come right out of a fashion magazine. Or at least their clothes do. Gwen Chambers is sexier than any of them. Sick as it seems, I like that, being with a pretty woman, that is. Even one I don't like or trust—one who has likely destroyed my life. I'm that superficial. Food's being served under silver and glass domes, like in old movies about rich people. The tablecloths shine unnaturally white.

I'm seated between Gwen Chambers and Daniel, along one half of a round table so we're all three facing out into the restaurant. I'm the sullen kid being forced to go out to eat with his parents. A sullen rich kid, that is, because people like me almost never went out to dinner with their parents and, if they ever did, never acted sullen— you'd get walloped if you did. When the waiter puts menus the size of double record albums in front of us, I say, "Not hungry." Totally not true. Reflexive resistance. I'm still waiting for the promised fantastic news.

Ignoring what I say, Daniel tells me, "The squab is delicious."

"Squab?"

"Pigeon. But you would likely prefer the medallions of boeuf with hollandaise."

How would he know what I would prefer or not prefer? And *medallions*? *Boeuf*? *Hollandaise*?

"Wine?" he asks. I don't so much as nod or shake my head. The waiter returns, and Daniel orders for all of us. Again, like a dad. The squab for himself, a *salade* with some French name for the lady, and the *boeuf* for me. It's weird that he's speaking English to the waiter and using French words for the dishes because this is his and the waiter's country and they have their own language, Danish, which is, as far as I can tell, nothing like either English or French.

The wine smells like a basement. I lift the huge globe set on a perilously thin stem and gulp the dark liquid because I need anything at all to calm my nerves.

Gwen Chambers shimmies in her seat as she starts to speak: "I want to share the marvelous news with you!" Why's she always exclaiming? She leans over her wineglass. Deep-purple reflections play across her freckled face. I really, really don't trust her but am most definitely in lust. To trust or not to trust? To lust or not to lust? These are the questions . . . I prepare myself to respond with a firm no to whatever she's about to propose. I try reducing her voice to rhythm, but the meaning of the words keeps seeping through, and I'm hearing not just good news but insanely—and Daniel was right—*fantastic* news, impossibly fantastic news. I'm blinking fast and hard. Apparently, Daniel helped her convince her boss Willy to sign a contract with the whole band. Daniel's smiling, not like a father this time, more like a kid. He's even blushing. In that instant, my whole sense of him changes yet again, this time from sinister to gallant.

He then goes all grown-up on me again as he explains, "The studio will work with you on new material. You will, however, maintain complete artistic control." He swirls his wine. "I am your biggest fan; however, I do think you can become even better."

"Oh?"

Gwen Chambers purses her lips before saying, "The songs that you now have hit the nerve of our time but they are maybe a little too . . . how should I say . . . catchy. They could use more complexity. I would not want the songs to become complicated or arty, only a little more . . . complex."

I actually like the distinction she's making. Complex, complicated. What she means, I think, is what Bobby calls poetry without getting poetic. She wants poetry. I agree with her, though not out loud. She's smart.

The money for a new album sounds insane—too good to be true?—and is probably as much as my dad made in all his years at the refinery put together. I can't wait to tell the guys. They'll go out of their minds.

"What do you think?" Daniel asks with an uncharacteristic grin.

I can't help but greet his idiot grin with one that's probably even more idiotic. It's the first grin either of them has seen crossing my face. Then I look at Gwen Chambers, who suddenly and most definitely seems simply Gwen. I say, "A-ma-zing," mocking her gently. She's looking all smug.

A parade of uniformed waiters arrives with the food. They lift the domes in unison, with a flourish. The beef looks all glossy and colorful, like in a magazine, and smells a-ma-zing. I'm now all-out ravenous. Just as I'm about to pounce on the meat, Gwen raises her glass for a toast. Definitely not a custom I've been raised with. As the three deep-red orbs touch and make an outer space ping, she trills, "To music!"

As Daniel echoes her (minus the trill), I'm already cutting into the meat. The first bloody hunk I shove into my mouth tastes better than anything I've ever known, even better than the surf 'n' turf with Pete in Niagara Falls. Only after devouring half the plate do I look up and catch Daniel observing me, like he's somehow pleased. By what? My hunger? The two of them talk and laugh, picking at their food, while I keep going at mine, definitely not like a human being.

When we're done with dinner, Gwen invites us up to her suite. But the guys. I want to give them the news. And I want to make things right with Pete. Maybe he's wondering why I'm not doing that right now? Maybe he's even worried about where I might be? Gwen and Daniel stand up to leave. I hesitate. I'm about to say I've got to get going when Gwen touches me on the cheek and says in a sweet voice, "Come on, we'll celebrate!" I offer half a smile, get up, and we head out.

I'm all nerves on the elevator, though a second bottle of wine has taken a bit of the edge off.

We enter the suite. It reminds me of someplace you see on the news when the President travels overseas and meets another president or a king or a dictator. Crystal chandeliers turned low make everything golden. She motions for Daniel and me to sit on a sofa covered in satin or silk—something like that—while she puts a reel-to-reel on a tape player I guess she must have brought from London. It's piano music, classical. The sound's almost as good as live, bouncing off all the marble and plasterwork but softened by oriental carpets and tapestries. The piece is beautiful, but beautiful is way too weak a word for what it is. Gwen sits down across the dark, glowing coffee table from us, on a kind of mini throne.

"So, what do you think?" she asks Daniel.

He answers blandly, "It's fine."

As it turns out, it's him playing. She's brought the tracks he recorded last month in London, sonatas by Haydn. This time hearing him play I don't get agitated like I did at his house. I'm kind of what? *Elated?* Daniel is telling Gwen he would like another go at this passage or that passage, and she's giving him super technical advice, but I'm not really listening to them. I'm lost, totally lost, in the intricate patterns of sound filling the rooms. At some point I don't know if I'm asleep or awake or in some other state that's neither.

It feels days later when I open my eyes. I freak out a little to find Daniel asleep beside me on the sofa, or more like half under me, my head resting on his hip, and I freak out even more to find Gwen asleep with her head resting on my hip. The suite is no longer golden but bathed in the same diffuse silver light as the room above the bar was after making porn. It's like being in a black-and-white photo.

In the next moment Gwen wakes up, like she's sensed my eyes moving or a change in my breathing. I look down at her. Her eyelids flutter slowly as she reaches a hand up to rest on my belly, bare because my T-shirt hiked up while I slept. I take hold of her hand kind of romantic-like, but more so she doesn't brush the morning wood poking above the waist of my jeans. Next thing I know, she's rising from the sofa with this incredible grace, still holding my hand, pulling me along with her. We move through the room kind of like this Roman statue that Pete loves. It's of a girl leading a guy somewhere, or maybe—I forget—they're fleeing from something or someone or someplace. We whirl and tumble onto a canopied bed in the adjoining room. To an onlooker, we'd appear tiny and lost in this cave within the canyon of the suite. She's kissing me, though not desperate like some girls I've been with, or mushy and weak like others. She kisses in a definite way, like maybe it's part of a performance she's choreographing. She then does what seems impossible: she strips both of us at the same time, like it's something she's rehearsed. It all does feel a little staged, but that doesn't matter, I'm into it. I have grown to like her, though I am still a little afraid of her, of how perceptive she is, of how she just seems to *know*.

My jeans are down around my ankles, and I rise above her pale body. She looks less skinny naked than with clothes on. More voluptuous. I like that. We kiss and touch each other all over for a long time. And then, with her slim hand, she guides my dick down between her legs. Everything's about to go outer space when suddenly everything crashes. My eye catches the ridiculously ornate clock on the nightstand. It's got two silver statuettes posing on either side of a blue enamel face. One figure is asleep, seated, chin resting on her fist, the moon on her lap, and the other one's standing, raising the sun above his head. Greek or Roman gods, I guess. It's almost seven! I totally forgot I was supposed to go with Pete at six for his lunatic Byron swim across the sound to Sweden. I push up into the kneeling position, cock bobbing. I scramble out of bed, pulling my underwear and jeans up, ready to tear on out of here. Gwen's staring up at me, confused, maybe even scared. This isn't in the script. She starts to pull the sheet up around her, under her delicate chin. She looks beautiful, red hair veiling her face, one hip uncovered, looking so milky, so soft. Suddenly I find myself thinking about Wordsworth—of all absurd things—the passage in *The Prelude* where he's been hiking up and across the Alps for days, anticipating the Continental Divide from where he'll be able to see all of Europe spread below him. He's pumped, can hardly wait for that moment he expects will hold the Sublime he's wanted so bad. But he never gets that moment. Dark clouds, heavy rainstorms, followed by nightfall and even more storms, cause him to miss the Continental Divide and the Sublime altogether. Thing is, he doesn't even know he's missing it until it's too late. Only when the sky eventually clears does the morning light reveal that he's already trudged far past the Divide and is well along the descent. It's understandable that he gets depressed when he discovers what's happened. If I leave Gwen now, I'll be like Wordsworth crossing the Alps. All the girls I did not have sex with leading up to the sublime Gwen, and then—just like that—I miss out on my moment with her. Having sex with a female will be for me like the Sublime was for Wordsworth. The moment lost. Maybe forever. Ridiculous, I know, but that's how I'm feeling.

I tug my jeans and underwear back down, kicking them aside. Pete will understand. It's because of having had sex with him that I can even do this. Besides, he's had lots of girls. He can swim some other sound or bay, river or lake—even the whole ocean if he wants to—some other time, and I'll be there for him, I will. I most definitely want to finish what I've started with Gwen, or, rather, what she started with me. As I slip back in between her legs, she smiles. For a second, I think I should have a rubber but then forget about it. For once, I'm not afraid. She's definitely not the kind of girl who would let herself get pregnant. She's got places to go even higher than she's already gone. I get my rhythm and she synchronizes her body with mine. It's weird and surprising that none of it seems awkward. She makes it seem like I know what I'm doing. It's amazing— she's amazing—but there's one thing, just one thing: as hard as I try not to, I can't help hearing Pete saying how I've got him, how I've got him soul-wise and body-wise.

When I wake for the second time, the Roman numerals between Night and Day show that it's almost eleven! Damn. Now I've really got to run. The guys and I need to hit the road. Pete might be sore at me for a while, for missing his swim, but only until he hears the unimaginable news: a record deal with a major label!

Gwen's still asleep. As quiet as possible, I get dressed. She looks so beautiful lying there, the shiny sheets twisted around her. I'd love to kiss her cheek but don't want to disturb her. I tiptoe from the room, then run, soft as I can, through the other rooms. No sign of Daniel, though only now do I get the feeling that maybe he was watching the whole thing from under the threshold between the rooms, like it really was a performance, maybe even one created for him.

I slow to a fast walk through the lobby so as not to look as much like an intruder as I feel. Once outside, I start running again. I'm running because I'm late but also because I feel so unbelievable having been with Gwen, and because the guys and me are going to be rock stars, and because this is my life! The narrow streets are crowded with people not in any hurry at all. Women with baskets on their arms, students with satchels and collared shirts, hippies who stepped right out of *The Hobbit*. Everyone and everything so damn *picturesque*. To make time, I run behind the stalls piled high with flowers and fruit and vegetables. The ferry that crosses the harbor is loading up. I manage to jump on right as the gangplank's being lifted, like I'm in some Hollywood caper. Above the ferry, gulls bob in the breeze. All the spires and domes of this, my Visible City, glitter better than in any postcard because the sky is a real blue and the sun is shining for real and everything is real. *I'm here. I'm here,* I keep saying to myself, which almost makes me feel that I am real.

JUNE–JULY 1994, ISAAC

I felt like I was turning into that girl (was it Victor Hugo's daughter?) in a movie our French teacher made us watch. She literally goes insane obsessing over some military guy who doesn't love her anymore. Except the pathetic fact is I've never even met my version of the military guy—that is, the No Names—except on vinyl. I still haven't found a single picture of them. In any case, after leaving the salt cave with Daniel and dropping him off at his hotel to catch the airport shuttle, I didn't hear from him. And I wrote five times. A bit much, I know. When I left him at the airport, he hadn't acted like we'd never see each other again, let alone not be in touch. I guess he hadn't acted like we would, either. I thought our talks had been pretty deep, though, almost philosophical. About music, math, the universe. Maybe to a guy like him they were ordinary, and maybe my going on and on about the band in my letters got to be too much. I gave what probably seemed like obsessively detailed interpretations of every song on *Invisible City*. Couldn't help it. Without Daniel, my obsession with the No Names hit a brick wall. I had no luck finding Pete Lac, the only other possibility. No one's ever at his parents' house when I've stopped by, and no one picks up the phone and there's no answering machine.

Despite all this, I continued listening to *Invisible City* pretty much constantly. Each time, I would focus on a different musician's playing. All of them blow me away, but for me Pete's guitar probably reigns supreme. I don't know how he got such creaminess out of an electric guitar while still getting it to slice through walls. Other than that, I spent my time playing guitar and getting high. I also finished planning my South American adventure, hoping the epic journey itself would help me forget about the No Names.

More than six weeks after Daniel left, a short letter from him finally arrived. He hadn't, he apologized, answered my letters because he had been on tour in Asia and only received them upon his recent return. In his calm, collected manner, he suggested I consider coming for a visit to Copenhagen. He would send an airline ticket. He put this out there like it was no big deal, so in my cooler-than-antifreeze response I pretended it wasn't. Of course, it was. As crazy as my plotting and planning had been up to this point, by comparison his invitation made it all seem sane. After all, Daniel Beck is, well, Daniel Beck, and I am me. Suddenly it seemed like one of those stories that doesn't end well. Like, for example, me chained to a dungeon wall and found only years later, naked, starving, babbling like a madman or, worse, me found dismembered in a trash bag with certain organs missing. At the very least, his offer made me feel like a gigolo. In any case, I told him that sounded great, I'd come.

Daniel's letter arrived exactly one week before I was going to take off on my motorcycle odyssey. I'd even gotten my passport, no thanks to Vashti. Went to city hall and paid for a copy of the birth certificate she supposedly couldn't find. In any case, I nixed my dream—the Che thing—just like that. Funny how nothing is ever what you think it's going to be. The big adventure evaporates and a different one, maybe not so big, appears. First, I told him not to worry about the plane ticket, I'd get it. That way I wouldn't owe him. Besides, I could use it to my advantage with Vashti. I told her she'd been right. The more I thought about it, South America seemed dangerous and how about me taking a trip to Europe instead? She was so thrilled she didn't suspect anything was up and paid for the airline ticket, just like that. It was as if her finely tuned, always activated suspicion monitor had gotten disconnected. Though I'm nineteen and an adult, still, I didn't see the point of being disowned by telling the truth. Explaining the whole Daniel and No Names situation to her would've been not only impossible but a serious risk to my finances and to her health. Not difficult to imagine the veins at her temples bursting.

What could be better than arriving at Daniel's door drunk, right? Free booze on my first overseas flight was so cool, thanks to the first-class upgrade Vashti purchased with frequent flyer miles. That said, sober or drunk, what am I doing here? Plane fare paid for by him, or not, I am kind of like a common hustler. Such are the thoughts floating through my head as I stand in front of a house older than probably anything in the whole us, located in a maze of streets as complicated as history. The black paint on the door shines so bright I can't avoid my guilty reflection in it. I'm hustling this perfectly decent guy and am about to lose my nerve. From the get-go, this quest for the No Names has been unrealistic at best and now feels like it's about to become what Vashti would call a fiasco. At this moment I could be experiencing the first true freedom of my life, buzzing along some awesome *camino* towards Patagonia, my very own La Poderosa full throttle. Instead, I'm wasting my life in pursuit of what? A long-defunct band. *Okay,* I mutter to myself, *buck the fuck up, you're here.* I lift the hefty door knocker, let it go, and stand there wowed by the clear *thump!* announcing me, the young writer. Yeah, right.

A woman, who looks like she could be Daniel's twin, answers the door, not smiling. When I ask for Mr. Beck, she asks, in slightly accented English, if he is expecting me? "Yes," I say, trying to sound upbeat, "he's expecting me."

"He is in a recording session upstairs," she informs me. "He should be finished in not more than half an hour. If you would like, please take a seat."

I thank her, give my name, and sit down on the weird modern couch she directs me to. I flip through Danish lifestyle magazines on the end table, looking at pictures and wondering about the imported English—*Super! Sexy! Must-Have!* Posters and photographs of Daniel Beck and other classical musicians, either performing or holding their instruments, plaster the walls.

Down the steep, narrow staircase precisely twenty-six minutes later comes Daniel Beck, looking like an ad for a luxury watch. And when he gets closer, I swear, clamped to his wrist, is the Audemars Piguet Vashti swore she was going to buy me if I got into Princeton or Harvard. He even smiles elegantly. He's casual and classic, as they say, in a blue, probably cashmere, v-neck, navy cords, loafers with no socks. Until like a minute ago I would have thought this style of his—the kind Vashti drools over—both lame and pretentious, but somehow, here in his natural habitat, it works. Or else, maybe jet lag's warping my judgment.

"Good to see you, Isaac!" he calls out, shaking my hand like an enthusiastic politician.

His voice kind of makes me think of a robot—a warm and friendly robot but a robot nonetheless. He tells me to come on up to the studio, he's just finishing. I follow him upstairs. He says something to the engineers—three guys about his age, as unkempt as he is kempt—who are leaving.

In this ancient house, they've built a high-tech recording studio, in the middle of which stands the high tech of the last century, an outrageously shiny grand piano. Daniel pulls the padded bench away from the keyboard and sits, motioning me to take the nearby rolling desk chair.

"Your studio's cool." I sound totally idiotic and totally unlike a robot. I'm jittery because now that I'm here it's actually sinking in that I'm not just sort of like a hustler, I *am* a hustler, hustling the world-famous Daniel Beck in order to find one forgotten Mike Abramczyk.

"Why, thank you. Though it's not mine, I am lucky enough to be able to use it."

I can't stop my mouth from running: "It would be cool to hit the music scene here. You'll show me where the No Names played, right?"

He laughs, "Perhaps! But let me take you to your hotel now, so you can freshen up and have a rest. I'll come by for you this evening at seven. We'll dine together."

Oh. I'd assumed I'd be staying with him. Maybe he has a partner or family that he's never mentioned and puts his extra-curriculars up at hotels? Though we talked the whole night through at the salt mine, and it seemed to me there was some sort of intimacy between us, I now realize I know exactly nothing about his personal life.

The cab pulls up to an überfancy hotel on a big circular plaza. Daniel's been nice the whole ride but nothing more. When we get out of the car, he waves away the doorman, takes my suitcase inside, and checks me in. The place is definitely five-star, if not more, if there are more. He will not be escorting me to the room, he tells me, and hands the key to the bellboy.

The digs are totally luxe. Once the bellboy has settled me in, I feel more than a little uneasy. I stare out the window onto the plaza. Pigeons circle an enormous green equestrian statue, then land all along it, from the exaggerated waves of the forelock to the tail blowing dramatically in an imaginary wind sweeping across an imaginary battlefield. The birds rise, circling the plaza before landing along horse and rider again. Circle and land, circle and land. I decide to take a bath. The tub is huge and marble, fit for a Roman emperor. Calms my nerves a little, the hot water. After drying off, I'm too lazy to go to my suitcase and fall asleep completely naked in a bed fit for a princess, waiting to be summoned by the prince.

Instead of coming up to the room to get me, Daniel calls from the lobby. It must have taken a lot of rings to wake me, because I think I heard the ringing in my dream for a long time. I jump up, put on the CK suit I wore to his concert back home, and head down to the lobby.

He greets me, friendly enough, though still way formal. "I've reserved a table for us here. I hope that's alright."

His formality's beginning to creep me out. It's as if he's figured out my game and is just playing along, kind of cat and mouse. A maître d'—who must be like ninety—takes us to a corner table that looks out on all the other diners. What with all the chandeliers, the place positively glitters. The old guy and Daniel talk to each other in Danish. It seems like they go way back.

"I'm glad you're here," Daniel says, opening the leather menu. It's the first personal thing he's said. "Wine?"

"Sure."

"The squab is delicious."

"I never say no to squab." He doesn't smile. Not sure he gets my humor.

The waiters move like parodies, noses pointed up toward the ceiling, enormous silver trays hoisted above their shoulders. When the wine guy arrives, gold cup on a chain around his neck, Daniel of course does the selecting, tasting, approving, and when the waiter comes, he orders the squab for both of us. I feel like a girl on a date from like fifty years ago.

We small talk. The whole situation seems so out of whack with our sort of mystical night in the salt cave on Deep Lake. Even though we didn't have sex then, and I was—and am—playing him, at least there I felt close to him.

After the pair of squabs arrive, looking right out of one of Vashti's gourmet mags, I tell him, "If it's weird having me here, I don't have to stay. I can bum around the rest of Europe." I pop a fake laugh: "Never seen the world!"

For a second Daniel looks confused—his usually placid face twisting slightly, blue eyes flashing—but in the next second his features relax, and he says with his usual robotic calm, "That won't be necessary." He raises his glass, red wine throbbing in the candlelight. "To the future!"

I raise my glass slowly—me now probably the one looking confused—and echo, "To the future?" though I don't manage to get the question out of my voice.

The corners of Daniel's mouth turn slightly downward, his voice becoming serious, his language even more formal than usual. "We have an important matter at hand. Perhaps I should have explained via post, but that would have taken too long, what with the back-and-forth."

At this point, I'm on edge. Not used to feeling unsure of myself in very many situations, I chug the wine. My squab, shiny and dark with plum sauce, stays untouched, even as Daniel slices the breast in front of him, forking pink morsel after pink morsel into his mouth with absurd grace. After a minute or two, he places the knife and fork on the scalloped edge of the plate, lifts the napkin, and pats his mouth. He looks me right in the eye. "I have come to believe that you should meet Michael."

It's like the busy dining room has gone completely still and silent except for the slow blinking of Daniel's eyes and the thumping of my own heart. His announcement echoes around in my head, but not a word comes out of me for a stretch of time. I finally manage to stammer, "Wow."

He rests what I'm guessing are million-dollar hands on the white tablecloth. "Let me ask, how much time do you have?"

I take a deep breath. "Um, as much as I want?"

He nods. "Good."

I walk into Christiania, still high on Gwen, trying to figure out how I can see her again, and even how to bring her into Pete's and my life. Then reality strikes. We're leaving and she lives in London. She's posh, I'm most definitely not. Outside the building where we're crashing, a skinny skinhead is on his knees weeding a haphazard vegetable patch fenced in by rusted pieces of scrap metal and driftwood. We smoked with him the other night. He looks up and tells me, like he's reading the weather on TV, "Police were here looking for you and your bandmates. One of them OD'd." He looks down again at the task before him.

The sun goes black.

I want to smash his face in just for being so matter-of-fact even as I'm not really registering the fact. I try to think, can't, to breathe, can't, then at last manage, "Where are they?"

He shrugs. I finally get how totally obnoxious my shrug probably seems to people.

I spin away from him, fly in through the dim portal, nearly crashing into Matt and Bobby. They're on their way out, loaded up with their instruments and duffel bags. So, it's Pete. And they're leaving? Matt drops his stuff and hugs me hard and tight.

I pull away, take a huge step back, because if I don't, I'll deck him. "Is he dead?" Not sure how I even got that question out.

Bobby's crying. "No, no. Hospital. They took him to the hospital."

Matt tries explaining, "We shot up together this morning, when Bobby and I were getting back from the night with our girls. After, Pete said he was going down to the harbor to swim. You know him. We didn't really think anything of it. He nearly drowned."

Guilt shuts my anger down. I wasn't there to row, to watch over him. Matt and Bobby are shaking with nerves, like real junkies. Christ, they *are* real junkies.

Bobby blurts out, "We gotta split. Cops came by looking for us."

And, as if it is a cop show, Matt adds, "Gotta make ourselves invisible."

Invisible. Exactly. I don't so much as nod as they push their way out into the all too visible decay of the world.

The reflection in the glass of the hospital door scares me. It's my father, face pale as a mushroom, circles under his eyes dark as dirt. I shake my head hard and enter the bright lobby, like a zombie on speed. A nurse stops me. She doesn't speak English. She escorts me to the front desk. The nurse there asks in English if she may help me.

I can't even get a simple question out. Panic jolts each syllable, syntax goes haywire. I must sound deranged. Man, I am deranged. Sobs erupt from my gut. I finally get Pete's name out, if not a fully formed question: "Peter Ichiro Lac." I pause before adding, "American."

"Are you family?" She doesn't blink her bloodshot eyes as she waits for me to reply. I don't know why I don't lie and tell her that yes, I am family, yes, I am his brother. She clarifies: "Only family members and partners are allowed in intensive care." She can read something in my gestures or on my face that's maybe afraid to admit anything, so she asks, "Are you his partner?" She's trying to help me. She directs this question to me matter-of-factly, and yet I swear, also with some kind of huge understanding that I don't even begin to understand about myself. I'd been acting like she was a generic nurse, like on TV, the one you know isn't going to have a big part. I'm so wrong. She knows love and I know nothing. She repeats, "Are you his partner?" And then, maybe thinking I don't understand what that might mean, she adds, "His lover?"

The word reverberates inside my head. I don't understand why, but it feels almost as right as it does wrong. I answer, frantic and hesitant all at the same time, "Yes. Yes, I am."

She nods. Her acknowledgment nearly floors me. She tells me the room number then walks me to a bank of elevators. I ride up, feeling calmer, thanks to her, than when I entered the hospital.

I stop at the threshold of the room. I can't see Pete. The bed's swarmed by nurses and doctors. The situation can't be good. They've placed a balloon thing above the bed. One doctor—bald and baby-faced—has a deep, serious look as he presses the balloon slowly between his palms until all the air gets pushed out. The balloon fills again, and he repeats the action. He does this three times. I move into the room, about halfway to the bed. Though Pete's features are obstructed by tubes, I can make out his root beer hair. His strong body looks so small and weak under the white sheets. God, he'd hate to be tucked in like this. After some minutes, the doctors and one of the nurses turn to leave. Each of them notices me. They seem wary, like I'm going to do something.

The doctor with the baby face does stop, even as the others continue on their way out of the room. "Are you with Mr. Lac?"

I manage a nod.

He looks me right in the eye. "Mr. Lac nearly drowned, in the middle of the Øresund. It was his good fortune that a fishing boat happened along. However, he had been unconscious for a time and his lungs filled with water."

He pauses, maybe waiting for me to respond. I only blink—one, two, three times.

"Mr. Lac's recovery is complicated by heroin in his bloodstream. We have administered a narcotic antagonist, or antidote, but we will not know for twenty-four to forty-eight hours whether it has worked or not. The heroin has slowed his breathing and lowered his blood pressure dramatically. He is in a coma. We have contacted his family in America."

Coma? The word causes something inside of me to collapse. I try to imagine the Lacs getting the news. I want to tell Mrs. Lac that I'm sorry for not keeping my promise to her. Watching out for Pete. That's what I was supposed to do. I broke my promise, I failed.

I nod to the doctor as I move to the bedside. Pete's lips and fingernails have turned an even darker blue than when he came out of San Francisco Bay. They're cobalt. I see myself reacting in a hundred different ways. I see myself standing there, gripping the metal bed railing, sniffling politely. I see myself throwing my body on top of his and wailing like one of those women from the Middle East you see on the news when her son or husband or brother has been killed. I also see the whole range of reactions between the two. And yet, here I stand, dry-eyed, mind shattered, for what seems like hours. The light from the window has moved a good ways across the room by the time I shift my weight from one foot to the other. At some point, I lift my hand and reach for him. With my index finger, I brush his lower lip, then draw the finger back to touch my own. His eyes flutter briefly. It's like there are no pupils. I rest my hand on his forearm and stand like that until the sunlight disappears from the room.

Doctors, nurses, orderlies come and go. At one point a guy nurse—they have guy nurses here—shows me to a chair in the near corner. I have this crazy thought that once the doctors and nurses have all gone, I'll kiss Pete on the lips and he'll wake up.

I'm now alone with him. I stand up, lean over his body and sweep the wave of hair from his forehead. I put my mouth close to his ear and whisper, "I'm sorry." I don't know how to pray, except for the prayers in Latin I was forced to learn as an altar boy. I try one, just in case: *"Ave Maria, gratia plena, Dominus tecum . . ."* I don't even remember what it means, feel it's meaningless anyway, and that I'm a hypocrite.

A nurse dims the lights, leaves. I'm desperate to bust out of this hospital scene. I want to make it all different, make it somehow have more meaning, or at least a different meaning. I want to transcend all that goes with *hospital*. Weird as it sounds, the desire to transcend is what brought me to punk—brought *us* to punk—and this situation seems to be the harshest example of how we're all bound to this earth and its expectations, of how we can't transcend a thing. Bed, machines, people in white, worry, grief. Nothing.

I'm thinking music might at least change the silence, the expected silence. I sing, meekly at first:

Maybe I come off strong and silent, but I'm not that type.
Maybe I come off strong and silent, but inside me there's a lot
    to fight.

One day I'm gonna break out and be strong and loud.
One day I'm gonna break out and be strong and loud.
One day I'm gonna be strong and break this world that shuts
    me down,
Then I'll be loud, I'll be loud, I'll be loud, loud, loud . . .

I somehow succeed in making our loudest song sound like a lullaby. I just have to believe Pete heard me. I sit down and stare into his expressionless face. A different nurse comes in every fifteen minutes or so to check on him. One brings me a footstool and a blanket. Pete's face looks different from when he's asleep. It's stiller—not a flicker, not a twitch—as if there aren't any dreams rippling under the surface. I promise out loud, "If you pull through, I'll never leave your side." I make myself sick with my promises.

The night hours don't go slow, don't go fast. A continual present. Sleepless. Dawn comes on like a headache. The sun looks crooked. I wince like a vampire. I get up to take a leak. In the mirror, I see my father again and I avoid him. An orderly brings me breakfast. I drink the tea. The day continues on without me. Nurses, doctors, and others do what they do. People are nice to me, they really are. They bring meals even though I don't eat them. The water tastes good, though. I'm pissed off at Bobby and Matt for abandoning me and Pete, but even still, I'd like to see them now. There's a part of me that can't blame them. It's a foreign country. No one wants to land in prison overseas.

It's afternoon. I go into the bathroom, splash cold water on my face, sit on the toilet. When I come out, the sun's going down. I must have fallen asleep. My blood's turned to sand.

It's past midnight. I stand up and start shaking, like it's cold in the room, except it's not. I move right up against the bed. The machines show Pete is breathing, though I can't see it, can't hear it. I put my ear right down to his mouth and there I do feel it, so shallow, so faint—but it is there, and it is warm.

Something inside me that's so outside of how I think of myself gets me to lift my T-shirt up. Then, carefully, because of all the tubes and wires, I raise Pete's left arm and, as gentle as I know how, open his curled hand and move his palm across my belly. Can't believe I'm doing this, but I swear I sense something from inside of him, like a car's ignition clicking on a subzero morning. I'm desperate. I need to do something that will bring him back. Right there—with night nurses and orderlies passing by the open door—I unzip my jeans. I move Pete's hand down from my abdomen so he's cupping my balls. At the same time, I slip my hand under the sheets and under his hospital gown to cup his. The heat of him is so beautiful. I whisper, "I swear I wasn't lying, Pete, about being with you forever. It was negligence. That's what it was. I was negligent. I promise I won't let you down again." The makeshift ritual over, I tuck my equipment back in, zip up, and slouch back into the chair. The nurses still come and go, the sun rises, I keep my vigil, and everything feels good.

JULY 1994, DANIEL

We sail past South Island, then around Sand Island. At three nautical miles I of course cannot see Michael, but I can tell he is out herding by the dozens of dots moving in perfect unison down from the mountainside and over to the headland. I am certain he sees us or, rather, he sees the *First Movement's* spinnaker and probably has for some time. As we sail closer in, navigating all the way past Sand Island, his vague figure, followed by black-and-white splashes of dog, heads down to the landing. At a quarter nautical mile, Michael appears standing on the ledge, arms akimbo, wind whipping his black hair across his face. Alpha and Omega leap around him. He has certainly noticed someone else on deck with me, though his expression remains inscrutable. As we coast in, he steps forward to grab the prow, steadying the craft while I lash it to the cleats bolted into the rock. At this moment of contact, I am afraid the whole idea has been a great mistake. Presumptuous and arrogant of me to think I could bring Michael out into the world, to think this stranger—this strange boy—could be a tool to help me do it. Without a word, Michael takes the luggage Isaac and I lift up to him. The boat is rocking sharply. He gives me his hand. Isaac doesn't wait, leaping to the landing on his own. Michael embraces me less spontaneously than usual. He says nothing, not even to ask who this person is who has arrived with me. He glances over at Isaac who is now kneeling, wrapping his arms around the dogs and letting them lap at his face. Isaac is laughing, Michael is not. I force a smile.

"The trip came up all of a sudden," I start to explain, "and a letter would not have reached you in time." This is not really an explanation at all. I am arriving a month early and, more significantly, with someone else, two things I have never done before. In addition, he knows I am not a man of surprises. To the contrary, I am a man of plans, agendas, schedules. "This is Isaac Burns," I say, pausing slightly, "the one who sent you a letter, the writer interested in the No Names."

Michael's expression leaches the light out of the sky.

Isaac glances up at us, smiling, hopeful. Perhaps a smidgin of anxiety flickers in his eyes as he offers a quintessentially American, "Hey."

Michael responds with less than half a nod. He lifts the baggage and turns away, carrying it up to the house. The dogs bound after him.

This is going to be more difficult than I had anticipated. Under Michael's ice I am certain that rage is ablaze. He has undoubtedly woven a whole conspiracy theory together in his head as he tries to make sense of how this letter writer from his hometown even found me, let alone convinced me to bring him here to violate his sanctuary.

I look at Isaac, force a smile, then offer a hearty, "Let's go!" We lift the remaining bags and head up after Michael and the dogs.

A few splashes of rain come with the wind, followed by enormous black clouds galloping in across the empty sky. By the time we get to the door, a deluge is upon us.

Daniel and I duck into the cottage just as the sky lets everything go. The dogs scurry in between our legs. *Click, click, click* of nails on the floor.

This place is unbelievable. Would give the Flintstones a run for their money. Stone floor, stone walls, and all the furniture looks dinosaur-proof.

Mike (or is it *Michael,* as Daniel says?) has disappeared. Daniel shows me to the room where I'll be staying, tells me to relax and make myself at home while he prepares dinner. Obviously, I want Mike to like me, though the chances of that aren't looking too good. I start unpacking. I need to figure out how I got here. *Here,* as in the middle of the ocean, but also *here,* as in this insane situation. Insane, for sure, and of my own making.

The only thing Daniel told me when I met him at the marina back in Copenhagen was that we had a four-day voyage ahead of us, if the weather remained fair, but more likely five. I didn't have a clue as to where we were headed, except toward the setting sun. The name Færoes meant nothing to me. He taught me how to trim the sails and to take the helm so I could spell him. This was probably more responsibility than I've been given in the entire nineteen years of my pampered existence. Watching him deal with the forces of wind and ocean made me respect him big-time.

The voyage was, I suppose, the experience of a lifetime, or it probably would have been to most anyone else. Seeing a pod of white-sided dolphins arcing along starboard, or a blue shark slowly circling the boat for hours and stuff like that was pretty cool, but to be honest, I got unbelievably bored by day two. I have the attention span of a macaque. Even with some not insignificant squalls and one fierce storm, I was like the whiny kid in the backseat on vacation, wondering are we there yet, wherever *there* was. When I asked Daniel if he ever got bored at sea, he answered, without a shred of doubt or irony, "No, not at all. Being out here is a time for me to consider life." From anyone else that would have annoyed the fuck out of me. "Sailing," he went on, "brings me back to myself and out of myself all at once." Man, did I feel superficial.

He went on to describe how sailing on the open sea was like playing a concerto. The sailor being the soloist and the ocean both orchestra and music. Only the sailor, he added, was the most insignificant and foolhardy of musicians, and the ocean was all music together, none of it written down. "And of course, there was much more at stake than a good performance," he concluded, "for instance, your life."

Who says lofty shit like that? Though I've got to admit I'm becoming more and more envious of this guy. He's the living symbol of self-reliance. He's forced me to see that there's something profound about his type and something unprofound about mine. Even realizing this about myself has possibly been a major step.

After nearly three days with no land in sight, the wind completely died. It was like being indoors on a hot summer day with windows closed and no AC. A couple hours into this, Daniel stated the obvious: "We are becalmed." Even so, his old-timey word choice added a note of seriousness to the situation. Becalmed. We were becalmed. This, he explained, in great meteorological detail, was extremely unusual for this zone of ocean. He had experienced dead stillness in the Mediterranean many times, as well as in the Indian Ocean and South Atlantic, but never before here, the stretch of ocean he was, in fact, most familiar with.

During the calm, and the super-sized boredom that went along with it, like any reptile I couldn't help but feel horny big-time. I mean, I wasn't *that* attracted to the guy, but I was not *not* attracted either. In any case, the sorry-no-sex attitude Daniel had shown consistently from the hotel and salt mines back in Hallein to the hotel in Copenhagen continued onboard the *First Movement*. So, what's a guy to do? Well, I broke out the duty-free from my flight over—two liters of cheap-shit Russian vodka—and offered my captain, who was diligently studying scores for the upcoming concert season, a drink.

To my surprise, he said, "That would be lovely." He then added, "No harm in just one, what with this calm and all." Just one. Of course.

So, I poured what probably amounted to two overflowing shots into each of our aluminum cups. He raised his, looked me in the eye, nodded. Before tossing back the poison, we toasted to the wind gods. To my not unexpected disappointment, Daniel immediately went back to his scores. I had with me only the few issues of *Adventure Motorcycle* that I'd already paged to death on the flight over, and so, as any reasonable person would, I continued to drink, slow and steady. And the more I drank, the more Daniel sitting there with no shirt on turned me on, despite the total loser seersucker shorts. Fortunately, or unfortunately, depending on your perspective, my inhibitions lowered with each pour. I lay down on the deck, eyeing him as I fiddled with my junk through my Nautica trunks, none too subtly. Very pretty, I know. Even after I peeled the trunks off and was lying there at half-mast, so to speak, he kept right on with his work. As nonchalantly as a naked guy with a boner possibly could, I asked if he'd like another shot.

He looked up and handed me his cup. "Why not?"

A little victory, or so I thought. I poured for us both, and then, dick bobbing, moseyed on over and handed him his drink, putting on a seductive look plagiarized from Sharon Stone in *Basic Instinct*.

"Thank you," he said, obviously uninterested in faux Stone. Then, as casual as can be, he nodded at my dick. "You can take care of that belowdecks, if you'd like."

Totally humiliated, I stammered, "Um, that's okay," and tugged my trunks back up over my rapidly shrinking dick. What did I expect? I tied the drawstring so tight it burned my waist.

Maybe two hours after my well-earned humiliation, a light breeze began rippling the water. It gradually picked up so we began tightening the sails.

Once underway, Daniel said he wanted to talk.

Uh-oh.

"I should prepare you a little for meeting Michael." It was his scary lecture tone. "What I am about to say may sound harsh; however, I am saying it only because I care about Michael, and I care about you."

Looking toward the blank horizon, I gulped big-time, glad I wasn't sober.

"This is difficult to say," he continued. "You are an attractive, intelligent, and interesting young man, that much is clear, but you have . . . you have a quality—and I do not know how to describe it precisely— that I want to caution you about." His tone was completely disinterested, like he was a marine biologist and I was some invertebrate washed up on the deck that he was about to dissect. "In my language, we have a word for this quality that lacks an English equivalent. It means something like, lacking in seriousness, intent, or direction. It also means having an overly ironic attitude toward life, which, arguably, is not a productive stance given the world in which we live."

A total smackdown. I gripped the gunwale. At this point, I didn't dare turn around to face him. I would rather have thrown myself overboard than meet his eyes.

"I'm saying this now," he went on, solemn as a judge at sentencing, "because I want you to have the best encounter possible with Michael. He is a very serious person. Things have happened to him to make him this way, things he may or may not choose to share with you."

He was saying *Mike* is serious? Unbelievable. Daniel is by far the most serious person I've ever met. I interpreted what he was saying as me being a superficial slacker. And, I had to admit, that was pretty much spot-on. Swallowing this truth was harsh as potassium cyanide, though at some level I had known it for a long time and not done a thing about it. The guy should be a therapist.

I finally dared look over at him. His tanned cheeks reddened as he finished. Was he blushing? That would be out of character. He peered at me, almost nervous, but he's not the nervous type either. Then, one hand steadying the tiller, he leaned under the boom and, with his other hand, patted me on the shoulder. "I'm sorry if I was tough on you." His voice had warmed.

I shook my bowed head. Maybe it's only wishful thinking, but I believe Daniel's words changed me—well, maybe not in a huge way, but at least a little.

Twenty-four hours after the come-to-Jesus-meeting, Daniel called out, "Land ahoy!" like we were in a pirate movie.

I thought that I have good eyes, yet I couldn't make out any-thing on the horizon. Daniel laughed at my confused expression and directed me to look up in the sky. Whoa! There, projected on the cloud bank, shone the ghostly image of a group of mountain-ous islands. A *cloud map*, he called it. Cloud maps, he explained in his science-guy mode, occur when the sun is at a certain angle and enough ice crystals fill the atmosphere to allow for this bizarre phenomenon. It can happen any season, though mostly in winter. We were seeing the islands virtually. This blew even my jaded mind.

Within five hours, the actual Færoes appeared—these out-rageously high peaks jutting straight out of churning ocean. Seabirds everywhere. Puffins! I'd only ever seen one as a stuffed toy. I'm not much of a nature guy, but the enormous flocks of birds were almost inspiring. Villages along the shore of the islands looked lost under the mountains. The houses, painted either white or black, had sod or corrugated-metal roofs. Sheep dotted the lower slopes. We skirted the southern edge of the archipelago, which looked to be about a dozen or more islands, before tacking north between them.

"There it is," Daniel called out, motioning ahead to what appeared to be one of the smaller islands. It looked like an arrowhead point-ing into the sky. He told me that their island is known simply as *the Island* because its actual name is nearly unpronounceable, even to natives, and, unlike all the other island names, is of completely unknown origin. The other islands have simple names that translate to, for example, Bird Island, Colt Island, Horse Island, and the like. His family's island might mean "Echoland" or "Shadowland," but nobody's sure. The Island consists of a solitary, narrow, and very high mountain on the one side and a single flat-topped hill on the other, with a small stretch of low-lying land between the two. In the lowland stands a black house and a black barn, both with green sod roofs that shone almost fluorescent in the bright afternoon sun. It's not close to the other islands but it's also not the farthest out. A place that could go unnoticed. As we got within maybe a couple hundred yards, a man with crow-black hair appeared, heading down from the hill in the company of two black-and-white dogs, some kind of sheepdog. This was obviously Mike. Mike, the invisible object of my desire for all these months, was becoming more and more visible. In some ways he was just a regular looking guy. Kind of boyish for being in his thirties. Wiry. Sharp features. His dark eyes flashed, giving him an intensity that scared me as much as it attracted me. His greeting was definitely not friendly.

It does seem like it was important to have *recounted* the voyage right now, as a kind of *accounting* of myself for myself before facing up to what's here. The here that was here before I arrived and the here that my arrival seems to be in the process of making.

After unpacking, I head back out to the kitchen. In a deep, iron sink Daniel's gutting a monster. I've never seen such a huge fish outside of SeaWorld. Its scales glitter gold and silver and copper.

Daniel turns his head, offers a flaccid smile. He tells me to take a seat on one of the benches at the table. He lifts the slit-open fish. "Michael caught it this morning. Cod." The creature's got an enormous, gaping maw. I'm not too sure about eating it. We don't do much seafood in Hallein. He pours me a glass of dark beer. Now, that I can get into.

Instead of sitting on one of the benches, I kneel on the flagstones where the dogs are sprawled. I start rubbing their gray-spotted, pink bellies. So soft. They wriggle and growl, all happy. A good diversion. Daniel smiles.

"What breed are they?" I ask.

"They're a landrace particular to the Færoes."

"Landrace?"

"Oh? That's an English word, isn't it?" I shrug. "It means they're not exactly a breed but a local mix." They look a little like border collies, black and white, with blue eyes. I lie down on the floor, nuzzling and cuddling them.

"It will take time, don't worry." I'm guessing he means with Michael, not the fish. He lays the fish on a giant cutting board and starts filleting it as he's telling me about the Færoes, the farm, his family's insanely long history here. We're talking Vikings. Like they've lived right here for a freaking millennium. The sheep have been around that long too. Came with them. They're small, like sheep were back then, and not white but all different colors of brown as well as black.

At first, I think Mike might not eat dinner with us, but when Daniel announces it's ready, he appears out of nowhere. We sit down. It's difficult to tell if Mike is sullen or indifferent. The silence gets punctuated by poor Daniel launching small talk. It's awkward, and Daniel's the least awkward person I know.

"Where did you catch the fish?" he asks.

"West side," comes the full answer.

"It's a beauty, and lucky for us. Reports say the cod are even lower this year, and last year was simply awful."

"I guess."

Here we sit, those two on the one bench, me on the other facing them. The dogs are lying perfectly still under the table, raising their eyes without raising their heads whenever I glance down at them.

The mood's gloomy, as if the sky's come inside. It's raining harder than I've ever seen. The bizarre night-sun, now behind clouds, has turned the sky scorching gray. Never thought of gray as scorching before, but this is. Looks like we're shut in for the night. Not that there's really anywhere to go.

After dinner, Mike starts clearing the table. I volunteer to help but Daniel tells me, "Not your first night." He claps me on the shoulder, a friendly gesture that feels a bit forced. "Do you play chess?"

I nod. In my vast experience, when things get weird, doing something beats doing nothing. Which explains the obsession I had all through my growing up with building model cars that had as many pieces as I could find (Mustang LX 5.0 Drag Racer!). Daniel brings out a wooden chess set from a cabinet. Looks hand carved. Like most chess sets, it's medieval style, but I get the feeling this one might actually *be* medieval. We sit at the table playing while Mike washes the dishes. If you were outside looking in, you might think we're the picture of domestic bliss. In my dreams.

When Mike's finished doing dishes, he doesn't say anything as he passes by, the dogs right behind him. And yet, he doesn't retreat to another room, as I thought he might. I guess that's good. He sits down in the main room where we are, but away from us, by the peat stove, the dogs at his feet.

I'm getting creamed at chess. I thought I was good—captain of the high school chess club junior year and all—but Daniel is—no big surprise—a wizard. When he's about to capture a second of my knights, notes start coming from an acoustic guitar. I don't dare look. Like I'm afraid I'll turn to stone if I see the mythic musician I've only ever heard on a record playing for real. The music is objectively gentle, yet it jolts me. As the sound grows more and more complex, it takes hold of me hard and fast, deranging my brain. I glance over. He's sitting there, curled around the instrument. The music sounds classical—what with the intricate fingerpicking—but with more strumming—sometimes hard—blended in. There's a blurring and complicating of chords. Some moments it sounds like two guitars playing. Johnny Ramone meets Segovia! It would, I'm positive, be a mistake to say a word, even to tell him how great his playing sounds. After a while I can't keep my amazement to myself. I look at Daniel with a *like wow!* expression. He smiles. For whole long passages it's as if the air in the room's being carved into a labyrinth that I'm either wandering through or, more likely, lost or trapped in. And yet I feel a strange sort of contentment—contentment shot through with stress, if that's even possible.

More than anything, I want to break up the iceberg in the room. I'm guessing the nocino Mike's sister gave me might just do the trick. When I get checkmated a second game, I excuse myself and go and get the bottle from my suitcase, where it's carefully wrapped in a hoodie. I bring it out and set it on the table. Mike eyes it without pausing in his playing. It's a normal deep-green wine bottle, with a masking tape label that reads Nocino 1970. Then he stops mid-chord. He seems to have registered what the bottle is. He directs his eyes at me. There's nothing in his look that tells me bringing the bottle out was a good idea. I can't help but wince. "Your sister gave it to me," I practically whimper, "to give to you. That is, if I ever saw you."

He sets his guitar on the sideboard, comes over to the table, picks the bottle up, and I swear he's going to break it over my head. Instead, he stands there holding it in both hands, studying the label, even though there's really nothing to study. It's as if he's in a trance.

"She told me you made it," I offer.

Silence and more silence. Poor Daniel glances nervously between the two of us.

Finally, in a voice flat as death, Mike asks, "What is it you want?" He's shaking his head. "What is it you need?"

I open my mouth. Not a single one of the syllables forming will fall out.

"You're not writing any damn book, are you?" He sets the bottle down and leaves the room, the dogs slinking after him.

Daniel looks at me, obviously stressed out. He tells me not to worry, to get some sleep, things will be better in the morning, then follows Mike into the other room.

Not to worry. Get some sleep. Things will be better in the morning. Right. From the get-go, my lie was absurd. If there's no book, then what reason could I possibly have for invading their lives and this island? Nutjob fans are just that, nutjobs. I've got to get out of here. Only one problem: there's no place to go. Literally. The rain's now pounding down harder than ever. I open the door and push my way out into the storm.

JULY 1994, MIKE

Not a minute after I leave the room, Daniel follows. The diplomat. He lies down next to me on the bed, in the dark. We both stay completely still, staring straight up at the ceiling. Rain hammers the window. Lightning flickers across the walls.

After what seems a very long while, he says, "You're a good man, Michael."

Sounds like the prologue to something I don't want to hear. I don't respond. I don't feel remotely like a good man. I don't know what I feel like, let alone what I feel. Lost? Maybe. How easy it was to lose the solitude that had become my existence.

I sense his face turning toward me. I don't look. He whispers, "You have every right to be angry with me."

If it were only that simple.

"I know," he continues, "it was like playing God, me bringing Isaac here unannounced, especially since you had no intention of even replying to his letter. I am sorry for that, I truly am."

He tells the story of their meeting. It's hard to understand how the Daniel I know went along with, or was taken in by, such a bizarre scheme. Was this kid Isaac that convincing? That charming? That clever a charlatan? And his one eye is dark, the other light, giving him an unbalanced appearance. Maybe he *is* unbalanced. Daniel reaches over and presses his palm against my cheek. "With his interest in the band, and the fact he comes from your hometown, I thought he would make a good connection to your past and to the world. At the time it seemed like it might be a good thing."

It's obvious Daniel thinks I need to get a life. I get that, I do. That he somehow saw Isaac as the solution? That makes me angry.

Not angry at Daniel, though, or even at Isaac, but angry with myself for being in this position. For being so dependent. He calls me the caretaker of the Island, but really, he has been taking care of me by letting me stay. For a while now, I've gotten the feeling that Daniel, like any rational person, thinks it would be better for me if I left the Island, that fifteen years ought to be enough time wasted in any one life. Yes, I've gotten the feeling but have ignored it. He should have just asked me to leave. I wish he had. No, he would never have asked me to leave, he would have asked me to come live with him in Copenhagen. I couldn't do that. That wouldn't be us. Whatever us implies. After passing through miles of silence, I manage to say, "Okay," though I'm not sure what I mean by that, not sure what I'm okaying.

"Don't worry," he assures me, "Isaac and I will be leaving in a couple of days."

Thunder rattles the windowpanes. Daniel rolls onto his side to face me. Lightning flashes through the water flowing down the glass, turning his face to marble, melted marble. "Okay," I repeat. I touch his shoulder and he rolls onto his other side so I can wrap around him. It's been a long time.

It's four o'clock and I'm wide awake. What with the certainty of my life now so uncertain. Certainty? Or do I really mean security? Maybe Daniel's unspoken conclusion is right. Maybe I am just hiding out here, keeping myself safe from the world, living the fairy tale of being a shepherd. His shepherd. Maybe it's as simple as that: I'm afraid. I should just get up now. Let Daniel get some rest undisturbed by my restlessness.

The dense clouds have begun to break up. The sun pushes through, revealing the mountain's outline. As gently as I can, I push a lock of Daniel's hair away from his closed eyes and tuck it behind his ear. Then I pull on my underwear, jeans, and flannel shirt and leave the room, Alpha and Omega close behind.

Something's not right. The lights are all on and the door to Isaac's room is wide open. I go over and peer in. Bed hasn't been slept in. I say his name. No answer. I slip on socks and work boots, go outside with the dogs and look around, calling for him. The only answer is the wind, the waves. The dogs bound around the farm. Now I'm worried. As small an island as this may be, it still holds plenty of dangers. Especially at night. Especially for someone unfamiliar with the network of ravines, crevices, cliffs. I don't understand what happened, or at least not exactly. Do I come off as so hateful and inhuman that he would run out into the night in a strange place in the middle of a storm? I didn't tell him to get out, yet somehow, I communicated that. I've put him in danger.

The sky's clearing fast. The night-sun becomes a morning one.

I head over to the barn, turn on the lone overhead light dangling there, and call his name. Only echo. I even climb up into the loft to look around. Empty.

A terrifying thought hits me: he has tried to sail away. I hurry with the dogs down to the boat-launch. The rowboat and the sailboat are both still there. A huge relief. Trying to cross to Stream Island in a storm like last night's would be certain death, even for an experienced sailor.

The dogs and I make several widening circles beyond the farmyard. I continue calling for Isaac. This is so crazy. Sure, I was angry, but his reaction is over the top. I should go wake Daniel up. As I'm about to head back to the house, the dogs start barking at me decisively as they move in the opposite direction. They're demanding I follow. They start up the base of the mountain. No way could he have made it up the mountain in that storm. I call them back, and they do come but only to bark even more insistently for me to come their way. I give in. More like goats than dogs, Alpha and Omega leap easily from rock to rock, up the steep, rain-slick incline, as I struggle and strain behind them. The waterfall's gushing wildly at our side from all the rain, covering us in spray. Definitely tougher climbing in these conditions. Luckily, I know the mountain well. By the time we make it to the top of the waterfall—about three-quarters of the way to the summit—I'm exhausted. I bend over to catch my breath.

My guides now lead me toward what appears to be a small gap in the face of the sunlit cliff that wasn't there before. There's a pile of gravel and mud in front of it. The rain has washed part of the slope away, exposing what, I can now see as I get closer, is definitely an opening. The dogs are wagging their tails fiercely as they poke their heads in. They keep looking back at me, crazy with excitement. I bend low, stepping into what turns out to be a small cave. Sunlight pushes its way around me. I have to crouch in order to move farther in. And there, to my huge relief, curled up among the mossy stones, is Isaac, asleep, breathing deeply. A single ray of sun lights him. The space isn't much wider than his body. Something about him lying here, soaking wet, face flushed, makes it hard to think of him as my antagonist. The whole mystery (if I can call it that) of his presence in my world still disturbs me, but no way did I want him to come to harm. I move all the way into the cave, kneel and touch his shoulder. I have to nudge him a few times before he opens his eyes. It takes a moment or two for him to orient himself and to recognize me.

"Come on," is all I say. "Let's go. You need dry clothes, you need some rest." I don't ask all the questions filling my head. I stick to the here and now.

Alpha and Omega push in on either side of me and start licking him all over. He laughs, so full, so natural. I help him up and out of the cave, and let the dogs lead us back down the mountainside to the house.

As we walk in the door, Daniel greets us with a complicated smile. He can only guess what has happened and can probably tell by my expression I don't want to get into any of it in front of Isaac. Not what happened, not what I'm thinking, not what I'm feeling. Isaac says he's sorry about everything. He offers that he left the house because he needed someplace to think, and besides, he laughs, he's a rock climber and couldn't resist the mountain. His sense of humor bothers me. Or maybe I'm just envious that he can find anything at all humorous about the situation. Pete always said I take everything too seriously. I get Isaac a towel and tell him to go warm up in the shower before getting some rest.

When I woke up, I could hear Mike and Daniel talking in the other room. They're headed out to reapply peat tar to the windward side of the barn. *Peat tar, windward, barn.* So outside my reality. After the two of them have gone, I crawl out of bed, back still stiff from lying in the cave. I pull on my basketball shorts and head to the bathroom on the other side of the house. The shorts and pissing feel familiar, while the rest of me feels unfamiliar.

On my way back, a guitar on a shelf right below the ceiling catches my eye. The wood glows in the afternoon light. I hadn't noticed it before. It's not the one Mike was playing. As with nearly everything else here, it looks ancient, like it belongs in a museum and shouldn't be touched. It distracts me the way forbidden things tend to. Not that anyone said I couldn't play it, but no one said I could, either. More than a distraction, it starts acting like juju on me. Good juju or bad juju, can't tell. I step away from it, I step back toward it. I can't help myself. I get a chair, climb up and reach to take the instrument down. The rose-colored wood has been worn almost white in places, with a fine web of cracks over the entire surface. The body's smaller than a modern guitar, the neck thinner. The strings appear to be gut, not nylon or steel like I'm used to. I run my fingers across the strings a few times and automatically start tuning it. The sound's not bad at all. I diddle around, playing a few chords, some scales. It's not as loud as a modern guitar, though the sound seems more focused. I like it. My fingers aren't working quite the way I want them to, maybe because the strings are closer together. The windows and doors are all open, so I play softly, like it's a secret. Daniel and Mike should be a while yet with their painting.

I play stray notes, a few random chords, searching for some music that will anchor me. I eventually work into the Bowie covers I'd been learning with Rongo. Bowie seems right for this alternative universe and this alternative version of me. I play through my repertoire, all obvious choices: "Changes," "Heroes," "The Man Who Sold the World," "Rebel, Rebel," "Space Oddity."

In the middle of a second time through "Changes," I hear Mike and Daniel. I'd fallen so deep into the zone that they've managed to make it nearly to the doorway without me noticing. I stop playing, like I've been busted. They stand at the threshold, jeans and T-shirts splattered with the tarry paint, both kind of staring at me. A streak runs down Mike's left cheek, like the tracks of a black tear. A small yellow bird—a kind I've never seen before—lands on top of the open door behind them, cocking its head this way and that, as if trying to figure the situation out. Daniel sort of smiles. Mike doesn't even sort of smile. He looks pissed off, like I've disrespected him by playing in his space and/or playing that guitar. Another massive mistake.

Daniel's eyes dart to Mike before he moves across the room, announcing weakly, "I am going to get cleaned up and start preparing some food." Not sure what his strategy is, other than escaping the next chapter in this disaster.

Mike stays planted where he is for precisely an eon.

When he finally speaks, it's to tell me to go on. He steps into the room. I look up at him, confused, then back down at the strings. He repeats, "Go on." I swallow hard, then start where I left off:

I watch the ripples change their size
But never leave the stream
Of warm impermanence and
So the days float through my eyes
But still the days seem the same . . .

I stare down into the sound hole in order to avoid his eyes, otherwise I wouldn't be able to play at all. I can sense that he has now moved further into the room.

Before I see it, I hear it. For fuck's sake, he's joining in. His guitar sounds bigger and mellower than this one. I can't believe it, can't believe this great blank in my life is getting filled in right here, right now. What turned things around? He sits on the bench beside me, playing, though not singing. I don't stop. This is hell, this is nirvana.

I shift my gaze from the sound hole slightly, now focusing on the iridescent rosette inlay that outlines it.

As the song is coming to an end, he says, "Pick another."

By now Daniel's in the kitchen, in clean clothes, working quietly.

I start to ask Mike if he knows "The Man Who Sold the World," but before I can get the whole title out, he answers, "Don't worry." I start, and he follows me for a few measures. It's clear he knows the song way better than I do.

We finish playing all the Bowie I know. When I tell him that, he starts in on "Starman," solo. I'm hearing my idol live. He makes the song all his own. His version sounds like Gregorian chant for the age we're in, if that doesn't sound too crazy. And when he sings,

> There's a starman waiting in the sky
> He'd like to come and meet us
> But he thinks he'd blow our minds
> There's a starman waiting in the sky
> He's told us not to blow it
> Cause he knows it's all worthwhile . . .

I know that if I believed in blessings then I am blessed.

We play for more than an hour, till Daniel calls us to dinner. I could go on forever. The meal set before us comes off as totally abstract. A golden still life. Mackerel. Potatoes. Rutabaga. Beer. Aquavit. It's as if the supper symbolizes that we—or really, only I—have left the familiar world behind. Under Daniel's usual calm expression, I think I can detect he's busting-out happy that Mike and I are finally hitting it off. It's in his eyes—the way they blink a little more frequently—and in his mouth—the way it's slightly tauter, as if he's holding back a grin. This is, I'll bet, how Daniel does excited. He asks, "Why haven't you said you play guitar?"

"I guess I was a little intimidated, what with all you guys have accomplished."

It's Mike who says, "You play well. I mean it." I'm blown away.

It's only when we're well into our third beers that I ask Mike if the No Names did any Bowie covers.

He doesn't get mad or anything, but he does say with some finality, "Hey, let's stick with the present."

So, we talk Bowie. Daniel also seems to be something of an expert. It's maybe the best night of my life, hanging out in this otherworld with these two out-of-this-world musicians, almost like we're friends.

At one point, Mike asks what he asked the first night, though this time without the scornful edge, "You're not writing a book, are you?" Before I can answer, he adds, "I don't mean to be a jerk, it's just that I've moved on. It's cool you're into the band, but it's cooler playing together with you in the present."

That it's cool to be playing with me is by far the most radical thing anyone's ever said to me.

At the end of the meal, Mike gets up and brings the bottle of nocino out from one of the kitchen cupboards, along with three glasses. He was like twelve when the liqueur was made, and I was still five years away from being born. He pours, we toast. If we aren't *talking* about the past, at least we are *drinking* it, and it is thick and dark and strong.

Mike and I have been playing music together for over a week now. He got into classical after he got to the Island, through Daniel of course. But Daniel never forced it on him. Mike wanted to learn to read music and Daniel was, he laughed, patient enough to teach him. He started him with *Bridges: Guitar Repertoire and Etudes* from the Royal Conservatory of Music. He then gave him modified arrangements of Bach chorales. Stuff he'd never heard about. Once he managed to read music, every time he played, especially the Bach, he got so calm it was like entering into a trance. He would spend maybe a hundred hours perfecting just one of the chorales. Daniel also gave him something called Carulli country dances, as well as Giuliani arpeggio studies and Ferrer's *Three Easy Pieces*. I'm learning the Giuliani from him.

Mike and I usually play right after breakfast, before we begin doing work around the farm, then again after dinner. He's been showing me how the farm runs, which is cool. I've never done a chore in my life and am kind of liking it. Maybe just because it's a novelty? I fantasize Suburb Kid turning Country Boy with these guys. He tells me that being a shepherd is easier than you might think. Or at least it is here. No predators and no neighbors, so no need for fences. And though the winters do get cold and dark, they're not bitter like back home. There's green grass for grazing year-round and clean water that never freezes from the stream pouring down the mountain. Mostly what makes the work easy, though, are the dogs. On command, Alpha and Omega herd the three dozen sheep up and down the mountain or across the headland to switch grazing areas. It's a beautiful thing to watch. The instant the dogs hup to the whole herd shifts on the mountainside, like a flock of birds against the sky. Twice a year they get herded into the barn for two days so the wool's dry for shearing. Once a week or so during winter he'll give them hay or a few buckets of oats with molasses to supplement their diet. He also has to replace the salt lick when they've worn it down. He stresses that it's easy work, though Daniel acts like it's a big deal and pays him more than it's probably worth.

Delusional as the idea most definitely is, still I'm getting my hopes up for a new life here. Two days ago, Daniel sailed back to Copenhagen. He has big concerts coming up in Milan and Rome. Before he left, he asked me if I'd like to stay on the Island with Mike for the month he'd be away or head back to Copenhagen with him. I guess he'd already talked to Mike because he asked me this right in front of him, at breakfast. I set my coffee cup down on the table very slowly to give myself time to process this, and then, trying not to sound too pumped, I told him, that yes, I wouldn't mind staying. The best part was when Mike added, "Cool," and not *cool* as in *I'm okay with that* but *cool* as in *that sounds good.* Or at least that's how I interpreted it.

Today, Mike and I got up from an after-breakfast jam session to herd the sheep from the headland over to the mountainside. The hike's not all that far, but the terrain's rocky and uneven so it takes longer than you'd think. Alpha and Omega whirl around us, eager to do Mike's bidding. When he says *heel,* they're right at his side, in lock-step. We spot the sheep gathered in a depression where they've gone for protection from the wind. With the slightest move of his hand, Mike signals the dogs to get down, and they do, crawling along rap-idly on their bellies, like snipers. As we get nearer, he gives another signal and they leap forward, Alpha going to one side of the flock, Omega to the other. The sheep lift their heads from grazing, freeze for a second, then stampede. It's only a couple of seconds before the dogs get control of the chaos. They move the herd from side to side, at will, or, really, at Mike's will. He signals them to take the herd to the left, to the right, then toward us, every single sheep in unison. Sheep and dogs speed past, the pounding of hooves reverberating through the ground.

Right as Mike whistles for the dogs to slow the herd down, a lamb skittering along the edge of a ravine slips. The little guy free-falls, turning over once, twice, before landing in a heap on rocks about fifty feet below. He—and I don't know why but I'm thinking it's a he—is bleating. Sounds like a human baby.

In a flash I'm over the edge, scrambling down the side. I catch a glimpse of Mike. He looks like he's about to signal with his arms or shout for me to stop. When I reach the stony bottom, the brown sugar lamb looks at me with those freaky eyes sheep have—rectangular pupils, yellowish irises—like he's pleading for help. He's wedged between several boulders, can't move. As careful as I can, I move aside each lichen-encrusted hunk of rock, gently pull-ing the soft body into my arms. His bleating calms as I whisper, "Everything's going to be okay, okay," over and over again, my lips touching his soft ear. I lift him up and place him around my neck—front legs over one shoulder, hind legs over the other—to free my hands for the climb.

When I get to the top, Mike reaches down and lifts the lamb from my shoulders. He sits on the ground, cross-legged, the injured baby in his lap. I kneel in front of them.

"You could've killed yourself the way you flew down there." Mike looks at me, then at the lamb. "Once in a while we lose one." He coughs into his hand. "All the cliffs." He sweeps his arm in a half circle over the landscape. "Seems both front legs are broken. Maybe his back, too."

"What should we do?"

"Afraid there's not much we can do."

"Take him to the vet?"

"Isn't one."

"There's got to be something we can do."

He shakes his head, probably more a reaction to the whine in my voice than anything else. Super quiet now, he says, "There's nothing we can do."

"Please . . ." Then, seeing what looks to be disappointment in Mike's eyes, I stop. I glance around at the cliffs, the ocean, the sky. Since coming to the Island, I'm maybe finally starting to understand, at least a little, a more real world than the Heights. I've never even had a dog or a cat to put down. For the first time in my sheltered life, I'm faced with death—and it's not even a human death—and I can't deal. That part of me that's so good at manipulating to get what I want is about to start begging. It's practically involuntary. Miraculously, though, I manage to shut that part down. One little victory. I'm beginning to learn there are forces greater than my needs that make up the world. Without a word, I lift the lamb gently from Mike's lap, cradle it in my arms, and we head back toward the barn. The dogs already have the rest of the flock up the mountain, grazing fresh grass.

At the barn door, Mike says, "I'll take it from here." He reaches for the lamb.

I keep hold of the creature, like its Fate is literally in my hands. "If it's alright, I'd like to come."

Mike flashes an expression I've never seen from him—or really anyone else—before. It's kind of stoic, yet not, kind of compassionate, yet not. It's like a negative of a color photograph. You see both the color and its complement at the same time. As green is to red, so stoicism is to compassion. I swear that's what's crossing his features, and it's beautiful. I follow him into the low, dark space.

"You'll get used to it," he assures me. I like that he's assuming I might be around the Island long enough to get used to it or anything. He leaves to find the one proper knife in the house. I nuzzle my face into the oily wool, loving the soapy smell. The warm body feels so freaking good against my chest. I stick my pinky into the tiny mouth. The lamb starts sucking away like mad, maybe finding some small comfort here at the end of his brief existence.

Mike returns. "Set him up on the shearing table. On his side."

I do.

"Hold the front hooves in your left hand, the rear in your right."

I do.

The lamb seems amazingly—or disturbingly?—calm, like he believes we're helping him. And maybe we are. Mike holds the head gently in the crook of his arm, and then, with one swift motion, pulls the blade along the fleecy throat, from shoulder to shoulder. This living creature convulses three times, blood bubbling fast out of the deep cut before running in smooth scarlet rivers down the brown wool. Then, his life is over and I let go. Mike quickly makes another cut along the underside—from where the ribs join, down to the anus—revealing convolutions of intestine and all the rest of what was bright-red life. He scoops the steaming organs out with bare hands, dropping them into a metal bucket. Next, he swings a rope over a beam, tying a knot that looks like a noose, and hangs the lamb by its hind legs so the rest of the blood can drain out into the bucket.

"Come on," he says, wiping his hands on an old undershirt, and we leave.

Rain on my face wakes me from a nap. I left the window by my head open. A pair of demon clouds swoops away, leaving the sky blank blue. The weather's like that here. Rain, sun—sometimes even snow—all in an afternoon. A new season practically every hour. A warm breeze replaces the cool one and moves through the room. Smoke floats in, though not the usual smell of peat. I close the window, roll out of bed, and go looking for Mike.

I find him out behind the barn, at the stone oven. When he sees me, he nods. From the top of the chimney, he pulls up an iron bar with hooks attached to it from which hang crackling hunks of meat. I smack down my default sentimentality, reminding myself that over the years I've probably eaten herds of anonymous animals in plastic wrap from the supermarket and in boxes from McDonald's and never shed a tear. In the late afternoon light, the fat and skin glint red and orange, purple and black. He places the pieces on a platter, and we go in.

Mike takes the pot of potatoes sitting in hot water on the stove to the sink, drains them, then mashes them with a wooden fork. He opens a can of peas and heats them up in a saucepan. When everything's ready, we go to the table. Mike carves the meat fast and sure, like a pro, putting the first rosy slice on my plate, the second on his. We sit across from each other. He cuts his meat and puts a forkful into his mouth, nodding for me to go ahead, eat. I cut a piece off, breathe deep and urge the fork toward my mouth. In my head, I give thanks to the little guy and eat.

Mike takes a swig of beer. "So, what music you listening to these days?"

I finish chewing, swallow. The meat tastes good and I tell him so before answering. "Well, the No Names for one." I don't say this to be sly. It's the truth.

He snorts. "I mean new stuff."

I lift a few of the soft, pale peas to my mouth, pop them in. "I'm all over the place, though right now I'd say the Dead Kennedys, Pavement. Unwritten Law."

He shakes his head and takes another bite of meat. As he chews, he says, "I'm Rip Van Winkle. Tell me what's going on."

So, I give him the lay of musicland today, thumbnail. My take, of course. "I think you'd be totally simpatico with Pavement. Also, a band called Hüsker Du."

"Ramones still around?"

"You bet!" My enthusiasm more high school cheerleader than jaded punk.

"Good to hear, good to hear."

I talk about more bands, especially the surge of the more political Bad Religion. My mini presentation ends lamenting the death of punk, real punk, what with the likes of Green Day. "They're a big deal," I explain, "but kind of joke with real punkers."

"Sounds like I've missed a lot," he says, maybe wistful but also something else I can't quite name.

"I don't know about that. Everything comes and goes." I look down at my plate. "Ever want to go back?"

He wipes his mouth with his sleeve. "To the music scene?"

I nod.

He finishes his beer and pours us both more before answering, "Not really."

There's a very full full stop there, like I'm not supposed to ask follow-ups.

"Maybe when you get back home you can send me a mixtape of stuff you're into," he offers with a tired smile.

I don't want to think about leaving. Now for sure I can't tell him about my crazy dream of never going back, of staying here with him and Daniel, of making this home. I'm not that stupid. Besides, it's laughable.

When we're done with the feast, we get up, leaving the dishes on the table. We top our glasses off before heading over to the bench. We don't have to say anything; we tune the guitars as we've done every night for nearly two weeks. As usual, he starts. He's been showing me some Fernando Sor etudes. I always tried skipping the classical stuff back home with Rongo, but with Mike it seems kind of cool—that's what desire will do. After the etudes, he shows me a modern Italian classical piece for two guitars. It's intricate and kind of a blast once I get the hang of it.

Maybe because I'm feeling pretty wasted, I really want the forbidden fruit: I want to finally hear him play from *Invisible City*. He said he doesn't want to talk about the past, but I think, spinning out a good length of what Vashti calls my trademark sophistry, music is music, not the same as life. Besides, it would be solo, it would be acoustic. Temptation keeps nudging me. When we're through the Italian piece a second time, I ask, trying to iron the tremor out of my voice, "Would you be cool with showing me some songs from *Invisible City*?"

During the silence that answers me, I'm cringing. After forever, a note or two make a hairline crack on the still air. Then, all of a sudden, it gets totally shattered by the opening chords of "All Your Finery at the Refinery." He delivers the lyrics in that totally honest voice of his, so unchanged, so changed:

Down Petroleum Avenue you come
Wearing all your finery to the refinery,
Down Petroleum Avenue you come
In the Signal Red Triumph from your daddy . . .

He plays the song with the same stark rhythms as on the record, though not at the same frantic speed, and obviously not at the same volume. He sings the words without the full-blown rage from back then, more like a fuck you letter to someone you maybe once dated. His voice has the same hot-cold steel to it, only now there are breaks that weren't there before. The breaks make the voice sound more fragile, but they also make it sound even more profound, even more beautiful. When the song finishes, he's looking at me, but really, it's more like through me.

Lame as it sounds, I mutter, "Thanks." That miserable word stands for all the anxiety and ecstasy swirling around inside of me.

After a pause, without my even asking, he continues playing. More and then more. The whole amazing album. Nonstop. When he's finished the eighth and final song, he bends over his guitar, shaking his head slowly for a long time. I put my arm around him, hoping that gesture says more than another *thanks* or an equally feeble *awesome*.

A minute or so later, he sits up. "Choose one," he says.

"To play?"

He nods. I, of course, know all the words and chords, but still, I'm scared shitless. I automatically choose "Polluted," maybe because it's sort of about our hometown. The chords start out dissonant but it's probably the softest song on a hard album:

Doesn't matter that we never met,
doesn't matter that only two percent
of the universe is visible matter.
What's the matter?
The universe is all made up.
Doesn't matter the universe is all made up
of invisible matter, doesn't matter,
doesn't matter that we never met,
'cause in some other time and space we met
down by a river, down by a river we met
under a river of stars, a river of stars . . .

Mike looks happy and sad and maybe a little shell-shocked all at the same time. As he stands up, he touches me between my shoulder blades. I know to follow him. It's like he's talking from dream: "Let's go find that river of stars."

By now, it's the middle of the night. We stand up. The sleeping dogs stir. As we head to the door they rise and follow. At first, the poor guys appear confused by the hour, but in a sec they're as eager as ever.

As we leave, Mike turns all the lights off. "So the dark will be even bigger."

We walk the rugged half mile to the south side of the Island, the only part, he explains, where the water's shallow enough for kelp to grow. Over the centuries, the Færoese dried enormous stacks of kelp fronds to then bundle and take to burn. No trees, so kelp and peat were the main sources of heat. Stars bubble up from the dark; the Milky Way flows like white water. On the flat, black plane of rock are piles of dried kelp I guess he has harvested. He arranges the long, flat fronds crisscross, until the stack rises nearly shoulder high. The fronds clatter in the wind. He strikes a wooden match on the ground and ignites the lightweight tower at its base. A single frond crackles and sputters for a long time before spreading slowly into a decent flame that slithers its way up. Being so thin and so brittle, you'd expect the fronds to burn fast, but the oil found in kelp, he tells me, makes for a steady burn.

The dogs curl up at the border between firelight and darkness. We sit down on the flat stone beside them and look up into what's more than a river of stars. It's an ocean. We listen to the actual waves unfold on the rocks. We don't say anything for a long time.

Mike places a hand on my shoulder before breaking the silence: "I have something to say." I turn toward him. His eyes appear black as the space between the stars. In a voice as clear as starlight he tells me, "It was good hearing you play that old tune." His features seem to be saying something different, though. It's like he's falling out of this time and place. Now I'm the one thinking it might not be such a great idea to muck around in the past.

I start to speak, then don't. I reach my hand toward him, as if to pull him back into the present, then stop, closing my hand around nothing but air. A monster wave of silence crashes over us. No words drift in to save us. Not knowing what to say or do, I give him a quick kiss on the cheek, as if such a random gesture might help. No reaction at all, so I give it another shot. This time, he takes hold of the back of my head and pulls me in close. He covers my mouth with his and sucks the air right out of me, then pushes every last atom right back in. We fall onto the rock, mouths locked together. The dogs lift their heads, blue eyes reflecting blood red in the firelight. When Mike finally unlatches his mouth from mine, he rolls onto his back. Lying there, he seems to be looking beyond me—to the stars maybe? into the past?—and says in a voice so flat it almost gets lost in the crash of waves, "This is what you wanted, right?"

The moments move past like when you're dreaming and don't know whether the dream's going in the direction of sweet or nightmare. The smart thing would, of course, be to wake up.

He puts his hand on my crotch and holds on. Not rough, not gentle. He pulls me on top of him, kissing with more passion this time, or at least it seems that way. Some version of me that I don't know takes both his arms and raises them over his head, pinning them to the rock. This strange me starts kissing his unshaven face and then on down his throat. I continue, like it's a script I'm reading for the very first time right as I'm doing the scene. Amazed and scared as I am, I start being almost okay with it, start almost liking what's happening. I find myself lifting his T-shirt and licking his chest and underarms. I run my tongue down the line of hair on his belly. He's kind of sighing. I ask if it's okay, and he says, "Do whatever you want." I unbuckle his belt, the leather worn nearly thin as paper, hesitating big-time before unzipping his jeans. I look into his eyes for some signal either way. It doesn't come. I pause before tugging the holey denim down his thighs. He doesn't help. "Okay?" I ask. He murmurs something I can't make out. "What?" I ask. He places one hand on the back of my head and pulls it toward his waist. I start going down on him. I take a deep breath, then exhale long, heating the fly of his briefs. Very slowly, I pull them down. I lick his soft cock a little before taking the head in my mouth. I look up to see how he's doing. His eyes meet mine. At first, they appear glazed over, then in the next instant they're bright, focused. In some micro-split of time, he slams upward, throwing me across the rock shelf. I land on my back. In the next split he's on top of me, straddling me, lifting me up by the front of my shirt and smashing me against the rock ground again and again. I don't even try defending myself. I don't scream or cry out and, warped as it might seem, I don't feel afraid. The dogs get up, circling us with worried looks. And right when I'm thinking how Mike and I are out here totally alone in the middle of the ocean and that he is going to kill me and that maybe no one will find out for a long time, if ever, he stops and, arms outstretched, looks to the sky in what—misery? His face, slick with tears, shines in the firelight. He gasps long and deep then leaps to his feet and tears off into the dark, in the opposite direction of the house, Alpha and Omega bounding after him. I lie by the fire, unable to move.

JULY 1994, MIKE

I wake to Omega lapping at my cheek, Alpha at my hands. I can't remember falling asleep. Flexing my fingers feels like a small miracle. Stretching my limbs, an even bigger one. After just three breaths, I unfortunately recognize where I am. The old shepherd's hut. It's only on the far side of the mountain yet feels like the far side of the planet. Worse, after five breaths I remember how I came to be here. Morning seeps in through cracks between the stones. My body aches from the hard ground. Yet my only complaint is that the aches remind me I still have a body. The dogs go berserk when I finally kick open the weatherworn boards lashed together that serve as a door. The two of them spring out into the light and wind, nostrils quivering with the bounty of the world. I stay where I am, enclosed in stone, sick of my existence. The dogs circle back to see what's become of their master. They lick me all over, paw me. Only then do I rise and leave the windowless shelter, blinking in the sunlight. I cover my face with my hands. If I were to take a dozen paces straight ahead, I'd fall a thousand feet into perfect oblivion and the ocean would forget me before I even broke its surface. That might be a blessing.

All my years on this island I've tried to live without a story—that is, without conflict—by not having contact with anyone besides of course Daniel on his yearly visit. Haven't written a single letter, not even a postcard. But now I've reentered the story of my life in about the most dramatic way possible. I've got to deal with the consequences of what I've done. I've got to go down and find Isaac. I pray to God he's not injured. I've got to let him know I won't harm him anymore, will stay up here until Daniel returns. At the very least he needs to know my remorse, though any words I might come up with can't possibly help him or free me from guilt. Still, I've got to tell him to *not* forgive me.

I scramble down the mountainside, following Alpha and Omega along the fall line they know by instinct. On the rock ledge running along the shore, we pass the circle of snowy ash where I destroyed the brief happiness Isaac had given me. I scoop up a handful of the fine white flakes, releasing it to the wind. I lick my palm, as if it's possible to taste the remains of happiness.

Further along, a pod of pilot whales gathers in close to the cliff. I stop, as if this meeting has been arranged. I lean over the edge, waiting for counsel. They lift their dark, shiny heads out of the water, aiming their sidewise eyes right at me. They click and whistle as if they are wanting to tell me something, something important. I reach down. I can nearly touch them. I can see my reflection on their foreheads. Then, before I can interpret anything at all, they turn in unison and swim away, dorsal fins dipping and rising, dipping and rising. If I could, I would follow them into the deep.

The bright-red door to the house stands wide open. I enter this particular silence I know so well: the light jangling of brass rings on the rod as the curtains sway in the breeze, the fluttering of sheet music on the piano, the soft growling of the ancient refrigerator, the crisp ticking of the grandfather clock. Under and over all of this, the omniscient toning of the ocean. I call Isaac's name. I move through the rooms, making believe I'll find him.

I head down to the landing and curse out loud. Boat's gone, its canvas cover lying in a heap. The ocean's all deep swells flecked with white. Not the best of conditions, not the worst. The thought of the boat capsizing and Isaac's pale body, arms and legs outstretched, turning and turning in the waves, brings me down to zero. I'm stuck here until the postal ferry arrives in two days. I look at Alpha and Omega and urge them on with as much excitement as I can muster, "Let's go! Find Isaac!" They cock their heads, prick their ears. Alpha barks and the two take off. We spend half the day hiking the perimeter of the Island, searching for the boat on the water, aright or capsized, or else ashore, beached or wrecked among the rocks. Nothing.

From the day I got the random letter from Isaac posing as a writer, I sensed danger. But I thought the danger would be to me. As it turns out, I'm the danger. When I saw the *First Movement* approaching—weeks early and unannounced—with someone onboard with Daniel, I knew my world had already changed. I didn't know how. I only knew it had.

But the secret. I couldn't have anticipated it. Or that Daniel kept it from me. That first night they arrived, he lay there in bed with me, talking in a way I took to be sincere, all the while waiting for me to find out on my own. In all our years together, he never showed even the slightest trace of deceit. It's humiliating to think of the two of them conspiring against me.

Playing No Names songs after all these years really got to me. For a while it almost felt good, but it soon began opening too many closed-off spaces and I began free-falling into the past. I had to get out into the night and find the strange comfort of infinity that the stars offer. But when Isaac started throwing rocks into the bonfire, it reminded me too much of the old days down by the river with Pete. I got really depressed. When Isaac kissed me, for some reason I went with the flow. It seemed to take my mind out of itself. It felt okay, it really did. When he started going down on me, I didn't mind that either. Then he looked up into my face and it happened. At first, I couldn't understand. Something in his expression. It was an exact echo of that look Pete had pretty much patented: demon-like and ridiculous and sweet all at the same time. Had to be a hallucination. When he took his mouth off my cock, he broke into a smile. Then everything was lost. That tooth—the overlapping canine, same as both Pete and Mrs. Lac—I hadn't noticed before. With that one detail, a whole resemblance fell into place. And I flipped out: I was about to have sex with Pete's son.

Like a psychopath, I attacked him. Did I beat the hell out of him because I found myself making out with the son of the guy who had, in all but name, been my lover? Or had I been making out with him in the first place because in my subconscious I was making out with my lost lover? My lost lover, who I had never made love with outside of porn. Like a psychopath, I attacked him. Like a deranged figure from one of Pete's ancient myths. That too.

Isaac had hunted me down. I did the math and figured his mother was the girl in the sumac thicket at that kegger down by the river when we were sixteen. Maybe she told him when he turned eighteen and he started searching for his father? Whatever the case may be, with Daniel's help, he deceived me big time. They deceived me. But that in no way justifies what I did. The violence I thought I had detached myself from over these years of seclusion, and was sure had drifted away, had not. Violence still marked me, still *made* me, and this makes me sick.

When the dogs and I finish scouring the Island, I start falling into what feels like dream. I can't stop it. Dream, yet more logical and methodical than any dream. Back at the house, I wrap my bankbook and wallet in three plastic bags. Next, I take my guitar out of its case, kiss the strings, and set it on the shelf next to the parlor guitar. After that, I strip down right there in the kitchen. I strip down, dip my hands into the vat of cooking lard and rub it over my whole body, including head and face, like I saw someone about to swim the English Channel do on TV when I was a kid. The dogs are so perplexed they don't even try to lap the lard from my legs. With kitchen shears I cut off my jeans, put them back on, and secure the plastic packet in the front pocket. I fill the dog bowls with plenty of food and place them outside the door. I go back in and pick up the empty guitar case before heading down to the boat landing. The dogs follow.

From the landing, I heave the case into the ocean. It plunges beneath turbulent gray, then bobs back up and bounces between the waves.

I dive in after it.

The world goes dark.

I wake to light so pure it startles me. White, crystalline. In this cave from another life.

The cold and deep had split my brain wide open. Blacked me out. But something in the universe must have wanted to mess around with me a while longer because, beyond all reason, I came to and resurfaced. I saw the guitar case being tossed among the waves, lunged for it, grabbed ahold. But unlike the coffin Ishmael grabs on to when the *Pequod* sinks at the end of *Moby-Dick,* the guitar case took on water and sank within seconds. By then, the waves had already taken me a couple hundred yards from shore. Weirdly enough, my body felt both numb and hyperaware from the cold. I decided (if you can call such lack of judgment *deciding*) that I was dead *and* that I would go for Stream Island. I flailed amid the waves, completely blind to the massive irony of me, of all people, attempting anything even vaguely resembling an epic swim. Or maybe somewhere in my subconscious I did see the irony and wanted to prove something *in earnest*? But *swim* is too generous a term for what I was doing. I rolled onto my back and floundered my way up and down the steep slopes of water. Must have caught a lucky current, or else maybe the sea eagle floating overhead was a lucky charm, because I was headed across the channel fast. When I finally drifted onto Stream Island, I could barely pull myself over the rocks and out of the water. My body shone fluorescent blue. Streams of blood ran from cuts on my hands and knees I got on the rocks. I was shaking so violently that I could not, no matter how hard I tried, stand up. I felt panicked and drowsy and confused all at the same time. Luckily, the sun was out, making the air warm, at least for the Færoes—somewhere around sixty-five, I'd guess. I spread out on the rocks to recover, only to find myself terrorized by a skua, the meanest bird on earth, according to Daniel. The winged savage dive-bombed me over and over. I was convinced this creature had been sent by unknown gods to rip my eyes out as punishment for my crime. At some point I stopped shaking enough to crawl out of the skua's territory and stumble my way onto a path that led the couple of miles into town.

When people saw this nearly naked blue man staggering through the streets of Tòrshavn, they looked scared. They practically ran from me, like I was Frankenstein's monster. Can't say I blame them.

I made it to the bank and got money from the account Daniel had long ago set up for me (and deposited monthly the too generous pay he gave me as caretaker and shepherd). Then I could buy clothes, food, and passage to Copenhagen. The whole situation seemed kind of comical. The security guard at the bank is probably the only one on the Færoes, and, courtesy of me, he had a red-letter day. Though he doesn't have a gun to draw, he got to grip his nightstick as he approached such a clearly disturbed individual, *the* alien everyone knew of but who no one *knew*. He was practically trembling as he leaned in to take a look at the bankbook that I held out in front of me as proof of my humanity. When I entered the general store for clothes, I waved a fistful of money around as similar proof. The other customers backed away or left the store altogether. I kept repeating the shibboleth, *jeans,* to let the whole store know I was, or at least wanted to be, a member of that sect called humanity. Three panicked clerks jumped to it and got this naked beast outfitted in no time at all, so he might at least resemble a real human being.

In the few hours before the ship was to depart for Copenhagen, I'd hoped to find Isaac there in Tòrshavn. It's really only a village, but still no luck. Then I convinced myself he was already onboard. I boarded but couldn't find him anywhere. Thinking of what might have happened to him crossing the channel from the Island shook me to the core.

I slept the entire day-and-a-half voyage to Copenhagen. The berth was dark—no porthole—dark as my dreams.

Being off the Island and in a city as big as Copenhagen freaked me out. I'd been away from people, buildings, traffic, and all the other things that makes up civilization for too long.

First thing I did was take the train up the Øresund to Daniel's, to see if he, and hopefully Isaac, were there. Strange, how the walk down the hill through the trees to the glass house seemed familiar

after so many years. In the middle of the space, facing the sparkling sound and with his back to me, was someone much shorter
than Daniel, and with dark hair, playing a cello or bass violin.
I hadn't expected this. I stood there for a long while watching the
silent music before knocking. The person turned around abruptly,
apparently bothered by the interruption. He leaned the instrument
against a stand and headed toward me. When he opened the door,
he asked, "Yes?" Not a word more. The crease between his eyes
deepened.

"Is Daniel here?"

"No, he's not." Not exactly forthcoming. Who was this guy? A
musician, obviously. He looked to be about Daniel's and my age,
though his hair had silver in it.

"Do you know when he'll be back?"

"I don't. Now if you'll excuse me." With a nod, he closed the
glass door slowly and turned away. Did he know who I was and
that's why he was so reticent? I stayed there and watched as he
returned to the cello and resumed playing. Only then did I turn
away and walk back up through the woods. Was he the house sitter? A friend? Lover? I've never asked and Daniel's never offered
much about his life outside of us and outside of music.

It got all Kafka mixed with Rip Van Winkle when I showed up at
the US embassy in Copenhagen to get a passport. Explaining that
I'd lost it fifteen years ago and had spent the entire time abroad
without one made the situation sound even weirder than it was. For
a while it seemed I would not only be a man without a country but
a man without an identity. To prove I was me was not a slam dunk.
The battery of questions about the United States and where I had
learned to speak English nearly defeated me. The consular officer
(as he was called) who grilled me looked like a rich college kid. He
claimed my English sounded stilted, the vocabulary unnatural. I
guess that's what years of solitude on top of Mrs. Homer's vocab
lists will do. After two days of interrogation, endless phone calls
and faxes, with a wise-guy smirk the consular officer finally issued

me a passport. Another miracle. The passport, not the smirk. The photo made me look like a refugee from some war-torn country, all wide-eyed, haggard, scared and scary looking. I suppose the war's inside of me.

By far the cheapest flight was to JFK. When I arrived after sleeping across the Atlantic, I didn't mind the two-day Greyhound to Hallein. The bus gave me time to think.

Not much by way of nostalgia hit me as I walked out of the Greyhound Station in what's supposedly my old hometown for the first time in fifteen years. Maybe I'll feel different when I make it out to the Flats? Or maybe it's that I don't have feelings? That maybe I'm not a human being after all?

And so many people! Hard to get used to that. They looked like phantoms as they rushed past me, and I bet I looked the same to them. Maybe we're all phantoms to each other and that's life?

I needed to call Isaac's house, so I went to a newsstand to get some change. I swear the sunken-in man at the register said, "Stan?" Like he thought I was my dad. A hallucination? In any case, I panicked, did an about-face, and ducked into a florist for quarters. Definitely the wrong kind of nostalgia to be mistaken for one's dad, one's dad who's doing life. If that even counts as nostalgia.

I'd tried calling Isaac's house from JFK but an answering machine came on, so I hung up. Answering machines are new to me. They sort of creep me out. I haven't thought through the implications of leaving a message. I found a phone booth on a quiet side street and fed the slot. This time a woman answered. His mother, I suppose. She shouted, "Isaac, it's for you!"—*He's alive!* is all I could think—and he yelled back, "Tell them I'll call back." And so again, I hung up. Right then I decided that whatever it is I'm going to say to him, it's got to be in person.

As I stepped out of the booth, a guy approached me. Needle-thin. Skin so white it looked powdered. Shock of hair as black as a Halloween wig. Clothes black, too. A kabuki version of those French guys back in Copenhagen, I swear. Before I could get away, he floated right up to me, so close I could feel his warm, moist breath on my face as he whispered, "Smack?" With that one syllable, every nerve in my body craved that old euphoria, that old terror. Like Fate, he had come to me out of nowhere, or possibly a nowhere deep inside of me? I'd considered a lot of possible scenarios after leaving the Island, but this was not one of them. Hadn't thought about the junk in forever. "No thank you," I answered. Not sure why, but I wanted to be polite. His resemblance to the Frenchmen aside, I felt for him. As he and I joined together for that one moment in our separate falls through the universe, I felt for him. I turned away, slipping into the neon-dark streets, and I swear he was calling after me, "Welcome home!"

I spun back around. He was nowhere to be seen. Suddenly I needed him. I ran in the direction I thought he'd gone, glancing in shops and doorways. I ran for blocks. I even looked skyward. Did I think he was able to crawl like a vampire up the sides of buildings? He had vanished so completely I wondered if maybe I really had made him up. I stood there, lost in the space between us, lost between now and several thens, between me and several mes. Forgotten thens, forgotten mes. I tried to stop the remembering. I could not.

I was afraid of what I might do out there on the street, what I might do if I found Jean-Kabuki. I had to get away. I thought about Pete and instantly knew I had to come here, to our salt cave, the place of my sweetest memories. I spent the first night huddling and shaking uncontrollably. I huddled and shook just the same as way back then in Copenhagen when I was coming down off a high without another hit in sight. I huddled and shook until, at last, I plummeted into the kind of sleep that felt as if my mind and self were being erased.

Sifting salt dust through my fingers as I woke, I start thinking how I must be a man of miracles. Unasked for miracles. It was a miracle when I found sanctuary on the Island and a miracle when I made it off the Island. For better or for worse, there seems to be some filament flickering inside of me that won't go out.

I hadn't bothered to think about, let alone plan, where I was going to stay when I got back to Hallein. After three nights sleeping in the salt cave, drinking lake water and eating candy bars from duty-free, I forced myself to find an apartment. A major adventure into the real world. I took the cheapest place advertised in the paper. A walk-up on the fourth and top floor of a worn-out brick building the color of dried blood. It has the absurd name *Arkadia* written in fake Greek letters over the entry. It's anything but. Pete would find it funny. The building stands in a neglected pocket of the city that, weirdly enough, is close to downtown. It's at an on-ramp to the freeway and a short two blocks from the metal warehouse where garbage is sent until it gets hauled away on barges. Grit coats the Arkadia inside and out. Oddly, the largest of my three rooms is the closet. It has two windows. I'm using it as my bedroom. Pretty funny, if you think about it. The main room has one window and a kitchenette. The third room's tiny, with a piano window that's got cool stained glass of some kind of flower, maybe a lily. It'll be my music room when I get a new guitar. Much of the caulking has fallen away from the windowpanes and the paint's chipped off the sills. The first time I pulled the blinds up, soot snowed down.

Hallein has changed, and it hasn't. A couple of shiny new skyscrapers make it look like a more prosperous place. The river of course still runs through it and the lake hasn't disappeared, but along the banks of both there are a lot more apartments and condos. It's still tough getting around without a car, so I haven't gotten over to the Flats yet. From what Isaac's letter last year described, it sounds as if my sisters have gone off some sort of deep end—my words, not his. I have to prepare myself mentally. I have to prepare myself for lots of things.

A week after getting back, I found a job. It's two bus transfers then a long walk, so I had to get a car. Found a cheap beater, a '78 Fury, in Spinnaker White (Daniel would dig the color's maritime name). Think cop car. Think rust. I'll give it a new paint job. It'll be nice to paint again. If I'm recalling Plymouth's colors from back then correctly, the Sunfire Yellow or Burgundy Poly would look good.

I searched for jobs you wouldn't need a resume for. High school diploma, gas station attendant, punk rocker, shepherd, don't exactly add up to *career*. I got one busing tables at the Yacht and Country Club, of all places. I went in to apply for the waiter job in the paper but with no prior experience I didn't get it. They had a dishwasher position too, but I could tell by the way the lady doing the hiring half-flirted with me that she thought I'd look good out in the dining room, so she made me busboy, even though they hadn't been advertising for one. It's a wonder what a shave and a haircut (I cut my own) and a clean shirt can do. She suggested I could maybe make the leap to waiter in a few months. In any case, I get a split of the tips. Very first shift, made double wage.

It's my first day off. Finally, a chance to drive out to the Flats. Taking the old river road instead of the freeway. Whereas the ocean kept me in a state of low-grade ecstasy alternating with melancholy, the river only soothes me. There's my nostalgia. The refinery looks bigger than I remember, the houses smaller. A couple of the ramblers along Petroleum Avenue have been boarded up. I turn onto Magnolia. A lot of mailboxes have different names on them now. I drive to the end, to the house I once called *our* house or *my* house. It was never kept up very well but now it's at a whole other level of chaos, like it should probably be condemned. A thicket of junk trees has taken over the yard. Strips of siding and patches of roofing are missing.

I slide out of the Fury, head up the broken concrete walk, and almost walk right in, for a second forgetting I'm a stranger here. Even after all these years the doorbell's still not working. I knock. Both girls come to the door, like they're expecting someone. After fifteen years they actually don't look much different, Anne-Marie maybe a little thinner, Terri maybe a little heavier.

"Jesus Christ," Terri whispers from behind the rusty screen.

"Hey," is all I manage for what should be a big emotional moment.

"We thought you were dead."

Anne-Marie echoes, "We thought you were dead."

I shake my head, as if a response is necessary.

They don't open the door; I don't ask to come in. My heart's a wasteland. In the doorframe are what appear to be bullet holes. I examine closer. They *are* bullet holes. I look past the girls. It doesn't seem like the rooms have been painted since I left, the white walls now the color of smog. I fake cough. Can't help it. "Mom here?"

Terri laughs. Like snakes falling from her mouth.

Anne-Marie starts to clarify, "Haven't seen her since . . ."

And Terri finishes the sentence, ". . . since Dad's funeral."

My knees lock. I stop breathing. I struggle like mad to get words to form but can't stutter even one into the space between us. After forever, I'm able to suck in barely enough air to ask, "When?" I suck in a bit more, "When did Dad die?" Doesn't either of them want to step out and give their little brother a hug, regardless of how cold-blooded and not like a human being he's been since birth? It feels like I'm crying but my eyes are a desert. I once read somewhere that animals don't have tears.

"A good six, seven years ago," Terri answers, lobotomy-calm.

I study their faces, so like mine—pallid, sharply angled, without emotion. "How?" I ask, trying to give it a little feeling. "How'd it happen?"

"Heart attack," they tell me in unison.

"Hadn't seen him since he was sent up," Anne-Marie offers. "He wouldn't see any of us. Not ever. Prison Service called to tell us. There was a funeral."

Terri adds, "What they call the Prison Service Order. Basics only. Surprised Mom came. All dolled up too. You wouldn't have recognized her. Made her money in real estate out there in Vegas. Came and left, just like that." She snaps her fingers.

"Later," Anne-Marie explains, "we got the birthday card we sent her returned, stamped *No forwarding address,* and her phone number was no longer in service. Couldn't find a new listing. That was that. She was wearing a big rock, an engagement ring we supposed. Figured she must've got married, changed her name, moved."

All this seriously depresses me. "Any pictures?" I rub my temples. "Of Mom, I mean." Crazy to ask, but I need something—any kind of proof—to anchor this.

"There is one, from the funeral," Anne-Marie answers, disappearing deep into the house.

She returns with a color snapshot in a white-painted metal frame. She props the screen door open with her hip, holding on to the frame while I look at the picture, as if she's afraid I might snatch it from her. Hard to tell it's Mom, though. Little glares bounce off her from what look to be diamonds. A necklace, a bracelet, earrings, the ring. She's wearing a white lady-suit. "It's leather," Terri announces, as she notices me noticing it. The leather looks thin, soft, fits tight. Her hair's platinum, done up in sort of a beehive. Her natural color's dark, like all of ours. She never used to dye it. Mom a blond, in white leather and diamonds. Now that's something. Like a movie star.

"The diamonds are real," Terri informs me, as if I'm wondering. "All of them. Bought them herself, she wanted us to be sure to know. When Aunt Blondie asked her if they were real, she looked at her, all insulted, and told her, 'Damn straight!' just as proud as proud could be."

Mom's also wearing silver sandals in the picture. Fingernails, toenails, eyelids, all painted silvery white. Everything on her—and done to her—shines so bright against her skin that turned the color of caramel from the sun out there. The picture doesn't look like Mom but it's how I'll remember her because I'm guessing that's how she wants to be remembered.

I know I shouldn't ask if I can keep the picture, so I don't, but then, like she's once again read my mind, Anne-Marie nods, removes it from the frame, and hands it to me. "Here, take it. She'd want you to have it."

"You sure?"

Both girls nod. Then Terri adds, like it's a matter of fact, "You were always her favorite anyways."

"Favorite?" I shake my head. "Doubt it."

"Seriously," Anne-Marie insists, "she always thought you would get the hell out of this place, like she wanted to, and you did. Even though you became a ghost, she was proud. Probably still is."

I can't help but laugh. "That's why she never had a good word to say about me?"

"She treated you rough," Terri says, as if she's the designated explainer, "because she didn't want you to settle for normal stuff. Even through all that was happening with Dad, she thought you were going to be a rock star."

No need to mention how well that worked out.

"You gave her the gumption to finally get the hell out of here." Terri looks at me with an intensity I didn't know she still had, like when she was a girl. "You know, about the only things she took from the house after the funeral were that double-frame picture of Nana and Papa and that record you made."

From the pocket of her smock, Anne-Marie brings out a tissue-thin, light-blue envelope, hands it to me. "Yours," she says, but I already know that. I recognized it instantly.

The screen door closes, them behind it.

I look down at my scuffed work shoes, waiting for I don't know what. Not sure what kind of homecoming I'd expected but maybe more than this. Though really, it's not much different from when I lived here. It's the news of Dad's death—the weight of it—that's making me wish for something else, something more. It makes me sick to the core that I never wrote to him. Like Mrs. Lac said I should. Thought it would be too painful. I'm a selfish bastard. He was the one in pain, way worse pain than mine, and I thought writing to him would be too painful for *me*. No one says a word. Not a question as to where I've been or what I've been up to. I turn to go, then can't, at least not without turning back to ask, "You two okay?"

They look out at me through the screen. Makes me think of those flying squirrels Frankie Champagne from down the street caught when they were kits. He raised them, kept them in a wire-mesh cage that took up half the bedroom he shared with his two brothers. Those squirrel eyes appeared anxious and resigned at the same time—what with no forest and not enough space to fly around in. My sisters again answer in unison, "Sure, we're fine."

"Need anything?"

"We're set," Anne-Marie says. "I'm up to the Family Bargain Center, stocking shelves." She sort of smiles. "It's a job." She wants to assure me that they really are okay, at least moneywise, which is nice of her, it is.

Terri adds, "I'm at a daycare across town. I like working with kids."

These scraps of news come as somewhat of a relief, though I can't stop thinking about the two of them when they were girls. Both of them a whole lot smarter than me. Anne-Marie especially. Great at math. And Terri, she was something else at softball. So damn *ebullient*. She wanted to be an astronaut.

My eye catches the bullet holes again. "What's with those?" I rub my index finger over the splinters.

They both shrug. Then Terri offers, "Whole neighborhood's gone to hell."

I shrug back involuntarily. A family trait, I suppose. "You two take care of yourselves." I walk away, slow, my feet heavy with grief, my whole body drained by a misplaced or long-delayed guilt about family, about home.

"Say," Terri calls out when I'm halfway to the curb, "some kid came by looking for you a few months ago."

I look back again, nod.

Once back in my Spinnaker White boat, I sail away fast, though as soon as I can't see the smokestacks of the refinery anymore, I pull over, get out, walk down, and sit by the sluggish river. I take ·the letter out, unfold it. For some reason, I've got to read it aloud, to the sky:

October 1970

Hey Little Brother,

Believe me, there are lots of places I'd rather be right now than here in the middle of this godforsaken jungle. For instance, with you and Dad and Kev out to Bethel Grove. We had a blast, didn't we? Getting all those walnuts? And that was some battle we had! Though I now have to admit you and Kev really did win. When I get out of here, you'll be about old enough to handle my bike all by yourself, so you won't have to hold on to me for dear life anymore. It was fun anyways, wasn't it? Riding out in the country. Popping wheelies down the river road.

Kind of tough here. One of the guys from our platoon had his butt blown off this past week. Poor fella was in terrible pain, worse than you could imagine. They coptered him out. We hear he's doing okay in the field hospital. Lots of cute nurses there! We're keeping our spirits up playing cards, some touch football (don't want us playing tackle for fear we'll injure ourselves— never mind the grenades!), getting mail and writing letters, etc. And that book Mrs. Homer gave me when I was called up, Leaves of Grass, there's some great stuff in it, though a lot of it's kind of weird too. I'll send it to you when I'm finished.

Lying in my cot the other night, trying to get to sleep, what with all the monkeys chattering away in the trees and machine-gun fire in the distance, I was thinking that hopefully, if someday I'm lucky enough to have a family, I'll have a kid just like you.

You look after Mom and the girls, okay? Dad can't do it alone. Oh, and send me one of your new school pictures (wallet-size, please).

Your Ever-Lovin' Brother,
John

God, I wish he was here. To help me deal with Dad, with Mom. I also wish Daniel was here. As mad as I am at him, still, I wish he was here. We have this bond around grief. He just so happened to be on the Island when he got the news of his parents' death. It was, I believe, in my fourth year. Their plane had crashed over the South China Sea. Abraham rowed over from his place on Sand Island with the news, because he has phone service there and relatives from Copenhagen had called. I of course couldn't understand the Færoese, but Daniel's face turned gray as clay. The two of them stood on the boat landing for the longest time, not saying a word. Eventually, they embraced in a weirdly calm kind of way. Abraham came up to the house and waited while Daniel packed. It was then Daniel told me what had happened. His voice had no emotion. He returned a few weeks later and stayed a whole month, instead of his usual two weeks. It was during that time we grew closer. He wasn't at all dramatic in his grief, but I could tell that he—the most together person I've ever met—was a wreck. I listened to him when he wanted to talk. I stayed by his side. I held him close in bed. I think that being with him through his grief I learned to be a better person, at least a little. I'll never see him again, but he always knew the right words, the right silences. With him, I would have someone to share at least some of my grief with.

Once again, my life is made absurd, and once again it's made that way by me and me alone. I start parking outside Isaac's house—a severe modern place in the Heights—in my cop car. A stakeout. I don't want to go to the door on the chance his mother answers. The image of her underneath Pete has been haunting me of late. He shot his wad in the sand. I'll bet. To make myself less conspicuous, I show up at a different time each day, waiting exactly thirty minutes before leaving. In this neighborhood of luxury imports, the beat-up Fury sticks out like a donkey at the Kentucky Derby. Today's my ninth time. If nothing else, I'm patient. It's a little before ten. The last of the morning mist begins to burn off, giving a strange clarity—a gauzy clarity?—to everything. I've got only four minutes left when one of the three garage doors slowly lifts and out rolls a Kawasaki! I can't believe my eyes. An H1 Mach III, 500cc, a '69 or '70. Virtually identical to John's bike, except for the color. This one's their Peacock Gray; his was Midnight White. Could it possibly be his bike with a new paint job? Isaac's in the saddle. Or I believe it's Isaac. Hard to tell with the helmet on, dark visor down and in full leathers. Maybe he has a brother? Or maybe a ghost's riding this ghost machine? I'm being ridiculous. Of course it's him. And I know it's only a motorcycle yet can't help thinking of it as our dream machine. John's, Pete's, mine. Obviously Isaac's as well. John took a lot of shit for getting a Japanese bike. There weren't many around back then, but he knew engineering and he knew they were better than Hogs or Brit bikes.

I hop out of the Fury as this Maybe-Isaac on this mythic Kawasaki coasts down the driveway and onto the street. At first, I'm not sure he notices me. Then he stops. He doesn't get out of the saddle, simply directs his shiny black insect face toward me. He cocks his head, which I take as a gesture to get on. I do. It's like the kind of dream where you're doing things you wouldn't normally do and know you probably should be afraid but for some reason aren't. He should want to kill me after what I did to him on the Island. Before I'm completely on, he tears off. I grab hold around his waist, like I always did with John. And in fact, the last time I was on a bike was with John. The Kawasaki soars like a hawk in great loops all the way down from the Heights and onto the boulevard. Once we're through town, he turns to head up the lake. On the narrow two-lane we buzz past yellow truck after yellow truck loaded with dusty apples. The wind feels good, the speed feels good. We zip past the Yacht and Country Club. He eventually turns off to the salt mines, dodging around the gate, through thick weeds and out onto the salt flats. He opens up and we fly, the speedometer hitting one-ten. He attacks the ridge at such insane speed I swear we're going to soar on off into the lake, and to tell the truth I wouldn't mind that ending at all. But he stops just short of oblivion, looks back at me, and I think I detect a grin behind the visor. I don't know why he'd be grinning at me, the guy who attacked him. He pulls the helmet off, red hair falling down. And yes, he is grinning, and yes, there's that overlapping canine. We don't greet each other with words, hug, or even handshake. We simply dismount in unison. Even though he's the one who brought us here, I take the lead around the ridge and along the ledge above the water.

I duck into what was Pete's and my favorite cave, Isaac close behind. Here, with him, at the hideaway, the retreat, the hermitage, the sanctuary, where his father and I came to think and be away from everything and to be ourselves. Where we wrote songs, drank, smoked, made out with girls. Where he talked philosophy and history and myths and dreams, while I mostly listened, and where, when I came back to this country, I found refuge. Isaac's over six feet, so his head almost grazes the ceiling. We face each other. He's still grinning. I don't get it. I lift my right hand to touch his left cheek—a gesture of healing I must have copycatted from somewhere—then don't. No touch from me, no matter how gentle, could make amends for what I did. Still, after all these weeks to think about it, I have yet to untangle the words in my head that I need to say.

He's the one to finally break the silence: "You left the Island?"

I know what he means by this statement of fact posed as a question, so I nod.

"Weird," he says, suddenly distracted, looking around the white space, "but I wasn't ever here at the salt mines before Daniel asked me to bring him here."

Not so weird. Kids from the Heights have their luxe cottages and their Yacht and Country Club. They own most of the damn lake. In any case, it's almost impossible to imagine Daniel here. Would be my two worlds crashing together. I take a long, shallow breath. The jumble of words inside me keeps me from taking a deeper one. The words that do manage to come seep out half voiced: "I left so I could make things right. With you."

Isaac wraps his arms around himself, like an Egyptian mummy.

"I don't expect you to forgive me." My voice sounds so full it startles me.

"You left the Island," he repeats, though not as a question this time. The grin has now disappeared. He presses his face into my shoulder, like he's the one who should be sorry.

My instinct is to pull away. I fight it. "Doesn't matter. Important thing is, I'm here. Here to say I'm sorry." Then I add, less abstractly, "For what I did. For attacking you like I did. There's no excuse."

He steps away, head shaking. "No, not true. I made the first move. I was out of line. Sometimes I come on too strong. I do."

"That's not it. I was good with that, really, I was." I lower myself to the cave floor, motioning him to come sit down beside me. He does. "In any case," I continue, "what I did to you aside, I'm almost glad it's come down the way it has." I'm about to rest my hand on his shoulder, then pull back. I fake cough. "It's just that I'm the kind of guy who hates surprises. I'm guessing you and Daniel thought it would be cool for me to find out for myself?"

He looks confused.

I laugh. It's so unlike me to find anything funny about anything, let alone something as life-altering as this, but I can't help it. "It was right out of one of those Greek tragedies Pete loved so much: without knowing it, man sleeps with brother's son. Guess I was supposed to gouge my eyes out or something."

Isaac sits upright, eyes strafing me.

"What?" This time I fake laugh. "It's a metaphor. Pete's not my brother! I'm not your uncle!"

"Are you messing with me?"

"Messing with you?"

He shakes his head. "You're telling me Pete—your Pete—is—"

Now I'm the one who's confused. Completely confused. If someone can both nod and shake their head at the same time, I'm doing just that.

"—is my dad?" His body starts trembling.

This makes no sense at all. Him tracking me down to find some connection with the father he never knew is what this whole debacle is about. Part of me wants to yell at him to cut the head games, but the torment in his voice, in his body, comes off as too real.

He's barely whispering now. "Pete . . . Peter Lac . . . Pete is my dad?"

A paranoid thought comes to me: that Isaac and I are Daniel's marionettes. I steady my bobbling head to a nod, even though now

I'm not sure about anything at all. I inspect his face, wondering if that canine tooth is not, in fact, like a lot of other people's. Maybe we humans find resemblances because we want to find them? Like when everyone used to think Pete and I were brothers. No, it's got to be true. I was there. I was there when Isaac was conceived. His age is pretty much right. He's said his mother went to high school with us. I nod to him again. "You didn't . . . you really didn't know?"

It sounds like he's hyperventilating or about to have a seizure. He shakes his head fast, then asks, "So, you knew her, my mom? Lynn Burns?"

The name sounds familiar. Not sure, yet I nod anyway, I nod before going all vertigo. I have to close my eyes. I somehow manage to tell him, "I didn't know, I didn't know it myself, didn't know Pete had a kid. And I'm positive he didn't know." I close my eyes to steady myself. "I didn't know till the night you and I were by the fire. It hit me like lightning. I swear, I had no idea." I give him the story. Not the whole story, just a brief outline. I lean down to kiss his forehead because I think that's what a human being would do, an avuncular human being, but then, right before my lips make contact, I pull up short.

"Where is he? Where's my father?"

AUGUST 1978, MIKE

One of the monitors is glowing 7:27 a.m. when the machines hooked up to Pete start going berserk, breaking my trance. A platoon of nurses and doctors slips into the room. One NBA-tall doctor starts pounding on Pete's chest. The rest of the crew stand at the ready. A lady doctor leans over and starts performing mouth-to-mouth. I can't help thinking of a scene from one of the Greek myths Pete told me about, where a god molds a person out of clay and a goddess breathes life into him. An orderly rolls a portable machine into the room. They hook it up to Pete. His body convulses. They're shocking him. They shock him two more times, and I believe he's going to rise out of the bed because don't they say magic happens in threes? There's more mouth-to-mouth. Then the goddess doctor stops. The intense focus on Pete lets up, the whole space seems to collapse, and I know he is dead. The myth turns out to be a lie. I stand up. I need to be standing.

The goddess doctor is no longer a goddess doctor but only a woman bending toward me—trying not to appear awkward—to tell me she's sorry, she's so sorry. Two of the nurses say the same. I don't hate them for this convention, for being unable to transcend the scene. I don't, I can't. All my attempts at transcendence have come to nothing, have ended in the misery of *this*: Pete's body, dead, lying on *this* bed, in *this* hospital room. The nurses methodically liberate Pete from the machines. He lies there, unadorned, but in the kaleidoscope of memory arranging and disarranging inside my head he is magnificent. He's laughing and shaking his head at me because I don't know anything about anything. He's doing a three sixty off a picnic table at Dreamland while laying out some arabesque riff on his guitar. He's diving into the sun-shattered lake from the salt caves. He's putting his face close to mine, under starlight, saying, "Promise?"

A young nurse comes in and asks, "Would you like to be alone with your friend?" I barely nod.

She leaves, closing the door gently behind her. I press my left ear against Pete's chest, checking to make sure there really is no life. I stay like this for I don't know how long, paralyzed by regret. If only I had kept following him after the concert or agreed to rent a barge here where we two could live, or to buy a beat-up van and headed east for Katmandu together. If only I had let him quit the band in San Francisco or not sabotaged his attempt to join the Army. When I finally lift my head, I'm blind. Dense colors fill the center of my field of vision. I can see only peripherally. This doesn't freak me out. I take it as punishment from the gods up there on Pete's Olympus, as punishment deserved. I sit down, put my face on the edge of the bed. I want to howl into the sheets but can't.

I wake to voices coming near. I can see normal again. The baby-faced doctor is entering the room and with him Mrs. Lac! I desperately wish I could switch places with Pete. The doctor is guiding her, his hand on her bare upper arm. Time and space get mixed up. She stops short when she sees the body. Then, swift as a bird, she's at the bed, arms outstretched. She falls and covers her son with her body, as if to protect him, her head turned to the side. A deep stillness occupies every square millimeter of her face, and yet this lack of expression expresses the tragedy more profoundly than any expression ever could. I'm as sure as I've ever been of anything: that her feelings are way, way deeper than any I have ever felt or could ever feel. It seems as if she had no idea he was already dead when she arrived at the hospital. She must have gotten the first flight possible from Hallein after hearing he was in a coma. She likely thought she would be at her only child's bedside as he recuperated. She looks at me briefly—less than briefly—and doesn't say a word. Her eyes flash and it's the most terrible thing I've ever seen. The most terrible, and yet, the look contains not a trace of malice, or at least I pray it doesn't. Maybe it holds something like pity? Pity not for me, or not for me only, but pity radiating out for the whole world because a son is dead. Not simply her son but a son for everyone. It's maybe also the look of one betrayed, though she isn't, I think (or hope?) directing it towards me, or not me alone but outwardly, out into the world. That expression—without any intention or any will at all on her part, or so it seems—dismisses me, sends me falling from on high. In that momentless moment, I know for certain that I no longer exist for her. She and Pete are the only two people who have ever even come close to knowing me, and now I've got to face the fact that I have lost them both. I open my mouth. Not a word will form. What does it matter? What could any word do, especially coming from me? She must hear the one cracking sound—barely a syllable—that does fall from my mouth, but she doesn't acknowledge it. I slip out of the room, as one cast out.

After my regular coaching session with the maestro at Symphony Hall, I was heading to the platform for the train home when in an instant my mind short-circuited. There before me, splashed across the evening papers at the kiosk, was a body my eye knew yet my brain refused to acknowledge. It was a grainy news photo, and yet one filled with beauty, with pathos. As my gaze dwelt there, my mind was at last forced to register the image was of Peter, his body—limp, pale, naked—being lifted from a fishing boat.

I grab ahold of a pillar. This image collides with the one of Peter in my head, of him swimming in the Øresund. There, he was so vital, so strong, pulling me into the cold waves with him and afterwards holding onto me for warmth as we lay on the sun-soaked sand. One headline announces an overdose. The lead-in states that he died three days after a fisherman found him unconscious and rescued him from the water. I go up to the counter, buy the paper, then sit down on a bench amid the swirl of commuters. Trains come and go in rapid succession. From this moment on, I know for certain my life is changed. The front-page news is of course not simply an incident (an accident?) to which I have only a loose connection. I am, after all, the one who told Peter the best way to swim the sound (advice he apparently did not take, as this happened right outside the city harbor). I turn the black-and-white image face down on the bench, stand up, but cannot move. I am frozen here, studying a flock of pigeons spiraling high above, amid the lacework of glass and iron. The mutual anonymity holding any crowd together anywhere breaks apart as I become the Man of Tears. People rush past, glancing at me, disturbed to varying (though all subtle) degrees by an emotional display in our shared societal space, a space that is, by unspoken agreement, meant to be neutral, uninflected by deep feeling. They are certainly unaware of the cause, or of any connection between me and the tabloids they have also likely seen in passing.

Michael. I need to find Michael. I go to the telephone stalls at the post office on the other side of the station in order to call the airlines. There is not another flight to Hallein until morning, which likely means he is still here. I phone Gwen's hotel, but she has already checked out. I hurry to the taxi queue and ask to be taken out to Christiania.

The driver lets me off at the ruined archway. People avoid me, a bourgeois figure intruding on their counterculture haven. Or, quite possibly, I look like an undercover police officer? Regardless, I ask around. Everyone seems on edge. No one will say much. They want nothing to do with the case of a foreigner overdosing. The incident has brought trouble, a wild-eyed young fellow tells me. "There have," he whispers, "been raids on several squats after they found out it was heroin." Hash is one thing, heroin quite another. Two of the Americans, he informs me, disappeared after their band member was pulled from the water. The poor fellow talking to me suddenly becomes frenzied. He grabs me by the elbow and leads me inside the building. He hands me a guitar left behind, as if it is evidence he wants removed. It is Michael's, not Peter's.

Morning comes on slow, ponderous. I make my way out to the airport. Michael is not on the passenger list. However, one Mariko Lac is. I would not presume to speak with her. I simply want to see her, to see Peter's mother. There is only one Asian woman in the boarding queue. She stands there, pale, silent, though no more so than other passengers. No one in the crowd would be able to tell she is grieving. I wait until every passenger has boarded and the gate is shut before turning to leave. Out the great wall of glass, a coffin is being loaded into the hold. I slump down in a seat in the departure area and stare. Sleep comes quickly, deeply, as if I have been given a sedative.

I awaken, still in the airport terminal. I am completely disoriented. Never before have I fallen asleep in any public place. I pull myself together and head out from the airport by taxi in search of Michael. I ask the driver to stop at the conservatory so I can store the guitar in my studio and then to take me back to Christiania. I need to try again to get information. The ride gives me time to think.

I have the driver wait at the entrance. I get out and approach people randomly, asking if they have any information at all. Most of them still won't speak with me, although a frighteningly thin girl does tell me she might have seen Michael in the red-light district. I thank her and get back in the taxi. It's a vague lead but nonetheless a lead. On the way, I ask the driver to head to the French fellows' place in Nyhavn, where I last saw Peter.

Like any other nightclub would be during the day, it stands empty, dim. One of the Frenchmen is seated at the bar, bent over stacks of what appear to be bills or receipts. I greet him. He lifts his head. His thin face is barely recognizable, swollen and bruised. When he sees me, he appears angry.

He looks back down at the pieces of paper. "What do you want?"

"My friends I came in with the other night—"

He interrupts, practically spitting, "Those Americans are trouble."

He obviously hasn't heard the news. I tell him what has happened. He is not surprised that one of them is dead and mutters, "As far as I'm concerned, the other one can go to hell too." He stands up, gathers his work and stalks away.

This interaction shakes me. The driver next takes me over to the red-light district. I push my way through the crowd of tourists in search of pornography and sex along the main thoroughfare. Not surprisingly, I don't find Michael, so I wend my way down shadowy side streets, where one could become invisible if one so wished. I show several of the corner grocers a picture of Michael onstage that I tore from the newspaper. None of them claims to have seen him. I have no luck at the mission shelter either. Most of the men huddled in alcoves and entryways along these streets are too far gone to answer my questions, even after I place some coins in their hands. An oddly cherubic bouncer at a strip club merely shrugs. One of the hustlers pacing the sidewalk—a very tall fellow, around my age—appears alert and watchful. I approach him. His eyes shine amber under the streetlight. When I start asking questions, he seems disappointed that I am not a john. Eventually, he brightens.

"Hey, wait a minute," he says with a Færoese accent, "don't I know you from somewhere? From TV or something?"

"Perhaps," I answer in Færoese, showing the picture of Michael. "Have you seen this fellow?"

"You're from the Færoes?" He seems surprised and switches languages.

"No, my mother."

"That makes more sense. Otherwise, I would have known you." Our connection seems to relax him. He takes the black-and-white image from me. His fingernails are worn down, dirty. We move into a well-lit passageway. After examining it for a moment, he says, "Sure. Seen him hanging around the past few days. He's been kicked out of the sauna twice." He laughs sharply. Then, mocking an official-sounding voice, he adds, "No sleeping allowed!" He thinks it likely that Michael now spends the night in the park, under the bushes behind the equestrian statue. "A lot of us sleep there."

I'm not sure exactly who he means by *us*. I thank him, handing over more money than I probably need to, simply because I am relieved to know Michael is—or at least recently was—in the vicinity.

"Anytime," he says, running a hand through his long, tawny hair. "If you need me, just ask around. Ask for Albert."

Though the red-light district effectively begins directly out the back entrance of Central Station, I've never been here before, nor have I been to the park that borders it on the other side. The park is renowned, not only for its romantic design but also for being the main drug market for anything harder than hashish. I walk along the wrought iron fence that encloses the park, running my fingers over the spikes in the shape of lilies. Entering through the ornate gateway, I am greeted with a shuffle or a nod by a handful of deal-ers. It is nearly three in the morning, yet business appears brisk. The small, amorphous lake at the heart of the park shimmers in moon-light. Bronze statues of classical gods and goddesses shine, those of marble glow. At the far end of the water rises a grand equestrian statue of one of our less noble kings. I walk toward the rearing horse, skirting the bank of the lake. A white cat streaks across my path, then stops, looking at me first curiously, then indignantly, eyes flashing amber quite like Albert's. The little ghost raises its right forepaw before carrying on and soon disappears into the shadows. I have to duck low to get underneath the shrubbery. Once in, I find myself in an astonishing labyrinth, where indeed, as I crawl through, men are sleeping, some soundly, others restlessly, in dens, amid used condoms and syringes, empty bottles of beer and spirits. The close air smells of decay. No Michael to be found. I emerge from this miniature underworld and continue around the shore, discouraged.

After walking a short while, I see at the north end of the lake what appears to be a human form lying curled around the plinth of a marble Apollo. How strange, the sun god glowing so brightly in moonlight. When I get within a few feet, I can see that, yes, it is Michael! I am so relieved. I call his name quietly. He doesn't respond. I call twice more. He doesn't so much as stir. I kneel beside him. The moonlight reveals bruises and scabs along his left arm. I lean over, touching him lightly on the shoulder. He slowly turns his face toward me. The emptiness of his expression startles me. In these few days, his features have become hard, drained of vitality, not quite human. His head nods involuntarily. He doesn't recognize me. He turns away.

"It's me, Daniel." He folds in on himself. Mosquitoes halo his head. At this time, there is no use saying how sad or sorry I am about Peter, or how, at this very moment, I apprehend how tightly our fates have been bound together. "Come on," I urge, "we should really get out of this place." I pull him gently by the arm. "You can stay with me until things get sorted."

He doesn't respond. He keeps his face pressed against the base of the statue.

I plead for a long time, at last sitting down beside him. I wait in silence until the moon has set and sunlight begins to seep through the high beech canopy. When the rays strike Apollo, Michael responds, as if to a signal meant expressly for him, and rises to his feet. I reach for him, but he brushes me aside, lurching his way down the white gravel path toward the park's entrance. I follow, calling his name once, twice, three times. He heads back into the streets. Before I know it, he has slipped into an alleyway and disappears in a foyer. The door opens and shuts quickly behind him. I knock and knock, calling his name, until a voice—not his—tells me to fuck off and stay the hell away. I pound the locked door and call his name. It's hopeless. And in only a few hours I must depart for a series of concerts across the Soviet Union.

AUGUST 1978, MARIKO

My passport and my boarding pass are in hand, as if I am that person pictured there, with those statistics, as if I am that person in time and space, as if I am that person in a line about to board a plane with her son's coffin in the hold.

Within this body I hardly recognize anymore, I become a raging *kijo*, an unbound demoness. The fire of grief and anger have burned away any goodness that was within me. How can I survive a world that would take my son in this way?

AUGUST 1978, MIKE

. . . it's dark in here . . . do whatever you want, do whatever you want to me . . . so dark.

SEPTEMBER 1978, DANIEL

I'm in the middle of Liszt's crazy transcriptions of Beethoven's Ninth, improvising between the score for two hands and the score for four, when a feeling so uncanny as to raise the hair on the back of my neck causes me to turn around and look out the window. I catch a glance of two men heading down the wooded slope. This distracts me from the fiendishly difficult—if not impossible—music. Before I can get a good look, they are out of my line of sight. There comes a knock. Mother answers the door and I return my attention to the keyboard, proceeding deep into the final movement, the choral, with its alternating dark dissonance and manic melody. Something in Mother's voice from the kitchen—a sternness perhaps—distracts me again. Silence follows, yet my focus continues to waver. I barely manage to make it to the end of the movement. As the last giant chord reverberates clumsily through the house, I look up, at which point I can see Mother nodding for the two behind the partition to proceed into the room.

At first glance, I don't recognize Michael. His once ethereally white skin is stained, as if rubbed with bicycle grease. His glossy black hair has dulled to gray with dust. He now has a full beard flecked with lint, crumbs of dirt, bits of dried grass and leaves. The presence of a ghost would be more believable. I say his name but there is no recognition. His head is bobbing, his body swaying. Though he appears otherwise expressionless, tears stream down his face, like one of those wooden statues of saints that, by either miracle or some mysterious natural phenomenon, weeps. Sweat beads his brow, his nose is running. It is difficult to tell from his dull, unfocused eyes whether he knows who I am or not. I embrace him. The stench of sweat and urine is nearly overpowering. I offer hopelessly conventional words he does not respond to with so much as a blink. My usually serene mother looks on, disconcerted, her left eye twitching. The other man stands there, arms folded across his chest.

When I returned from the Soviet tour a week ago, the first thing I did was continue my search for Michael. I spent the week combing the red-light district, the park, Christiania. I checked hospitals, jails, shelters but found no sign of him. Not so much as a clue, let alone a lead, from anyone I asked. My two weeks away had been, I regretted, too long. My one hope was that he had left the country and was safely back home in the States. I had been forced to concede that our lives, so briefly entwined, had come unraveled.

It took me another few moments to recognize the other fellow as Albert, from the Færoes. His long auburn hair has been cropped short and bleached white and his hands and nails are clean. He looks more boyish in daylight. I exchange glances with Mother, and she politely heads off to her weaving studio.

I have to place my hand on Michael's shoulder to steady him as I lead him and Albert out into the garden. Today the dew has remained until late morning, glittering in the grass and on the surfaces of the sculptures. I sit Michael down on the marble bench overlooking the sound. He appears even more abject there, in sunlight. He hunches over, as if cramping. Nearby, Albert and I pace around each other as we talk.

"I didn't think your friend was going to make it," he tells me. "He's in bad shape."

I push the hair off my forehead. "I don't know how to thank you. I'm so glad he knew to come here."

Albert shakes his head. "He didn't. I finally remembered who you are, from TV. You're the piano player. He needs help, so I found out where you live."

"What happened?" I ask, pausing to look over at Michael.

Albert opens his amber eyes wide and stares at me. "Those French guys, the ones who own some clubs and the bathhouse. It wasn't pretty. There's nothing a junkie won't do for a hit." He lets out a short, bitter laugh. "Trust me, I know. How do you think I got where I am today?" He shakes his head. "You don't want to know."

"What don't I want to know?"

"All I'll say is that there's nothing a junkie won't do." His lively features seal right up, making it clear he has no intention of telling anything more. "Believe me, it's all for the best you don't know." He looks up at the sun to tell the time, the way the Færoese do. "I've got to get back to work."

I nod, frustrated he won't tell me anything more, though of course relieved that, thanks to him, Michael is here and safe.

Albert draws an impatient breath. "This isn't charity."

"What?"

He raises his right hand, rubbing his middle and index fingers against his thumb. "I figure it's worth two tricks."

Sometimes it takes me a while to catch on. "Oh," I say, turning my back to the house and asking how much. The figure seems exorbitant, though the truth is I have no idea whether it is or not. I pull the cash from my wallet and slip it into his hand.

"Plus, transportation."

I hand over another bill that more than covers two train fares from town and back. He merely nods, then he's off, disappearing like a phantasm around the corner of the house.

I sit down beside Michael. He remains doubled over. I stare at the horizon, having no idea of what needs to happen. A regimented and protected life, such as mine, I am now learning, is not adept in crisis. I will have to somehow learn. Embarrassing as it is for me to admit even to myself, this is the first true crisis I've faced in my twenty years.

The only things I come up with to say are anodyne: "It is a difficult time, I know . . . It is good that you are here . . ." He doesn't so much as look at me. I ask a few questions about his general state, but he either cannot or will not answer.

Taking him gently by the elbow, I guide him back across the lawn and into the house. I go to Mother's studio and tell her, "I need to help my friend. I will explain later."

"Of course." Though nothing like this has ever happened in our immediate family, she trusts me, and for all her refinement she is nonetheless compassionate. She came from what she calls the pastoral poverty of the Island, and she witnessed and experienced much hardship in childhood during the War, when her family had to evacuate the Færoes. Once here in Denmark, at great risk to themselves, they helped hide Resistance fighters. Mother is a proper person, certainly, but above all else she is a decent one. It is fortunate, however, that Father is on business in the Far East. He would most definitely not approve of any of this.

What am I getting myself into? I lead Michael to my room. The windows don't view the sound but face up the hill, into the trees. In the filtered green light, he looks like a creature of the forest recently arisen from the humus. I suggest he bathe, and while he does, I will put his clothes in the wash. I motion toward the open bathroom door, telling him there are towels on the shelf and soap and shampoo on the edge of the tub and that I will bring a clean bathrobe. He doesn't respond. I wait some moments before asking him to please undress and I'll get the bath ready. He doesn't react to this either. I wait again, ask again. It becomes apparent that I will have to do it. I'm unprepared for anything like this. With utmost awkwardness, I begin the necessary duty of removing his clothing. I try coaxing him to help as I pull the T-shirt over his head. The black fabric has turned brown from sweat and living on the street. He doesn't cooperate but neither does he resist. Next, I unfasten his jeans and take them down to his ankles. His white undershorts are filthy. Most disturbingly, there are blood-stains. Gingerly, I pull them down. I am taken aback by how emaciated he has become since our day out sailing only a few weeks ago. Bones jut out. His body resembles those in photos of victims of torture. I say this without exaggeration. His chest, his thighs, his back, his buttocks are a map of bruises.

I put the soiled clothes in a laundry bag and step away to run the bath. When the tub is full, I guide him over, having to lift first his one leg and then the other into the water. I can't help noticing his anus is ringed by dried blood and that there are abrasions along his penis. I force myself to stop imagining what the Frenchmen did to him or else I'll go crazy with thoughts of revenge. Then, a foreign feeling overwhelms me, and these words come automatically: "Don't worry about anything, I will take care of you, I will be with you." I lower him into the hot bath. The water turns to sewage. Through some long-dormant instinct, I, who have never had to care for another person in any bodily way, do not hesitate to take up a cloth to wash this man I barely know. I focus intently on the task before me. It's not as though erotic feelings I felt toward him and his bandmates fall away entirely, but they transform into a compassion I never knew I had. I begin by soaping every part of him, then scrubbing gently, taking special care with the injuries. He remains inanimate. His limbs float like driftwood, his genitals like a sea anemone. I shampoo and rinse his hair three times, working the suds down into his scalp with my fingers. At last, I help him rise from the water. He stands there, fresh pink. I open the drain. The superficial evidence of his tribulations disappears in a muddy maelstrom.

Next, I seat him on the edge of the tub in order to shave his face. Before using the razor, I have to clip the beard with scissors. It is surprisingly thick. The black whiskers fall like spruce needles onto the snow-white tile. I sharpen the razor on the leather strap, whisk soap up into a lather in the mug, and brush the foam over his bony face. Then, ever so slowly, cautiously, I pull the blade down his hollow cheeks. I am so afraid of cutting him. Flecks of black gather in the foam. I negotiate the intricacies of his cleft chin before moving down his throat, especially careful not to nick the prominent Adam's apple. It becomes something more than mechanical, this ordinary act, something intimate. I am learning who he is and who I am in a way that cannot be put into words. It is ritual, it is revelation: the trinity of dark moles displayed below his left cheekbone, the crimson scar in the shape of a small newt along his jawline. I lose myself in the slow rhythm of shaving. When I have finished, I lift his chin and hold his face between my hands, turning it from side to side, examining my workmanship. His eyes remain blank, do not meet mine. I lather him up again and go over his face a second time. When at last I've finished, I put him back in the empty tub, where, with the handheld shower, I wash his entire body one final time. After helping him to step out and drying him off, I take a tube of antibiotic ointment from the drawer. I ask him if he would like to put some on his cuts. As expected, he doesn't answer. So, as gently as I can, I rub a fingerful around his anus and then some more on the cuts along his penis.

Although I have only ever seen it unkempt, I comb his hair. It shines, glossy as mink. I part it in the center. He looks like a young gentleman from a century ago. Finally, I dress him in clean clothes from my closet. It is necessary to cuff the trousers and roll the shirt-sleeves up, but he looks fine. His shoes are ruined so I put him in a pair of my loafers. They are a little big, but with thick socks they fit well enough until we get him some new ones. There is something uncanny about seeing him groomed and dressed in this way. Color has returned to his face, though it remains without expression.

Mother has cooked a hearty dinner for us. She is wonderful. She serves it in the dining room, adding politely that she will not be joining us. Michael does not touch the pork cutlet, potatoes, or beets. He still has not spoken a word.

After I clear the plates, Mother and I are alone in the kitchen. She asks if she should make up the guestroom. I now explain to her what is going on, or what I think is going on, not sparing the details. I tell her, no, it is necessary that Michael sleep in my room so I can care for him, as I do not trust he will stay in the house. He would, I suspect, crave a fix and leave in the night if I am not there. She expresses concern, tells me to be careful, but does not object. It dawns on me that she may well consider this the start of a worldly and practical education she and Father neglected to give me in their efforts to provide me with so much.

I get Michael into bed. He lies under the duvet, shivering. When I crawl in, instantly he grabs onto me. He grips me from behind, shuddering violently and gasping, until at last, he drops into something resembling sleep. Perhaps an hour later, he cries out, in a voice haunted and ragged, over and over again: "Do what you want to me, whatever you want . . ."

This delirium goes on for some time, until he begins to heave. Before I can move away, a sudden burst of burning liquid covers my back. It is difficult for me to understand my calm. Some unknown part deep inside of me has accepted the situation in its entirety. To the astonishment of my former self, my present self is not horrified. In fact, I remain completely levelheaded. I simply get Michael up,

remove our pajamas, shower us both thoroughly, change the bed-
clothes, and dress us in clean pajamas. We get into bed and I urge him
back to sleep, murmuring, "Don't worry, nothing will harm you . . ."

In the morning, I telephone my agent to cancel all engagements
for the coming six weeks.

SEPTEMBER 1978, MIKE

Sunlight slipping between billowing curtains woke me slowly. I kept
trying to push the rays away with my hands. Feels like I've been
asleep for a whole day on whichever planet it is in that Ray Bradbury
story where a day lasts an Earth year. Venus maybe? And wherever
I now am does seem like another world—*otherworldly*, I guess. This
room's right out of the Bible. Or at least Bible movies. Simple like
that. Rough-plastered stone walls, wood beams across a low ceiling,
a clay pitcher and cup on a plain table beside a bed. Nothing modern. Unnerves me.

The smell of ocean is getting to me. Keeps the feeling I had for
those days—how many was it? Four? Five?—on the boat, the feeling of wanting to disappear into the waves. Those days and nights of
sleepless sleep. I was so out of it I didn't even register what direction
we were sailing. But I can clearly see Daniel Beck standing there at
the tiller, bathed in sunlight and spray, telling me important things.
I can't for the life of me recall a word of it. Scary, this remembering not remembering. A wave would wash over the deck, its cold
force bringing me back to life for only a few moments before I'd
drop back into blankness. I still don't know what our destination
was, which *is* of course *here*. Only now am I beginning to remember *there*. That weird un-house of Daniel Beck's on the sound
where Pete drowned. But how did I get *there*, to his house, to him?
Memory is starting to reassemble. Slow, unsteady. Only sensations
for now, not really memories yet. Sensations of being in a dark place
where everything inside and outside my head was erased.

I can't account for even the small things. Like the fact I'm wearing pajamas. Striped, like people on TV wear. I haven't worn pajamas since the footsie kind when I was a little kid. I reach for the
pitcher on the nightstand, pour a cup of water. The clay of the cup
tastes like life. A single drop hits my tongue and I gulp the rest down.
I pour another cupful and another, until the pitcher's empty.

There is one familiar thing in the room, just one: my guitar case
standing in the corner. The stickers of all the motorcycles I never
got plaster the entire surface. I study the collage for a long time.
This is what finally draws me out of bed. I move across the floor,
stiff, unsteady. I open the case slowly, cautiously, as if expecting
something like a bomb or jewels or snakes. But there it is, my guitar. Once my appendage, it now appears phantom. All that it has
meant—both for good and for bad—washes over me. I lift it from
the blue velvet. I turn it around and around before sitting down on
the edge of the bed, cradling it. I move my hand from lower bout to
upper bout, then on along the neck, hesitating a few times before
daring to strum just a little. An electric guitar unplugged is a strange
thing, unless you're used to it, in which case you do hear the proper
sound in your head. I focus on the fretboard. Without me willing it,
my fingers begin "May This Be Love." The playing's shaky, and at
first my voice doesn't work at all. Finally, it cracks and croaks the
words that have meant so much to me, to me and Pete:

Waterfall, nothing can harm me at all,
my worries seem so very small
with my waterfall . . .

I'm losing it.
I can't continue.
I jump to my feet. In a single warp speed motion I swing the guitar over my head, arching my back all the way till the output jack
hits my heels. Then, full force, I whip it in a great arc all the way
back around, exploding it on the stone floor in front of me. A million pieces ricochet everywhere. I'm left with just the headstock in

my hands. I curl down on the floor into a tight crouch, sobbing myself out of myself.

The next thing I know, Daniel's there, kneeling by my side, hand on my back, not saying a word. How horrible that he had to witness this. I'm so ashamed.

It's been maybe a week since I smashed the guitar. It was like destroying a part of myself. I still haven't left this archetype of a house, though when I hear Daniel go outside, I've started wandering around the other rooms. From the window I watch him with two dogs herding sheep. I watch him while at the same time trying to avoid the general view. The vastness of the ocean and sky freaks me out. Ocean, right smack in the face. And sky, sky, sky. It's way too much. A giant mountain oppresses. It dominates what looks to be a small island that we're on. Other islands in view have similar crazy high peaks.

Daniel brings a meal to the room three times a day. It's good of him. More than good. At first, I didn't touch any of it. Now, I've started eating some. I eat the white bread at breakfast, the black bread at lunch, and the boiled potatoes at dinner. I can't stomach the stinky cheese, pickled herring, lamb, or cabbage. He offers the food, never coaxes. And he talks about things like the weather without expecting me to respond. I try to make my presence an absence, though I probably just come off as sullen, resentful.

After breakfast this morning, Daniel comes to the threshold of the room to tell me he's going to sail across to Tórshavn, on the main island of Stream Island, for supplies. Would I care to come along? I don't answer. "That's fine," he says. "I'll be back in a few hours."

Once I see him sail away, I venture out of the room. I go sit in the middle of the floor of the main area of the house. I sit there a long time, petting both dogs. This feels good. They are good. Some kind of collie, maybe. He calls them Goofy and Pluto.

Musical instruments rest on a shelf above me: a violin, a flute, a concertina, a guitar. There's also an upright piano in the corner furthest from the windows. Some of the keys are chipped, others missing ivory altogether. Weird for a pianist to have a piano in that condition, but then he hasn't played it since we've been here. All the instruments look really old. I hadn't thought I would want to touch a guitar again but now I find that I do. I avoid the temptation by studying the bookcase. Most of the books are not in English. I take down one I know and have loved, *Moby-Dick*, and start reading from the random page I open to. Whales are calving.

But the guitar pulls like a magnet. Eventually, I get up off the floor and stand there studying the craftsmanship, wondering how old it is, where it came from, who made it. I reach up to the shelf in slow motion. I tap the soundboard lightly. I balk a couple times before lifting it down and carrying it over to one of the benches by the window. There I sit, holding the curved wood against my torso. I hold it for a long time without playing. In the end, I can't stop myself. I start strumming as soft as possible, making almost no sound at all. Then I pluck a few notes, twisting the tuning pegs as I do. When I get the instrument as close to tuned as it's going to get, I breathe deep and begin playing for real. A song comes automatically, like a miracle. It's no song I've ever played before, or even heard. It's not improv, though, or not only improv. Definitely a song. No tight form like punk or even mainstream rock, but still, a song. As if it's coming onto the strings from the wind flowing through the open window. Maybe this is what the Aeolian harp Pete used to talk about is like? Music from someplace beyond intention? In the wind? From the spheres? Some undersong, as Daniel would say, of the universe? Variations I couldn't ever think of consciously come to me. I lose myself in the music, and that feels almost good at this time when feeling good was a forgotten thing. The words, too, come from somewhere else:

Even through forgetting,
I remember you.
Even blind,
I watch you
Return from unknown latitudes
And then with all my strength,

And then with all my will,
I try forgetting you.
And then with all my strength,
And then with all my will,
I show you how to never go
To unknown latitudes . . .

Maybe the fifth time through, Daniel appears out the window, mooring the boat. My first impulse is to stop, to get back to the room and pretend I'm asleep. But something tells me to stay with the music. No, not something: I have decided this. In a minute, Daniel enters with a wooden crate piled high with supplies. He looks over at me and smiles, like he's trying to make it not a big deal that I've finally emerged from someplace way farther away than the other room. I nod and assemble something resembling a smile. I've decided this: to nod, to smile. I continue playing. I've decided this. I want to let Daniel into my life. Yes, I've decided this.

Pale sausages sputter among potatoes, onions, and cabbage in a cast-iron skillet. Daniel serves it onto big blue-and-white plates, slabs of butter melting over everything. We sit down together for the first time. He looks so content. He holds his knife in one hand, fork in the other, and digs in. Not since the fancy hotel with him and Gwen have I felt hunger like this. I find myself wanting to tell him everything that I'm starting to feel and starting to remember. But I can't. Can't will it.

He handles my silence well. He speaks into it: "You don't have to make any decisions, and I don't want to make a speech, but I want you to know that you of course may leave this island whenever you wish. Simply ask, and I will take you. I also want you to know that you may stay as long as you wish."

I'm trying to understand his kindness, his generosity, his love (as hard as it is to accept, that's what it is, love). None of which I deserve. I lift a flaky piece of potato with my fork to my mouth. I place it on my tongue. The buttery morsel brings me into the here and now. For the first time, I look Daniel in the eye and tell myself, *Stop being such a freak, try acting like a normal human being,* and so I say, "Thank you." This scrap of gratitude is the first thing I've said in forever. I'm not sure if I mean it, or really, I'm not sure what I mean by it, or maybe it's just that I don't know what it means to be grateful.

He takes a swallow of the thick, black beer. "Don't mention it. I brought you here because I thought, given everything, it may well be the best place for you. Solitude, nature—you know." He kind of sighs and laughs softly at the same time. "Besides, my friend, you have no passport, so I couldn't exactly send you home, and I wasn't so sure it was a good idea to take you to your embassy in Copenhagen, given the state you were in."

Hadn't realized my passport went missing.

After dinner, I want to help out. It hadn't occurred to me before. Now I make another decision. A small one, yet still, a decision. I take the sponge—real sponge out of the ocean—from Daniel and start washing the dishes. He looks surprised, then steps aside. I'm completely caught up in the task of moving the sponge over the plates and scrubbing the silverware. Simple as the work is, it feels good to be doing something useful. Daniel dries, placing the plates on a rack above the cabinets, the silverware in a drawer. There's beauty in these everyday things and in his simple movements that I would've never noticed before. Every detail of the kitchen and of life suddenly and miraculously seems to have meaning.

When we're done washing up, more than anything I want to return to the guitar. I ask if that would be okay. He laughs and tells me of course it is. I don't have to ask. He sits in a wooden chair nearby, reading Kierkegaard, a name I recognize from a Great Books list Mrs. Homer once handed out. I always meant to read the whole list but never did, barely made a dent in it. Sitting with Daniel like this, I almost feel like a real human being.

When I get into bed my body starts feeling real for the first time in a long, long time. I take off the pajamas Daniel gave me and touch my face, my throat, my ribs, my thighs, lightly, lightly, lighter than even tickling. It feels like when I was about to drop my body into the crowd at a concert, that trembling, though much fainter. It's not too long before I can't stand it—it being the very fact of having a body. I get up, leave the room, and float through the moonlit house. But I'm no ghost. I'm a person. I head into Daniel's room. He never closes the door or the curtains. He's wearing only pajama bottoms, lying there on his left side on top of the covers, bathed in moonlight, sound asleep. Looks like he's cast in silver. I don't hesitate, I get into bed with him, I wrap myself around his back. I've got to hold onto his body or else I'll fall away from everything. I hold on tight, pressing into him. This is real: my body, his body, my body against his body. The warmth is a gift. He smells clean as mountain air. He stirs, then reaches around to touch my unshaven cheek.

My own breath feels hot coming off his neck. I whisper, "You can do whatever you want."

He loosens himself from my grip and rolls over to face me. He takes my head between his hands, holds it there, looks into my eyes, and tells me in a voice as calm as the moonlight filling the room, "I don't want to *do* anything to you, do you understand?"

Pathetic that I don't know any other way to express what I want or need, or even how to want or need. Now it seems urgent for me to have Daniel know me, to know me beyond dead, to know my desire. I pull him in so we're chest to chest, belly to belly, crotch to crotch. I bury my face in the depression under his jaw, taking a long, deep breath. I lick at the hair curling down behind his ear before resting my lips on his earlobe and whispering, "I understand, I do," as I press my whole body into his.

NOVEMBER 1979, MARIKO

Dearest Keiko,

Bless you for coming all the way from California for Richard's funeral. You are the only family I have, as well as my truest friend.

257

We did not get a chance to talk alone together, or rather, at that time I could not talk with anyone beyond formalities.

Richard never really recovered from the shock of Peter's death. That is my opinion, not the doctors'. They describe a series of coronary artery spasms, or silent heart attacks, over the year after Peter died, leading to the final myocardial infarction, or heart attack. I blame myself in part. After Peter died, I became withdrawn and angry and was not caring for him as I should have. It was as if I had become one of the ikiryō from the tales of our childhood. Indeed, I felt as if my disembodied spirit was scouring the earth ceaselessly to avenge Peter's death, even as my living body stayed within my home. I cursed the day we ever came to Hallein and the day he met his friend Mike.

At times, I wasn't sure I could carry on. I pitied myself. Pity and anger, an ugly alliance if ever there was! It took you to remind me that my own mother carried on after losing both husband and son in a single day, and that I carried on after losing father and brother.

Thank you, dear cousin, for inviting me to come stay with you. It would be lovely to celebrate the new year with you. As for moving back to California? I don't think so. At least not now. I feel that I am meant to stay here.

With All My Love,
Mariko

AUGUST 1994, MIKE

I know what Isaac's about to ask. My mind tries disappearing into the swirling stripes—what I think geologists call striations?—of the salt walls that enclose us.

"He's dead, isn't he?" His features flicker in the light reflecting off the walls.

Silence and silence and silence, until it can't go on any longer without me being massively sanctioned by whatever powers of justice rule the universe. I answer, blunt as a hammer, "Yes." One sound, one syllable, one word to express fifteen years of grief.

He burrows his collapsing face into my chest and starts sobbing. Thick grief for a man he never met.

I owe him more. I gather strength. I pat his back, a kind of emotional filler. In fits and starts I try to tell something resembling a story. I fake cough before beginning: "That's when the No Names ended. That's when I went—I mean, when Daniel brought me—to the Island."

Isaac and I stay in the sparkling white space, him holding onto me as I try fitting together fragments of me and Pete and the No Names. I'm not sure how long the telling takes, only that when I've done as much as I'm able to do the light's almost gone.

Isaac lifts his head and stares past me, eyes narrowed. I move a little ways away. He shakes his head. "I hate her for this. Her keeping this secret. It's why she and I have always lived together in mortal combat." His eyes widen. He aims his gaze at me. "What right did she have?"

The ancient image of the girl—the one I think would become his mother—lying under Pete in the sumacs resurfaces.

Why would she do this to her own son?

I've got to respond. I owe it to her, to him, to the universe. I leave his arms and step away. "Look," I begin, rubbing my face, "it was one of those high school parties. Down by the river. They didn't know each other. The school was all about cliques, all about where you came from. You know—the Heights, the Flats. They never got together again after that." This is so vague and so stupid sounding. I step back toward him and place my arm around his shoulder. "She has her reasons, I'm sure."

He shakes his head again, this time fast. "She always has her reasons. It's all about power with her. Power over me. And now, power over him—a dead man. Noble as fuck. I even asked her if she knew you guys in high school and she said she didn't."

"Okay, okay. But now you do know. You know, and so you've got to try and get past this." Me dispensing advice—especially this advice—now that's a laugh. "If not for your mother's sake, for your grandmother's."

His face has fallen into shadow. "Grandmother?"

I wasn't going to bring Mrs. Lac into this, but in all the mess it suddenly seems important, as if somehow it will verify all the rest. I nod, telling him, "She has no idea. She has no idea about you."

"Holy shit." His voice seems to lighten. He blows his nose on the back of his hand—just like Pete—and wipes it on the salt floor. "Can we go see her?"

It's my turn to shake my head. "If you want to meet her, you need to go by yourself." I can't explain to him or even myself the look she gave me in the hospital all those years ago, how final it was. Even if she said she wanted to see me—and if I believed she really did—it would be wrong. Isaac's not a gift for me to give to her. It was too much like playing God, me telling him she exists, even if this god is only a god of mistakes.

"But Pete—I mean, my dad—was your boyfriend, right?"

That word seems as accurate as any. "Yes, he was."

AUGUST 1994, ISAAC

I'm no longer me. Which isn't necessarily such a bad thing.

I take Mike back to the house for his car. When he gets off the bike, he gives me my grandmother's address. I don't tell him I already know it. He crosses the street to his car. I don't invite him in because I know he'd say no thanks, and besides, I want to get going. Haven't even taken my helmet off.

I call out, "Where you staying?"

"Arkadia," he laughs.

I look at him, puzzled.

He gets in his car and is pulling out before I get a chance to ask for more specific contact info. Then, jittery as a cokehead, I kick-start the bike and tear on out of the Heights. I'm going to meet my grandmother. "My grandmother," I say out loud. It's got a sweet ring to it that even a sarcastic bastard like me can love.

The sun's going down. Long shadows cover the house that only yesterday was to me just the house of one of the guitarists for the No Names. The windows are lit. I practically bounce up the front walk and ring the bell. No answer. I wait, ring again. A third time. Every light is on, though it doesn't look like anyone's home. Maybe she's in the back of the house and doesn't hear me? I go around to the backdoor and knock. I can see right into the kitchen. No one there either. I press my face to the glass.

The instant I turn away from the door, I'm a monkey glimpsing the shadow of a snake, frozen and freaking out at the same time. Thousands upon thousands of TV and movie images have conditioned me so completely that it's like genetic, my reaction to a pistol in my face. I know for certain that every moment of my life that has led to this one has been an absurd mistake. I put my hands up—also like I've been conditioned to do. A woman's holding the gun on me. She's Asian, about five-seven, slim, late forties/early fifties. These details in case it ever comes to me having to ID her.

"Face down on the ground," she orders. She has a foreign accent.

As I fall on my knees, I whimper, "I'm just looking to talk with Mrs. Lac."

"So you can what?" she asks with a laugh. "So this time you can ask her permission to rob her house?" With her foot, she pushes my shoulder down. "Didn't you get everything you wanted the last *two* times?"

I'm now flat on my stomach, stammering, "I don't know anything about that, I swear." I get how she could think that, though, me like a burglar looking in the window, casing the place. She nudges the nose of the gun against the base of my skull, and I yell, "I'm her grandson! I'm Mrs. Lac's grandson!"

With her free hand she pulls me by the head of hair. "What did you say?"

I barely manage to repeat, "I'm . . . I'm Mrs. Lac's . . . I'm her grandson."

She draws a sharp breath. She jerks my head to the side, examining my face.

I'm sweating, trembling. In a last-ditch effort to keep a bullet from exploding any future thoughts that might be crawling around in my brain, I blurt out the improbable facts of Copenhagen, the Færoes, Michael on the Island, until finally I'm begging, "Please, believe me!"

After long silence, she says, voice barely audible, "I am Mariko Lac," the gun now aimed at my face, "and my son has no children."

"It's a long story."

"And you look nothing like him."

Never seen a picture of him, but I certainly don't look anything like her. Even as I'm feeling the very real possibility of dying right here, right now, knowing my grandmother is Asian gives me a weird satisfaction. I'm blown away by the fact that, even genetically—not to mention socially or sociologically, ethically or ethnically, psychically or psychologically—we know next to nothing about ourselves, or at least I know next to nothing about myself.

"Listen," I tell her between gasps I can't control, "I know it sounds crazy, but, swear to God, I'm telling the truth."

An even deeper silence falls between us. Then, at last, lowering the gun to her side, she says, "Please, accept my apology. Come inside." She even takes me by the arm and helps me up.

There's no other clue that she thinks what I'm saying is true, or even that it might not be true, but it's clear she thinks I'm harmless. She puts the gun in her pocketbook, picks up a bag of groceries and a set of keys from the lawn. She'd apparently been coming from the garage at the back of the yard when she spotted me in what were clearly sketchy circumstances. I take the bag from her; she thanks me. I follow her inside, into the kitchen, like this is our usual domestic routine. We still don't speak. I put the bag on the counter. As if

I'm not a stranger, let alone an intruder, she goes about unpacking the groceries, quickly, efficiently, while I stand there in the space between us and the space between me and my old self.

When she's done, she tells me to come. We leave the kitchen, me trailing behind, and go on into the living room. I'm almost afraid she'll disappear the way dreams do. She motions to a turquoise sofa. We sit down together, side by side. I spot what looks to be a high school graduation picture on the mantel. He—my dad!—looks like her, though he looks like a white guy too. A white guy like me, sure, but she's right, I don't really look anything like him.

My *grandmother* and I sit there not looking at each other. The last rays of sun fall in through the front window. Roses the color and size of peaches bounce in the warm breeze, their shadows playing on the walls and ceiling. It's as if neither one of us dares to disturb this feeling. She nods, stands, breaks the silence by excusing herself, she will bring refreshments. I tell her she doesn't have to. She quietly insists. A short time later, she returns with a tray of soft drinks, a little blue-and-white bowl of stick pretzels and another of macadamia nuts. I choose Mountain Dew. She pours it over ice in a tall glass with wheat stalks painted on the outside.

"Perhaps now it is time for us to talk," she says.

I nod. A sunbeam pierces the glass of Mountain Dew. It glows, radioactive. I take two big gulps before beginning to fill in the blanks of the mess I blurted out on the lawn. I try sticking to the facts and not letting my amped-up desire seep into the story. I avoid anything that sounds like I'm trying to convince her of anything. She sits, hands folded on her lap, head turned to face me, listening without interrupting. She doesn't take a sip of the ginger ale she's poured for herself, not for the whole long tale. When I finally come to the end, I say, "That brings us to now."

She lifts her hands and places them on either side of her face. There's no sign as to whether she believes what I've just finished telling her or not. The only thing she says is, "I don't even know your name."

I shove a big handful of macadamia nuts in my mouth because I'm nervous, scared. I chew and chew, finally telling her slowly, quietly, "It's Isaac. Isaac Burns."

"Well, Isaac Burns, unless this is some cruel joke, I am your grandmother."

It seems like we should be screaming or crying, or screaming *and* crying, blitzed by emotions, but we just stay seated there, staring at each other. I think we should be making a big scene because that's the default mode for Vashti and me. But then, I find I can't help myself from starting to talk a little crazy about how crazy the whole situation is.

My grandmother puts her index finger to her lips to stop the shit that's coming out of my mouth. She leans in toward me, whispering, "Yes, yes, yes." She pulls me towards her, and we hold each other for a long, long time, as if to be sure we're not illusions of each other. Finally, she says, "I feel like . . . like this is a new beginning."

AUGUST 1994, MIKE

I'm just finishing setting a round six-top for the second seating when in walk the party—four businessmen and two business ladies—ten minutes early. I don't recognize her right away. Her long brown hair is now kind of red and spiky, her figure curvier, plus she's wearing grown-up clothes. But the instant I do recognize it's Lisa right in front of me, I'm all messed up. For some non-reason, I never expected to meet anyone I knew from back then, especially not in foreign territory, like here at the Yacht and Country Club. I think I might know the other woman, too.

When Lisa finally registers it's me, she looks like she's seen a ghost, and maybe she has. Next second, she smiles super happy, practically shouting, "Mike!" The men look at me weird, but she doesn't seem to care. The other woman smiles. I'm pretty sure it's Doi Sargent, Afro now gone, hair cut super close, also in grown-up clothes. Yes, definitely her. Lisa runs over and gives me a big warm hug. God, she smells good. She keeps saying, "Wow!"

I have no idea what to say, so I say, "Hey, Lisa," like I suppose a real human being would.

The rest of her party is sitting down. I have to go and get the water pitcher.

"You're our waiter!" she says with that same old not fake smile of hers. "Cool."

I shake my head. "Busboy."

"Nice," she says, as if it really is.

Doi wonders, "Aren't you that boy from music class way back when?"

I nod.

"My, my, my," she says, shaking her head, "but you've turned into a fine-looking man!"

I blush, then blush double recalling the totally messed-up slave auction I took part in, and the look of indignation Doi aimed at me from the back of the auditorium. The slave auction where I met Pete, where Pete bought me. And then I blush triple, wondering how she could be nice to me, even after all these years.

"Look," Lisa says, "when do you get off?"

By the time I'm done vacuuming the dining room it's around eleven. "Late," is all I say.

"Want to grab a drink?"

What would be a totally routine question for most people, to me sounds like a foreign custom. I'm feeling like the waiters passing by are wondering what's up, so I answer as fast as I can, "Sure."

"What about you, Doi?" she asks. "Want to join us?"

Doi smiles. "That would be wonderful, thank you, but I've got to get home right after this to relieve the husband of three young hellions." She breaks out laughing, tossing her head back, and I swear I've never seen anything so beautiful. Funny, how someone from the periphery of the past can have such a central effect on you when they appear out of nowhere in the present. I want to find out everything about her. I want to apologize for what happened back then.

"The Pines is open late," Lisa says, kissing me on the cheek like a movie star. "See you there when you get there." She turns toward her party and sits down, graceful as a queen.

Lisa and Doi have gotten me hard in my polyester work slacks. I shift to try and adjust this reborn horniness, then turn away. "I'll be right back with water."

The two of them have obviously made it. Good for them. This is a normal scene in their world. I mean, going out to dinner, having nice food, drinks, conversation, like real human beings. At this moment, every scene of my life seems to have been part of some antisocial drama. That is, until it became one absurdly long antisocial soliloquy on the Island.

When I take a plate away, bring bread or pour more water, I avoid Lisa's light-brown eyes. But I can't avoid those hands of hers—strong yet delicate, that in another world I've held, hands that have touched me all over. She has on a sleek wristwatch and pretty bracelet—don't know if they're expensive or not, but they look nice—and no wedding ring, something I wouldn't normally notice except I'm trying to look only at her hands. Of course, I also notice the food Rudy puts down in front of her. She starts with the Putting Green Salad. For the main, she has the Almond Crusted Gulf Snapper. "Chardonnay," he says, when he pours her wine. Key lime pie for dessert. Unlike most ladies at the club, she eats everything. I like that.

When the group is done with their meal, Rudy brings the check to Lisa. As I'm clearing, I can see she puts it on a member tab. I know it's totally ridiculous, not to mention hypocritical, but I like it that a girl from the Flats has made good.

When the party gets up to leave, Lisa looks into my eyes so intense and happy that I'm forced to stop shifting mine. She smiles. "Catch you later."

As I finish clearing the table, the six real human beings stand around in the parking lot, talking before going to their separate cars. Lisa gets into a car I didn't know before coming back to the States, an Acura Legend. Pretty slick. A coupe, in a metallic gray

I've never seen before. Have to find out what name they came up with for that cool color.

I reset the tables for tomorrow, then vacuum. When I finally roll the vacuum cleaner back into the utility closet, I go to the locker room and change back into my jeans and T-shirt, wishing they were cleaner. Last thing I do is wave so long to the waiters and other bussers before slipping out into the night. The sprinklers on the golf course begin to whirl and hiss. I hop in the Fury, surprised at how eager I suddenly am, and head out for the Pines. After all this time, I could still drive the winding lake road in my sleep. How many pitchers and cocktails did Lisa and I have there with Pete? Back when the legal age was eighteen—everything's changed, even the small things. I'm excited about meeting her, that is until memories start freaking me out. If it were anyone else except Lisa, I'd be a no-show. But she's the kind of girl you don't want to treat bad, you just don't.

The scent of pines mixed with lake hits me as I open the car door. Almost forgot what this world smells like. No pines on the Færoes. No trees at all. And the smell and feel of salt spray, constant there. I walk into the tavern and I'm walking into a past. The shellacked knotty pine paneling and booths glow yellow in the light from hurricane lamps, same as before, or maybe yellower with age. The place is crowded with no one I know, except of course Lisa. In the same corner booth where the three of us used to huddle, she's wrapped around a cocktail. It shines darkly in the candlelight. The benches, hard as pews, she somehow always made look cozy and still does. She's changed into nice-fitting jeans. When she stands up, her blouse—the kind that ties at the waist—shows some of her sexy belly. She looks great. She hugs me tight and long, repeating my name over and over. I'm scared and getting hard at the same time. The last woman I touched was Gwen Chambers. A fact that weirds me out.

"God," Lisa sighs, "I thought you were gone." She pauses, her features tense. "Like the rest of the band."

The waitress comes over. The same one from way back when. Doris was it? My mind is mobbed by death. I barely get the word *draft* out of my mouth.

"After you guys didn't come back from Europe when you said you were, I kept waiting. I finally went to your houses, yours and Pete's. Your sisters didn't know. Then I went to Pete's. I wasn't expecting anything like that. I couldn't breathe, couldn't move. There hadn't been an obituary. And his mom, his mom . . . She'd always been the nicest person, so I was kind of scared as she practically spat the news at me from behind the screen door. She didn't know what had happened to you. She looked terrible. Like she was wasting away. Who could blame her? She closed the door before I could ask any more questions. And her garden, her beautiful garden, was overgrown, full of weeds. The lawn hadn't even been mown. Grass knee-high."

She reaches across the table, takes hold of my hands. "You knew about Bobby and Matt, right?"

I did but I didn't. From Isaac I'd learned Bobby and Matt are dead—he'd said *passed* the way people here seem to do nowadays—but not how or when. I attempt to shake my head and nod at the same time.

"Bobby about ten years ago, Matt three." She'd read about them in the paper—paid death notices—not news at all. No mention of the No Names or that they'd been musicians. No causes of death listed. She'd asked around. Bobby, heroin. Matt, heart attack—super young for that.

The beer comes. To keep from breaking down and bawling like a baby, I empty the mugful in three long swallows.

"You were there, huh?" She means Pete.

Even telling a radically shortened version of what happened is going to be tough. I stare into a knot on the table like it's the abyss. Telling her that I wasn't exactly *there* is even tougher. I haven't had to fit the details into a story before.

"You know," she says, "I loved him." She runs both hands through her hair. "I loved you guys."

She touches my cheek and I recall every whorl of fingerprint. "So, where've you been?"

A simple enough question. At least geographically. But how I wound up on the Island and why I stayed for fifteen years will take some major explaining. It's a good long time before I can begin to answer. My brain won't work. She takes two sips of her drink. Even the way she does something as ordinary as that is so incredibly pretty, her shiny lips agile. It occurs to me for the first time how absurd the truth will sound: *Oh, I lived alone on an island in the middle of the ocean, herding sheep, messing around with the guitar, and beating off. For fifteen years.* Or better yet: *I was kept by a man on his family's private island.* It hadn't occurred to me I'd ever be telling my story to anyone. Still, I've got to tell her something. I owe her that. "Lisa," I begin, then stop. Some old metal anthem I almost recognize is playing on the jukebox. She has changed her life so much. It now has less than nothing to do with mine. "Lisa," I begin again with an unintended sigh, "I've been nowhere."

She blinks twice, fast. "You've been *here* all this time?"

Hallein's not that small, so you could possibly not run into someone for fifteen years. Possibly, though not likely. I'd of course meant *nowhere* as a figure of speech. But how could she know that? What I'd really meant is, *I'm a nobody,* but I keep that to myself. "No, let's just say I was missing in action." That's not fair. She deserves at least an outline.

I catch Doris's eye. She nods and delivers another beer fast, like she can tell I'm desperate. I gulp nervously. The velvety head soothes my upper lip. I lick it away.

I try to make the story sound reasonable: "A friend needed help with his family's sheep farm. Seeing how I was in pretty rough shape after what happened with Pete and had nothing going on back here . . ." That's the truth, simplified, slanted.

With her questions that follow I turn into a cagey bastard, giving only enough detail to satisfy her without allowing her into the reality of it. She thinks the Island sounds so romantic. Maybe she means romantic both ways; maybe she imagines there was a girl involved.

Lisa's story is everything mine is not. She's worked hard, gotten ahead, gotten a life, without ever having left Hallein. She started in the steno pool at the refinery and took night courses at the new community college. Then she transferred to the university, all the while continuing to work. She majored in computers. That's what people do nowadays. She tells me with a laugh that she was into them before anyone. After graduating, she, along with two of the guys I saw her with at the Club, started a company that does something I don't understand at all. Something that will help people manage their computer files, is it? She was married for almost ten years to an out-of-state guy she met in college, but that ended over a year ago.

"And Doi?" I wonder.

"She's great, isn't she? Didn't really know her back in school. She's a client. She's a hospital administrator, at St. Joe's."

I nod, happy for both of them.

We skirt the subject of Pete. Don't know how to tell her that the whole fifteen years on the Island was about him. Or that *now* is still about him. Every note, every chord, every word, every thought is, in some way—no matter how oblique—a coming to terms with him.

We sit, hands again knotted together.

"So, why'd you come back?"

It hadn't occurred to me she'd ask this. Of course, anyone would. I'm that slow on the uptake. The melting ice in her glass glitters. I raise two fingers for another round. "For Pete," I tell Lisa. "I came back for Pete."

She cocks her head and wrinkles her brow. "I'm not following."

I look away.

The drinks arrive during the silence between us, a silence made all the deeper by the noise of this place. I take swallow after swallow of beer for courage, finally blurting out, "I came back for Pete . . . and his son."

"Whoa." She lets go of my hand. "His son? You're telling me Pete's got a son?"

I take a deep breath. "He didn't know. I didn't know. The son found me. So, I came back. I owe it to him. I mean, his son."

"His son's here?"

I nod.

"What is he, like fifteen? Sixteen?"

"Nineteen."

"Nineteen?" I can hear her doing the math in her head.

"Do you remember Lynn Burns?"

Her face screws up. "She's the mother?"

I nod as I fake cough into my sleeve. "They got together down by the river. Remember that one bonfire she was at with those other rich girls?"

"Sort of?" She folds her hands together, resolute. "But really, I never would have thought that kid was Pete's son. I mean, I've watched him growing up these past at least eight years at the Club. He looks nothing at all like Pete. And when she left school because she was pregnant, the girls said it was her ex-boyfriend's baby. Doug Something. He left school that Christmas break. Went to some prep school out East."

"So, you know her?" Her take on the situation jars me. I squeeze the mug tight.

"We're friendly, not friends." She explains how they're competitors. They both got into computers, started companies. Seems like the girls have done well for themselves.

"Never even knew she left school, let alone got pregnant." I shake my head. "In case you don't remember, I was generally too stoned to pay attention to most high school stuff." I laugh to get past the doubt she's put in my head. I laugh to get past the fact I didn't tell her I'm the one who told Isaac that Pete's his father, that he didn't hunt me down for that. I laugh again.

"It's going okay with him?" she asks.

"He basically wants to know everything about Pete and the No Names." I'm on the verge of losing it. I've really got to change the subject. "But enough of the past." I raise my glass, she raises hers, we clink. "To seeing you again." I force a smile.

"To seeing you again," she says with a smile that's deep and true. "You're looking good."

I shake my head. "You're drunk. Last I checked, I look like hell." I take a couple more deep gulps of beer.

"Hey," she laughs, "don't *you* get drunk. You probably didn't get the memo. We don't drive that way anymore." She's had three of her Jack and TaBs. Plus, wine with dinner. I'm on only my third beer.

"Oh, yeah?" I say, imitating some flirty smirk I maybe picked up from Pete. "Then how you going to get yourself home?"

This banter almost starts to sound real, or at least like a bad rom-com.

She tilts her head, looks me in the eye. "Guess I'll call myself a cab, then."

I settle the bill with my tip money. "Let's hail one." We're twelve miles from town and no cab has probably ever ventured out here, let alone cruised for a trick. I put my arm around her as we walk outside, like we're on a real date. "We'll come back first thing in the morning for yours."

She giggles. "First thing?"

I open the passenger door of the Fury, close her in, go around, hop in, and we're off.

Lisa lives only four avenues over from the Arkadia, but it's definitely a better neighborhood. Better, though not that fancy. She and her ex sold their house in the Heights when they divorced. "Tudor just wasn't me," she jokes. "Heights wasn't either."

"What about the Yacht and Country Club." I turn to look at her. "That you?"

"Corporate membership."

I don't remind her that *she* is the corporation.

The apartment building we pull up to is modern, like from back when everything was so modern. It's yellow brick, with turquoise tiles around the windows. The glass entryway goes the three-story height of the building, holding the floating staircase. Three white globes hanging at different heights, step-like, light it up. On the expanse of glass above the entrance, written in gold script, is the building's name: *The Margaret Anne.* Carved into the cornerstone is *1958,* the year we were born.

"We're here," she says.

I put the car in park but keep the engine running. I guess I'm supposed to come up. I guess I'm getting cold feet. I guess I've forgotten how to be with a girl. What I always loved about Lisa is that she can tell things. In some way, we're back in the salt cave before I let Pete have her—as if anyone could *have* anyone, like we thought they could in those days.

She leans over and gives me a G-rated kiss. "No need to rush things."

I'm relieved. "I'll stop by in the morning and drive you back out to the Pines. What time?"

She opens the door. "I can catch the bus to work. How about swinging by here after work? Say six?"

"Sure." I feel good, or at least like I haven't blown it entirely.

I'm actually starting to resemble a real human being. Working a full-time job. Paying rent. And now dating. All nice and proper: going to restaurants and movies, kissing goodnight outside the Margaret Anne. I bought a button-down shirt, khakis, and hard shoes, and was good to go. We haven't slept together yet, maybe because the one time we both dozed off in the car down at Dreamland I got embarrassed when I woke her with one of my nightmares. She said I kept calling out something about the dark. And though she hasn't said as much, I get the idea she's not into casual sex, and I guess, given my non-track record, I'm not either. She's been dating since her divorce and is looking for someone to settle down with and have kids. She doesn't say so, not exactly, but that's what I'm picking up. I don't mind the idea, at least not in theory, but it would be impossible for me anytime soon. I mind a little that she usually picks up the tab when we're out, though she doesn't seem to care. She makes probably a hundred times what I do. She also doesn't seem to care that she's a bona fide executive and that I am, at age thirty-five, a bona fide busboy. She likely thinks that I do care, which actually I do. Lisa's not a snob, though. No, not at all. She's still the same great girl from the Flats.

Sometimes I do pay for things. I'll buy a six-pack and some kind of chips or pretzels and take her to the drive-in, like we did in the old days with Pete. One Saturday afternoon, I picked up a couple of boxes of Kentucky Fried Chicken, and we drove to Dreamland for a picnic. It was a nice day, so we didn't need to go for one of the pavilions. We sat on the only blanket I own—a ratty plaid one from a flea market—under a giant willow. A crowd started gathering at a nearby pavilion. Then a kid got up on one of the picnic tables, plugged a rhythm machine and mic in, and started rapping. He was really good. Rapping's new to me. I like it. Back in the day, I suppose I was the punk version of that boy performing here at the park.

We opened our boxes. I gave her my breast; she gave me her drumstick. I gave her my coleslaw; she gave me her biscuit and honey. I drank four beers, she drank two. I loved how carefully she licked the grease from her lips with her bud-like tongue and just as carefully wiped her fingers with the napkin.

Dating still feels weird, though. Especially without Pete. Which I know is an even weirder thing to think. And being around people in general still feels weird. Especially without him. Which is maybe a less weird thing to think. The point is, living still feels weird without Pete, which is maybe or maybe not a weird thing to think.

"I want to hear some real music," she said. Obviously not a rap fan. "Yours, for instance."

"Don't want to upstage him," I laughed, nodding in the kid's direction.

"How about the salt mines, then? You can serenade me there."

I sat cross-legged in the cave, facing the lake, Lisa sat cross-legged, facing me. I started tuning the guitar, a not great Yamaha I found at Goodwill.

"Can you play 'The Heart's Just Another Muscle?'"

Hadn't thought about that one ever. It came before the No Names. One of the first songs Pete and I wrote. I kept my eyes on the tuning pegs, as if I could make her request go away. I didn't know how to get out of it without sounding like a jerk. And the song's too simple for me to have pretended I didn't remember how it goes. Gulls hovered and dipped in the sky behind her. I played the first two chords. My mouth felt dry as I began to sing, "The heart's just another muscle, and I don't pump iron . . ." It starts out cynical but the ending's a little cheesy: "You do the heavy lifting, baby, and I'll follow . . ." Not our best by any means, but it's from the time the three of us were hanging out. The memory nearly sent me into a tailspin.

The song finished. I switched to newer stuff. After I'd played a few, we started making out. I leaned forward to kiss her in the middle of a long piece called "Air," and it went from there. Mid-kiss I lay the guitar back in its case. I was making out with Lisa, and she was taking off her blouse. I was holding her beautiful breasts, when Pete appeared. She was unbuckling my belt, and Pete was watching. I hesitated. Nothing abrupt. But Lisa isn't clueless. She pulled out from under me, asking in a truly kind way, "What's the matter?"

I couldn't explain. I told her, "You deserve more." Vague, cliché.

She started buttoning her shirt back up. "What do you mean by that?"

I didn't want to lie, though I continued down the path of vagueness: "You have plans."

She looked at me, blinking twice. "You don't?"

I pushed up to a kneeling position. "I don't know what I'm doing with my life." That's the truth, the easy truth. I felt like I'd ruined everything. She knows my past—by which I mean Pete—and would accept me in a way most any other girl would not. She knows my past and maybe that's the problem.

We headed home, not exactly sullen but real quiet. We drove along the lake. It was shining like Achilles's shield, something Pete once compared it to.

Before she got out of the car, she turned for me to kiss her on the cheek. "Maybe we should cool it for a while," she said. "When you're ready, let me know." She looked at me directly, not hurt or blaming or accusing. It was a look of deep feeling, maybe sympathy. She then added, "I think you're still in love with Pete."

As I say, Lisa's not clueless.

A whimper, not a bang. I hate T.S. Eliot.

Out of a diamond-blue sky a vagrant cloud, more silver than gray, appears over the Øresund. A few random raindrops fleck the score of the impossible *Hammerklavier* spread out in front of me on the table. The morning has been a titanic struggle with Beethoven. The rhythm of the unexpected rain quickens, forcing me to sweep the sheets up. I retreat from the terrace into the house, less confident about the piece than when I started going over it right after breakfast. This sonata has always vexed me. I'm doubtful it will be ready for the all-Beethoven recital in New York later in the fall. I wish I had another year to get it right, whatever *right* could possibly mean with this music. Today I've been only studying the score, avoiding the keyboard, and still, it appears to me as hieroglyphics. It feels new to me, which is ridiculous, as I have twice recorded it. It's my signature piece, or so critics say, but I'm still deeply dissatisfied with my interpretations to date, and likely will have a similar feeling about any future attempts as well.

I force myself to sit down at the piano. Before I can think too much and call it quits for the day I begin to play. It doesn't take long before I am lost in the complexity, thinking, what do I know about music? About art? To be sure, this loss of confidence is, at least in part, the effect of Michael and Isaac disappearing from the Island and from my life without a word of explanation. That, however, does not make these questions any less honest. By the time I get to the fourth movement, with its three-voice fugue in triple meter, I am defeated. I really do know nothing.

I stop before even completing a decent run-through of any one of the movements. I am so distracted I head into the study, suddenly desperate to find the record I made with the No Names, as if listening to it will somehow, someway act as antidote to my musical and personal crisis. I have not played the recording since the day after we left the studio all those years ago. I have avoided it. I find the plain white jacket exactly where I placed it that day, on the lowest shelf of the wall of recordings in the study, among the miscellaneous.

I remove the record from its sleeve, place it on the turntable, lower the needle. As the music begins, I lean back on the sofa, locking my hands behind my head. I focus on Michael's playing. Those Möbius-strip riffs are impossible wonders. Within a few measures, he torques them into something orbitoid. A weird geometry, like Bach's contrapuntal, though twisted. And yet, through this complexity, he still somehow maintains a primal pulse. Beyond all analysis, there is something in his music, in his playing—on recordings and in person—that I cannot account for. It's as if he taps into some vast undersong running through the infinitely intricate network of caverns that make up the aural universe. The music flows into my head and body, estranging me from myself.

It simply doesn't make sense that Michael left his guitar on the Island yet took the case. Even if I could understand why he and Isaac left without letting me know, I cannot figure out leaving the guitar behind. When I finally reached the Island after my tour ended, I had, perhaps naively, expected a joyous reunion with the two of them, my newfound family. As I docked, the sky was fading. The dogs bounded down to greet me and, much to my surprise, were followed by Abraham. He explained how, some weeks earlier, he had received an unsigned message at the post office—in English, so obviously from Michael—asking him to please come look after the dogs and the sheep. I spent only a day on the Island before sailing back home. There was no message for me here, either.

SEPTEMBER 1994, ISAAC

The night I met Obaachan (once she determined I wasn't a burglar and didn't blow my brains out!), the two of us sat on her sofa talking until the sun started coming up. Her stories were not only about my dad, though. Things she told me got me thinking about more than myself for a change. For instance, about her American cousin Keiko in California. During the War, Keiko's family had their strawberry farm in the Bay Area confiscated and were sent to an internment camp far away, at a place on the Oregon border called Tule Lake. Not just them but thousands of other Japanese Americans were sent to camps. I can't believe I'd never heard about this before. Obaachan also told me how my grandfather's family had disowned him for marrying her because she wasn't white. People can be pretty shitty.

Obaachan said that, if I wanted to, I could get some rest in my dad's room before starting the day. Needy freak that I am, I took this as an invitation into the life I'd missed, whether she meant it that way or not. It felt as if Fate herself was leading me up the stairs. Entering the room was like entering a time warp. Twin beds with matching plaid bedspreads and plaid curtains like "the boys' room" on really old TV shows. Sports pennants, some from teams that no longer exist, like the Brooklyn Dodgers and Minnesota North Stars. Two rows of autographed glossies of sports heroes from back before my day. I recognized only the really famous ones: Joe Namath, Roberto Clemente, Pistol Pete, Bobby Orr. A poster of Mark Spitz, in a patriotic Speedo, with his haul of gold medals hanging from his neck. Somehow, the Hendrix poster seems timeless in the way the rest of the room does not.

As she put sheets on the one bed for me, she told me I may call her Obaachan, which is Japanese for grandmother, if I'd like. She would like that. I told her I'd like that too. Very much. And that I'd also like to learn the language. She smiled.

Within a week, I was practically living with Obaachan. When it gets late, and we've maybe had too much to drink, I stay over. Our running joke is how lucky we both are that she wasn't more trigger-happy the night we met. After dinner we sometimes watch TV together, like a real family, like Vashti and I never do. My picks are *Doogie Howser, M.D.* and *Beavis and Butt-Head;* hers, *Dr. Quinn, Medicine Woman* and *Missing Persons.* But mostly we talk, and mostly we of course talk about Dad. It does seem kind of weird calling someone you never met Dad, but it feels wicked good. I can't get enough of her stories about him, or even just plain facts. His first words were Japanese—*inu* (dog), *oshiri* (butt). I get a kick hearing about the quirky things too. Before he even started school, he was catching lizards in their backyard in California and putting them on leashes he made from strands of Obaachan's hair. He also loved snakes. A few times when she would go in at night to cover him up (he hated covers), she'd find a snake he'd caught coiled beside him for warmth. Not knowing whether it was poisonous or not, she put on thick gardening gloves and, using my grandfather's long-handled fishing net, scoop the snake up from the mattress, dump it in a burlap sack, and drive far into the surrounding wilderness to release it. When he was in elementary school, Dad would lie on the sofa for hours reading biography after biography of famous people because he, as he often announced, would one day be famous. He wanted to be the next Alexander the Great or Beethoven or Jim Thorpe. She imitated the way he played the cello, head shaking, face twisted into a super intense expression. *What size were his shoes? Ten. His shirts? Fifteen collar. His jeans? Twenty-eight, thirty-two. Favorite snacks? Fritos and dried seaweed.* No detail was too random or obscure. I'd even like to know what his shit smelled like, if it wasn't rude to ask.

The best story, though, is about the time she returned to Japan with him when he was eleven. Just the two of them because the flight was too expensive for my grandfather to go along. It was the only time she has ever returned. The trip was to visit her dying mother. She wanted her to meet her grandson. When my dad saw his mother change into what's called a yukata, a kind of informal kimono, he asked if he could wear one too. Obaachan was pleased. She borrowed one in his size from a cousin. She beamed when she showed me a Polaroid of her and my dad in the cotton robes, him looking so proud, chin stuck in the air, arms folded across his chest like a samurai. He was fascinated by the family house made of wood and paper and set on a rock above the sea.

It made her so happy, and also nearly broke her heart, when he entered his grandmother's room quietly, totally aware of the seriousness of the situation, and in perfect, formal—maybe a bit too formal—Japanese, said, "I am so happy to finally meet you, Grandmother. I have looked forward to this day for a very long time." Then, his grandmother—my great-grandmother!—too weak to speak, lifted her hand and touched his cheek. She died the next day. I love this image of him as the good boy almost as much as the one of him as the punk bad boy he'd later become.

Since I wormed my way into Obaachan's life, I'm happier than I've ever been. If happiness even counted before her. Happiness always seemed kind of lame, something for losers. There seemed to be more important things in this messed-up world. For instance, not taking things too seriously (except for gnarly math problems!). Besides, getting stoned seemed a better option. The small things that I used to blow off, I'm now finding I like. Such as chores. Unlike at home, here I'll make my bed, put my clothes in the laundry, take the trash out, and all that stuff. Or Obaachan and I will do yardwork together. I'll be mowing the lawn and she'll be pruning bushes. It feels weirdly satisfying, this family kind of thing. At home, we've always had a house cleaner and lawn service.

Today, we scraped and painted storm windows to put up next week. It's pretty detailed work. You have to be careful to not get any paint on the glass. It took most of the day. After cleaning the brushes in turpentine and showering, we grill trout that one of the men on her sharpshooting team caught and gave to her. To go with it, Obaachan made her amazing coleslaw. We sit on the same side of the picnic table, pouring glass after glass for each other from a gallon jug of Pink Catawba. By the time we finish eating, the light's disappearing from the sky. We watch the nightly flood of bats pouring out from an oak the size of God.

"I feel fortunate to share such a beautiful evening with you," she says, resting her hand on mine. I like how formal her language can be. It takes ordinary things out of the ordinary.

"Same here. No place else I'd rather be."

She shifts on the bench so she's facing me. "It is wonderful, Isaac, it is, but I'm wondering if your being here so much is alright with your mother. You haven't been home in a while."

Mom/Vashti crashes the party. I knew this moment would come but haven't planned how to respond. I mumble-blurt, "She doesn't know I'm here. Besides, I'm an adult."

Obaachan doesn't say a word, but her look says it all: perplexed, concerned, maybe even a little hurt having only now realized that she's a secret, or at least part of one.

"She's kept things from me for nineteen years. Maybe in nineteen years I'll tell her about you, and that I found out who my father is." As the words are coming out, I can hear I sound like a jerk.

Obaachan tilts her face slowly upward, studying the sky. The last light tints the clouds lilac; the last of the bats flit out of the tree right as a mass of starlings enter. Nature's changing of the guard. She then lowers her face and looks me directly in the eye, saying softly but firmly, "Be forgiving, Isaac." She can tell I'm about to protest so raises a finger to her lips. "Your mother was very young when all of this happened. You can't blame her. Such matters are always complicated . . . difficult . . . especially so back then. The one thing I regret is not knowing, not knowing you existed. I would have helped your mother and you in any way possible."

I stop myself from describing the out of whack dynamic between Vashti and me. When I was five or six, I'd started asking, "Where's my daddy?" and she'd always give the same answer: "Some kids are special and have only a mommy." And how, since hitting puberty, I hadn't been buying that so much. Once I even sneered, "Like Jesus." On more than one occasion, usually when I'd come home stoned, I'd get up in her face. I'd demand to know who my father is, and she'd snap, "Case closed." By eighteen, I'd stopped asking. None of this would reflect well on me if I told Obaachan.

She places her arm around my shoulder. "Think about it, Isaac. She was only fifteen. A girl." She goes silent, returning her gaze to the darkening sky. Then, as if getting a signal from a star, she says: "Let me tell the story of how your grandfather and I met."

"Sure," I say, though I'm not at all sure where this is going. I pour us each another glass.

"Thank you." She nods, taking two sips. "Your grandfather was a young American soldier stationed in Japan, I was a girl on my own. He was twenty, I was seventeen. This was 1957. We didn't meet in the most wholesome of places. A kind of cocktail bar—what in Japan we call, in our borrowed, quirky English, a *snack*. It was on Okinawa, far away from my hometown, Kobe. I had gone to Okinawa to earn money. Like most Japanese families at that time, we had little, and around the US military bases there was some money to be made. I washed glasses, wiped down the bar, and filled bowls with peanuts and sesame crackers for the hostess, the mama-san. For this, I received a small wage, as well as a tiny room behind the kitchen, plus all my meals."

She explains how Mama-san's snack was a place typical for the time: dimly lit, room for only ten customers, cozy in its way. Hers was frequented by gai-jin, almost all of them American service-men. At first, the foreigners frightened Obaachan. They seemed like giants, these conquerors. Mama-san was strict with the customers, even as she flirted and chatted with them. That was how she was supposed to act, and that was what they paid for: the chatting, the scolding, the flirting.

"If Mama-san had not kept me under her—what was to me, glamorous—wing and not negotiated the courtship with your grandfather, I might well have found myself in an unfortunate cir-cumstance. You see, I was pregnant." My grandfather spoke not a word of Japanese and Obaachan not a word of English, and so, besides negotiating a difficult situation, Mama-san also acted as interpreter.

"Thanks to Mama-san, your grandfather and I found respect for each other and, gradually, love and happiness. We married after only a month because of the baby coming and because your grand-father's time in the Army was up shortly. We moved to California. He did not want to return to Missouri, where he was from, and I had family in the San Francisco area. Although I had never met them, having them did make the change easier for me. My cousin Keiko became a sister to me. Your grandfather went to college while working as a night janitor at a hospital. Peter was born later that year. It was only then that I wrote to my mother and told her my secrets and that I had left Japan. As you know, I wouldn't see her again for nearly twelve years."

I press my palms against the sides of my face, take a deep sigh. I thank her for trusting me with her story. I get the point. Still, I have to ask: "I understand my mother not wanting her parents and other people to know, but why couldn't she tell me who my father is when I got older?"

Obaachan lowers her voice, as if someone might be listening in from beyond the dark hedge. "I cannot say for certain, Isaac, but I would suspect it became harder and harder to tell the secret the longer it was kept."

A solo bat dips low above our heads.

OCTOBER 1994, MIKE

From way down deep in a whisky sleep I somehow managed to register a soft knocking on the door and woke slow, so slow, dragging my way up to where my senses could start kicking in. The knocking comes across way too polite to be one of the vagrants who wanders into the building pretty much regularly. They tend to pound and yell. A woman downstairs told me the Arkadia's intercom system broke over a year ago, and the landlord has yet to fix it, so some residents leave the outside door ajar for friends, lovers, dealers—whoever— which means anyone can just walk in off the street and come to any apartment. This has got to be Lisa. She's the only living soul who knows I'm here. Giving me a second chance? I stumble out of the closet/bedroom, trying to get the morning wood tenting my underwear to go down. I open the chained door a crack and peer out.

I blink hard. *Daniel?* It's got to be dream garbage spilling out of my drunk head. I blink again. No, it really is Daniel. Daniel on this continent. Daniel standing in my doorway. Daniel standing in my doorway with a guitar case in hand. Disbelief mixes with the alcohol still in my blood, diluting weeks of anger that have built up. As much as I'd like to, I can't not unlatch the chain. I just can't. I slip it loose. We stand on either side of the threshold of the partly opened door in silence, me looking back on all the years that have joined us, him probably doing the same. Eventually he sets the case down, nudges the door open further with his shoulder, and before I can pull away, he has wrapped me in his arms. Now I'm wide awake and sober as a nun, feeling nakeder than naked, and lost.

"So, we meet again," he says slyly, tugging at my boner. I knock his hand off and step back.

His appearance is disorienting, to say the least. Daniel visible in my Invisible City. Daniel here after all that's happened. Daniel acting playful after all that's happened. I owe him everything, including my life, but still, that messed-up Isaac stratagem of his went way too far. If it were anyone else, I'd wipe that suave smile off their face. I turn away, head over to the streaked window overlooking the highway on-ramp.

"May I come in?" he asks, voice sweet like he doesn't get what's gone down.

I glance over my shoulder, don't respond. He picks the case up and steps in anyway. I turn back around to face him as he shuts the door, wondering what this place must look like to him. Wondering not because I'm embarrassed but wondering how he sees me in my natural habitat, so to speak. The only furniture is a folding lawn chair with yellow and white webbing in this room and a bare mattress I picked up off the curb in the adjoining one. Other possessions: a few odd dishes, a hot pot, a copy of *The Complete Poems of Emily Dickinson*, all from rummage sales. No phone, no radio, no TV. The few clothes I own are folded neatly in a stack on the floor, a shoring up against the ruin. What rays of morning sun that do make their way through the filthy panes can't wash the shabbiness away. I flatten my voice. "How'd you find me?"

He laughs, not at all nervous, as he should be. "I had Isaac's address from his letters, so I stopped by there when my plane got in last evening. His mother answered the door. She seemed angry and called for him from the other room. Like you, he was surprised to see me. He said they were in the middle of a fight, so he couldn't talk, but would get ahold of me at my hotel today. However, when I asked, he did tell me he wasn't sure where you were but recalled you joking about living in Arcadia. I asked around at shops, newsstands, a bank. Finally, a cabdriver recalled the building."

I fold my arms across my chest. "Well, your plan worked. You succeeded. I left your island."

Daniel's expression changes. He appears what—confounded? Upset? Not any look I've seen cross his face before. Still holding onto the guitar case, he moves in closer. He stops at arm's length in front of me. "Listen . . ." he begins, then pauses, eyes turning toward the ceiling. "Listen . . . it is true I wanted you to connect with the world a little more." He brings his eyes back down to meet mine. "I did not want you to leave. No, not at all. Please, go back. I want you to, I really do. It's your home."

Home? No word could sound more foreign. I squat, directing my speech to the scratched and gouged floorboards: "I was the guest who overstayed his visit. By a long shot. More like a freeloader." I glance up.

He's shaking his head. "Don't say that." There's panic in his voice, him the least panicky person on Earth. He kneels next to me.

I can't help mirroring his shaking head. I've lost all sense of anything. Or anyone. "I would have left if you'd just asked. Did you really have to go that far?"

"What do you mean by that?"

"Oh, come off it!" I get up and head toward the other room.

"What?" he calls after me.

I stop, wheel around. "Do I really have to say it? Isaac. Isaac is what I mean. Or rather, who. Isaac."

He stays there on his knees. "I know. I know I should never have brought him to the Island without asking you. That wasn't right. Again, I can't tell you how sorry I am."

"It's not just that you brought him. You thought it would be funny for Isaac and me to find out ourselves? It nearly killed the both of us."

"Find out what?"

"Oh, nothing much."

"What?"

I can't keep the sarcasm out of my voice: "Just that he's Pete's son."

His mouth opens wide, as if he's about to say something, but not a word comes out. Then he starts laughing. A weird half laugh, like a madman. Super sane Daniel as a madman scares me. Eventually he looks up. "I have no idea in the world what you're talking about."

"Come off it!"

"You really think that I, of all people, could know anything about what you're saying, even if it were true?" He gestures again and again at his chest with both hands. "I live in Europe. I know nothing about Isaac's past or Peter's."

I don't know how to react. I stay in the middle of the room, about to say something. Nothing comes. Only silence. The silence of my life. The silence of the story that's supposed to be my life.

He looks at me, jaw clenched, eyes blinking fast. "How could I have known what you are saying? How?"

Deeper silence.

At last, his features start to calm. "I had no idea. Truly." His voice now gentle. "I would never have imagined he is Peter's son."

I want to not believe Daniel. I want to believe that he knew all along and had plotted against me. It would be easier that way. To keep things between us ended. I hadn't expected to ever see him again. I'm fatalistic that way. Even though nearly half my remembered life has been spent with him, when I left the Island I felt that was it, that Fate had severed our bond forever. I owe him so much, and he's the only real human connection I've got, and still, I felt that way.

If it wasn't him, and if it wasn't Isaac, then is it me and only me who discovered (or desired?) the resemblance to Pete?

But I don't want to explain or talk things out. That's not how I work. That's not how I work, and that's the problem with my whole life. I have no idea what to think, what to say, not now, not ever. I go back over to Daniel, reach out my hand, pull him to his feet, and all I say is, "I think we both could use some rest." I lead him into what goes for my bedroom. We lie down on the foul, bare mattress, me on my back, him on his side close to me, facing me. He rests his hand flat on my sternum and rubs gently. He knows this calms me. Maybe I am an animal, after all. We fall asleep. It's not even noon, and we fall asleep.

It's dark when I wake and I'm screaming. It's dark and I'm bolt upright and Daniel is holding me, telling me everything's going to be alright, alright. Dark dreams tumble into dark memories and now into the dark bedroom. Daniel is holding me and I am holding on to him. From the instant I blacked out diving into the ocean to swim away from the Island these memories have been trying to force their way out of my mind's cellar. In the hold of the ship to Copenhagen, on the plane to New York, on the bus to Hallein, and then outside the bus station in Hallein when I met Jean-Kabuki, and then in the salt cave those first nights back. Only now have the memories finally busted out, free and clear. Something about Daniel's presence here has allowed this.

We lie back down together. Me on my back, him on his side, facing me. He runs his fingers through my hair. "Tell me," he whispers. "Please tell me what happened."

We both know too well the years of my not telling, of not being able to tell.

"What did they do to you?"

I could pretend I don't know what or who he's talking about. Reticence has been my trademark. I think again about all we've been through, all he's done for me, and understand that, at this point, silence would be unfair to this person who has loved me without expecting anything in return. Not only unfair, it would be unjust.

And so, I begin. I begin by telling Daniel that they did nothing to me. I tell him I made a choice. I went to them. After Pete died, I went to the French guys. I went for a fix, I went for what I guess I'd hoped would be the end—same as Pete's end, same as my brother's end—if I was even thinking that coherently. I suppose I was seeking some kind of union with them.

Jean-Marc and Jean-Luc were drinking wine with their girlfriends in their club when I walked in. It was early, no one else was there. I didn't tell Daniel that the one Jean's face was still bruised from when I'd beaten him up after the porn shoot. I didn't tell him about that either, the porn shoot. When I walked in, the one Jean signaled the girls to split and they did, like they were used to whatever was about to happen. The other Jean grabbed hold of me and twisted my arm behind my back. When I told them what I had come for, they laughed. They laughed as they took me, arm still behind my back, to a room in the basement. Except for a few random chairs in a row by a doorway opposite the one we'd entered through, the room was empty. With exaggerated politeness they offered me a seat. They told me the price and I paid. Then they shot me up and I was free to go. Just like that. But that was only the beginning. I kept coming back. I still had my ticket home to the States from London, but I didn't even try to use it.

When my money ran out, they said they could offer me work. Without euphemism they explained I'd be selling my body, and without hesitating I accepted. It didn't matter. I hardly knew I had a body anymore. Besides, sex had always been alien to me. They said they had a room I could work from. I wouldn't have to be out on the street. They'd bring the johns to me.

They took me through the other doorway in the basement. It led into a small and dimly lit room. They told me to undress and had me lie down naked on what looked like a wrestling mat. Then they turned the light off and left. Soon someone came in. He lay on top of me. When he was done, another came. There were three more that first night.

As the door opened, I would sometimes catch a glimpse of the man entering, the one whose turn it was. There were men of all ages. Some in business suits, some in coveralls, some in jeans and T-shirts. Some thin, some fat, some weak, some strong. Some silent, some loud. The sharpest memories, though, are of smells. Colognes and aftershaves, toothpaste and liquor, sweat and even shit. And of sensations. Hot breath, hands on me, all over me, in me, some rough, others gentle. Of dicks pressing into me. At first, great pain. Pain and more pain, and then, gradually, it lessened until I felt no pain, until I felt nothing at all. Daniel didn't need the details, so I spared him. Each night one of the French guys would give me a hit, right there, naked on the gym mat, and hand me the rest of my earnings in cash. After that, I was free to get my clothes and leave. But I always returned. I always returned.

When I'm finished telling, we lie together in the dark for a long time. He doesn't say a word, only caresses me. It has started to rain hard. I get up and extend a hand to Daniel. In silence I lead him to the narrow bathroom. The bare bulb in the ceiling shows the cracked and broken tiles around the tub and in the honeycomb pattern on the floor, as well as the black mold in the grout I tried to scrub away when I first moved in. The mirror has cracks yet still reflects my pale, haggard face without mercy.

I'm still in just my underwear; Daniel's in his usual cords and dress shirt. I take his wrist and unclasp his watch, setting it with a heavy clink on the glass shelf above the sink. Then he lets me unbutton his shirt. I've never unbuttoned his shirt before. The buttons are iridescent, the cloth soft and fine. I undo the cuffs, lift the shirt off his freckled shoulders, pull his arms out and hang it on a broken ceramic hook fixed to the back of the door. His familiar torso is suddenly not. I'm seeing him differently. He's no longer an abstract need. He is a specific desire. His pronounced clavicle and sharp shoulder blades make me think of bows and arrows, of birds. A constellation of moles in the shape of a dragon plays over his chest. He lets me unbuckle his belt, unbutton and unzip his corduroys. I pull them down to his ankles and lift his feet out, one at a time.

I then take his socks off. I'd forgotten how muscly his legs are from all the walking and biking he does. The white-blond hairs glisten in this harsh light. His feet are like flippers. I hang the corduroys on the hook with the shirt. We stand there in our underwear (mine cotton briefs, his silk boxers) studying each other for a moment. I pull the moldy plastic shower curtain outside of the tub, bend over, and turn the squeaky spigots on, adjusting to get the temperature right. I turn back to Daniel and, still crouching, pull his boxers down. Like his shoulder blades, his hip bones are sharply angled. These are things I of course have seen but have never really noticed, if that makes sense. His uncircumcised penis, even flaccid, is oversized and curves like a scimitar to the right. I've seen his body and felt his body many times, but why now have the details become so vivid to the point of overwhelming me? It's as if only now, after the dark has been spoken, that I know him and he can know me.

I test the water. He lets me lift his feet, again one at a time, into the tub, even though he could do it—or any of this—himself. He of course understands what scene from the past is playing out here. I lower him into the water. I soap him up and scrub him with an old T-shirt I've been using as a washcloth. He lies there, looking content. I drain the tub, stand him up, shower him, wash his hair. The last thing I do is dry him with my one coarse, gray towel. At last, I lead him back to the bed.

"You got a place to stay?" I ask, though I know the answer. It's a feeble gesture, an attempt at giving back. "You can stay here, if you'd like." Lying on this dirty mattress with a ratty blanket, no sheets, fully clothed is one thing, but naked is quite another.

Unbelievably, he says he'd like that.

Our bodies here, stripped of mountain, ocean, sky. Our bodies here.

When I wake up, Daniel's lying on his side, one arm propping his head, smiling at me. He kisses me on the forehead and rolls out of bed. After all the rain, morning comes on brighter than I can recall since being back. I'd forgotten to close the blinds. He heads into the other room and brings the guitar case back over. Something funny about a naked man carrying a guitar case. He sits on the edge of the bed with the case on his lap. "You left something behind," he says, opening it.

My guitar! His great gift to me now given again. It glows as sweet as ever inside a new case. It was so long ago, my second summer on the Island, when Daniel arrived with it. He said I deserved better than his family's old parlor guitar. The Martin D-35 Dreadnought is such a beauty, top-of-the-line. That bound solid spruce top, a black-and-white rosette, rosewood back and sides, ebony fretboard. I'm floored. I give him a big hug and thank him again and again. Some other time I might tell him about the ridiculous circumstance in which the original case was lost.

He smiles. "You'll need it." He lifts the instrument from its velvet bed. "We have to rehearse."

I look at him, confused. He hands it to me like he's handing me a child.

"The music school at the university here has invited us to play."

"Us?" This is completely unexpected, not to mention weird.

He nods. "I was listening to the old recording we did with the band. That, and what you've been doing the last few years, made me think we should give it a go. Now that we're away from the Island, may as well. It will be low stakes. The music hall seats an intimate five hundred. I thought it would be a good place. Neutral territory." He smiles a little brighter.

It doesn't surprise me that he could have arranged a concert here on such short notice—if Daniel Beck wanted to play Carnegie Hall tomorrow, they'd make it happen—but this is monumentally crazy. How did he even know he'd find me? It's been way too long since I've performed. Besides, I don't think I even want to perform. How could he assume I'd want to and go ahead with these arrangements? Low stakes? For who? And neutral territory? More like enemy territory. I've hardly ever stepped foot on campus and it's right here in my so-called hometown. I don't bother explaining. All I say is, "I'm not ready."

"Don't worry, it will be great. You'll be great." It's as if he didn't hear me. He lies back on the mattress, next to me. "Look," he continues, "music is what you do. You could make a good living performing on your own. I'm sure of that."

As if I've already agreed to this scheme, he explains how it will go. He'll play with me here and a couple of other places, just to get things rolling, and then he'll help me arrange more venues and dates to do on my own. He even has the program planned for this first one.

When he's done explaining, I roll onto my stomach, hiding my face in the musty batten.

"We'll split the fifteen thousand dollars."

That number works like an emergency brake on my train of thought. It's obviously more than I've ever seen, though probably a huge pay cut for him. I roll over onto my back again.

"You'll be great." He rubs my stomach.

"Okay," I sigh, though I'm not at all convinced. Maybe I do need this—need him, his motivation. Left to my own devices, nothing would happen. Then again, I'm not sure I want anything to happen. For a few moments, I picture moving to his invisible house up the coast from his Visible City. I know that's probably what he wants in the long run. Some part of me wants it too. We could spend our days together there, with music, and spend our summers on the Island. Idyllic. But idyllic's not really me.

Back at the River Club, where it all started. Not sure Isaac knew this when he invited me. He thought I'd like the band, and once I got the past pushed out the door, I'm finding I do, I really do. They're called Fugazi and they're kind of amazing. Between sets, I tell Isaac, "They're a whole lot more sophisticated than the No Names ever were."

"But not better," he insists.

"Not so sure about that. Their anger has focus, purpose."

"So did yours."

"Besides, they're cooler."

"Definitely not."

I give my usual shrug paired with a fake cough. Classic me. We stay in the back of the room. I'm trying to lie low. As if anyone's going to recognize me. Most of the people who came to the No Names shows are probably married by now, with kids, holed up in the suburbs. Just as I'm thinking this, up in front I spot what looks to be a version of Jimmy Ryder. He's seriously at least a hundred pounds heavier, in a wheelchair, on oxygen. You can hear the machine going *click-click-click* between songs. Definitely don't want him to see me, don't want to hear his surprise, let alone any way belated condolences.

Isaac and I have a bunch of beers and are feeling pretty good. The show ends. It was great. Starting to almost feel back in my former world. He asks if I want to get high. I say sure. I don't add that it'll my first time since '78. We leave the club and wander down to the riverbank. Other people have the same idea. Pairs and groups huddle around glowing bowls and joints. Miles above, a jet unzips the bright night. Venus throbs.

Because I'm still not that used to being around people, watching them transfixes me in a way it never did before. It's as if either I or they are some strange species. Three long-haired women in way high-heeled shoes and way short skirts are smoking from a glass pipe. Isaac tells me it's likely something called crack. They're talking loud. The one tells the other about the third, like she's not even there: "I gave her a diamond ring and everything, and she goes stealing my brand-new color television set!"

The third, sucking her teeth, looks sideways at the one who made the comment. "Shit," she mutters, "it was just a chip."

Isaac nudges me to move on down the river.

"Good seeing you, man," I tell him, and I mean it.

"You too." He fake punches my shoulder.

Then, behind us, all hell breaks loose. Screaming and shouting—lots of *fuck* and *bitch*. We look back around. The three ladies are going at it, rolling on down the bank and into the river, tearing at each other's clothes and hair. They're punching and kicking, even as they're trying to stay afloat. People run down to break it up, cheer them on, or both. The scene seems like all humanity in a nut-shell: love and betrayal, connection and disconnection.

"Come on," Isaac says, pulling me by the arm.

He tamps the weed down in his little brass one-hitter as we carry on downriver. He's wearing a T-shirt that says *Fermat's Last Theorem* on the front. On the back are a bunch of proofs, each one crossed out. One of the things besides music that we bonded over on the Island was math. I *feel* numbers and am interested in math but was a terrible student. He feels them too but is a whiz. Which is cool. He can explain things.

He sparks up, takes a long toke. On the exhale he says, "I'm spend-ing a lot of time with Mrs. Lac—I mean, my grandmother!—now." He passes the pipe to me. "Most nights I stay at her place."

"You're kidding?" I'm more than a little surprised but guess this is a good development.

He puts his arm around my shoulder in a dad kind of way that's become part of the jokey rapport developing between us. Making his voice deeper than normal, he says, "I kid you not." He laughs. "Seriously, it's better this way. I can't get over what my mom did. Keeping me in the dark all these years. Keeping me from this awe-some grandma."

"What does your mom think?"

"Not much, I'd guess," he says with a weird old-man chuckle, "as she doesn't know. It's my turn to keep her in the dark."

I take a hit. The archaic memory of Pete and Lynn Burns in the sumacs resurfaces again. Isaac's looking at me like he's expecting I'll side with him. But I can't. I turn away. I never knew his mother, or, rather the girl I'm pretty sure became his mother, but still, I can't dismiss her, can't condemn how she's dealt with her kid. It's her kid, her life. I don't want to piece back together that night down at the river—*this* river—half my lifetime ago, but the pieces won't scatter. The moment I turn back toward Isaac, the scene starts play-ing inside my head.

I wasn't looking for Pete, that much I know. I literally stumbled upon him and this girl who now, all these years later, is looming large in my life. I've got to turn away again. I take a few steps toward the riverbank and toe a rock into the current. The air's warm for October but I'm feeling cold, sweaty and cold at the same time.

Isaac wants to know what do I think, what do I think, isn't she a real bitch?

I don't know, so I tell him, "I don't know."

"What do you mean, you don't know?"

The traffic on the new interstate bridge in the middle distance—or at least new since I left—sings through our silence.

"I was there. I saw them."

"What?"

I squat at the edge of the water. He doesn't come down beside me. Laughter in the distance. Real life in the distance. I see us, hear us, from the perspective of those people partying along the bank. Maybe one of them looks over at Isaac and me and in that instant understands our knot of hurt and loss better than we—or at least I—do?

"This is tough," I say, twisting my neck to look up at him. Now he does come down next to me. He shuffles his feet in the pebbles. Looking nowhere but into the past, I begin. I remind him we were at a kegger, as if that's part of an explanation or just an excuse. I emphasize that Pete and I were sixteen, his mom fifteen. I tell him how a lot of kids were pairing off, finding someplace to make out. I tell him how embarrassed I was when I came upon them having sex. I don't tell him that I never saw her clearly there in the shadows, that I couldn't swear to God it was her. I also don't tell him that at first it sort of turned me on a little, her lying there under Pete. I remind him that I left after a moment but don't say how long a moment it was. Lucky for me, I guess, that language is like that, imprecise. I cannot bring myself to confess that my hand touched the breast that nursed him or held his father's cock when he was about to shoot the load that would create him. Only now does it occur to me I was like the opposite of a midwife—a midhusband?—aiding in conception instead of birth. Unlike a midwife, though, my role was hardly wholesome. I was looking on, I tell him, and leave it at that.

I explain to Isaac how, as far as I know, they never got together again. Then I recall—or at least I think I recall—the same girl was here, right here at the River Club, at our first show ever, and neither Pete or I talked to her or with any of the other rich girls she was there with. It dawns on me only now that by then Isaac was already born. I don't tell him this. I don't know why, I just don't.

I finish by saying, with as much integrity as an unethical jerk like me can call up or fake, "I loved him—I mean, I love him—you know that—but sometimes he didn't treat girls right, didn't respect them. Sure, we were young, but still. I'm thinking maybe your mom has never wanted reminders, doesn't want to acknowledge him in any way. You've got to cut her some slack."

Isaac presses his forehead to his knees. He doesn't say anything.

OCTOBER 1994, ISAAC

I open the throttle wide. The Kawasaki loves to run. Mike and I spent the whole night down by the river talking, and now it's finally late enough in the morning that I can go see Vashti and talk with her about everything. I haven't been to her house very much in the past couple weeks. I mean, I haven't been *home*. Sure, I'm stressed about confronting her, but after talking with Obaachan, and now Mike, everything's clear, or at least clearer than it was. Finally have to admit, they're right, I can't not talk to her.

As I pull onto our street, Vashti's there, out in the driveway with two blue plastic buckets, hose running in one. It's overflowing, creating a narrow river down the sloped pavement. I pull in. One of those huge aquariums from up in the attic is sitting in the middle of the driveway. How the hell did she get it down from there? And why now, after like fifteen years? She's working on the crusty insides. I cut the engine. She doesn't so much as glance up from the job of peeling away layers of khaki-colored film from the glass with a razor blade.

I lift my helmet off and say, "Hey," but quickly correct myself, "Hi." She hates *hey*. Still no response. "What're you doing?"

Not a word.

I dismount. "Sorry haven't been around much." I rub the toe of my Van across the concrete. "Can we talk, Mom?" Took some effort not to call her *Vashti*.

She sets the razor blade down on a sheet of wet newspaper and peers up. Eventually, she stands. The sun now rising above the garage roof illuminates her face. She looks sad. In that moment I feel for probably the first time ever as if I'm seeing her as a person. The mother-of-pearl snaps on her blouse glow, as if they have pinhead-sized electric lights inside of them or bits of moonlight.

"You just disappear, and I'm not supposed to worry?"

She's all mom again and I'm all little kid.

I rub my forehead. "Sorry," I say, me the one who stopped saying sorry when I was like ten.

"Where've you been?" Before I can answer, she elaborates, "Where've you been sleeping?"

And before I can answer either question, she's heading into the garage and I'm following. Even yesterday, I wouldn't have. She goes into the kitchen, and, like a puppy, I'm right behind. On the blue soapstone island sits the other large aquarium from the attic, this one perfectly clean, full of water, and containing an amazingly realistic forest in miniature. A bonsai-size forest. Neon fish dip and dart among the branches and rocky outcroppings. After all these years she's suddenly into aquaculture again? We circle the island, her picking up as she goes a half-full coffee mug, a plate of toast crumbs, some coupons. I'm searching like crazy for words. I look around at the Brazilian cherry cabinets and German appliances. All of a sudden, the house I grew up in appears unfamiliar, though maybe it never was familiar, not really.

I'm building up the momentum to tell her I've been staying at my grandmother's. That's the plan. A bit of a jolt maybe, yet a perfectly natural entry point for telling her all that I've found out. But there's not a chance to say anything. As she opens a cupboard to put the coffee grinder away, she says, just as calm as she never is, "It doesn't really matter. You're moving out."

Oblivious to whatever human drama may or may not be taking place, the fish flock calmly, like birds, above the forest.

She turns back to face me. "And because I'm not going to live up to being the bitch you always make me out to be, I'm not throwing you out."

I look at her, stunned, puzzled.

"You're nineteen. It's about time you get a life. And I need mine back. The lease is up on the condo at the end of the month and the renters aren't renewing, so to get you set up, I'll let you have it for a year. If you decide to go to college, you can stay past that, and I'll continue your allowance. Otherwise, at that point, you'll have to get a job."

Not sure what to say or do, I run my nails back and forth on the soapstone, making faint scratches on the surface. The fish glide in unison to the surface of the aquarium.

Amid the ordinariness—the ordinary luxury—of this kitchen, I'm trying to find extraordinary words to make everything okay. I fail.

The fish spiral down into the depths of the tank, disappearing behind the base of the mountain.

The sicko bond between us finally gets severed. And she's the one who had the guts to finally do it. All drama now evaporated, our relationship instantly becomes more or less a business contract. Not how I thought this would play out, not at all. I'd pictured her face going full-on gargoyle as she gestalted the whole story in my bomb about staying at my grandmother's. I could just hear her bad-actress routine, full of *How dare yous* and the like. I'd even pictured us going mano a mano—and I don't mean figuratively—like we used to but haven't since the night I came home high from a dance in tenth grade and she, practically strip-searching me, found E in my sock. We went at it till I let her pin me on the kitchen floor, let her pin me because you don't want to be fighting your mom physically, let alone winning, you just don't. And after the fight I'd imagined we'd have over my dad and Obaachan, there'd be lots of crying and wailing, which would sputter out into psychobabble picked up from all our times in family therapy (which we would always bomb out of). I thought my whole big announcement would be combo *Medea, Dynasty* (especially the episodes with catfights), and *Donahue*.

In some way I'm relieved, though. What if she denied it? Every time I see Pete's picture, a slight shadow of doubt is cast. What if she dragged my ass to get one of those new DNA paternity tests and it turned out Mike was wrong? I mean, they just found out after decades that the skeleton in some mass grave really was the Czar. Then my life with Obaachan would be wrecked. Not sure I could take that. I reach to touch Mom's shoulder but she's already moving away from me, back toward the garage. I follow as she heads to the Audi and opens the door. "I have an acupuncture appointment," she tells me as she slides in and starts the engine. "I'll take you to the Club for dinner tomorrow night. We'll talk details then." She's backing out, head turned to look behind.

It's seriously great speeding across the countryside with Mike on the back of the bike. Antidote to the breakup with Mom two days ago. Wish we could ride forever. We're headed out to Bethel Grove, where his dad's family's from. He wants to get walnuts so he can start a batch of that nocino drink. We're going to surprise Obaachan. He's finally agreed to come see her, after me asking like a hundred times. Maybe because he was drunk? It was last night, after the Bikini Kill show at the River Club. In any case, he said yes. For my dad he's doing it, he said, for my dad.

In about an hour, we come to the miniscule town, village, hamlet—or whatever it is—of Bethel Grove. An old mill straddles the creek running through the center. There's a shut IGA, a boarded-up two-story brick Catholic school. A church, also brick, with the bizarre name of St. Caspar del Bufalo (looks like they're missing an *f*?), and the adjoining convent with the equally bizarre name of St. Germana Cousin, both of which look like they're still in business. Further on, an old-timey gas station—the kind that looks like Hansel and Gretel's cottage, only with pumps out front—is collapsing in on itself. About two dozen large Victorians, some of which look vacant, line the main street, while smaller houses run along the three side streets. At the edge of town, Mike directs me to the cemetery. We cruise through a rusted iron archway. A good breeze pushes compact little clouds across the sun, setting the place in motion.

The second we're on the grounds, Mike tells me to pull over, like there's something wrong. He jumps off the bike.

"My God," he says, shaking his head as he looks all around.

"What?"

He lowers his head and stands there looking like a defeated warrior. "They're gone," he mumbles, "totally gone." He looks up and lifts his hands to massage his temples.

"I don't understand." He walks off the blacktop, placing his sneaker on a tree stump the diameter of a car tire. He goes maybe twenty feet farther and puts his foot on another.

"Every one of them," he says, waving his hand up and down the drive. "Dozens of the best walnut trees in the world. Gone." He continues surveying the grounds, as if he's going to find the trees hidden somewhere. Anger flares in his dark eyes. "My dad used to tell me how the parish was routinely offered a fortune for them, for lumber, because the boles were so incredibly straight. The priest always swore they'd never do a thing like that, sell."

He walks away from me, like he needs to mourn alone. Along the drive he goes, maybe counting stumps. After a while he heads in among the graves, stopping in front of a group of pink granite headstones. I hang back, counting the rings of one of the stumps. More than a hundred.

I go over and stand beside him. All five stones have *Abramczyk* carved into them. Brown ants march over their surfaces, climbing in and out of the chiseled letters. Three of the Abramczyks died before Mike was born, all in 1949, though different days. Faustina Martyna and Tadeusz Benedikt, both thirty; Ewa Angelika, age ten. The other two stones show *John James Abramczyk, May 1, 1952–November 3, 1970* and *Stanislaw Krzysztof Abramczyk, April 7, 1929–December 7, 1986.*

He licks his thumb, leans down and tries wiping off purple and white bird shit that's dried right above the *John* and the *James*. He only manages to smear it. He wipes his thumb on his thigh, stands back up to look at his work, then leans down again to give it another go.

We're standing there, when out of the blue he asks in a voice that's both empty and angry, "Where'd you get the bike?" Before I can answer, he's already turned and starts walking away.

Trailing behind, I tell him what I know: "My mom got it. From some collector, upriver. For my birthday. I'd always wanted an early 500cc Kawasaki.

Mike shrugs. "Let's go." He obviously doesn't want to talk about it.

"Still up for Obaachan's?"

He shrugs again, his face a funeral.

I say, "You drive, okay?"

He nods, mounts the bike, kick-starts it. I hop on and we whip off like he's been riding this bike his whole life.

Obaachan's out weeding on hands and knees. She looks up when she hears the familiar engine, her face partly hidden by dahlias. She leaps to her feet, dropping her trowel, and runs through the gate toward us. She's laughing full out, like I've never seen anyone laugh, not ever. Mike grins, breaking his whole face wide open. She grabs hold of him with both arms, hugging him and shaking him.

"I knew that one day you would come!" She's gasping for air. "I am so happy!" She stands back to get a good long look at him, eventually hooking her arm in his. "Come in, come in. I was about to start dinner. You'll stay?"

I feel like I'm in a Western, when the long-lost hero comes from out of nowhere in a vast landscape that's all mesas and canyons, appearing at the homestead he left forever ago. I answer for him, "Of course he will!"

Mike is uncharacteristically goofy, almost giddy. "Sure, why not?"

Obaachan is making yosenabe, this amazing stew I love. It's got salmon and clams, as well as weird kinds of mushrooms and chrysanthemum greens. Mike recalls it from back in the day, licking his chops like a cartoon wolf.

"Please pour some beer, Isaac," Obaachan asks, slicing at super speed a head of Chinese cabbage into perfectly even thin ribbons.

I go to the fridge, bring out one of the twenty-two-ounce bottles of the Japanese stuff and pour three small glasses, which is how they do it over in Japan.

Mike looks so relaxed slouched in one of the yellow kitchen chairs, sipping beer. He's practically purring.

Obaachan tells him with that pure smile of hers, "I don't know how to thank you for this one!" She points to me with the knife. I'm sure I blush.

She sets the hotplate on the maple dining table, plugs it in, then goes back to the kitchen and gets the pot and places it down on the orange coil. The seafood is arranged on a sea-colored platter, ready to go in when the broth returns to a simmer. She has me bust out the sake and light candles while she runs upstairs to change.

A few minutes later she returns, looking amazing in a red silk blouse and tan skirt. We sit down. With giant chopsticks, she picks up the fish and shellfish a piece at a time, quickly, and drops them into the pot. Mike and I sit there mesmerized. She watches the stew carefully, so the fish won't overcook. When it's done, she serves overflowing ladlefuls into our black-and-red lacquer bowls.

With his first sip of broth, Mike announces, "This was my favorite dish."

Obaachan laughs. "I thought tonkatsu was."

Mouth now full of fish, he laughs right back at her, "That too!" He slurps more broth, then sets his ceramic spoon down.

The faint sound from Obaachan's AM big-band station filters in from the vintage GE Tabletop on the kitchen counter. The crimson blouse sets off her pale face. The dangling pearl earrings glow supernaturally in the candlelight. She looks like a goddess—a real goddess, not just a figure-of-speech goddess. Everything's perfect, as if the occasion hadn't been spontaneous and she was some famous hostess who had planned the evening carefully for weeks in advance. Mike sits there, the guest of honor, appearing maybe relieved but definitely content to be back in her realm.

Even with all this happiness, a current of sadness flows between the two of them. It likely won't ever disappear, at least not completely. This is probably how it has to be or even should be. It's like the thin stream of cold air that rose out from a deep crevice on a hot summer day once when Vashti and I went hiking in the Tetons. Of course, my father's the source of their sadness. It's weird how similar their fates have been since his death. Both living in isolation, both creating worlds of their own—he with his music, she with her garden.

Obaachan laughs at something Mike says and happiness returns, sealing the crevice up, at least for now. I take one of the chrysanthemums from the vase in the middle of the table. It's the color of a seashell. I reach over and tuck it behind Mike's ear. He doesn't seem to mind. He's leaning back, sake cup in hand. He smiles. Obaachan smiles.

"Come on," he says, taking Obaachan by the hand, "let's go into the night."

His words are a weird echo of my last night on the Island, but I like how he says that, *go into the night*. Sounds almost archaic.

I pour more sake. Then, with cups in hand, the three of us step into the garden. Her little paradise. It's an act of will, love, imagination. Once we've moved past the yellow rectangles of light cast onto the lawn, we stop and look into the night sky.

Mike turns to Obaachan and says, "I have to apologize." He coughs. "I promised I'd take care of Pete. I failed."

She gasps slightly, then pauses before responding, "I should never have asked you to promise such a thing. I was so angry for too long before I understood this."

Silence comes over us. The last fireflies of the season flicker in the hedge. I raise my cup: "To the memory of my father." They raise their cups, nod, and offer smiles that sail off somewhere into the dark, somewhere unknown to me.

We sit at the picnic table drinking sake and talking about my dad till the edge of the horizon starts turning milky, at which point we all rise, as if on command, and head back into the house.

"We'll have another party soon," Obaachan says as the three of us go up the stairs, as if our going up the stairs were the most natural thing in the world. "I hope it will be with your mother, Isaac, and with this Daniel you boys talk so much about."

Maybe Daniel, I think. But there's a long way to go before Vashti becomes a part of anything having to do with the me she knows let alone with the me she doesn't know. At our divorce dinner at the Club, I asked her, now that I was going to be out of the house, if she would tell me who my father is. I didn't even hint that I knew. Over enormous slabs of prime rib, she told me no. She added that she needed a total break from family stuff. Estranged from her parents for years because of the very existence of me, and having a relentless antagonist in me, I kind of get it. She has a feeling that she and I will get along better now that we'll be apart. Strange as it seems, after my not-so-great experience with family—basically just her—for the first time in my life I think how maybe one day I'd like to give family a whirl.

I take my father's bed, Mike takes what Obaachan calls "Mike's bed." As we're nodding off, he reaches across the space between us and, touching me on the shoulder, whispers, "Hey, thanks."

"For what?"

"I needed to come here, to her."

Suddenly I'm obsessed with the idea of the two of us living here with Obaachan.

Before the concert I stopped backstage to wish Mike and Daniel luck. Both are wearing jeans with dress shirts. The one probably more dressed up than usual for a performance, the other less. Maybe they planned it that way. Daniel looked completely at ease, smiling and talking with well-wishers who seem to know him. Maybe from the Hallein Orchestra? Mike stood in a corner, unreadable.

The house is full. It's a small concert hall but still, this has got to boost Mike's confidence. The place is Gothic, lit by heavy brass chandeliers with red and amber glass shades that match the narrow stained-glass windows. I'm sitting with Obaachan. It's a little surprising to see Mike's sisters a few rows up, looking totally normal. An old girlfriend of his is also here. I think her name is Lisa.

The hall goes absurdly crazy when Daniel and Mike walk onstage together. It's obviously for Daniel. The two of them have their music under their arms, and Mike is of course also carrying his acoustic. Fans probably feel like they've won the lottery, getting tickets to a surprise concert by Daniel Beck at such a small venue.

Acknowledging the audience with a nod, Daniel sits down at the piano, hands positioned above the keyboard, ready to strike. The place goes silent. Mike takes a chair, shifts to get comfortable with his guitar. They'll be starting with Bach's Cello Suite 1. They've combined various arrangements for guitar with Daniel's own for piano. It will be a perfect opening, Daniel explained, a piece so familiar as to lull all the classical concertgoers in, so when he and Mike start fucking with it, they'll be there, at least part way. It was the first time I'd ever heard Daniel swear but, as would only be possible with him, *fucking* comes off polite.

Right as Daniel's fingers are about to meet the ivories, Mike kind of shakes his head and raises his arm. Keeping his eyes focused on the floor, he stands up and heads offstage with his guitar. Wow. He's backing out. He'd had his doubts, but this is crazy. The audience buzzes with confusion. Daniel furrows his brow, squinting into the wings, obviously as miffed as anyone. His face reddens. He doesn't go after Mike. I suppose, pro that he is, the show must go on. Daniel will have to play the duet solo. He takes a couple deep breaths and begins. He's like a magician casting a spell that fills the place instantly with something beyond beauty, calming the crowd. Then, unexpectedly, after ten or so measures the same melody echoes from far offstage, only it's not coming from an acoustic, it's from an electric. Whoa! Maybe another ten measures later, Mike strides back onstage, looking confident, playing the Bach on a flame-colored electric guitar, rolling an amp along behind him. Daniel might have gotten pissed off, sullen, walked out, or any number of things in response to this unbelievable change of plan, but he's actually smiling. Then he tosses his head back, laughing, as he and Mike continue the piece. Mike offers up a bit of Hendrix-like feedback, as if to serve notice, in case the audience hadn't already gotten the idea that this is going to be an out of the ordinary listening experience. According to the original plan, Daniel and Mike linger a fraction of a second longer on each note than is written, in order to take listeners to a place in Bach where they've never been before. The two alternate between Mike's more emotional style and Daniel's more cerebral. Halfway through, they pick up the tempo. It's like they've gone full tilt rock 'n' roll with ol' Johann Sebastian. The audience doesn't quite know how to react. When the piece is over, applause comes, a little hesitant, though not weak.

The next piece on the program, "Invisible Citizen," comes from the album Daniel did with the No Names, *Undersong*, the one that was never released. It's like nothing anyone in the audience has ever heard, that's for sure. All I can say is that it's like a punk opera-aria, which sounds ridiculous, I know, but that's the only way to describe this hard-hitting yet hummable melody that starts spinning out to absurd lengths over nearly ten minutes, interrupted by high-risk riffs that uglify it every now and then. Like a weird, wobbly gyre, the line expands and varies with every turn. Sometimes smoother, sometimes more jagged. And the words, while not artsy, have more what I'd call grace to them than the songs on *Invisible City*. Mike sings,

> City of fate, city of bad luck, we're your surplus, overflowing
>   parks and streets,
> City of fate don't worry, city of bad luck no need to give a
>   damn, we'll keep it all
>   invisible, so invisible.

No need to worry, we'll keep the riots invisible, our screams
    only echoes floating
        down the river that we loved so much that it became
        invisible . . .

After this, Daniel leaves the stage for Mike to perform some of his newer work solo. Mike's body folds itself even tighter around the guitar. The music starts soaring off to unknown places. These pieces mystified me on the Island and they mystify me now. It's difficult to explain because explaining risks making it sound like the music careens into obscurity. It doesn't. It might come off as crazy, but it's as if the sorrow of the whole world has entered the hall through the strings of his guitar, the narrow limits to which he has confined himself for all these years. Confined, but it's like he knew these limits contain the entire universe, or at least *an* entire universe, the way a seashell contains the entire sea. This awareness has got to be what accounts for the unbeliev-able power of the performance. But, as Daniel once told me, "The uncanny facility of Michael's compositions cannot in any way be fully accounted for." Sounds stiff, but he gets it. The result of his intense vision isn't in the specifics of the pieces but in their effects. Right this very second, the music's making a psychic emer-gency in me.

When intermission comes, the audience seems confused. For five intense seconds, there's not a sound. And then applause, cautious at first. It grows more enthusiastic—it does—though it doesn't get out of control the way I feel deep inside.

For the second half of the program, there are empty seats. The hall's now maybe three-quarters full. Because it's been forever since the No Names, most of the people have of course come to hear Daniel Beck and are probably disappointed to have anyone else take center stage, let alone a has-been punker. Adding to that, completely new stuff tends to put a lot of people off. But people are lame. Studies show that the more times a piece of music is heard, regardless of genre or quality, the more popular it is.

Mike's pieces in the second half are just as brilliant, though very short and more varied, like pebbles on a shore. He focuses intensely on those strings, his head keeping time. There's something so inward about his performance that it becomes outward. It's like he's giving the innermost part of himself to the outermost reaches of not just us but the world. By the way they're shifting in their seats, I get the feeling people are starting to think the music is inaccessible. Then Daniel joins in, and they do a few songs from *Invisible City*, just in case some old fans have shown up. These are perfect for me, and sad. In the middle of "Altared Boy," Mike and Daniel look at each other with what looks like grief in their eyes. Nothing overt. Really subtle. I'm probably the only one who picks up on it.

The recital closes with Haydn. They do a couple of familiar movements from his piano sonatas transcribed for guitar before falling into *The Creation* transcribed from the oratorio. Haydn on electric guitar. Awesome. They look beautiful playing up there, the one head blond, the other black, really communicating with each other, balancing each other with their styles.

When the concert finishes, some people stand for an ovation, some people hurry out. I spot Vashti! Hadn't seen her before the concert started or at intermission. She's in the back, under the balcony, and she slips out before I can signal to her or anything. What exactly brought her here? And, if she saw me, is she wondering the same thing?

There's a reception in the lobby afterward. All proper. Champagne and canapés served by students wearing lame clip-on bowties. Around a third of the remaining audience—maybe a hundred people—have stayed. They mostly ask Daniel for autographs and do their fan thing. But those who approach Mike also appear enthusiastic. Obaachan, of course. His friend Lisa gives him a big hug and a kiss. They both show affection that's genuine and deep, coming from connection longer than I can imagine. Lisa tells him, "I'm not exactly sure what I heard tonight, but it was the best!" The Black woman with her hugs him, shakes him, and says with a laugh, "I knew you had talent way back then on that ukulele!" There are also well-wishers he doesn't seem to know. They ask him to sign their programs.

Obaachan has moved to the edge of the room. Under a fake balcony carved with griffons, she's daubing her eyes with one of the beautiful silk handkerchiefs she brought with her when she moved away from Japan all those years ago.

I wait until the crowd thins out before going up to Daniel and Mike. "You guys rocked the hall, so to speak." Then I hug them both at the same time. "Seriously, what you did was something I could never do in a million years. Which goes without saying!"

Daniel's beaming and he's not a beamer. "I'm pleased," he says, "really pleased." Which is out of control enthusiastic for a guy like him.

I'm guessing they'll probably tour and hopefully make a record of this amazing stuff down the road. There's nothing like it out there.

Mike's sisters seem to have disappeared, though I did see them grinning when the lights came up, going gaga with applause, proud of their long-lost brother.

More people leave. Obaachan is one of the last to say good-night, thanking them both as she goes. Then it's pretty much me and the guys.

"Why don't we head to the hotel for a drink?" Daniel suggests.

There's a slightly awkward silence before Mike answers, "Thanks, but I'm drained, totally drained, and have to work in the morning."

"Oh," Daniel says, sounding disappointed, "you're not staying over?"

"I'd like to, but my work clothes are back at the apartment." Then, as if he thinks he might be sounding ungrateful, he adds, "Don't know how to thank you for this." He gestures toward the hall.

"Don't mention it," Daniel says. "In Isaac's lingo, together we'll rock the world."

Mike nods and offers a smile as he hugs Daniel good night. It's weird, neither one of them mentions when they'll see each other again, so I say, "We'll stop by the country club to see you tomorrow, when I take Daniel to the airport." I give Mike a lame hug and lame words. "You were great."

Mike nods again, lifts his two guitar cases and amp, and heads for the doors.

"See you later," Daniel says, walking ahead of him to hold the door open.

A few steps into the Arts Quad and Mike turns back around and echoes, "See you later."

After the concert, Daniel took me to his hotel for some wine. Expensive. French. We closed the bar down, at which point he announced he wasn't going to invite me to his room. Kind of predictable, but who does that? Why make a big deal of *not* inviting someone to your room? Why even mention it? Maybe it was said in some kind of weird loyalty to his weird relationship with Mike? To my amazement, he then suggested we ride up to the salt mines instead, like we did the night we met. *Cool,* I thought, and we headed out.

There, in the moonlit cave, we discussed music and philosophy and math and the whole freaking universe till dawn. It was perfect, the kind of conversation I'd wanted to have my whole life without even knowing I wanted it. At some point, we crashed. Just like before, we slept in the salt dust, chaste as monks. I mean, I spooned him tight, but still, it didn't go anywhere. Everything was great, but I just don't get his sorry-no-sex vibe, or really him at all, because it does seem like he's attracted to me. And I'm not flattering myself. I can just tell. By the way he looks at me, pupils all dilated. By how totally into it he is when we talk. He's the sexiest sexless guy I've ever met, or else the most sexless sexy guy? I guess it's that he's all about, as he puts it, living a meaningful life, while I, pretty much until I met him and Mike, led a willfully meaningless one.

From the salt mines, we drove down the shore to the Yacht and Country Club. The hostess told us Mike hadn't come in yet. He was supposed to have been there already. We hung around waiting, drinking coffee in the empty bar for about an hour. We finally had to give up and head for the airport.

Though I really do believe Daniel and I have gotten close, this is still the end of the road for us, so to speak. He's going back to

Copenhagen; I'm staying here in Hallein to be with Obaachan and, I guess, start classes at the university. She wants me to. My having aced the accelerated math classes back in high school, plus an astronomical math score on the SAT made up for a slackerish transcript, so they took me for spring semester, late application and all.

On the way to the airport, we stop at Dairy Queen because I'm hungry. We're sitting outside at a concrete table next to the hectic expressway. Grit blowing from passing cars and trucks pricks my face, gets in my eyes. The angle the sun is at causes everything to glow redgold. He licks the soft serve cone I ordered for him. He has never been to a Dairy Queen. I got him one as big as a Maglite, dipped in fluorescent-red to boot. I want to give this squab-eating, Bordeaux-sipping Euro-dude the full DQ experience. The red reflects off his face, like he's blushing neon. His blue eyes look fluorescent. I tackle a chilidog, washing it down with my usual thirty-two-ounce Coke.

Daniel smiles that other smile of his—the small, sly one. A bit of the red shell gets stuck to his lower lip as he raises his cone and announces, "Not bad."

I raise my chilidog. "Want a bite?"

"Next time."

That's the thinnest of threads into the future, but nevertheless, a thread. I take the last bites of chilidog then lick out what remains in the cardboard boat. "You going to make more music with Mike?"

"Definitely. I'll arrange for a few more concerts."

"It'd be cool to do one in Copenhagen. I'd come!" This is my not-so-subtle way of letting Daniel know I want to see him again.

"It's where the No Names had their last show," he reminds me, blinking twice slowly before closing his eyes. Now he's getting me all sad.

After long silence, I speak: "I just have to ask you something."

His eyelids flutter open, twin moths.

"Was my dad a good guy?" I rephrase it in his style: "Was my father a good person?"

Daniel sits there, looking to the sky—maybe for answers—before saying, "My time with him was so brief." He has to stop to lick his neglected and fast-melting cone and the drips of vanilla from his knuckles. He continues, "The only story I have to tell is hardly a story at all. It was the one time I spent alone with him, and it lasted less than an hour. It was this simple: he and I walked across a field on a small island near my parents' house outside Copenhagen, and we swam together in the sound." His tongue catches a few more drips. "And yet, it was memorable. It's difficult to put into words, but I'll tell you, I have met very few people so open to the world."

"What do you mean by that?"

"Oh, that is vague. Sorry. He would ask questions about every-thing. About history and philosophy, about the kind of bird flying overhead or about my favorite musicians—classical, rock, or jazz. He was a talker, sure, but even in the few days I knew him, there were also profound silences. Even when he wasn't talking, you wanted to know what he was thinking."

I can't help but laugh because what Daniel's saying makes me, well—old-fashioned as it sounds–*overjoyed*. Over-fucking-joyed that my father affected someone that much.

He takes a broad lick up the length of the twist and laughs at himself. "I'm making him sound too cerebral. He was also—how shall I put it?—earthy. He was earthy."

I joke, "Is that a way of saying he was sexy?"

"Or something like that." He gives a sly smile. "He was so easy to be around. He was so comfortable in his own body that you felt comfortable in your own when you were with him."

I almost ask if they had sex but stop myself, not sure I want to know.

The diesel from passing semis is almost overpowering.

"But was he a good person?"

"If you mean in a traditional, moral sense, then I don't know. I didn't spend enough time with him to find that out. If you mean, did he live authentically, acting on freedom, then yes. He was not playing a role and his considerations were deep."

Daniel's philosophy suddenly sounds obscure, even pretentious. I want more from him, I want something else, but he's looking at that ridiculous hyper-luxury watch of his and announces time's getting short. We get up from the sticky tabletop. I toss my trash into the battered plastic container; he drops half his dripping cone in.

At the airport, we both hop off the bike curbside and start saying good-bye and not saying good-bye. His bags had been sent from the hotel ahead of time. I'm resigned to the fact that he has his own life and I've got to try to make one for myself.

To my surprise, he hugs me, drawing me in close. His lips, brutally chapped from all the sailing, brush my ear. "Take care," he whispers, "take care of yourself, take care of Michael." Then, he kisses me squarely on the lips, turns away, and disappears through the automatic doors.

APRIL 2016, MARIKO

Dearest Cousin Keiko,

Yes indeed, you heard correctly from Tomoko. Very shortly, I will be living with my girls! As ever, I am grateful to her for these beautiful great-granddaughters! And to you, for having arranged everything. Next week, I leave this place I have called home for over forty years. I leave my house and garden forever. Certainly, it is sad to be giving up all that I have made, but out of unfortunate circumstances fortunate circumstances have come.

It should really come as no surprise to me, of all people, about having to leave, and yet, now that the time has come, it feels that way. It's not as if I didn't see surrounding houses getting boarded up as people lost their jobs at the refinery and moved away. You thought it was crazy after the refinery shut down completely, and my house was robbed a third time, that I still wanted to stay. That I didn't take you up on your offer to return to California. I thought I could hold the tide back. I became a one-woman Neighborhood Crime Watch. So crazy! I began patrolling at night with my trusty Smith & Wesson. On several occasions, I have actually helped the police apprehend burglars and vandals. Once I even blew out the rear tires of a fleeing vehicle! The girls will be amused to one day hear these stories, I'm sure.

By the time I finally admitted to myself that I really did have to leave, I could not sell the house. No one wanted to buy in the Flats, what with nearly half the houses standing empty. And strange as it seems, even to me, I am the one behind the neighborhood's final destruction. I told you a little bit about this a long time ago. It was already ten years ago when I had the soil in my garden tested as part of an educational initiative we were promoting in the Master Gardeners Program at the University Extension. Even with all the amending of the soil I had done over the years, significant traces of heavy metals were found in my yard. It was so hard to think of my little paradise— all the beautiful flowers, shrubs, and trees—as rising out of poisoned soil.

I began testing empty lots around the refinery and throughout the Flats. All with the same result, or in fact higher concentrations than in mine. I felt it my duty to report my findings to the municipal government. They ignored me. So too, the county government and the state. My letters to my congressman and senators and the Environmental Protection Agency went unanswered or were given a boilerplate reply. As the company that owned the refinery no longer existed, no one wanted to take responsibility. I began a petition drive to have this matter addressed. Over a nearly three-year period, I visited politicians' offices and attended hearings. In the end, it was the newspapers and radio and television reporters that helped me. I think I sent you a few clippings. They reported that the government itself had found high levels of heavy metals, such as cadmium, chromium, lead, and mercury, as well as what they called semi-volatile constituents, such as pyrene, chrysene, benzo-this, and benzo-that, just as I had, and that no one had acted. Politicians and media alike kept referring to me as "one determined little lady." This was condescending, but I did not let it distract me. Besides, I was simply acting as any responsible citizen would, given the information I had.

At last, in 2010, the whole 250-acre area was declared a Superfund site. The ground itself, the government declared, was toxic. But nothing happened. It took until this year for the site to be given over to the state's Environmental Quality Commission, for what they call Voluntary Cleanup. Last month, they imploded the refinery. You will recall how big it was. I walked down by the river to observe the fall of the great smokestacks and enormous tanks. It reminded me of when Peter was a boy and would knock down the towers and other structures he had made with his Erector Set. More darkly, it was not unlike the bombing of Kobe when I was a girl. When the 350-foot thermoform catalytic convertor—where all the millions of gallons of crude oil had been converted for all those years—fell, my whole world shook. My view for so many years of those smokestacks, while not beautiful or picturesque, had been familiar, and out of such familiarity came the simple reassurance that this was indeed my world.

All our houses were bought up. Market value and replacement value were not one in the same, yet the authorities insisted they were. The money was not enough to buy another house nearly as nice as this one. And toxic soil or no, until the very end I continued trying to make my house a home, keeping the windows washed, the paint fresh, the flowerbeds weeded. The houses have been knocked down these past two weeks, one by one. Mine is among the last to go. The crane comes soon. The house now looks so small, as if I could just pick it up and carry it to a cleaner place. So bright and shiny, like porcelain. As I have seen happen to the other houses, the wrecking ball will take mine with a single blow.

Beyond my personal sentiment, this is something good. The site will be reclaimed as a wildlife refuge, a wetland. There will be clean water reflecting the sky. Thoughts of great cranes (how funny the machine they used to destroy everything is also called a crane!) soaring in for a landing among the reeds, of herons wading through in their hunt for fish and frogs, of redwing blackbirds alighting on cattails swaying in the breeze, provide some solace. And perhaps most of all, the Flats might well become a place for the tundra swans on their annual migration. Maybe when the land and water are reclaimed, you and I can come and see these magnificent birds! Long ago, you taught me to love birds!

Yes, my life has changed and will continue to change profoundly. The few belongings I would like to keep are being packed up in a ship's container the boys leased for me. In a few days I am heading off to live with them and the girls across the ocean, in their beautiful glass house. The boys get a most willing live-in babysitter for Aiko and Miyo. I have always seen the girls twice a year, two weeks at the holidays there, three weeks in the summer here, but the new situation will be infinitely better. And each summer, we will all go to the mystical island in the middle of the ocean, a place I have heard so much about but have never seen. You and Tomoko will have to come and visit us in both these places.

With Love,
Mariko

JANUARY 2018, MICHAEL

The cassettes—the whole lot of them—were headed for the Dumpster out back when suddenly I had second thoughts. Halfway across the parking lot, some tinge of guilt, vague sense of posterity, or scrap of plain old vanity caused me to reverse course. I lugged the huge box back across the scorching pavement to the apartment. Instead, I'll pack them up and send them to the only place I can think to send them: to the Lacs. Who knows if Mrs. Lac is still there, or for that matter if she's even still alive? If she is, I'm guessing she'll pass the collection on to Isaac, wherever he might be. My sole companion in the present swirls between my legs, purring with approval. "Yes, Bast," I whisper, "sometimes there is a past."

The box contains one past. All the cassettes Pete and I made. In his bedroom, at Dreamland, at all the random places—the high school pool, the salt caves. Recordings from even before the No Names, along with those from rehearsals and shows. Then there are the six or seven tapes I made each of the years I lived on the Island. Those tapes are really just an extended and pathetic echo of my time with Pete, even though, unbelievable as it seems, they represent a time lasting more than three times as long as the time I had with him. Maybe I'm assuming too much in thinking Isaac will want any of this. More than likely the No Names were just a blip on the screen of his adolescence. My own adolescent blip continued blipping way too far into adulthood. I was thirty-five and had to move here to the desert before I came to my senses and gave music up. Don't even listen to it anymore.

Maybe I should enclose a letter? But what could I possibly say after—what is it?—a quarter century? I'd have to explain to Mrs. Lac—or maybe also to Isaac?—that, had I stuck with music, I wouldn't have survived. Music saved my life at one point, for sure, but it was also killing me. I know it would sound absurd, but the truth is, every note I wrote or played was elegy—for Pete, for John, for Dad—and it occurred to me way late in the game that once you *become* elegy yourself that means you're dead. The Island and our Invisible City, those places made me—they *are* me—but everything was finished and done for me in both. How would I say that gently in a letter without sounding like a self-involved, ungrateful jerk, which I may well be anyway? And how could I tell them that, had I stayed—with or without music—I would have only been in the way? Saying even that would only sound self-important. I'd have been in the way, in general, for sure, but also in the way specifically of what looked to be a great relationship developing between Mrs. Lac and Isaac, and what (although Daniel seemed to be denying it) was going on between him and Isaac. One other thing bothered me. I didn't want to ever let the doubt of Isaac's paternity show in any way at all. Didn't want anyone to even sense that maybe I'd been wrong. Isaac and Mrs. Lac had become family, regardless of genes, and I didn't want to wreck it.

Daniel and I had pretty much wrecked for each other any ability to have normal relationships with other people. I mean, a couple weeks—occasionally a month—a year spent together in isolation is not a normal relationship. No family, no friends, no coworkers interacting with us. In its own way it was perfect. For me. And that's the problem. I'm sure Daniel wanted a real relationship. More than likely, though, Pete had already done the wrecking, at least for me. With me gone, I figured Daniel would at least have a fighting chance. Besides, I could no longer remain not only dependent on Daniel but his dependent. Not that there really could have been much pride for me to salvage after those fifteen years. He'd already done way too much for me. I owed him everything. I *owe* him everything. When he showed up at the Arkadia, it was one of the most powerful and beautiful days of my life. But it was, I felt, a completion, a reckoning, not an opening or a beginning. Same with the concert. I had finished what I needed to do with music, and he made the ending happen perfectly.

Sure, all three of them—Daniel, Isaac, Mrs. Lac—loved me—I have no doubt—but I could not be part of the equation. Simple as that. Sure, since I left, I've been lonely at times, but all in all I've been okay with my decision. To them, my disappearance probably seemed like an evasion of everything—relationships, career, music— but it was, I swear, necessary. Leaving everyone and everything was, random as it seemed, me taking a whack at making my own life, at shaping my future.

Would they even believe me if I told them that my leaving after the concert wasn't premeditated? Was spontaneous? It started with the sudden and vague idea of finding Mom. I so wished she'd been there to hear the concert. Sentimental, I know. The laundress's son playing the university's concert hall! More than that, since I was finally back in the States, I wanted to at least say something to her in person about Dad, about his life and death, about my love for him, wanted to show her I could start acting like a real human being. So, *bam!* The instant I walked out of the concert hall, I felt a deep need to head to Vegas to find her. That she was nowhere to be found once I got there, hit me hard. As the girls said, she probably remarried, changed her name. I checked a bunch of real estate offices, looking for her. No luck. There are like hundreds of realtors in that town. Even went up and down the Strip, checking casinos. Don't know why, but I could easily picture Mom as a blackjack dealer. Every few months I still drive up to Vegas for the weekend in hopes of finding her. I still even go by a few real estate offices, a casino or two. It was, and is, a misplaced—and years and years belated—sense of filial piety and duty.

If everyone from back then could see me now, they'd probably think how sad, how pathetic. Sometimes on one of my Vegas trips I'll eat at a real restaurant instead of fast food and, depending on my mood, stop in at a bar afterwards. In my non-initiator way, I might even meet someone to spend some time with, though usually nothing happens. Trouble with Vegas is, a lot of times there's money involved in finding company. In a way, it's pretty hilarious. The first years going there, people would on occasion offer me money, but of late they want money from me. The Two Ages of Man, I suppose.

Sending this package off is starting to make me think I'd kind of like to see Mrs. Lac and Isaac. Daniel too. A scary thought. Also makes me wonder if maybe I'd have headed back to Hallein had the big auto show not been going on when I first arrived in Vegas. Wouldn't have wound up here, that's for sure. One conversation changed everything. Got talking to Ashkii at the auto show and that was that. I thought it was kind of funny he and others called themselves "automotive artists" when back in Hallein we used to say "car painters." His booth looked impressive, though—amazing custom colors and finishes—so maybe "artist" fits. Next thing I know he's offering me a job based on my body shop experience from when I was a teenager. That, and my bizarre knowledge and love of auto paint. Just like that, life torqued radically. Only now do

I understand how crazy it would seem to anyone else. It was the day after I told him sure, I'd join his shop, that I realized the job wasn't in Vegas. Not even nearby. But in the kind of small town I never dreamed I'd live. Maybe Mrs. Lac would see this as ironic, me winding up back where I started from—in a body shop—the very place I'd worried about being stuck in when I was a kid.

But I should feel lucky, and mostly I do. Like a messenger from some twisted god, Ashkii appeared and took me—this loser going nowhere—under his wing and brought me to the middle of a real *nowhere*. A little garage but due to his amazing talent people came from *everywhere*. They ventured all the way here, to the middle of the desert, from Vegas, LA, Dallas, and lots of other places, for "the Navajo," as they called him. When he brought me on, I had no idea he was looking for someone to take over the business. After three years, he turned the whole show over to me and retired. That sealed my fate. People continued coming, and from even farther away. And now it's finally time to leave. Once again, a strange kind of luck. I'd never thought of leaving here until Auto Louvre in LA offered me good money to buy me out. I'm bringing my customers to LA. The plan is to work for them a couple years, then retire.

The work's been good. It was only when Ashkii proposed me taking over the shop—now, unbelievably, more than twenty years ago—that I learned how much the gruff old guy appreciated my work. I wasn't aware of it at the time, but after my first solo job—a snakeskin design for an '81 Camaro—he claimed he knew I was the guy. "You don't," he told me those three years later, "just paint fire—you know, like pictures of flames—with you, that car becomes fire! You don't just paint the sky, with clouds and birds—that car becomes sky. I never been to the ocean—seen plenty of pictures—but I wanted you to paint my Monte Carlo SS so I could be *at* the ocean, and dammit, you did! That's what I wanted, me driving around the desert *in* the ocean."

I was glad to hear he liked my work, though style's nothing I'd ever really thought about. It's just how I see things, how I mix the paint. Enough people like Ashkii thought what I did was cool enough, though, so I've wound up making decent money all these years. And he treated me decent. He and his wife would have me over to their place for Sunday dinners, holidays, barbecues, and such.

"When I die, Mike," Ashkii told me, "I want you to do the hearse up like heaven or hell. Your choice!" He laughed.

I'd rather write to Mrs. Lac and Isaac about painting cars than about the past because at least paint is something I know. Which is pretty funny. And sad. And I'd definitely rather write to them about painting cars than my personal life because there is none. Which is even funnier. Could tell them how I lose myself in metal flakes, pearl paint, candy paint, neon paint, thermochromic paint, chameleon paint, and holographics. And how there are all sorts of different spray guns, brushes, stencils, etc. to consider for each project. I still won't call it art, but it's intricate enough work that it keeps me away from myself for ten, twelve, sometimes fifteen or sixteen hours a day. It's all about the customer, what they desire. Not about me.

Getting rid of stuff for the move to LA is cleansing. Even though I've tried to avoid accumulating a past for a quarter century, it somehow does accumulate, it does. The present has a funny way of becoming the past.

I tape the box up with duct tape, sealing every seam double, then address it from memory.

Bast disappears out the window, like smoke.

JULY 2018, MARIKO

Hopping off the rocking postal ferry, Aiko and Miyo screech like gulls at the sight of a white cat dashing up the path. They chase after it. The cat is a new addition since last summer. Mice managed to get onto the Island with one or another delivery of supplies, so Daniel had Cousin Abraham bring a mouser over to hunt them down. But only until the pests are gone. The sheep, the dogs, and, I suppose, us should be the only mammals on the Island, because,

Daniel explained, once the mice are gone the cat would start killing nesting seabirds and their chicks.

Daniel has paid the shipmate to bring the luggage up to the house. Daniel and Isaac will arrive by the *First Movement* next week. Only because nowadays there is cellphone and internet service, as well as an emergency helicopter on the main island, do they allow me to come here alone with the girls. They underestimate my capabilities. They forget I survived the War as well as the crime wave during my last years in Hallein. This is my second summer, and there is no place on earth I would rather be than here with my girls and their fathers.

Aiko cries out from above, "If we catch him, may we bring him home at the end of summer?" Miyo runs back to me, begging, "Oh, please, Hiibachan!"

I laugh. "You can't simply have any cat you see! It belongs to Cousin Abraham. We are only borrowing it."

Aiko stops and turns back toward me. "Then may we please get our own?"

She is eight, old enough to care for a pet. I answer, trying not to smile, "That's up to your fathers, girls."

"You always say that!" Miyo pouts.

"First one in the house gets first pick of pastries!" I call out, and they run through the door. We made it to a few shops, including the bakery, for a couple of things between our ship docking in Tórshavn and the postal ferry departing for here. Otherwise, Abraham has already brought all the supplies we will need.

When I get to the door, the girls are already swooping around the rooms, making familiar once again this place where they've spent a good part of every summer of their lives.

I motion the shipmate to leave the suitcases inside the door. I thank him, in Færoese, tip him, and tell him good-bye, also in his language. These are among the phrases I have learned on my language app.

Inside the door sits a package—a rather large cardboard box—with some miscellaneous envelopes resting on top of it. Very little mail arrives here over the year, and anything deemed important

Abraham forwards to Daniel in Copenhagen. I kneel down for a closer look. The surface is tattooed with a variety of postage stamps and ink stamps. It is addressed to Daniel and comes from the States. The postmark reads *Blindeye, AZ*. I place the pastry box on the larger box, then carry them over to the kitchen counter.

While the girls set plates and cups on the coffee table, I bring the suitcases to the bedroom the three of us share. Then, returning to the kitchen, I untie the pastry box and slide the pink and yellow teacakes onto the fluted, blue-and-white china cake stand. I pour chocolate milk into the crystal pitcher the girls love—a very modern one, with fanciful geese etched in the design—place everything on a wooden tray, and carry it in to them.

They are discussing the motion picture *A Wrinkle in Time* as they nibble their cakes. Aiko has read the book and, with great authority, deems the original far superior. Her younger sister disagrees, despite the fact she has yet to read the book. The ocean out the window is lively with waves and bright. After finishing the cakes, the girls head out to fulfill their great desire to catch a lamb to hold and pet.

In the kitchen sink, I gut the small cod Cousin Abraham caught yesterday and kindly put in the refrigerator. Such a good man. I slice off the fish's plump cheeks, setting them aside to fry up as a late-night delicacy for myself after the girls are asleep. From the window, I see that Miyo has indeed caught a lamb! Last year, no matter how much the girls schemed, the lambs eluded them. She sits on a stone, the little creature curled in her lap. Aiko stands above her, hand extended downward so the lamb is able to suck her thumb. The scene warms me. I grab my phone from the counter and take a picture. I send it to their mother Tomoko in San Francisco and ask her to please show it to her grandmother. Cousin Keiko still refuses to get a smartphone or a computer! I'm not sure how, in this day and age, she can run her jewelry shop without one or the other.

As I fillet the fish, I cannot stop thinking about the box from Arizona. After the cod is prepared for cooking and the potatoes peeled and set in a pot of salted water, I rinse my hands in the cold mountain water, dry them on the checked apron, and go look at the stamps on the box again, this time more closely. Oddly, there are several other postmarks, including two from Hallein, months apart. There is no return address. Daniel's name and this address—which is simply the name of this island and Færoes—are written with a Sharpie on a large index card taped to the box. I peel up the edge of the card to discover underneath are my name and address on Geranium Avenue written in the same hand! Stamped next to it: *ADDRESS UNKNOWN*. I don't know why that startles me so, but it does. Another, later stamp reads: *NO RETURN ADDRESS*. One, with an even later date, seems even more ominous: *Send to Postal Reclamation Center, Atlanta, GA*. From postmark to postmark, it seems to have taken the box nearly seven months to have arrived here. It is a miracle that it made it at all. Even after all these years, it must be, I am quite certain, from Mike. Oh, Mike!

After dinner, the girls and I Skype their fathers, to let them know we have made it safe and sound. The boys chat and laugh with the girls. When I mention the box, and that it might be from Mike, Isaac's face lights up. "Go ahead, open it!" He means right away. Daniel nods cautiously.

The girls carry on the conversation while I go and retrieve the box from the kitchen, along with a sharp knife. In front of the camera, I slice the cardboard open hesitantly, carefully. I then remove layers of crumpled newspaper, dated from last year, spread on top.

"What's in it?" Isaac is so eager. He puts his eyeglasses on and leans in closer, as if the space isn't virtual.

Underneath, packed neatly, are dozens of cassette tapes and compact disks, each one labeled in jagged handwriting, with a date.

"Music," I answer, holding up a few samples for them to see, "from Mike."

"*Holy . . .*" Isaac stops himself from swearing in front of the girls. Daniel's pale eyes grow wide. He swallows hard.

"Who's Mike again?" Miyo asks.

Aiko is first to answer, "He was grandfather's boyfriend."

"Best friends forever!" Isaac says with a sly grin.

"Yes," I say, "and he lived with us back in Hallein, when they were in high school, when they started their band." Aiko, and to a lesser extent Miyo, are familiar with swaths of the story, and though they sometimes forget, they basically know who's who.

"When do we get to meet him?" Miyo wonders.

This time it's Daniel who answers. "Maybe someday. But you can probably meet him through his music. That says a lot about a person, their music."

Isaac urges me to play something from the box. Though the old stereo here does have a cassette player, I feign helplessness, and oh my goodness I wouldn't know where to begin with all these tapes and CDs. We might just have to wait until they arrive.

After the boys disappear into the ether, I tuck the girls in and read to them from Hans Christian Andersen's "The Little Mermaid." It is quite different, they notice, from the Disney picture. "More intense," says Aiko. Yes, more intense, yet somehow the girls still manage to drift off to sleep right in the middle of the painful transformation of the mermaid's fishtail into human legs.

I sit on the edge of the bed the girls share, staring out the window, immersed in the sound of wind and ocean. The sky and water are still light—nearly white—though it's past ten. On this blankness before me, memories begin etching themselves too clearly. Peter and Mike at Geranium Avenue doing all the ordinary things of this world. I see them making cold-cut sandwiches while standing in front of the open refrigerator, cleaning the slimy black leaves out of the eavestroughs for me, slouching on the sofa together watching a football game, playing music in their room and in the garden, relishing a T-bone steak hot off the hibachi. But more powerful still, a lexicon of their expressions and gestures—some so simple—a smile of contentment, a blink of disbelief. Others go uncategorized, coming at moments where one of them appears deep in thought or daydream. So many memories. Surely, Mike must have often experienced something similar, perhaps sitting right here staring out this very same window, all those years he lived in this house. After the initial pain subsides, the memories become less distressing. Mike has his music, and I have to believe that it was in the music he placed and shaped his memories.

When next I look at my watch, it is past midnight. I touch each of the girls on the cheek lightly, saying quietly, *Anata o hontoni aishiteimasu,* I love you very much, to each of them. I say it in Japanese, as I always did with Peter, and do with Isaac as well, because, even after all these many years, the ideas and the feelings still mean more to me that way. Hopefully, one day the girls will learn Japanese. They both have my blood, through Tomoko, but language forges a far more important bond.

I leave the girls to their dreams. The sun is still bright enough that I don't need to turn a lamp on. I go to the box chock-full of the past, searching through its contents for a letter. There is none. The tapes and CDs are ordered by date. The first is from December 1975. I lift it up, this plastic case containing traces of Peter and Mike, and contemplate what it would mean to hear their voices from that time right now. I'm not sure I could bear it, and though it sounds funny, I am not sure it is even right for me to intrude on them. Though the box was initially addressed to me—and I can therefore presume Mike would want me to listen—still, it would feel like trespassing on their friendship, their love, their story. Obviously, I was a part of it—a small one—but in the end, it is their story, not mine. To distract myself, I fry up the cod cheeks, slide them onto a blue glass plate and pour myself a beer. It is red and strong. I sit on the bench facing the window. I am, however, too preoccupied to really savor my treat. I have a second beer. I pick up another cassette, examine it, then place it, too, back in the box. I close the lid and turn to look out over the ocean, hoping for some respite from memory.

JULY 2018, DANIEL

This night, a rare easterly comes, steady and strong. If it continues, we will make up time lost in yesterday's punishing squalls. The sky

glows psychedelic, exactly the way Michael loved it. This phenomenon brought him, he would say, to a state of ecstasy, or *ekstasis*—that
is, becoming entranced, being brought out of oneself. The whole
northern portion of the sky writhes and throbs neon green. From
there, it swirls into deeper and deeper currents of cyan splattered
with yellow stars. It always amazed Michael that the stars actually shone brighter through the overlapping swaths of colors. In the
middle of the night he would sometimes wake me, and we would
leave the house, heading with the dogs over to the promontory. We
would sit on the north cliff all night long, transfixed by the spectacle
aurora borealis offers the soul.

Sailing at night is usually when I am able to lose myself most
completely; however, these past three days, since Mariko's news of
the box from Michael, I cannot even lose other people, especially
not Michael, let alone myself. What has become of him?

Isaac sleeps belowdecks; our girls sleep two days away. They are
my life, my happiness. And yet, it could all be so easily disturbed
by these relics from the past that await us on the Island. It has been
nearly a quarter century since Michael left there—considerably longer
than the fifteen years of our bivouacked life together. I know, *fifteen
years* and *bivouacked*—especially in such a solid and ancient house—
make for something of a paradox. But our situation was perpetually
temporary. There was never any kind of understanding—let alone
an agreement—between us that our life together would continue, not
even from one day to the next. He could, and eventually did, leave,
and without a word. It is forty years since I met Michael and Peter,
and now their absence has become vivid again, painful. Michael and
I are now practically old men. A case of nostalgia, I suppose. In centuries past, nostalgia was a disease confined to Swiss mercenary soldiers
when away from their beloved Alps, and later expanded to include any
soldier away from home. In our time, nostalgia is general and seems
to afflict the old most acutely. Time has supplanted space in how
we think of it: those Alpine valleys have become years.

This pain brings with it a thought I had long ago learned to repress:
that Isaac has, for me, in some perverse way, served as emblem, or

totem, of both Peter and Michael. A terrible admission, but it was, I swear, enacted almost entirely in my subconscious. I would even go so far as to say that it was as likely in Isaac's subconscious as it was in mine.

Now it seems important to recount my early days together with Isaac, to reaffirm the beauty and the love we have. It was one warm Sunday afternoon, halfway through Isaac's Fulbright in Copenhagen, that our separate needs coalesced, and we fell in love. The two of us were sailing around the Øresund, amid a vast flotilla of other weekend sailors, when he announced that he would quit his PhD studies in mathematics. At first, I did not respond.

"While I like math," he explained, "and have some talent, I really don't have the passion for all the years of study ahead. It's a slog." The wind kept blowing his long red hair across his face and he kept pushing it away. I was, quite literally, seeing him and not seeing him eye to eye.

His announcement perturbed me. I did not say so, but I suspected he was leaving mathematics so that he and I might be together. He was in a top program in the States. "You know," I began cautiously, "we all have a calling." He frowned, staring off toward the pastel mansions along the shore. "And mathematics is yours. Down the road you may very well regret having abandoned it."

Isaac shifted to face me directly. His face tensed. He gripped his hair in his fist to hold it back so he could look at me directly. "Listen, I'm good at math, and I enjoy it, but that doesn't mean it's my *calling*, as you put it." He inflected the word *calling* with a shot of sarcasm. "I'm also a decent guitarist and enjoy playing, but that doesn't mean I have a calling or even want to be a musician." He paused, lasering in on me with those eyes of his, each a different color. "Just because you have a calling, Daniel, doesn't mean everyone does."

Until that very moment, I had not realized Isaac had never stood up to me before. Suddenly, I viewed myself as something of a tyrant. This was disconcerting. Yet, even as he was disagreeing with me—challenging me—it felt like a good thing. It was as if a barrier between us had been broken through. My respect for him grew tremendously, and I knew then, as he looked at me in what could almost be called defiance, that I loved him.

"I just want a life," he concluded, at last breaking into a smile. "I'd like to teach math to high school kids." He let go of his hair and the wind once again swept it across his face.

It was then I changed course, both literally and figuratively. I jibed quickly, bringing the boom around. Once I had the boat turned about, we set sail for the low, sandy island where I had taken the No Names all those years before. I had no plan in mind, at least not consciously, of recreating the only moments I ever spent alone with his father. Only in retrospect did I understand, or rather, admit to myself, that in those hours the past did indeed come alive.

We docked, walked up the gradual slope, and then, passing the descendants of the same herd of golden cows that have grazed there for generations, I took Isaac's hand. The tough marram grass scratched our ankles. A pair of sapphire-blue butterflies traced arabesques above our heads. A rabbit sat up on its hind legs, undisturbed by our intrusion, ears glowing pink in the afternoon sun. We crossed the tiny island, arriving at the same secluded swath of golden sand where Peter and I had gone so many years before. As if on cue, together we undressed, in silence, dropping our clothes onto the sand. We stood there for the longest time, naked, looking at one another, as if to determine that this was real and that we were real, before wading into the surf and diving in. The water was especially clear and blue on that day. We swam around and around each other, like dolphins at play, and when we finally emerged from the waves, we lay down in the warm sand and made love, the uncanny sweeping over us in time with the shadows of gulls.

The northern lights begin to fade. To starboard, a humpback blows. Usually, I would go down to the cabin and wake Isaac for such a sighting, but this time I will let him sleep. The approaching daylight washes my nostalgia out. There is no use subjecting him to my disconsolate mood. My first impulsive thought is to try and find Michael, to sail solo all the way to America. Indulging my imagination further, I see myself sailing up the Saint Lawrence Seaway, over the Great Lakes, and eventually docking the *First Movement* in the farthest western port of Lake Superior (Duluth, is it?). There, I would find a ship-sized American convertible to rent and drive all the way to Arizona. I would tell Michael he could return to the Island, that it is his for as long as he wants to live there. He and I would recreate the solitude we once shared at regular intervals. This is all of course as presumptuous as it is preposterous. Most likely, he has a perfectly happy life in this place called Blindeye, and I have faded from his memory. Certainly, he was deliberate in not providing a return address on the box.

It pains me and shames me to think how I could consider—even fleetingly—upending my life, one so filled with love. However, I am certain that to not allow this fantasy to play out in my imagination would have an insidious effect on my love for Isaac and our family. Michael is, I have to remind myself once again, the one who left the Island without letting me know, the one who vanished after our sole concert together—again, without a word. I have learned to recall all of this without bitterness. My love for Michael will, as it has, continue outside of the present, outside of any shared place. Yes, outside of time and place. There it must stay.

Although he has not said anything specifically, I can sense that the box awaiting us has reignited Isaac's original, unchecked passion for the No Names. After all, it contains the past he has always so intently desired to know and to have been a part of. But then, I need to remind myself, it was his passion for Michael and the No Names that brought our lives together in the first place and set these decades of love in motion.

Desire overwhelms me. I double-check the chart points I plotted, engage the jib and rudder self-steering, and go belowdecks. As I head to the v-shaped bed in the bow, I strip off my polo and Bermudas. Isaac is on his back asleep, breathing deep and steady. I move on top of him, covering his mouth with mine, and slowly he comes to that state between dream and sleep where his passion becomes unbridled. I pull his gym shorts off. He is already aroused. I wet his penis with my mouth, then straddle him, letting him enter me. All our beautiful history plays out in the rhythm of our bodies, making this familiar act suddenly unfamiliar. When he is spent, he opens his legs and guides me into him. I move steadily, I lose myself, I am no longer who I thought I was.

JULY 2018, ISAAC

"Daddy! Daddy! Papa! Papa!" the girls holler as they race down from the house to meet the boat. Miyo leaps into my arms as we step onto the landing, Aiko into Daniel's. Miyo gives my stubbly cheek a kiss, laughing, "That tickles, Daddy!"

Aiko asks Daniel, "Papa, why couldn't we sail here with you and Daddy?"

Daniel explains what he's already explained a hundred times before, that the girls must wait until they are ten. He of course doesn't tell them that he sailed across with his parents every year from when he was a newborn, or that he did his first solo voyage when he was fifteen, still a kid.

"But why?" Aiko persists.

"Sometimes there are storms, my darling," he answers, "and you have to be able to help reef the mainsail and hoist the storm-jib."

"I know how!"

"You do?"

She blushes.

Obaachan steps down onto the landing, gives me a kiss as she takes Miyo from me. She tells Aiko to hop down from Daniel and help carry the luggage. She then leans over on tiptoes to kiss Daniel on the chin.

After dinner, the five of us walked along the stream and up the mountainside to the pool at the base of the waterfall so the girls could take a swim. They'd been begging us. The water from the mountain is cold, though not nearly so cold as the ocean. Miyo ran over the rocks to the water and dove right in without a thought. She's fierce like that, like my mother, and looks like her too. I bet they'd have gotten along. Nearly every day I think how sad it is the cancer took her before either of them was born, years before. Aiko took her time, splashing her arms and thighs before launching herself gently and gracefully. Daniel and I went in the water with them, or, really, only Daniel did. He swam all the way across the pool and under the falls, to the girls' amazement. I only waded at the edge. Obaachan sat on a large rock above, watching over us.

Miyo shouted up to her, "Hiibachan, you're Queen of the Island!"

And I thought how beautiful all of this is and how beautiful our girls are, and how one day they will be the queens of the Island. From Daniel, they learn tales of their line of ancestors stretching back over the past millennium, and of a mythical musician who, for a time, dwelt here and filled the place with songs of one prince who drowned and another prince who died in war. And, in turn, the girls will make their own stories, making this island truly theirs.

Everyone else has gone to bed hours ago. I put my glasses on and open the laptop, feeling a little like Pandora as I begin searching *Mike Abramczyk.* I'm not finding anything. I search *The No Names, The No Names punk band,* and so on. It's as if they never existed. They're invisible like they said our city was. Finally, I search *Blindeye, Arizona.* It's in the middle of the desert, apparently the farthest place from anyplace in the continental US. Whatever that means. It's a place as opposite as opposite could be from this island, and yet maybe bizarrely similar in its obscurity and isolation. How intentional was that on his part? On Google Maps I cruise the bleak main street of Blindeye, and head out of town on the two-lane highway into the wasteland. Everything glare, everything impossible to imagine.

I want it to be possible to imagine Mike, to imagine him in our lives. I'm sure I could find him if I went there. Up till now, all these years I've felt complete without him, or at least I thought I was. And up till now, I've thought our family was complete without him, but maybe we aren't. The pathetic truth is that in these past two plus decades I've only ever allowed myself to miss him vaguely and in passing. The fact that good old-fashioned repression ruled someone like me—who has always prided himself on his raging id—is classic. But what is it that I'm looking for in him? At this late stage in the game, am I looking for a father figure? Some unimaginative shrink might come up with that one. It's more than that, though, or not only that. I don't know exactly what, but it's more than that. It's desire—or about desire—though not sexual desire, or at least not only or even mostly. It's desire for friendship and love in some ultimate and probably unknown and unworkable form, as I imagine he and my father had. It's about living life as if life were not meaningless, while at the same admitting that it is. There's a blank space in time left by my father/Mariko's son/the girls' grandfather/Mike's whatever/Pete/Peter/Peter Ichiro Lac, that only Mike, or the idea of Mike, can help each of us fill, and then only partially, for like a second or two. But that's throwing Mike into the role of savior or sacrifice, selfishly ignoring the fact that he experienced—and probably still experiences—the loss of Pete profoundly. And of course Mike himself creates a blankness—a blankness of a blankness!—for me, but obviously way more for Obaachan and Daniel.

My recharged desire will not go over well with Daniel. He'll sense it, for sure. I haven't thought through the risks and unintended consequences of bringing Mike into our family. Daniel will be sensible, of that I can be a hundred percent sure. He'll try talking sense into me, and he should. I can tell he's uneasy. First thing we got here, I wanted to listen to some of the tapes, but he keeps putting me off, saying we need to take care of things around the farm first. Obaachan acts evasive, preoccupying herself with the girls.

I get up from the table, then hesitate for a moment before going over to the box. In my Pandora mode I bring out the very first tape in the sequence, one from 1975. I turn on the vintage Beomaster 1900. It's probably from around the same year—yet it's one of the newest things here on the farm. I put the cassette in the player, lean back and press *Play:*

MIKE: Testing, testing, one, two, three . . .

PETE: We're speaking into the new tape player that the future badass facsimile of Simon and Garfunkel is gonna use to make a demo that's gonna get them signed by the grandiosest label in this whirling world.

[laughter, followed by two electric guitars playing, not too fast and not too loud, fairly intricate chords for thirty-four seconds, followed by laughter that's now a lot more raucous]

PETE: Unreal, my Orpheus! You nailed it!

MIKE: We nailed it!

PETE: Add the words this time.

MIKE: They're yours. You sing them.

PETE: I only do backups. *[he laughs, then sings falsetto, "Stop, in the name of love . . ."]*

MIKE: Come on. I'll do harmony. *[he starts playing]*

PETE: You're such an ass-wipe! *[he then sings in his real voice]* I thought I had to fall in love, /But one look at you and I was floating in a dream . . . *[the music stops]* That really sucks. That's way too sappy.

MIKE: No, it's alright, man.

PETE: Problem is, I listened to my inner Plato who tells me, "At the touch of love everyone becomes a poet." Unless of course the philosopher's being ironic, because as far as I can tell, every guy is touched by love every day and very few are poets. Take you, my horndog, for instance . . .

MIKE: I only fall in love every other day, so couldn't possibly be a poet *[laughs]*. Seriously, your song's not so bad.

PETE: Let's do one of your deluxified chassons, my man!

MIKE: No. Let's work on this one. It's got potential. We just need to shake it up.

PETE: Come on! It sucks.

MIKE: No, seriously, we've just got to work on it some more. Takes hard work. You want to make it to the top, don't you?

PETE: *[audibly sighs]* Damn straight. *[one guitar starts, followed by the other]*

MIKE: *[singing, improvising the lyrics]* I thought I had to fall / To be in love, / I thought I had to call / It love, / But I only had to look / To be in love, / I only had to look into your eyes / To know my eyes will never shut, / Like a sweet waking dream, a sweet dream waking . . .

Mariko: *[voice in the distance]* Boys! Time for dinner!

PETE: *[guitars continuing]* Be right there, Mom! *[then, to Mike]* You're a fucking genius, man! You're the poet ultimate! *[music stops]*

MIKE: *[laughing]* Couldn't do it without your sweet inspiration. Couldn't do it without you. Let's go. I'm starving. I could eat the world.

ACKNOWLEDGMENTS

My gratitude to Christopher Tradowsky for the patient and loving care you've taken with this book every step of the way, and for the inspiration your stories and novel have provided me.

Jonis Agee, your insights into a later draft of this story were invaluable. All the years of our friendship have made me a better person and your books have made me a better writer.

Many thanks to Chris Fischbach for nurturing this novel in the early stages, and for your incisive edits.

Annemarie Eayrs, thank you for your comments on a very early draft and for the meticulous copyediting at the end.

Thank you, Jeremy Davies, Abbie Phelps, Robyn Earhart, Linda Ewing, and Kelly Winton at Coffee House for steering the editorial process to the finish line.

I am grateful to Carleton College for the support and the time to write, and to my students for keeping literature central to our lives.

For your comments along the way, William Reichard, James Cihlar, Bonnie Nadzam and Ted Mathys, I am grateful.

Jessica Leiman, thanks for your friendship and being the best sounding board.

Thank you, Eve Raimon and Amelia Montes for reading the manuscript and for encouraging me.

Ebba Hentze and Janus Kamban, wherever your spirits now dwell, thank you for welcoming me to the Færoes and for sharing your wisdom and your art.

To the Italian girl who long, long ago introduced this boy to punk in London, thank you, wherever you may be.

A much belated thanks to Toni Morrison for guiding me into the stories I need to tell. To you, I am forever indebted.

Coffee House Press began as a small letterpress operation in 1972 and has grown into an internationally renowned nonprofit publisher of literary fiction, essay, poetry, and other work that doesn't fit neatly into genre categories.

Coffee House is both a publisher and an arts organization. Through our *Books in Action* program and publications, we've become interdisciplinary collaborators and incubators for new work and audience experiences. Our vision for the future is one where a publisher is a catalyst and connector.

LITERATURE
is not the same thing as
PUBLISHING

FUNDER ACKNOWLEDGMENTS

Coffee House Press is an internationally renowned independent book publisher and arts nonprofit based in Minneapolis, MN; through its literary publications and *Books in Action* program, Coffee House acts as a catalyst and connector—between authors and readers, ideas and resources, creativity and community, inspiration and action.

Coffee House Press books are made possible through the generous support of grants and donations from corporations, state and federal grant programs, family foundations, and the many individuals who believe in the transformational power of literature. This activity is made possible by the voters of Minnesota through a Minnesota State Arts Board Operating Support grant, thanks to the legislative appropriation from the Arts and Cultural Heritage Fund. Coffee House also receives major operating support from the Amazon Literary Partnership, Jerome Foundation, Literary Arts Emergency Fund, McKnight Foundation, and the National Endowment for the Arts (NEA). To find out more about how NEA grants impact individuals and communities, visit www.arts.gov.

Coffee House Press receives additional support from Bookmobile; the Buckley Charitable Fund; Dorsey & Whitney LLP; the Gaea Foundation; the Schwab Charitable Fund; and the U.S. Bank Foundation.

THE PUBLISHER'S CIRCLE OF COFFEE HOUSE PRESS

Publisher's Circle members make significant contributions to Coffee House Press's annual giving campaign. Understanding that a strong financial base is necessary for the press to meet the challenges and opportunities that arise each year, this group plays a crucial part in the success of Coffee House's mission.

Recent Publisher's Circle members include many anonymous donors, Patricia A. Beithon, Kelli Cloutier, Theodore Cornwell, Jane Dalrymple-Hollo, Mary Ebert and Paul Stembler, Kamilah Foreman, Eva Galiber, Roger Hale and Nor Hall, William Hardacker, Randy Hartten and Ron Lotz, Carl and Heidi Horsch, Amy L. Hubbard and Geoffrey J. Kehoe Fund of the St. Paul & Minnesota Foundation, Hyde Family Charitable Fund, Kenneth & Susan Kahn, the Kenneth Koch Literary Estate, Cinda Kornblum, the Lenfestey Family Foundation, Carol and Aaron Mack, Gillian McCain, Mary and Malcolm McDermid, Daniel N. Smith III and Maureen Millea Smith, Vance Opperman, Mr. Pancks' Fund in memory of Graham Kimpton, Alan Polsky, Robin Preble, Ronald Restrepo and Candace S. Baggett, Steve Smith, Jeffrey Sugerman and Sarah Schultz, Paul Thissen, Grant Wood, Margaret Wurtele, Jeremy M. Davies, Robin Chemers Neustein, Dorsey and Whitney Foundation, The Buckley Charitable Fund, Elizabeth Schnieders, Allyson Tucker, and Aptara Inc.

For more information about the Publisher's Circle and other ways to support Coffee House Press books, authors, and activities, please visit www.coffeehousepress.org/pages/donate or contact us at info@coffeehousepress.org.

GREG HEWETT is the author of five volumes of poetry, including *Blindsight* (Coffee House Press, 2016). The recipient of Fulbright fellowships to Denmark and Norway, he has also been a fellow at the Camargo Foundation in France, and is Professor of English at Carleton College. *No Names* is his first novel. He lives with his husband in Minneapolis.

No Names was designed by
Bookmobile Design & Digital Publisher Services.
Text is set in Ten Oldstyle.